The Architect of Song

A.G. Howard

**

For more information on A.G. Howard and her books, visit her website at www.aghoward.com

To my two moms:

Ola Faye Ruggles and Carol Rene Howard.

One of you brought me into this world and had to leave too soon. The other welcomed me into her family and treats me as her own.

Thank you both for believing in me, supporting me, and showing me the strength of a mother's love.

Architecture, in general, is frozen music.
~Friedrich von Schelling, German philosopher 1775-
1854

CHAPTER 1

A silent mouth is melodious.
An Irish Proverb

Melancholy. Melody. Separate words, separate meanings, united by a memory pressed upon my heart. In my childhood, my mama sang to me. In her gardens, in the midst of fragrant foxgloves and hollyhocks taller than my five-year-old head, her voice took wing—a sound more lovely than a nightingale, more moving than a storm-crested sea. At times, the tune would break with sorrow or poignant happiness, and her tears would flow. I treasured nothing more than the melancholy melody of those fractured notes.

Now that I am deaf, I'm haunted by two regrets: that I didn't memorize the sound of Mama's precious voice ... and the eternal absence of song in my soul.

Claringwell, England
November 3, 1883

During my mama's final days in this world, I read aloud

1

from her book of assorted proverbs to comfort her.

She used to say each important scene of our lives could be summed up by a proverb. Yet I found none that captured the pain of her body taken by consumption. For three months I watched, helpless, as winter settled in her blood and froze her from the inside out. Even at age nineteen, my heart suffered as that of a child.

"Juliet, my sweet China Rose ..." Her lips formed my nickname often toward the end, and I ached to hear her say it one last time. To really *hear* her.

In some ways, my impairment softened the torment, her coughs and whimpers falling on incapable ears. Still, my other senses gave no such reprieve. I felt her cries when her withered hand seized my fingers for anchor; my nostrils stung from the pungent mint oils slathered across her chest and throat in hopes to aid her labored breath; and I could never un-see the pale cloud of sickness dimming those beloved eyes, once filled with color and light.

Well-meaning friends visited during her last hours. I envied them the ability to hear her words as opposed to reading her lips. I brooded, composing songs of self-pity in my mind. If our guests had but stopped to listen, they would have heard.

Silence has a melody all its own.

After her death, people came in droves to attend the funeral. Mama was beloved by many. Papa's only brother, Uncle Owen, and my and Mama's live-in maid, Enya Alderdice, accompanied me in the carriage that followed the covered equipage hearse. My attire from head to toe matched the horses' ebony coats.

Arranged on a hill, the cemetery's headstones appeared small and insignificant in the late afternoon light—like an overgrowth of stony mushrooms bursting from the brown and yellow landscape. I shivered beneath my veiled cap and fur blanket as the carriage swayed on the gales of a north wind bearing ice and sleet. The scene chilled me—such a cruel foil to sweeter times when I would dance with Mama during warm spring showers, our bodies tingling with laughter and song.

The rain softened upon our arrival, easing the trek for the pall bearers who laid Mama's casket within the ground. Uncle Owen cradled one of my gloved hands. In the other, I clasped the silver locket which held my parent's portraits ... memories weighing heavier on my shoulders than the clouds draped across Cemetery Hill.

I lifted my veil to watch the priest's lips give a benediction.

At the age of eight, a severe case of mumps cost me my hearing, as well as my papa's life, for I gave him my illness. Uncle Owen, not only Papa's brother, but his partner and friend, stepped up to carry the family business and offered a lifeline to Mama and me. For eleven years thereafter, both of them supported me in living a lie. Never once did they force me to acknowledge my deafness to strangers. Instead, they showed me how to mask my differences, by using my other senses to compensate.

Unlike children born with a hearing defect, I had already mastered speech and could yield responses. The hardest feat was controlling the volume of my voice, but I soon learned to adjust the tension on my vocal cords. Mama told me I often spoke too quiet. Yet to be soft-spoken was considered a virtue for a lady, so strangers simply believed me well-mannered and refined.

Those strangers underestimated me, for I was putting each and every one of them upon the slide of a microscope. I honed the art of reading lips and facial expressions, and learned how often they contradicted one another. There had been scales covering my eyes that lifted away upon the absence of my ears, and I came to see the underlying truth behind every spoken word. In that respect, my "limitation" proved to be a gift. One I preferred to keep safely secreted within until I deemed it safe to reveal it.

My greatest defense against a silent and stoic world.

A cold droplet of rain splattered on my nose as everyone's eyes closed in prayer. I used the pause to search within the folds of my pelisse overcoat for a China rose—the apricot-pink of a summer sunset—to set upon Mama's grave.

I aimed a sidelong glance in Uncle's direction, waiting for his cue to place it. I resisted the urge to lean against him. To draw strength from him. I knew that today, he needed me to be strong on my own.

Even at thirty-seven, he retained a distinguished appearance, almost eagle-like. His large, golden-hazel eyes, wise with noble insight, his fair skin smooth with a hint of distinguished wrinkles, his prematurely white hair, wavy and thick beneath his cap like a nest of downy feathers. He looked more like my handsome papa with each year.

My attention fell to the weather-worn tombstone at the other side of my feet. *Lord Anston Emerline: Loving father and husband.*

A middle-class baronet, a dyer of fabrics and cloth. A doting father, cut-down by his daughter's childhood illness.

Adrift on memories, I didn't realize the prayer had ended until Uncle nudged me. I kissed the rose and tucked its stem into the slight opening where the ground met the base of her tombstone—in hopes to hold the blossom from blowing away in the storm. My gloved fingers traced her inscription, *Lady Emilia Emerline: Beloved wife, mother, and friend.* There was a catch in my throat that grew to a sob. I feared how loud it was when the faces around me looked on with pity. Uncle knelt beside me, arm draped over my shoulders, his body trembling alongside mine.

After some minutes, he tenderly blotted my cheeks with a handkerchief, followed by his own, then stood. While he dusted off his breeches, I plucked two petals from Mama's rosebud. One, I carried to Papa, stuffing it into the cracked facade of his aged stone. The other, I eased into the band of my glove, the petal cool against my palm as I slid it in—an attempt to bind the three of us together for the long and lonely night ahead.

The grave diggers began the task of sludging mud atop Mama's casket. Grief burned within my chest, and I turned my back as Uncle bid the mourners goodbye. They scattered to their carriages, black and gray cloaks gleaming like rotted leaves driven to the gutters.

I inhaled a cleansing breath as the last hackney-drawn coach pulled out onto the road. I was relieved that we were at last alone. A certain viscount had been vying for my family's estate the past few months. I'd refused to personally meet him, and had worried he might make an appearance at the burial today, to stake his claim when I was at my most vulnerable. My home was not for sale, regardless that he'd raised his bid to three times its worth.

All along, Uncle had been encouraging me to consider the offer. *"An unmarried maiden has no use for two acres of land and a townhouse with six bedrooms."* Even without working ears, I felt the bite of those well-intended words. That house was the only tangible piece of my father and mother still standing. Papa built it for her with his own hands, and Mama decorated each room for him with love. And I would never be parted from it.

As if hearing my thoughts, Uncle clasped my elbow. "Ready to go home?" he mouthed the question and I glanced at Enya waiting beside the carriage, studying her boots. Pink patches stained her pale skin where she'd blotted tears away.

"Not yet." Eyes stinging, I fiddled with the petal tucked inside my glove and looked at the graves surrounding us, aware of my hypocrisy. I didn't wish to part with my home. Yet, I had no desire to go there. To stand in the empty rooms once filled with laughter and life. At that moment, I felt as if I belonged with the dead.

Chest rising on a sigh, Uncle observed the heavy clouds

overhead. "The weather's ill-tempered, tiny sparrow." His lips, glistening with raindrops in the hazy light, framed the words. Sadness and exhaustion tugged his whitening eyebrows. "There is nothing more to do here. Let your mother rest. We will visit again another day."

I stood rooted to the ground. "Just a short walk amongst the headstones."

My uncle offered me the umbrella. He said something to Coachman Giddings. After helping Enya into the warmth of the carriage, the plump hearse driver leaned against the carriage and drew out a cheroot to gnaw upon.

Uncle Owen started to accompany me.

I stiffened. "Please. I should like to go alone. I am no longer a child."

A worry line scrawled his forehead. He would always see me as the dreamy-eyed little princess who used to drape daisy crowns on her head, who sat upon his knees as he shared picture books of castles and handsome heroes riding white steeds. He didn't want to accept that I'd given up on fairytales and princes years ago.

"Don't be long," he finally conceded. "The sun will set soon. And take care not to trip over any graves. They are difficult to see in the fog." Reluctant, he released me and settled next to the coachman.

Ribbons of water drizzled from my umbrella. I wove through crumbling headstones, past two life-sized angels of masculine granite perfection: one carved and ravaged by time, the other youthful and smooth. Despite their subtle differences, they both stood tall and stalwart, protecting the living from the dead.

Or perhaps the dead from the living ...

That unbidden thought made me shiver. My mood soothed as the rain softened to a gentle mist, and the scent of earth, damp and clean, drifted upward. The clouds parted and I closed the umbrella. Sloshing through puddles so deep my stockings soaked to the ankles, I stopped at the furthest end of the graveyard. Tentative rays of warm sunlight curled around my shoulders, illuminating a scene a few feet away at a fenced-in enclosure.

A man dressed in black stood with his back to me, built with the same tall stature and muscular grace as the angel monuments. A governor's cane crooked around his elbow as he clenched the outside of the ivy-wound gate with gloved hands. Glistening through particles of mist, a sunbeam fell upon a lone headstone centered inside the fence, spotlighting it. The man's shoulders shook as if he wept.

I glanced behind me. The carriage was hidden from view by a six-foot wall of English hedgerows. I considered reaching out to the mourner, knowing his pain intimately. Instead, I tugged my veil down and started to leave, stopping only when his head began to jerk back and forth, banging on the bars, as if a rage had broken loose—so intense, the thuds of metal against his skull shuddered through the ground and into the soles of my shoes.

I couldn't move, nailed in place by morbid fascination.

His hat flipped off. The wind carried it to my feet and he turned my direction. Gasping, I dropped my umbrella and backed up. My heel caught on the edge of a headstone, and I fell on my rump. The large crinoline cage that held my skirt's hem aloft so I could walk protruded like a bowl turned on its side and impeded my view. I couldn't see the stranger until his gloved palm appeared next to my shoulder.

A groan scalded my throat. I accepted his help, replaying his emotionally unstable outburst at the gate. I was alone here; would Uncle be able to get to me in time if I had cause to scream?

Upon standing, I sought the man's face, wondering if his forehead had suffered any bruises or gashing. The sun met the horizon, and in a final searing display, it burst behind him, blinding me. He'd replaced his hat over his thick, dark hair. The brim's shadow obscured his eyes, and lush whiskers blurred his squared jaw. For all intents and purposes, he remained faceless.

Only his lips stood out ... full and lovely. They formed words I couldn't read clearly through my lace veil, so I remained mute to hide my deafness. He crouched to wipe mud from my shoe with a hanky. His gloved fingers gently grazed my stockinged ankle and stirred a hot flush of sensation that tingled in my abdomen and rushed to my cheeks. I jerked away.

As if oblivious he'd touched me, he handed over my umbrella, tipped his hat, and left. His off-set gait might have been awkward on another man, but he held his spine straight, his shoulders and chest forming a counterbalance. His weight eased from the governor's cane to his good foot with a meter so rhythmic, he appeared to glide on the waves of an ocean.

Intrigued, I watched until he vanished around the hedges in the direction of my uncle and the carriage. I debated following. Uncle might worry that I'd been unchaperoned in the back of the cemetery with a man, but curiosity got the better of me.

I rushed to the padlocked gate to read the epitaph on the tomb within ... to see what had caused such a volatile reaction in the stranger.

One word stood out across the slight distance: *Hawk*. If ever there had been a surname, time's razor had shaved it away. Movement at the grave's base distracted me before I could look any closer. A flower—stem covered in prickles—danced on the chill wind in a fringe of dying, yellow grass. It was odd that a blossom would bloom so many weeks after the first frost.

The shimmering silver petals folded downward, hugging the stem like a woman's skirt, to expose a raised central cone the blue of an autumn twilight. During all the times I'd gardened with Mama while growing flowers for our hats, I'd never seen such an upended blossom, or such unique colors.

An overwhelming ache began to well within me. My fingers itched to touch the petals, to burn from the stem's prickles. I needed to absorb what the flower knew all the way to its roots. Seated atop a tomb, it was closer to death than I had ever been—closer to Mama and Papa than I could be now. If I held it in my hands, perhaps I would somehow be closer to them, too.

I dropped the umbrella and flipped back my veil. I glanced toward the hedgerow. No one had come searching for me yet, so I found a large stone and pummeled the rusted padlock on the gate until it snapped open with a pouf of red dust.

Inside the enclosure, I used a stick to dig up the flower with roots still intact. While shaking mud from the stem, I noticed another gate on the backside of the fence. It opened to a path worn through a wild and writhing thicket that hedged the enclosure. Someone from those woods had been keeping a vigil over this grave.

As though in reaction to my discovery, a sharp wind gusted from the north and the sky became a gray-green swirling mass.

I trembled in the dimness, my attention snapping to the overturned dirt at my feet, shocked at what I'd done. I had desecrated a holy resting place. Would God unleash his stony angels and condemn my soul to Purgatory? What would that faceless gentleman do, or the anonymous grave keeper in the thicket, were they to find me standing here, a robber cradling her plunder?

I swallowed the lump from my throat. My gloves squeezed the flower's stem. The silver petals glowed in the dimming light. A floral scent drifted up, redolent and spiced like cider—an exotic thrill that fed my waning courage.

The harshest bite of winter was just around the bend, and this beautiful creation—so unique, so fragile—would not survive. Its well-being was now my responsibly, and I would not abandon it, no matter the consequences.

I tucked the flower beneath the flap of my pelisse overcoat, raced out of the enclosure, shut the gate, and

A.G. HOWARD

snagged the umbrella.

When I arrived behind the English hedgerows, I spotted the top of the stranger's hat bobbing on the other side, a few inches taller than the six foot barrier. I peered through the leaves. Coachman Giddings and Uncle Owen leaned against the carriage, deep in conversation with him. His back was turned, broad shoulders tense in the dissipating light.

Perhaps he was relaying how a brash young woman had spied upon his private grief then fell on her backside with all the grace of a circus clown. I bided my time and stayed hidden, trusting Uncle to keep my secret.

Once the stranger had climbed a white steed and trotted cautiously down the road back to town, I plunged from the bushes and stumbled by Giddings' horses. The crinoline beneath my skirts slapped the lead mare. She bucked and reared, her mouth and eyes wide with terror, aiming to trample me beneath her forelegs.

Uncle lunged, thudding us both into the mud.

A dull pain rattled my shoulder blades, quickly passing as I gasped for air. Coachman Giddings settled the rigging while Uncle helped me stand and straighten the hateful contraption holding up my hems.

Lavender twilight bent shadows around us, but I could still make out his lips. Although I didn't need to read his words to know I was being scolded. He'd always forbidden me to be in proximity of horses, since they were flighty and I couldn't hear to react to them.

I patted my coat's flap to check the blossom underneath. Assured of its safety, I interrupted Uncle's concerned ranting with a question of my own. "Who was that man?"

The worry line across his brow deepened. "The Viscount, Lord Nicolas Thornton."

I snapped free of Uncle's grasp. "How dare he come! All these months, Mama couldn't even rest for his incessant missives to buy the house." Tears burned behind my eyes. "And now he storms her burial to feast upon her carcass."

Devastation twisted Uncle's features.

I bit my tongue. Because I couldn't hear, I tended to say whatever entered my mind without a thought as to how it would sound to another person. Uncle's gaping wound was proof of the sword I wielded so carelessly. "Please, forgive me."

He took my hand inside both of his. Cold, wet gusts whipped at my dress as I was dragged into the depths of sadness in his eyes: lost moments, never to be reclaimed ... nagging regrets and bittersweet longing.

Uncle was my rock, and nothing hurt more than hurting him. "Why was the viscount here?" I asked, lacing our fingers tighter to pull him back from his grief.

He squeezed my hand. "To meet you. He's a fine gentleman, Juliet. I've invited him to call before he returns to Worthington at week's end. He'll be by on Thursday."

"To what end?"

"He wishes to give you his condolences, naturally."

"No." I swallowed. "Condolences are only natural coming from a friend. He knows nothing of me, and nothing of the woman Mama was. He only knew her through missives he sent, all selfishly-motivated." It was common knowledge the viscount was an only child and didn't get along well with his father. Perhaps that made him less sympathetic to familial boundaries. "He's coming to offer again on the estate. The fool won't take no for an answer."

Uncle shook his head. "I truly hoped, after your mother's death, you would feel more amenable toward him."

"*Amenable*?" I held my vocal cords lax in hopes my voice remained soft and steady. I bit back the urge to tell Uncle about the viscount's strange actions earlier. Lord Thornton was twenty-seven years old and a nobleman. Men of his age and breeding were expected to suppress their passions, not bang their heads on iron fences. But I couldn't condemn him openly without outing myself as a grave robber.

He must be dual natured. For he seemed in control, even kind and gentle, when he freed me from the mud. My ankle shook on the memory. I wasn't sure what disturbed me more ... the fact that he'd touched me so intimately, or the fact that I liked the way it felt—and craved to know more of that foreign sensation.

"I do not trust him," I said simply. "Not as a gentleman. And most certainly not as a guest in *my* home."

Mouth clamped, Uncle cupped my elbow to assist me into the carriage next to Enya. He was too kind to flaunt the truth: that in reality, I didn't legally have claim to anything. With Mama's death, Uncle Owen had become the executor of the estate, so I now lived as his tenant. It was all a grand façade; a masquerade set into play to ensure I would keep the lands and money without contest. Yet, at any given time, he could force my hand to sell. I wasn't sure how long his patience would hold, now that Mama was gone and the place held nothing but painful memories for him.

I sniffled as I took my seat, averting my gaze when Enya's green eyes locked on me with pity. Uncle climbed in and I pulled down my veil, turning toward the darkening horizon.

Having been my stand-in father for so long, he was more adept at peering into my soul than the most masterful gypsy. I couldn't afford for him to read my face, to know that it wasn't sadness causing the warm flush in my cheeks, that instead, vindication radiated through me. I had ravaged a grave to which the unrelenting Lord Thornton appeared emotionally shackled.

The carriage bounced over pits in the road and the hard-backed seat offered little comfort for the bumpy ride, but I was snuggled within the cushion of my machinations.

Before now, I never understood why the viscount wanted my property. From what Uncle had told me, he was a gifted architect, with a passion for odd color pairings and design. Held to such standards, my home would be considered mundane. But, perhaps it wasn't the house he wanted. It was the location. No other estate stood as close to the graveyard and the grave that seemed to hold him in some dark, impassioned thrall.

Who was this "Hawk" I had stepped upon and defiled? Why did their tomb have such an impact on the viscount? And how could I use this knowledge to save my home and rid myself of Lord Thornton's manipulative persistence, once and for all?

I had two days before his visit in which to solve the riddles, or risk losing the one thing left of my parents. The one thing left of myself.

CHAPTER 2

A thorn defends the rose, harming only those
who would steal the blossom.
A Chinese proverb

The moment Uncle and Coachman Goodings delivered us to the doorstep, Enya slipped inside.

I stalled upon the threshold to wave goodbye to Uncle, then turned and observed my bleak prosperity. Withered bushes curved from the courtyard out back as if hugging the house. By morning, the moisture weighing on them would pearl the leaves in autumn frost. Just as winter had swallowed up Mama, soon it would swallow my home.

Shutting the door, I removed my hat and coat and hung them on the brass hook. Enya rushed upstairs to shed her wet clothes, so I didn't bother hiding the flower while I felt my way through the dark rooms and revived every available gas lamp. My palm curled around each glass globe to feel the vibrations through my glove as they buzzed and popped on.

I stepped into the dining room, and a waft of Mama's scent settled on my nose—rosewater and vanilla. I could sense her there, though she never would be again. Misery rained in my heart.

During my youth, Mama would offer hot chocolate and a lemon crumpet to chase away storms. I would squeeze my eyes closed upon the first bite of the snack's tartness, then snap them open as the chocolate's sweet warmth coated my tongue.

She was a skilled emotional strategist. She taught me that taste affected moods, but even more persuasive was color. That's why, even if it were just the two of us sharing tea, we would always don our brightest gowns and hats.

Now that I was in mourning, I'd not have the privilege of wearing anything other than mourning weeds for several months, and my mood would be as drab as the black fabric that imprisoned me.

As the room gradually lit, the porcelain dinnerware glistened along the cupboard's velveteen lined shelves. Each platter had a story ... each plate and bowl held a memory. Some had been used for grand meals with friends, others for cozy family suppers with Uncle, Mama, Enya and me.

Uncle had only been seventeen when Papa married Mama. When Papa died nine years later, he carried mama's heart with him to heaven, leaving no other man a chance to claim it.

Mama had known Uncle loved her. She helplessly watched it happen as he stepped into Papa's shoes to keep us afloat after his death. Mama tried to discourage his feelings tenderly. Out of respect, Uncle hid his affection away, tucked within his heart like a feather in a pocket— waiting to come out one day if the winds were favorable for flying.

He'd never married anyone because of that hope, yet still he took care of us, not holding a grudge, even giving us a healthy percentage of the monthly earnings from the family's baronet service.

Because of him, we'd never had to auction any of our heirlooms. And now they were even more precious, yet at the same time, harbingers of change. For if I was forced to sell my home, they would all be boxed up and wrapped in cloaks of dust and grief.

I felt so deeply alone, until beside the bay windows, my pet nightingale fluttered to life and rocked her standing cage. Moonlight filtered through the mossy green curtains behind her, casting shadows of her performance across the Turkish rug.

Smiling at Aria's antics, I set aside the stolen flower on the window seat's cushion so I might remove my gloves. The petal from Mama's rose fell out of my wristband and fluttered down beside my plunder.

I left it there and nudged my finger between the nightingale's wire bars. Her beak nipped me in greeting.

Uncle discovered the bird three years ago, hidden beneath his cottage's foundation. Her song gave her away. She was little more than a fledgling then—half of her left wing chewed off by some predator. Yet somehow, she'd escaped alive.

Knowing she would never fly again, Uncle brought her to me and Mama. She adjusted to the life of a captive, coming to love and trust us as we nursed her back to health.

She pecked my finger with vigor now, hungrily seeking

a snack. She hadn't any idea of the agony I faced today—no inkling that Mama wouldn't be coming back, or that someone wished to take our home away. As long as she was fed and coddled, life assumed its natural slant for her.

I looked down at Mama's fallen rose petal again. How I envied the bird's singularly-minded outlook.

A chunk of stale bread waited upon the table, hidden among the ribbons, feathers, and dried flowers I'd strewn about in a vain attempt at work earlier this afternoon. I picked up the stolen flower to carry with me on my search for the bread. The prickled stem caught my bare finger, puncturing it.

An ache wound around my knuckles and joints. The strange pain lasted only an instant—yet long enough to remind me this delicate treasure needed to be planted. Carefully, I wrapped the stem and scraggly roots in a length of grosgrain ribbon. A small droplet of blood oozed from my finger and I sucked it away.

After feeding Aria, I took down my waist-length hair and stepped out of the dreadful crinoline which had caused so much trouble today, both tripping me in front of the viscount and nearly getting me kicked in the teeth by a horse.

I crinkled my nose, wishing I could shed the strictures of society just as easily ... the mores and virtuous ignorance pressed upon us that influenced our clothes and every aspect of our lives.

Draping the excess length of my dress and petticoats around my arm, I ventured out the back door, lantern and flower in hand.

Mud flooded the path to the potting shed. Overhead, the birches shook their bare limbs as if to protect the shadowy gardens. For the first time in my life, I felt like an intruder. Yet the moment I stepped inside the shed, I belonged once more. Moonlight drifted through the green-tinged glass roof and walls. Thousands of dust motes swirled around the hooks where my flowers dried in bundles of twine—a glistening, mystical display.

I hung my lantern on the peg next to the door and stroked the petals of my stolen flower. I used to imagine this place was the realm of fairies. Even the scents were enchanting: overturned soil, flowers specked with water, and feathers stirring up dust.

This reconstructed greenhouse sheltered more than plants, pots, gardening tools and aprons; it was also a haven for Mama's bluebirds, purple grackles, green herons, and other decorative fowl that lined the back wall in cages. They were not simply her pets, they were her livelihood. During their molting periods, they provided plumage for her signature caps and bonnets, along with feathers for women who couldn't afford newer creations, so they might spruce up their old hats.

Now Mama's legacy and charitable reputation were mine to preserve. Standing here, admiring the birds' sleeping sweetness, I ached for one touch of her hand on my hair ... for one wisp of her breath on my cheek as she leaned over to see them in the dim light.

Hot tears raced down my cheeks, blurring my vision to the point I nearly missed the glow upon my fingers. It reminded me of the time in my childhood when I had accidentally crushed a firefly between my palms. The strange residue seemed to be oozing from the flower.

I separated the petals to look closer at the luminescent pollen. Before I could make sense of it, a song burst through my ears.

My spine tingled with sensation—alert.

Impossible. I had to be mistaken. Eleven years without a sound; so much time gone by with only the roar of emptiness—more desolate than living within a seashell.

How could I suddenly *hear*?

I jumped as the musical notes broke again as if to prove me wrong—hammering against my eardrums—a delicious itch I'd once taken for granted.

It was a lullaby in a masculine, affecting baritone, sung in a foreign tongue.

Two feet in front of me, a man came into view bit by bit, as if being painted in place by each lyrical pearl of sound, until there he was, seated upon Mama's stool. He held white-gloved hands over his ears and his clean-shaved jaw moved with the song. And his skin ... it glowed like the petals between my fingers.

The singing stopped as the man's head snapped up. He stared at me, his expression a mirror of my own surprise and confusion. He was close to my age, his face regal and exotic—all elegant lines and sharp angles: high-boned cheeks and square chin, a defined nose with a sloping tip, sensuous lips, and heavy brows over almond-shaped eyes.

"H-how did you get in here?" he asked.

Shrieking, I picked up an empty bucket and slung it. It soared *through* him, hit a cage, and stirred the birds from their slumber. They flapped in a silent, drunken craze.

So shaken, I dropped the flower. Only then did the intruder vanish.

Shoulders braced against the wall, I whimpered. My throat stung, as if I had swallowed a wad of needles.

Was this my punishment for digging up a grave? Was I to lose my mind?

Scanning the shed, I found no signs—other than the overturned bucket and fluttering birds—that the incident had ever happened. Even on my fingertips, the glow was gone. Yet I couldn't stop shaking.

There had to some explanation. The flower's venom had hallucinatory qualities. The thorn's prick from earlier had caused some sort of auditory apparition. My eyes would not betray me otherwise. I had trained them for over a decade to be astute and incontrovertible.

I seized a pot already filled with soil. Then, using the grosgrain ribbon again, I picked up the flower without touching it directly and trundled across the muddy path and back into my home, locking the door behind me.

I stood there panting, forehead pressed to the frame as the soggy hem of my dress formed brown puddles on the floor.

A tap on my shoulder shook a yelp from my lungs and I spun, coming face to face with Enya. Questions sparkled in her wide, green gaze.

"You startled me," I mumbled.

Frowning, she lifted the hem of her bed gown out of the muddy water at my feet. Then her gaze trailed the pot I held at my chest.

"Mama's favorite." I flashed the flower with a shaky hand, ashamed of the lie but seeing no alternative.

"You went to the greenhouse? At this hour?" Enya had cleared most of the table and started a fire in the hearth. Orange light glazed her face as I watched her lips. "Are you all right? You look as if you've seen a—" She stopped herself and adjusted an auburn curl that had fallen from her nightcap. "I-I didn't mean that."

I nodded. But the implication stirred a quiver behind my sternum. I moved away from the wet puddles and settled the pot on the floor. Enya bent to help but I pushed her back. She squinted as if I'd gone raving mad.

Perhaps I had. I was trying to keep the same thing from happening to her.

Wearing gloves to prevent another prick from the venomous stem, I tucked the roots into the soft soil. The petals perked after being watered.

"We could set it by the window." Enya crouched beside me again. "So when morning comes, it will be awash in sunlight." Her finger lifted as if to stroke the silvery flower.

I blocked her. "Please never touch it. Its petals are very fragile."

She drew back, her features folded to a mix of hurt and worry. At twenty-nine years of age, Enya was the closest thing to an older sister I had ever had. Mama had given her a position as our maid ten years ago, when Enya's father abandoned her family, leaving them impoverished. Though Enya and I often disagreed on societal strictures, we held a deep affection for one another. I regretted being so harsh tonight of all nights, but until I found out how dangerous the flower might be, I had to guard her well-being.

Dangerous. I studied the intricately downturned petals. What an odd descriptor for something so beautiful. It was a *flower*. Nothing more. Nothing less.

Enya backed away from me. "Perhaps a bath will calm you." Casting concerned sidelong glances my direction, she puttered about the room and set water to boil from our drawn reserve. She moved the empty tub next to the wood pile Uncle had gathered prior to the funeral.

As I pinned up my hair and shed my clothes, I wondered about Uncle, all alone in his stone cottage just over the hill, with nothing but a senile, arthritic spaniel and his regrets. I almost wished I had taken him up on his offer to stay tonight. Perhaps I wouldn't be teetering on insanity, had he been here for me to care for, to distract me from my own loss. But I'd been determined to prove my independence, to show him I could manage with only Enya and a nightingale for company.

Enya left the room, promising to return with my bed gown and some towels.

I dragged the flower pot close before I eased my weary limbs into the tub. Warm water folded over me. To keep my locket dry, I draped the chain behind my nape so it hung over the tub's edge.

Eyes half-closed, I peered at the flower.

Perhaps I imagined that man—that *hallucination*—because I needed proof of the afterlife, to be closer to Mama and Papa somehow. Grief could stroke the heart strings to play convincing melodies, all in the want of seeing a loved one again.

Many times in my past, I would pick out a tune from my memories, dust it off, and bring it to life. Although I'd forgotten the sound of Mama's voice, I had never misplaced the harmonies or lyrics she sang.

Yet the lullaby I'd heard was in a language I could not decipher. How could I have imagined a man's voice so sensual, so filled with emotion and depth, singing a melody I'd never known?

The flower's scent mingled with the charred wood. Overwhelmed by an urge to hear the music once more—on the chance it was even possible—I reached out, drizzling water across the floor to clasp a silvery petal between my fingers. I stiffened as the song was reborn, instantly.

The man—or mirage—emerged slowly in the corner, propped against the cupboard, his palms covering his ears again. He wasn't fully substantive, had only a hint of color to his image. Even the wrinkles of the creamy wall hangings shone through him. Tall and broad-shouldered, he was dressed in a black waistcoat and striped trousers that draped strong thighs and long legs. A cravat was knotted above his muscular chest.

Though my arm weakened with curiosity and shock, I kept my contact with the flower. The moment he noticed me, the notes broke in his throat, hands dropping in one graceful motion from his ears.

Silence wreathed us, all but for his labored breath.

I debated speaking, but what does one say to a hallucination?

"Well, Miss." He tapped one of the button boots donning his feet, blatant in his appraisal of my body. "You might consider more what you should wear, than what you should say. Not that I'm complaining of your choice thus far."

I gasped and released the flower. He vanished.

Scrambling from the tub, I covered myself with a woolen throw and slumped next to the planter. I arranged my necklace so the locket fell again between my breasts. My erratic pulse hammered my sternum beneath it.

A man had seen me naked in my bath.

But no. It was merely an apparition.

I studied the corner where he had stood. He'd seemed so real.

He even heard my *thoughts,* as if I had spoken them directly to him.

That had been wonderful—no straining to read his lips, no struggling to form answers without *sounding* deaf to him. I rarely engaged in conversation with anyone other than Uncle, Enya, Mama, or our female clientage. Communication was laborious, and in the past, the effort had yielded painful results. Most especially with men.

I'd inherited Mama's long, golden hair and soft brown eyes, and lashes uncharacteristically dark for one of my porcelain coloring. Paired with Papa's shapely lips and a small nose that earned me the nickname of China Rose— the nymph of all blossoms—my appearance garnered more attention than I desired. But I'd learned men could not be trusted once they discovered my "abnormality." So even had I been eligible for a coming out season to meet a suitable mate, I would have refused it. Something I'd made very clear to Mama and Uncle.

That didn't mean I was immune to curiosities or loneliness.

I flushed, thinking of how Lord Thornton touched my ankle at the cemetery. Society said it was wrong to have such stirrings. Enya constantly catechized me on proper codes of conduct. Only familial affection and the goal to one day be a mother were acceptable feelings for a lady to have. Heaven forbid we put any intellectual consideration into how those things came about.

Yet earlier, when I saw the viscount mourning at the gate, what I first noticed was his masculinity. I thought him attractive, and wounded. I was drawn to him, beyond my empathy for his loss. I knew better than to reach out. Not only because it would be improper with no chaperone between us ... but because I dared not step from the veil of diffidence that had cloaked me for so long. Being vulnerable was far more discomforting than being reprimanded by society.

Yet if there were someone who only I could see ... someone who could hear me without my tongue, and that I could hear without my ears, we wouldn't have those boundaries. We wouldn't have *any* boundaries.

And my solitude would be no more.

I glanced down at the flower. My chin trembled. I must indeed have lost my mind. For instead of fearing the implications of the apparition I'd imagined, I was desperate to conjure him again.

Wrapping the woolen throw around me, I touched the

petals. On cue, my translucent guest materialized in front of the windows beside my nightingale's cage, his form aglow with that otherworldly light.

Upon his appearance, Aria bustled behind the wires as if flames lit her tail feathers. The man kept his back to me, distracted by her. I stood with one hand on the flower, the other cradling the pot to help hold the throw where I had knotted it at my chest.

If the bird could see him, and he could see the bird, he wasn't a hallucination.

He *must* be real.

Clasping his gloved hands behind him, my visitor turned around. His eyes were soft like grey clouds of winter, though alive with light, as if the sun lingered behind them.

There was a shift as I saw him as an irrefutable entity, connected to me on some level defying all logic.

"Thank you." His voice curled through the air, warm like a vapor of coffee on a chill morn.

For? The query formed in my mind. I didn't even bother moving my lips.

"For showing me the way out of the darkness. I've been there since ..." He reached into the lapel of his jacket and pulled out a gold pocket watch of unusual shape, square instead of round. Upon gazing at it, my guest's jaw twitched. "What time is it? My watch is cracked." He held it up. Behind a crinkled glass face, the hands pointed to half-past twelve.

I appraised the clock on my mantle, and this time I answered aloud. "It's ten of the clock." Feeling exposed beneath his unfaltering stare, I averted my eyes to the floor. "Sir Hawk."

He tucked his watch away. "Hawk?"

I inched backward until I stood in a puddle of tepid bath water, a result of my swift withdrawal from the tub. "Yes. That's your name, is it not?"

"It does seem familiar." He ran a gloved palm through glossy, shoulder length waves—either black or a brown as rich as burnt chocolate. With his glowing translucence, it was hard to be sure. "I feel as if I'm expected somewhere. Do you know anything of that?"

I shook my head.

"I'm dressed for an occasion." His arms stretched out and he studied his clothes. Then he offered a roguish smile—an arresting flash of straight, white teeth. "Perchance I've just arrived, and we were to share a bath."

No! I tightened the throw around me, disconcerted yet titillated by the implication.

The smile slipped from his face. "Wait. Say something."

What should I say? I struggled to think over my heart's raucous pounding. Surely he could hear it.

"How are you doing that?" He discarded his gloves, revealing long, fine fingers. "Your lips—they don't move. Yet I still hear you." His gloves dispersed to dust upon hitting the floor. He didn't seem to notice, too intent on me. "Is that how you drew me out of the darkness? You are a witch?"

"I assure you. *I* am human." I moved my lips with the words this time, though my vocal cords and tongue played no part in this conversation.

His shoulders eased, as if relieved by my efforts. He backed up and glanced again at Aria. She preened her feathers while eyeing him suspiciously.

I dragged the flower's pot between my breasts to pull the woolen throw higher. My locket wedged beneath it, pinching me.

Such a tragedy, to have no idea the state he was in.

He straightened his posture. "What state? Have I been in an accident? Is that why I'm imagining such queer things? Are you my nurse?" Then his attention dropped to my covering. "What kind of hospital is this?"

Inching toward the windows, the throw trailing behind me through the puddles, I stepped onto the dry rug. Still pinching a flower petal, I sat on the window seat, keeping Aria's cage between me and my guest. My arm tightened around the flower pot. "I hardly believe it myself. If not for seeing you earlier in the shed, and your appearance now ... though you are not exactly *here*, are you?"

He furrowed his brow and stepped around the cage to sit beside me.

The cushion dented beneath his weight and I wondered upon the strange physical rules binding him. A bucket, when tossed his direction, couldn't touch him; yet he affected things around him to some degree.

"What do you mean, not here?" His voice lowered, tentative.

I looked him in the eyes, their light shadowed by thick, dusky lashes. "You are dead ... a spirit without a form. *A ghost.*"

CHAPTER 3

Better to light a candle than to curse the darkness.
Chinese Proverb

"A ... ghost." My guest looked on the verge of either amusement or hysterics. It was obvious he thought me mad.

I glanced at his boots, noticing for the first time that something was clumped and dried upon them. It seemed familiar, though I couldn't place it. "What is that?" I asked. It looked like blood, but was too thick. "Some sort of mud. Where is it from? Such an odd color."

He scraped his right heel with his left. "Color?" As if an afterthought, he glanced at the wavering fire. "No. Everything is varying shades of gray. Even the flames."

I shook my head. "There must be some sort of visual boundary between your realm and mine."

"My realm and—?" His mouth tensed to a line. "Not this death madness again. I've woken up in a bloody sanatorium."

"I agree it does feel like one. Considering I'm as deaf as the night is dark. Yet here I am conversing with you," I clamped my lips shut, sealing them tight to prove my point, *with or without using my tongue.*

He launched himself off the cushion and stumbled

backward several steps, staring at me in repulsion. "Stop doing that! It is you that is a ghost. You're haunting me!"

Aria ruffled her feathers and opened her bill on a screech that I couldn't hear. Worried her tantrums might bring Enya running, I draped her cage with the silken cloth used to settle her to sleep at night while still keeping my finger on the flower's petal.

"No, Sir Hawk." This time, I moved my lips. "I can hold and touch things." I rolled the flower pot at my sternum. "You cannot."

"You're daft."

I stood. The throw's fringe tickled my toes. "All right. What happened to your gloves?"

He shook his head. "I dropped them."

"Then find them."

His gaze jerked around the room, desperate. "But ... they fell. Right there." He gestured to Aria's cage. "Somewhere beneath."

I stiffened my chin. "They were only real while you wore them. Once you took them off, they vanished—ceased to exist."

He glared at me. Unbuttoning his jacket, he shrugged out of the sleeves and draped it over his elbow. Then, holding my gaze, he pulled off the cravat. His shirt lapels folded open to reveal a strong chest with a slight furring of dark hair.

I'd never seen a man's naked chest before and looking away proved a very difficult task.

"Interesting," he baited. "It appears my clothes are still here. You're playing me for a fool." The cravat dangled from his fingers like a white flag of surrender, a stark contrast to the challenge in his voice.

I'd been holding onto the pot and the flower for so long, my hands were falling asleep. "Let the jacket and cravat fall free of your touch."

He narrowed his eyes and released them. We both watched the clothing vanish the moment it met the floor, all but the pocket watch inside his jacket. It stayed intact and hit the rug with a thump I felt in my feet.

Why didn't it disappear, too? Perhaps it being made of metal played a role.

He started to tug his shirt from his pants, staring at the place on the floor where his jacket and cravat should have been. He studied my face. "Show me how you did that." He began to work his wrists free from his ruffled sleeves.

"You would do well not to relinquish the rest of your clothes." I moved back to the window and sat with the flower pot propped on my lap. My fingertips tingled as blood resumed its natural course. "I suspect if you strip yourself naked, you shall remain that way." *And your pocket watch has little hope of hiding your most prized attribute.* The wicked thought raced through me, unchecked, as the gleaming glass face caught my eye from the rug.

"You are a bold one," he said.

Shame burned my cheeks in a hot rush. "You weren't meant to hear that."

He eased his wrists back into place within the shirt then bent to pick up the watch. He tucked its chain within his waistband with the square face hanging outside his trousers. "What kind of scheme are you running? Summoning men to your bath and teasing them with visions of milky skin and perfect breasts. Purposely leading them on a nightmare journey into madness."

A forbidden delight stirred in my chest. "You think my breasts are perfect?"

He grimaced—an expression which on any other man would be off-putting. But framed by his opacity, it made him look like an avenging angel. "I owe you no pretty words. You're a thief. You've drugged me, so you may unhinge my mind and steal my purse."

"I am no thief." I steadied my gaze on his, determined to make him face his truth, however tragic it was. "And it would appear you have nothing real enough to steal, other than a most unusual broken watch."

"Is that so?" His lip twitched. "Why are you holding that blasted plant? Put it down." A dare laced his words. "Put it down and I'll give you something worth stealing. First, we start with a kiss. Then I'll show you how real the rest of my body is."

My mouth drained of moisture. I never realized a threat could double as an enticement.

Before I could react, he reached for my wrist. His hand dispersed like a rush of dandelion seeds then reappeared. It felt as if the wind had ruffled my skin. He cried out and my legs jerked in reaction, toppling the pot from my lap. Dirt hiccupped onto my bare feet as my guest vanished.

I cursed—a word which would've curled my mama's straight hair. The throw came unwound from my body as I fell to my knees.

Ignoring my nakedness, I scooped the soil back into the pot. I almost didn't notice the feet settling next to me.

I glanced up into Enya's horrified face. "What has gotten into you?" She dropped my bed gown to the floor. "Cover up. I'll clean this mess."

My cheeks grew hotter. Only after I patted the dirt in place around the flower and nudged the stem to assure it didn't snap did I slip the gown over my head.

Enya forced me to stand, cupping my chin so I'd look directly at her. "Your mother was your world. I understand. I loved her as my own. For all her generosity toward me and my family. For always treating me with respect and kindness. You are not alone in your grief, Juliet. Let me help you."

My chest clenched against a pain I refused to face.

Enya caressed my cheek sweetly. "I will fix you some chocolate to drink. We'll share our favorite memories of her. It is the only way to find peace and sense once more." She started for the cupboard.

"Wait," I said. I didn't want to find peace or sense. I wanted to be with the ghost again. Talking to him made me feel closer to Mama, and was much easier on the heart than dredging up bittersweet nostalgia. "I would prefer to be alone. Down here, among her and Papa's things. Just for tonight."

Enya's freckled features saddened, and I despised my selfishness. Omitting her from my grief as if she was nothing but a maid, when she was so much more. I debated sharing the secret, letting her see the captivating face of the afterlife as I had, but before I could form proper words, Enya was gone—into the hall and up the stairs.

Slapping tears from my cheeks, I bolted the double doors behind her, then touched the flower again. Sound was becoming a drunken obsession, having been so long without it. And that tickle in my ears was only the beginning of the sensations this experience was igniting in me.

Hawk appeared across the room this time, standing in front of the dying fire. The smoldering flames flapped behind him, as if showing through a curtain of sheer fabric. His hands cupped his ears. "Stop sending me back … please. I cannot abide the voices any longer."

"Voices?"

His hands inched down. "Why do you think I sing?" His dark brows drew low to contain some intense emotion.

Voices.

Could it be he was a madman in life, that he had killed someone and been put to death for the crime? Perhaps he was evil and cruel, and those voices were his eternal punishment.

For a moment, I considered uprooting the flower and throwing it out into the night, so by morning it and everything attached would be destroyed by the winter winds.

My guest's face grew agonized in the firelight—and I knew he weighed my every doubt against the ones he must be having himself.

As I mused upon this, the luminance behind his eyes danced. I realized it was music burning within him, not madness. He wasn't evil. He was simply confused, and needed help making peace with his death.

My companion held his pocket watch up with a trembling hand. *"Death."* The word shattered his baritone, as if he choked. He dropped to his knees. "I'm dead."

Before I could even wonder if a ghost was capable of feeling pain, moisture gathered along his lashes. His fingers clenched his knees, his agony punctuated by the bulging of his knuckles and the gouges in the fabric of his pants.

"Why do you not run away in horror?" he asked without looking at me.

My heart went out to him. I stepped closer and knelt. "I myself have been a ghost for many years. Haunting a muted world as others experience life in full. I understand isolation."

He studied each of his fingers, preoccupied with his phantom form. "How did this happen?"

"I don't know. When I buried my mama earlier today ..." I struggled with the lump in my throat. "I came across a tombstone. And I saw the name, 'Hawk.' The plant is from the gravesite, and you are obviously connected to it."

This caught his attention, and he stood, slowly. "You dug it up."

Wavering, I got to my feet with the pot cradled in front of me. "Yes. I defiled your grave. Are you angry?"

"Considering I threatened to defile you moments ago, I believe we're even now." He managed a tight, self-deprecating smile. "By taking the flower, you released me from Purgatory. I'm no longer alone in my darkness."

I glanced at my feet, still gritty with residual dirt. "Nor am I."

Our attention settled on one another—appraising and thoughtful. I wished I could read his thoughts as he did mine.

"No, Miss. You have no business probing the nightfall of uncertainty that is my mind." He clasped his wrist, as if searching for a pulse. "How long, according to the stone?"

I caressed the petal. "The flower distracted me from the epitaph."

Behind him, through the transparency of his chest, the fire snuffed to embers. It was a tragic image, as if I watched his hope die.

Silence stretched between us, a merciless roar.

Hawk cleared his throat. "Might I ask your name, Miss?"

The formality struck me as almost comical, given our situation, until it dawned on me how difficult it was to escape the confines of society, even after death. "You may call me Juliet."

He nodded. "Juliet, I'm sorry for the loss of your mother."

His kind sentiment was almost as beautiful as hearing my name spoken. "Thank you."

"She must have been an exceptional woman, to have left such a hole in your life."

I shut my eyes, framing her face in my mind. I would never forget her appearance as I had her voice. I would make sure of that.

"But you said you are deaf."

My eyes snapped open upon my guest's redundant observation.

"How could you have known your mother's voice to forget it?"

I studied my feet beneath the throw's fringe, tilting my left one to the side to shake dirt from between my toes. "A childhood illness took my hearing. Before that, my mama sang to me." I sighed. "Since then, so many years without music, so many nights without lullabies." The flower's incense rushed through me, comforting. "Until your song." I smiled. "So lovely. So unexpected."

Compassion and a hint of something else—humility?—flashed across his troubled features. "You flatter me."

"No. I would venture you have much in common with Aria."

"Your nightingale? Her melodies were far from harmonious earlier. She doesn't like me much." His lips formed a thoughtful line. "She seems to notice me even without touching the flower."

I glanced at Aria's covered cage. "I've read animals are endowed with an extra sense ... a perception humans don't possess. Could it be the same holds true for plants, and somehow, by touching the petals, such insight is imposed upon me?"

He tapped his chin thoughtfully. "Or somehow, that flower holds my very essence."

"Can you remember anything that would tie you to this plant? You apparently know a second language."

"Nothing. It is all a void. I couldn't even tell you the language of my songs." A muscle in his jaw fluttered.

"Although ..." He flipped his pocket watch to look at an engraving on the backside. "*Rat King*. Damned if I know what it means. But it's in English." He tucked the chain away again. "As is the name I keep hearing when I'm in hell."

Hell. The despondency in his voice over the acceptance of his fate sliced like a blade. "What name?" I asked.

Hawk's brow furrowed. "Thornton. The voices in my purgatory. They speak it often."

A horrified knot formed in my chest ... undeniable confirmation that the viscount was somehow bound to this tragic soul. For his name to be carried to Hawk's dead consciousness on a choir of haunting voices, paired with the outburst I'd earlier witnessed, Lord Thornton might be more dangerous than I ever imagined.

Hawk stepped closer. "What do you know of him?"

"Very little. I have never even seen his face. But he was at your grave today. He had no way in and appeared distraught about that. A padlock kept him at bay. There's a path that leads from the backside of the fence surrounding your tomb. A well-worn path. Someone else keeps a vigil at your grave. They have the key."

My ghostly guest's eyes grew wild. "You must return to the cemetery! I need to know my identity. How this fate befell me. Please ..."

My stomach flipped. I had already been planning to go so I might outmaneuver the viscount before he came at week's end. Yet, now, faced with the ever deepening chasm of my doubt about the man's emotional stability and the possibility he was involved with another man's death, I'd lost all courage.

A shiver ran through my spine as I realized how dark and chilly the room had grown.

Hawk looked over his shoulder at the embers. "Let me stir the fire for—" The statement broke and he bowed his head, cursing.

I wondered how anyone could bear such frustration.

He slumped onto the hearth. "God help me. I'm nothing more than a puff of wind or a passing chill. Just put the flower down and cast me back into the darkness! I can't expect you to carry a blasted pot around for the rest of the night."

"But you hate the darkness." After the accident I'd endured as a child, I of all people could empathize with the gruesome notions a lightless setting could inspire.

"What kind of accident?" Hawk asked, as though eager to turn the subject on my past and away from his own absent memories.

I didn't answer. My attention had caught upon the singular rose petal I'd earlier had in my glove. The one I'd taken from Mama's rose to hold her spirit close to me. It gave me an idea.

Biting my lip, I plucked the petal I'd been holding on Hawk's flower. I fisted my hand around it and set aside the pot. When I looked up, Hawk was still there.

I raised my eyebrows. The flower didn't have to be intact to bind us, so long as I held a petal.

He stood, tentative. "That's encouraging. But ..." He rubbed his chin. "It will prove a challenge to carry that around and never drop it. The chain on your neck. Did I see a locket earlier?"

I tugged on the necklace to expose the heart-shaped charm and the intricate rose embossed on its front.

"Is it pure silver?"

A "yes" was all I could manage as he strode closer, intent in his study of the necklace. A full head taller than me, had he been flesh, his breath would have warmed my brow. I wondered what he smelled like ... if the upturned hair at his shoulders was as soft as it appeared. Cradled in the safety of otherworldly isolation, I wondered all the things I'd never let myself wonder about any man.

Then, remembering my nakedness beneath my bed gown, I blushed.

Hawk's fingertip scattered upon attempting to touch the necklace's chain. A ripple of sensation grazed my collar bone, gone before my brain could even register it. "It seems I've stepped from one purgatory into another," he whispered.

"I'm sorry."

"As am I." He smiled, though sadness cluttered the curve. "Tuck the petal within your locket," he instructed. "Silver is the most conductive of all metals. Perchance it will allow the energy ... life force ... whatever I share with this flower, to find its way to you."

"I shall lose you in the transfer."

Anxious lines scrawled across his forehead, but he nodded.

"I'll be swift." I promised, then placed the petal in the pot.

He vanished.

With a sense of urgency, I picked up the pot and carried it to the dining table. It pained me to remove Mama and Papa's portraits from the locket. But if Hawk was correct, there must be nothing to interfere with the silver.

I caught a flicker of him as I placed the petal inside and latched the locket shut. The moment the charm slipped between my breasts beneath the throw and touched my skin, my ghostly companion reappeared. This time, to stay.

CHAPTER 4

*Stolen waters are sweet, and bread eaten
in secret is pleasant.*
Proverbs 9:17

I dreamt of a moving darkness with legs like centipedes. It crawled along my skin until nothing remained but bones. The shadows whispered, bidding my spirit to join them. I obeyed, no longer walking but flowing: a liquid, lightless void.

I became one with the night, oozing into the depths of some underground world, joined by the skeletons of others who had followed the shadows long before me. The only colors were black and white, and a red as deep as the mud coating Hawk's ghostly boots.

He hovered over me, his lips so close I could taste his breath—mint with a hint of chicory. As he started to sing, other voices gathered for the serenade, all of my friends and family who'd passed throughout my life. Their music swelled within my soul.

It was then I realized I no longer resided in the land of the living. And it wasn't so unpleasant here, in the world of the dead ...

⌒ ᵔ • ᵔ ⌒

"A man arrived with the sunrise."

The deep voice nudged at my subconscious, but I kept my eyes closed, basking in the afterglow of fading music. Mama was there by my side, listening to the final notes of the song, a contented smile on her face, the same look she always gave me after we'd spent a day together, stitching on our hats. Then I blinked, and the music was gone. Like a slice of winter wind the reality of Mama's absence from my life sucked the breath from my lungs. I bunched my knees to my chest and sobbed, willing the pain away.

"Dear Juliet." Hawk's compassion broke through my self-pity.

I opened my eyes to find him leaning over me, much like he'd been in my dream; though now I was atop a feather mattress and pillows instead of in an underground world, and there was no serenade.

"A serenade in another world." He smiled gently, his face close enough that if I but raised my head, I would disrupt his chin's image for an instant. "Sounds enchanting. You must tell me of this dream later." It was an obvious effort to cheer me.

I forced a smile, grateful that though he could read my thoughts, at least my subconscious remained private. My fingers clasped the locket pressed against my sternum. "What time is it?"

"A few hours past dawn."

I blotted my eyes with my quilt. "I slept through the night without waking even once?"

"Didn't hear a peep out of you," he answered.

I squinted at him, remembering what he had told me last night about how he no longer required sleep.

"I held true to my promise to sit at the desk and not stare at you. At least for the first few minutes." He winked.

I smirked, unable to resist his good humor. In truth, I was grateful for his vigil. I had struggled with sleep since Mama first became ill. Each time I closed my eyes, that near-death experience from my childhood resurfaced in my mind. I was only six when it happened, and the details were hazy. But flames of fear had crisped the memory to a nightmare, which snowed like ash over my dreams.

I didn't make it to bed until well after midnight. Having buried Mama, I anticipated tossing and turning. Yet after Hawk turned his back to allow me to crawl beneath the safety of my covers—proving even a ghost could be a gentleman—I fell away to the sound of his beautiful lullaby. And even if it was only a few hours, it was the most restful sleep I'd had in some time.

Hawk cleared his throat. "As for your visitor ... you told me of a maid, but didn't mention any male acquaintances."

"My Uncle Owen."

On Wednesdays, Uncle always came to sort through the greenhouse, choosing blossoms for his fabric dyes: sunflowers, geraniums, foxgloves, and bloodroot. In all of my emotional upheaval, I'd lost track of what day it was. The most tender part of me didn't think life should resume so quickly after Mama's death. But Uncle felt most at peace when he worked.

Hawk frowned. "Ah. I thought perhaps it was that

Thornton fellow, come early."

"Heaven forbid." My heart hammered at the thought of the viscount. I needed every hour and minute of the next two days to prepare for that encounter.

Slipping out from my sheets, I held a blanket across my chemise, waiting for Hawk to look away.

He crossed to the other side of the room and stopped beside my rosewood desk where I'd placed his flower and its pot. His gaze toured the south window. "Well, since it's your uncle, perhaps we might use his cart and sorrel for our post-breakfast expedition."

I glanced outside over Hawk's shoulder. Fog hugged the sky and cloaked the sun, thick and gray like a wolf's pelt. A miserable day for facing Mama's grave again. But on the bright side, this weather aggravated Uncle's back injury, which had inspired him to drive his two-wheeled sprung cart as opposed to walking.

All I needed was a way to keep Uncle and Enya from realizing I was gone until we returned.

Hawk's feet shifted, swishing the curtains at my window, once again affecting the world around me. "Shall we plan some elaborate scheme? Or would you prefer to follow my lead?"

I secured the steel knob clasps upon the front busk of my corset over my chemise, and eased into stockings and garters. "You wish to be my puppet-master?"

"Hmmm. Me in charge of all your strings? That could prove *most* entertaining." Hawk threatened to turn around but I yelped at him while slipping quickly into my wide-legged drawers.

His broad shoulders shook on a chortle. One thing I had learned in our short time together: he had a wicked wit and his laughter was infectious. Such a masculine, full-bodied sound. It purred through my ears, pulsed through my blood, and lifted my heart to soar—a refreshing counterpoise to the deep silence I had been wrapped within for so many years.

In that instant the sun broke through the fog. Gilded by the light, Hawk resembled a luminous, human-shaped bubble—even more breathtaking and ethereal than the shimmering silver petals of his flower.

"I'm not sure how to feel about that," he teased. "Being compared to a flower."

"Would you prefer a weed?"

He laughed again, and I smiled at his back while arranging a princess panel dress of black crape over my curves. I still hadn't learned how to hide my rampant thoughts and curiosities about him. For the most part, he was taking it all in stride, and was kind enough to make light of it, to ease my embarrassment.

"I must warn you," I said, brushing my hair and rolling it to a chignon at the base of my nape. "Chloe will be downstairs. Uncle always brings her."

"Chloe?"

"His spaniel."

"Ah. And judging by the way Aria reacts to me ..."

"A dog would be even harder to contain. I could wear my locket outside of my dress until I make it out the door." I hated to suggest it, knowing how he dreaded returning to his dark oblivion.

Last night, after he and I discovered we could connect via a petal within the locket, I learned to keep the necklace tucked beneath my corset so it would be held snug against my flesh. Otherwise, he faded from my vision and returned to his dark gloom until it touched my skin again.

We also realized we had to stay within fifteen feet or so of one another while I was wearing the necklace pressed to my skin, with nothing solid—such as a wall or closed door—standing between us. Otherwise, the petal would wither and have to be replaced with another.

Together, we chose never to be separated, except upon the most personal moments when I required privacy.

"Well thankfully," Hawk said from his post at the window, "separation won't be necessary this morn. I see the dog around the corner, secured beside your greenhouse out back."

Relieved, I smoothed my dress into place. The princess panels hugged my small waist and hips, eliminating the need for my nemesis crinoline. Better we were sneaking out. Enya would never let me leave the house otherwise. She would insist my dress was too form-fitting without the attachable long train connected by its hooks ... the one I'd left hanging in my wardrobe to make for ease in walking about.

"You may turn around now," I said.

Hawk did, and then whistled. The sound tickled my ears and made me feel desirable—a most welcome rarity.

"You are exquisite, Juliet. Surely men have told you that."

Before Hawk could see into my thoughts, I suppressed

the memory of the two suitors from my past. It was a pain too demeaning to share. With my mind a blank slate, I led the way downstairs to the dining room, focused only on our plan for escape.

⌒�•ᕐ⌒

Seated at the head of the table, I sorted through my milliner materials.

Just minutes earlier, Enya had peeled the cloth off Aria's cage. The bird fluttered impotently behind the bars, screaming at Hawk. I convinced my maid to cover her up again, that the bird missed Mama and needed a quiet space so she wouldn't be reminded of her absence, much like Uncle had been avoiding going upstairs in fear of crossing her room.

None of us wished to entertain nostalgia today.

I worked to cover a straw bonnet with periwinkle taffeta, wincing when the needle shoved into my tender thumb pad. I had already pricked that place four times.

Pleats were difficult. The tediousness of their construction bored me. This morning, though, I fought a new battle that had nothing to do with boredom. For one thing, the dusty brown of the ribbons waiting to trim my bonnet reminded me of Mama's eyes. And each time I thought on it, Hawk comforted me from over my shoulder where he stood to observe my work.

It was strange enough—to not even be safe in my own head with my musings. But even more unsettling was the fact that Enya and my uncle were bustling about like nervous mice. Each time one of them came close to Hawk,

I jumped and pricked my finger once more.

I worried they might step on him, or walk through him, or somehow feel his presence. Or worse, cause him to disappear—still unsure of the rules of the dead. In fact, in regard to the unusual flower now occupying the left bay window, I had forbidden either of them to touch it.

I claimed the petals too fragile, that the bloom would die with too much handling. All because I feared they might see him. That I might have to share him and his songs. Hawk was a treasure, more cherished than an extravagant ruby ring I might have stolen to keep tucked away and wear in private moments when I wished to feel decadent.

"You intend to wear me, aye?" Hawk's voice lowered and he leaned close, his phantom finger tracing an invisible pattern on the table next to my hat. "I believe I'm going to like being your secret."

Blushing at the seductive imagery, I folded another pleat into place.

While Uncle cleared out some ash to make a place for fresh kindling, Enya prepared his favorite bread pudding for breakfast. Her fingers, frosted with crumbs from the day-old slices she earlier cubed, sorted through a basket of cranberries and tossed out any pitted or specked subjects before adding everything to a heavy cauldron already laced with milk, vanilla, eggs and honey.

"By the way, your strategy to disappear after breakfast for a 'nap' is working," Hawk said, and I imagined the soft weave of his shirt could rake my temple as he pressed his palms on the table's corner—his sleeve just inches from my face. "They speak of how tired you look."

With a long needle, I pulled a basting stitch taut and regarded my family, deep in a clandestine conversation by the fireplace where flames now painted the walls with orange and rose-colored flashes. Enya watched my uncle strain to hang the heavy cauldron, patting his back in gratitude upon completion of the task.

Brushing his hands along his trousers, Uncle Owen gimped toward me. Enya studied him while stirring her pudding with a wooden spoon. She caught me watching and her pink skin brightened as she looked away.

Uncle patted my hand after I folded the final pleat in the taffeta and pinned it in place. I didn't have to look beyond his down-turned mouth to see his concern. His lips moved, and I focused to better read his words before remembering that with Hawk here to translate, I didn't have to read them at all.

"Did you have ill dreams last night, tiny sparrow?" Uncle asked. "You seem weary this morn."

"No nightmares. Just ... not enough sleep. I will nap later." Upon securing my pleats with a running stitch and knotting off the thread, I regarded the circles beneath his eyes. "You also appear tired, father bear."

He grinned at the familiar affectation. Mama had always called him this when he was being over-protective of me. His hazel irises sparkled for an instant, but the whites of his eyes retained evidence of his grief—swollen and veined. "I miss her."

"Then we are of one heart." My own eyes also stung on the admission.

He took the chair beside me, opposite where Hawk stood. We held hands for a moment, our foreheads pressed together—linking unspoken memories through osmosis.

Utilizing a trick he had mastered last night, Hawk drifted through the oak table like a knife slicing butter that folds upon itself in the utensil's wake, leaving no indication of ever being cut. Though it unbalanced me to see him perform such capers, I couldn't stifle a rush of bravado that he was conquering the challenges of his condition.

Hawk took a seat on the other side of Uncle Owen. "He loved your mother deeply. Much more than a brother-in-law should."

He did. I sent the answer back.

Hawk glanced over his shoulder at Enya, then clicked his teeth together in thought—the first I had heard of such a habit. His presence opened a whole new world of sounds for me.

My uncle pulled away and I picked up my scissors, cutting the excess thread from the bonnet.

Uncle nudged me with his elbow to get my attention. "Lovely work."

Before I could thank him, Enya cleared the table of my hat-making materials and placed a steaming bowl of pudding and dried apple wedges under our noses. Warmth eased through me, along with scents of nourishment and comfort. I had a passing curiosity if Hawk could smell them, as well.

"No." His answer draped my thoughts. "But it's all

right. I no longer have an appetite or need for food or drink."

As for me, my stomach growled. Despite my emotional turmoil over the past twenty-four hours, nothing could quell my body's instinctual will to go on. To rise above it all and survive ... whether or not my spirit complied.

For my spirit still remembered my secret dream of earlier, and the comfort of company, song, and sound that waited within the realm of death and darkness.

CHAPTER 5

Love enters a man through his eyes,
a woman through her ears.
Polish Proverb

"Enya is hanging laundry by the greenhouse," Hawk said, looking out my side window. "We should leave before she comes back in."

I tugged on my riding boots and laced them up to my knees beneath my skirt, tucking in the lacy hems of my drawers. After I shrugged into my pelisse overcoat, I grabbed my black veiled hat and a pair of open-fingered silk-knit mitts and followed Hawk down the winding staircase. Just as we entered the hall, he motioned me back toward the stairs.

"She's inside again," he growled. "Industrious, isn't she?"

I crept back up to my room, softening my footsteps under Hawk's insistence. Then I eased my door closed.

Hawk's fists clenched at his sides. "Just tell her you're leaving. Pull rank. She's a simple maid."

"You're wrong. She is so much more than that." Mama had not only given Enya a position to work for our family, but she also gave her an education right alongside me.

Intellectually, and in every other way, I considered us equals.

"Then ask your uncle to take you to visit your mother's grave."

"He'll never allow me to go off alone to explore some path inside an overgrown thicket. Besides, he can't even bring himself to walk by her room. It is too soon for him to face her grave again."

Hawk's lips pursed. He clasped the square face of his pocket watch and studied the cryptic engraving on the back.

Rat King.

The desperate need for answers settled in every shadow of his agonized face. I pressed my forehead to the east window's chilled glass. The oak tree Papa had planted upon his and Mama's nuptials reached up toward me in the fog, massive and sturdy. Withered vines clung to its branches like serpentine hair. I used to be an adept climber. Until the mines—the one time I fell.

"Wait." Hawk towered behind me, his voice gruff. "Is *that* the accident you had? A fall?"

I ignored the concern in his voice. This tree was an old friend, with branches so deftly aligned they formed a ladder in places. I could do it, without a doubt. And being at the front of the house, no one would see us leave. Enya and Uncle were preoccupied: her in the kitchen, and Uncle in the greenhouse out back.

"No," Hawk commanded, though he sounded shaken. "With the bark so wet from the melted frost, you're tempting fate."

I threw back the sash and a rush of chill wind lifted strands of my hair. The hat's lace veil stuck to my lashes, clinging with each blink. Though my heart pounded, I felt a calm—an exhilarating peace. The world in my dream had been beautiful. I wasn't afraid to face it.

"Juliet ... think this through."

I assured my locket remained tucked safely beneath my corset and chemise then drew up my skirts and swung a leg over the sill.

"Please, you don't wish to be where I am." Hawk reached for my arm, a passing sweep of air.

Shoving my other leg out next to my first, I gripped the closest branch and inched forward until one foot wedged in place upon a lower branch. The bark scraped my palms through my gloves. I tightened bare fingers around the narrowest end.

Ignoring Hawk's shouts, I pushed myself free of the sill and centered my weight on my fixed boot. My other foot found purchase on a separate branch and I started my descent.

I couldn't stop my smile as Hawk perched next to me, afloat in midair.

"Are you always this stubborn? Watch that branch!"

The juncture cracked apart and I lost my grip. My dress caught on a snag, pinching my midsection. The hem wound around my legs, tangling my feet.

I hung there, heart tapping an uneasy rhythm. Fog swirled in a dizzying whorl around me. My dress ripped and lowered me an inch. The fabric cinched around my lungs and I gasped for breath. I reached for the vines

Hawk instructed me to grab with a roaring yell.

They were too far. My dress ripped again. Terror clenched my throat.

I lost sight of my courage, forgot the beauty of my dream.

Just like when I was a child, hanging by a thread.

A scream swelled in my chest but before its release, Hawk—with a look of intense concentration—batted at a vine and made contact with his hand. It swung in my direction and I caught it, wrapping it around my wrist the instant the fabric in my dress gave.

I clung tightly to vines the rest of the way down. Once my feet touched, I wanted to kiss the ground. Though I wanted to kiss my rescuer even more. My cheeks warmed, knowing Hawk had heard the unspoken observation.

He scowled at me. "Why would you attempt something so foolhardy? Climbing an ice-slicked tree from those heights. Do you *want* to be dead?"

A stunned realization throttled through me, taking precedent over his insightful question. "You touched that vine and made it move. *Purposely.*" With shaky fingers, I buttoned my coat to cover the gaping tear in my dress.

We both looked over our shoulders at the tree, though our meditation was short lived. Feeling the press of time, we rushed to the stable. In spite of the sorrel's gentle nature, Chester startled at Hawk's presence. I offered a chunk of browned apple that I had tucked away from breakfast, settling him.

I patted his glistening chestnut coat, raw fingertips sliding over the satin of his mane as I walked him toward the gig.

After leading me through the steps of harnessing and securing the rigging, Hawk studied my face. "So, you know how to handle one of these?"

I climbed into the cab and perched on the cold, stiff squab. "Uncle taught me when I was twelve. I caught on as quickly as any boy. Until there was a fat toad." I shook my head. "He came out of nowhere and plopped into the road. I turned the horses sharply ... drove the gig into a ditch. The ruined axles were nothing to the damage on Uncle's lower back."

Hawk barked a laugh. "Well, at least you saved the toad."

"Actually, the left rear wheel flattened him."

Hawk burst into robust chuckles.

I grinned sheepishly. "Stop that. It's tragic." I'd never recovered from the guilt of wounding Uncle. I wore it around my neck like an albatross, along with the weight of Papa's death.

Hawk settled next to me. "You are not a god. Things happen, Juliet. That does not mean you're the cause of them. You're merely a thread in the fabric of life."

His kindness touched me. "All right, if I'm not all powerful, then why would you be concerned about my driving abilities? Nothing can harm you."

"You are my one connection to the living world. Should *you* get hurt, I would bleed more than if I severed my own arm."

The press of his observation made me stop and think. He needed me, as Mama once did. I would not let him down by being careless.

I snapped the lines and Chester trotted along the pebbled road. The misted scenery passed—a hazy glide—as if we skimmed atop clouds. On the climb to Cemetery Hill, bare-branched trees cut through the frothy air like gnarled fingers spinning cotton on a loom.

A damp film coated my face through my netted veil. I shivered. Hawk lifted an arm to draw me close and block the wind—an instinctual move. He couldn't hide his frustration when he realized we still could not touch, regardless his success with the vine.

My heart dropped heavier than a stone as I wondered how much more upset he'd be once we reached our destination. How could anyone withstand the sight of their own grave, knowing what lay beneath the dirt?

Patches of fog wrapped the tombs and statues like gauze.

I set the brake on the gig and secured Chester's reins to a tree. Hawk walked at my side, looking out of place in the cold with his thin, opened shirt, dress breeches, and muddied boots. His attention darted from one headstone to the next, anxiously searching for his body's home.

I paused beside Mama's grave. Hawk waited next to the angel statues in the distance, his silhouette an untouchable reflection of their physiques of marble and moss.

Kneeling, I swept the veil from my face. "Sweet Mama, how I miss you." My fingertip traced the engraving on her stone. "But I have a new friend. He's going to help me keep our estate." The rose I'd left the day before was gone.

A few remaining, withered petals fluttered around my knees, as if to taunt me that my mother was gone, too, and that she would never be here again to offer her wisdom or approval. My eyes stung and I silently promised to bring her a fresh rose on my next visit.

I stood. Mud puckered around my boots as I wove around the hedges, sniffling.

Hawk joined me, focused solely on my face. "Forgive me for asking you to visit so soon."

"I would've come, with or without you," I assured him.

We arrived at his tomb. Another padlock replaced the one I'd broken the day before. His grave keeper had been by and left muddy prints, too small to be a man's.

It dawned on me that my ghostly companion might have a wife who missed him. And children that adored him. And I'd earlier wanted to kiss him ... more than just to thank him for saving me. I wanted to taste his breath of chicory and mint. To savor the mouth that gave me such beautiful songs and sounds. Shame splashed through me, hot and scalding. Enya would say I was a trollop ... that only men should have such carnal thoughts.

"No." Hawk squinted toward the tomb centered within the fence. "I would remember, had I given my heart to someone. This much I'm sure of." His eyes—glittering to match the mist-dampened stone that marked his grave—came to rest on mine. "And having desire to be close to another person is natural. Intrinsic, not only to a man, but to any human. Such attraction goes beyond the physical, and reaches into the spiritual, as I know now. For although I've no need for food or sleep, those other appetites still beg appeasement." His gaze ran the length of me and I basked in the huskiness of his voice, remembering the night before when he had tried to touch my necklace. When I had melted beneath a phantom caress.

Hawk offered his hand. And though we could not touch, I removed my glove and hovered my palm over his.

"We're playing make-believe." His free hand reached up as if to tuck a wayfaring lock of hair into my hat. I leaned forward, pretending he could. "I am inaccessible. I am safe. You are a perceptive young woman, more attuned to your senses than most, and curious about the intimacies between two people, after having witnessed the great love of your mother and father. We live in a society that stifles emotions. It is no wonder you would allow your thoughts free reign now that you are provided such an outlet. I'm honored, to have inspired such a restricted spirit's attempt at flight."

I regarded every exotic angle and turn to his beautiful face, stopping at the bow of his lips. In truth, this was the first time I'd ever longed so much for wings.

Hawk mimed a kiss along my wrist, at first rushing my skin like a tender breeze. Then something changed. His mouth vanished and his spirit became part of my flesh, in much how a droplet of rain on a window merges with another. His lips reappeared with a slight tug as he stepped back, as shocked as I.

A breath burned in my lungs, locked in place. Though not tangible, not in the way of a physical touch, we had connected. So fleeting ... so brief ... yet purely sensual—as if I were a lake, and he immersed himself in me.

That was not make-believe.

He held my gaze, his jaw twitching in acknowledgment of my unspoken words.

Overwhelmed by the heat of his glowing stare, I glanced toward his tombstone. "Are you ready to see it?" I pulled my glove over the place he had tried to kiss, determined to preserve the invisible impression his phantom mouth had left behind.

His attention never strayed from me as he backed up and slipped through the bars, materializing on the other side.

We stood there, facing one another—he, inside his fenced-in prison, and me outside. The iron separated us, just as it had yesterday when I first saw his flower.

At last, he turned toward his grave. I found a stone and tried to bust the lock free. Yet no matter how hard I chiseled the new padlock, it held. Forced to watch from outside, I clutched the bars much the way Lord Thornton had.

Hawk crouched with his forearm propped on the stone. At its base, the mud was still overturned from the day before, though the hole appeared wider than I'd left it. As he stared at the epitaph, his ruffled sleeve flapped in time to some otherworldly breeze, out of rhythm with the gusts tugging my torn skirt.

"Nothing." The longer he sat there, the more his broad shoulders drooped. "No date. No good son or beloved brother, or dear friend. Simply ... Hawk." He growled. "I don't even know how old I am. Or was. Or ..." He fisted his hands and wailed—a gut wrenching sound that throttled my spine.

I couldn't stand to witness his devastation. "Hawk, all is not lost. There is yet the path outside the back gate." I swiped at my eyes with the back of my gloves.

His tortured expression gave way to tentative hope. He glanced at the teary streaks on my face and smiled gently. "Meet me there."

I hiked up my skirt and thrashed along the fence's border, through nettles and yellowed grasses as tall as my knees. The thicket of birch trees and spiny shrubs surrendered to a three-foot wall of gooseberry bushes. There, I used a fallen tree limb to slash at thorny branches. By the time I plunged to the other side where Hawk waited, sweat sprung up beneath my layers of clothes.

"Keep the tree branch," he insisted. "I don't want you defenseless should we cross any stray animals or degenerate strangers."

His concern spurred a shrinking flutter in my chest, a reminder that for all intents and purposes, I was alone, regardless of my powerfully built companion.

My dragging branch stirred a fragrant carpet of pine needles and cones piled up on one side of the trail. The path forked after several yards. I glanced above at scraps of cloth draped from the tops of the firs along the trail to the right. Some a dingy white, some red, others puffy, multi-colored patches with bits of stuffing strung out from the corners, like mutilated quilts hung in effigy.

"It must be some kind of sign," Hawk said before I

could ask. "Like the trail of white pebbles left by the children in that Grimm's fable my father used to tell me."

I gasped in delight, despite my unease of what hung above our heads. "Your first memory. Do you remember your father's name? His face? Where you lived?"

Hawk raised his hand as if I were a dog nipping at his ankles. "All I remember is the fable, and a man reading it to me. I can't see his face. I still know nothing more than I did. But"—he beamed—"it is a start."

Again I looked at the trees. "Who do you suppose left such a trail of pebbles? And is it there to lead us, or warn us?"

Hawk started forward, veering right. "Only one way to find out." He turned on his heel, looming over me. "Stay several paces behind. And be ready to run at my signal."

I nodded.

The end of the path opened to a sunlit glade. Hawk motioned for me to stay hidden and stepped out. I couldn't see or hear him for what seemed an eternity. I feared he had wandered too far and fallen back into his purgatory. Just as I debated checking the petal within my locket, he reappeared.

"You must see this." His smile was blissful.

I stepped into the glade. Above, the sun reflected off of more cloth scraps where they decked the fir trees circling the clearing. A canvas tent stood several feet away—shaped like an egg propped upon its wide end, with five-foot rods supporting the roof. A laundry line stretched from one rod to a pole embedded in the mud. Everywhere else, woven baskets, iron pans, pewter plates and trenchers cluttered the ground.

Hawk grinned again. "This is a gypsy camp. Although there's just one living here."

"Romanies?" My blood raced. Lord Thornton was an English nobleman. Their kind disdained the gypsy race. This proved without a doubt he was not friends with the grave keeper. "How do you know there's only one here? Did you see him?"

"No. The camp is unattended. But I peered in where the flap curled on the breeze. It's a woman's clothes. Had it been a man's things, I would have turned you about immediately." His eyebrows furrowed, but his eager smile stayed intact. "This place feels familiar somehow."

To me, nothing had ever felt more foreign. I knew very little of the gypsy life. According to the rumor mills, they were dark-skinned heretics who practiced no religion or morals and made their living by deceiving innocent victims with false fortune readings.

Uncle Owen disparaged such rumors. The Romanies he had known pursued legitimate trades. Some bottomed chairs, some sold handmade earthenware and baskets. Others served the community and worked as rat-catchers or handy men, even manning bellows—a sweaty, uncomfortable task most genteel men balked at.

To look at this campsite, they appeared every bit as backward as society conceived. But I'd never put much stock in society's conceptions.

I couldn't deny a desire to slip into the tent and walk in the shoes of this complex, superstitious woman, to uncover what secrets she might have on Lord Thornton, perhaps on death itself.

Still, I paused. I had already violated a man's grave and lied to Enya and Uncle countless times. What did it speak of me should I disturb a woman's private sanctuary?

Hawk bent slightly forward to meet my gaze. "She'll never know. We will not compromise anything. Are you with me ... *Gretel*?"

I nudged the locket beneath my layers of clothes. "All right, Hansel. But if there's a witch waiting to fatten me up and eat me, I will spend the rest of eternity haunting you."

"I'll hold you to that." His roguish wit made me brave.

I used my branch to prop the tent flap open, and sunlight torched the surroundings with brilliant illumination.

CHAPTER 6

Unless you enter the tiger's den
you cannot take the cubs.
Japanese Proverb

I stepped inside, inundated by the scent of cinnamon, cedar, and scorched pine needles.

No chairs or tables were in sight. It appeared the woman arranged meals upon one of her two trunks then sat on the ground, cushioned by the hand-woven carpet beneath my boots.

Though she had an abundance of pots and dishes outside, her sole utensils were a knife and three spoons made of bone. At the tent's farthest end, the remains of the quilt I'd seen hanging upon the trees covered a thin mattress. A few threadbare skirts had been rolled together to make a pillow.

A three-legged iron pot sat in the midst, complete with holes in the sides. Tapping the lid to ensure it wasn't hot, I opened it to find a pile of cool, porous rocks. "Coal?"

Hawk looked over my shoulder, thoughtful. "Coke. The solid remains of coal after it's been distilled. Emits no flame and little smoke. Yet still casts considerable heat. Perfect for life in a tent."

I stared at him in awe. "How do you know that?"

He tugged on the chain at his waist so the watch swung next to his thigh, a troubled turn to his brow. "A hazy memory. But nothing substantial."

Another jagged piece of puzzle, yet still no frame in which to fit it.

I dropped to my knees beside the first trunk. Upon opening it, I looked back where Hawk kept guard at the flap and smiled.

"Find something?" He came to stand over me.

I peeled off my gloves and plunged up to my elbows within the trunk. "A hat maker's heaven." My fingers swam in a gluttonous sea of sashes, shawls, strands of bells; pouches with trinkets pinned or stitched upon them; amulets, beads, exotic earrings, rings and anklets with gemstones too grandiose and craggy to be genuine.

I could hardly tear myself away from the opulent stash to open the next trunk.

When I did, a rainbow of bloomers, bodices, skirts, and head scarves greeted my hungry eyes. The under-things were lacy like my own, yet hedonistic in their vivid hues—blues, greens, burgundies, golds, and oranges as bright as pumpkins.

"Her kind are nomads." Hawk stood at the door flap once more, fiddling with the cracks in his watch's face. "They travel to distant lands where dyes are plentiful and cheap."

I didn't question his knowledge again, for not having the answer would only frustrate him. Instead, I stood to drape a beautiful dress across my body. It was one I would love to wear for its vivid color and daring fashion: a velvety red brocade bodice, full skirt, and long sleeves, with lace trim as black as ink.

Hawk watched me from his post. "Those are items of personal value. Nothing which will further our cause. We need to look through the books before the Romani returns."

Shame scalded my cheeks—for treating this like a game of dress-up and pretend when for him the urgency was all too real. "Forgive me."

Framed within the tent's opening, he turned his translucent profile—masculine and harsh, yet softened to delicacy by long, sweeping lashes slanted downward. "No. Forgive me. Watching you ... enthralled with wonder, like a child dancing beneath a snow of dandelion bonnets. For a moment, I felt alive." The edges of his eyes crinkled. "But then I tried to picture the colors, how the dress lit your features and complimented your skin and hair. And damned if I don't even know the hue of the fabric, the depth your eyes, or the glow of your hair in the sunlight. Everything is gray. For I am dead. And no matter what we find here, there is no recovering from such a fate."

Next to this despairing finality, I felt inadequate. What could I offer him? Comfort was meaningless without the touch of a friend, condolences empty without a warm breath whispered upon the ear. So I gave him the only thing I could—a description tempered with the sensory he was now deprived of on a daily basis. "My eyes are brown ... dusty and soft, like a fawn's pelt. And my hair is the warm glimmer of golden coins beneath the sun."

He turned back to the tent flap. "Thank you. Least now, I can pretend to imagine it."

Saddened beyond words, I folded the lush dress and put it away, then reached for the pile of books, skimming a palm along their spines. I paused at a smaller ledger-sized book.

Clumps of dirt snowed from the pages as if it had recently been dug up. I could not decipher the language of the handwritten script, but it appeared to be a journal. One of the pages pulled free from the spine with ease—not a part of the book, but folded within it. I opened the parchment to reveal a disturbing drawing.

A circle of rats laid with their bellies in the air, legs flailing as their tails tangled between them in a macabre jungle of cartilage and flexible bones. Blood-red ink formed the image with such mastery the rodents looked ready to scuttle off the page.

I studied the lower left corner where two English words slanted in a fevered scrawl: *Rat King.*

Catching a breath, I held it up. "Hawk ..."

Turning my direction, he took three steps my way, then stalled, his head cocked. "I hear someone coming. You must leave, *now.*"

The hairs along my nape stood on end. I tucked the drawing between the journal's pages and shoved the book within my coat. As I ducked through the tent's flap, two white-hot eyes faced me—attached to a snarling black wolf.

Her hot breath, rank with blood, cloaked my face. A shriek scalded my throat.

"Slowly ..." Hawk's voice remained calm. "Back away

slowly." As he spoke, he inched toward me, and I knew he thought upon Aria's volatile reaction to his presence.

I managed a few backward steps. It must've started misting outside again, judging by the scent of wet fur. As if reinforcing that observation, sunlight tipped the she-wolf's dark scruff and lit each individual droplet to pinhead stars. She resembled a mythological beast, carrying the midnight sky upon her back.

Streaks of white fringed her eyes, paws, and neck—a token of age. Her tail thrashed, dislodging the branch where it propped the flap and casting the background in muted yellow light.

The limb slanted on its fall and rolled next to the beast's feet. Her corded muscles tensed. The thunder-roll of her growl reverberated in the soles of my boots.

Terror shivered along my spine all the way into my arms and legs, leaving them numb and unresponsive.

"Juliet, beside the mattress. There is a heavy pot you can use for a shield."

I couldn't budge another inch ... frozen in the predator's icy gaze.

"Juliet!" Hawk yelled.

The wolf leapt toward me, fangs snapping in a violent fury. I felt a shove atop my coat between my shoulder blades and crumpled to the ground as the beast soared over me. Rolling to my side, I watched her clamber to her feet with Hawk in her sights.

He had been her target all along. I was the one solid barrier between them, and had he not pushed me out of the way ...

Had he not *pushed* me.

Hawk narrowed his eyes, intuiting what I had just realized: he was getting stronger.

"Aye there, lovely pup." He clucked his tongue at the wolf, and she bared her teeth again. "Juliet." Hawk held her attention as he backed up. "Leave, now. I'll keep her occupied."

Concern for his safety slowed my response until I remembered what he was. I barely managed to duck under the tent flap again when the cold prick of a knife met the side of my neck and forced me back inside.

The woman couldn't have been more than four and half feet tall, with features as rough as a horse's. She wore no coat. A green chemise with sleeves the yellow of winter squash peered out from under a fur-trimmed vest. A trio of skirts piled one atop another at her waist, each knotted so the side seams revealed an evolution of color, from pink to orange to green.

"Nye-nye, Naldi!" The old woman's lips formed words I could never have read had Hawk not been there to repeat them. In my peripheral view, the wolf craned its head to attention. "Naldi, caught a rhubarb. I allers did say you the jam on my rye."

The beast trotted over to lick the gypsy's stockinged feet through the strands of her sandals, then nudged the fallen branch that earlier held the tent's flap, a plea to play fetch.

My captor jerked my elbow until the tip of my nose aligned with hers. Her breath—tart and spiced with tobacco—scorched my nostrils and her wrinkled face reminded me of a walnut's meat. Braids, as white as untouched snow, looped beneath a broad-brimmed hat tied over her ears with a crimson sash, distracting me as I tried to concentrate on her pruned mouth.

"My vurma you followed. The straightway made crooked. Little rhubarb ... cheat an old woman of her sumadji. Black-hearted trot."

Hawk relayed the strange, senseless words. I struggled against her grasp, stopping when she jabbed the knife at my neck. Hawk's swift appearance at my side offered little comfort as my pulse throbbed against the blade's tip.

"Don't struggle, Juliet. She thinks you followed her trail in the trees to steal her stash. We must reason with her to get you out of this."

Trail in the trees? Stash? When did she say that?

"Vurma," he answered without pause. "It means a trail; and sumadji is a treasured heirloom."

Before I could even respond, my captor nudged the knife against the book beneath my coat. Her neck veins strained in a shout. "What ye hide give back, rhubarb!"

In spite of my noodling legs, I wouldn't surrender. We needed this book; judging from Hawk's knowledge of the gypsy tongue, he could decipher the pages. To think that all along the songs he'd been singing were Romani ...

Hawk hadn't budged from his place at my side, but there was little he could do. I had to save myself.

Taking shallow breaths to prevent the knife from sinking deeper into the journal, I looked the woman square on and hoped she would understand English. "I've been visited by the one whose grave you keep. I seek the truth about the *Rat King*."

"Mulo ...?" The old woman's face paled and she dropped the knife. "O Bengh!" She clutched her chest. Her eyes lolled into their sockets and she fainted, knocking the back of her head on the branch behind her.

CHAPTER 7

A bar of iron continually ground becomes a needle.
Chinese Proverb

I sat next to the fireplace and sipped the spiced cider Enya had warmed. She watched from her place at the table, preparing a mud poultice for our untimely guest. I didn't wish to give an explanation yet. Not when I would have to repeat it upon my uncle's return.

I couldn't have left the gypsy bleeding and groggy. She might very well be Hawk's family. I hadn't even considered the possibility that he might be of another race. A foolish oversight, considering his mastery of a foreign tongue and his exotic features. But with his opacity, I never had a clear glimpse of his coloring. And his English attire offered another contradiction.

On the way home, Hawk had deciphered the gypsy's last words. She'd said something about a masculine spirit before fainting dead away. The Romanies obviously knew more of the afterlife than the English did.

Small though she was, it had been no easy feat to drag the woman along the path through the forest and back to the cemetery. Hawk had instructed me on crafting a stretcher with some branches and one of the gypsy's skirts. The carriage's boot was low enough to the ground that I managed to push her motionless form into Uncle's cab.

If not for Hawk's help, I would never have slipped the woman past Naldi and out of the tent in the first place. The wolf tried once to attack me until a shove from Hawk sent her sprawling on her back. After that, he stood between us and she dared not cross him again. Yet the loyal pet stayed with us, not letting her mistress out of her sight, even following behind the rig.

Upon our arrival home, Enya helped me carry our guest across the threshold. We stretched her out in the sitting room upon a velvet settee, draping the woolen throw up to her chin. When last I looked in on them, Naldi lay on the floor beside her, powerful muzzle cradled between delicate front paws.

I reached the bottom of my cider where the cloves overpowered the juice, leaving my tongue numb. Even without looking over my shoulder, I sensed Enya's angry glare.

Earlier, when Uncle had noticed the absence of his cab-fronted gig and saw my window lagging open, he had left to follow the wheel tracks. He went on foot—despite his gimp back. For Hawk and I to miss him on our ride in, he must have taken the foot trail to the cemetery as opposed to the road. I could not imagine what horrific scenarios raced through his mind. No doubt he thought me too distressed to make any sound decisions.

I stood and put down the cider, casting a glance at Hawk but speaking to Enya. "I must search for him."

Enya's hardened scowl came into view as she stepped

into the circle of firelight. "Haven't you caused trouble enough? He shan't be physically able to chase you another step today." No sooner had she said this, than her head snapped toward the front of the house.

I rushed into the hall. Upon slamming the door shut, Uncle drew me into an embrace against the rough nap of his great coat. His scent of dusty citrus filled my nose and his lips moved atop my head, scolding me, while knowing I wouldn't hear a word.

What he didn't know was that a ghost relayed them for me: how he would not survive losing me after losing Mama, how I was all he had now—the daughter of his heart.

I heard the tenderness in Hawk's recitation of each sentiment, and wondered if it was respect for my uncle's devotion to me, or regret for his lack of memory of any such relationship in his past.

"Both," Hawk whispered, and with my cheek pressed to my uncle's chest, I met my friend's ghostly gaze to assure him he had a family now.

He smiled in grateful acknowledgment.

Our quiet moment shattered as my uncle stretched me out to arm's length so I could see his lips. "Never leave like that again, tiny sparrow." His eyes glistened with tears as he stared at my waistline where the strip of fabric formed a limp tail. "Did someone hurt you? Did someone touch you?"

My cheeks flamed. "No, I'm fine. It happened when I climbed down the tree."

His face paled as if just the thought made him faint.

"I've been in turmoil for hours. I could only think of that day ... at the quarry ... the mud, so red on your frock I thought you were bleeding. I cannot relive that. Ever."

Mud as red as blood. I glanced at Hawk's boots. *That's* where I had seen such a color before. My accident at the ochre mines when I was a child.

Hawk gave me a meaningful frown, seeking more details, but I pressed him to wait. First I had to show Uncle Owen our guest ... and I had no idea what to offer as explanation.

⌒ ᴐ•ᴄ ⌒

"That was the perfect ruse, Juliet. Your uncle believed you stumbled upon her on the road, already unconscious. So why so distraught?"

I stiffened at the edge of my bed. Hawk stood in front of my picture window, his palms splayed on the desk top to appraise the strange drawing of the rats that I had spread open. Evening's blush filtered through him— making him unsettlingly beautiful once again.

"Why am I upset?" I wasn't even sure if I spoke aloud. "Not only have I proved myself a resourceful thief—I am also a masterful liar. And I've had wanton thoughts about a ghostly man who lives in the petals of a flower. Who am I since my mother has left me? I don't know anymore."

Hawk strode over. The mattress sunk beneath him as he settled, and again I spurned the physical laws so intent on taunting us.

"Everything you have done is for the greater good. Yes, you filched the flower ... but in the process, you liberated my spirit. And yes, we stole from the gypsy. But this book could very well be about me—which in turn makes it mine. And as for your uncle, would he have believed the truth? Or would he have imagined you crushed with grief to the point of insanity, and become ill with worry himself? Now he's off to retrieve the physician who will heal the woman. When she wakes, we can learn her relation to me. And lastly,"—his palm drifted through the back of my hand, dipped into my flesh, then released with a slight tug, just as his lips had done earlier—"by having *wanton* thoughts of me, you're making me feel alive."

Our gazes joined and I smiled. "You are becoming stronger."

He grinned back. "I'm learning how to connect on another level. It seems to be a form of osmosis ... triggered by my spirit touching your flesh. As if I'm being absorbed by your body. So, what should we try next? My lips upon your cheek?"

I lowered my lashes, self-conscious beneath the intensity of his stare. "I fear there's no time for that. We need to study the journal."

"Ah, coy Juliet." Amusement smoothed his husky murmur. "You do like to pretend. But you always manage to change the subject when things harken too close to reality."

"That's not it at all." It was impossible to lie to a spirit who could see my thoughts. "We should look now." I struggled against the tickle in my chest. "While we have time alone."

"Of course. While we're alone. Were I a man of flesh, I could surely find better use of such moments."

I shook my head and leafed through the journal—an effort to appear in control.

Hawk's teasing chuckle silenced as I came to the first page with writing on it. "There. Hold it there," he said, pointing to the signature. "The book's owner is someone named 'Chaine Kaldera'."

On the next page we found a dated entry. Hawk began to read the foreign words in silence until I folded the page down. "If I'm to be your doorway into the world of the living, you will bar no secrets from me. Read aloud."

He seemed hesitant, but nodded.

I pressed out the crease with a fingertip then held the page at its corner.

"The monster came tonight when Papa left," Hawk relayed the script, his gaze tense and focused. "I hate him. He howls at me. He tears my clothes and skin until I bleed and the stains will never come out. Papa is angry when he sees them. The monster doesn't care. He hates me, too. He throws me into the pit. I don't like it there. The shadows whisper and snarl ..."

Hawk stalled as my hand covered the page, as if by holding the script I could ease the anguish etched into each loop and curve. It was a child's voice—a boy, judging by the name. I never imagined anyone could treat a child with such maliciousness.

Hawk regarded my face. "Are you sure you wish to continue? It seems rather severe for a lady's sensibilities."

My eyebrows pinched together. "I am in constant company of a dead man, yet you're worried for my delicate sensibilities?"

He pursed his mouth. "Fair point." He regarded the page again, this time reading the child's words in a tentative voice. "You belong there, the monster says. You are born of dirt and filth, he says. Then he takes the light from me. I wait alone. In the dark, I wait. When I feel their claws in my hair ... I know they have come. The monster dumps them from a bag onto my head. They scuttle down my arms. Their eyes are beaded like glowing buttons; I want to poke them out. I want to wear them so I might see in the dark as they do ... but I can't. The monster says I must make of them a living crown. I must tie each to the other by their tails. For I am their king. I will always be their king. The king of rats, the monster says. The king of rats." Hawk's vocal cords faltered.

He glanced at me, his cheeks streaked with tears. Though I'd been crying, I hadn't realized he'd wept, too. His voice had remained strong throughout the reading until the very end.

"God help me." He swiped at the moisture with his shirt cuffs and leapt to his feet. "Wake the gypsy! I must know. Did I terrorize this poor child? How could I have lived with myself?" His expression darkened. "Perhaps I couldn't ... perhaps I took my own life and am better off alone in darkness with the voices."

"No." I stood, casting the offending book atop my pillows. "You have never been anything but kind to me. Even as a ghost, you practice more empathy for my infirmity than most living men I've met." I kneaded my hands, afraid to give too much of my past away. "Your watch is engraved with the words 'Rat King'. If anything is to be gleaned from that detail, *you* are the child. You are Chaine."

Evening shadows swathed the room, but with his soft, otherworldly glow, I could still make out his tortured face. Such a harsh twist of the knife, to have gone from the warm, loving memory he had earlier of a father reading a fairytale, to this.

"Someone is coming." He gestured toward the door I'd left ajar.

I folded down my quilt to cover the journal before Uncle's concerned face appeared, illumined by the glow of the candle he held. "Why are you standing alone in the dark, still in your torn dress? Why have you not lit your lamp and changed?"

Tucking the ripped fabric in at my waist, I shrugged.

He leaned his temple against the doorframe. "The physician wants to take the old woman to his home. He needs to monitor her for the night. If you wish, I shall carry you to visit her on the morrow."

Seeing Hawk's downtrodden cast, I nodded, then rethought. "What of Lord Thornton? Isn't he to visit tomorrow?"

"He had a business emergency and left town," Uncle answered.

A burst of relief warmed my chest. This would give us more time to uncover his part in all of this. "But the viscount will be coming back?" I asked.

Uncle held onto the doorframe, something akin to hope in his eyes. "Of course. I invited him to return in three weeks, at month's end. I told him you needed more time to grieve, as it stands. I am sorry I rushed you." He started to close the door, then paused, opening it wider. "The physician refuses to take the wolf for fear it might harm his children. Enya mentioned you have a way with the beast?"

I nodded again, although it was Hawk who had tamed the wolf.

"All right. I gave it some wine to daze it. I've roped its neck and tied it in the shed. I will come back after depositing the old woman at the doctor's. I'm staying tonight to help you care for the animal. I'll sleep on the settee downstairs. If you wish to come down and explain your earlier escapade ... I'll be there to listen."

Receiving no response, he frowned and closed the door between us. It hurt, being so secretive toward the one man who had always supported my peculiar inner-workings. But this he would never understand.

Hawk paced the room and I turned on the gas lamp at my desk to study the gruesome portrait of the rat crown, the same blood red shade as the mud on Hawk's boots. Following an intuition, I lifted the paper to taste the ink. A familiar acrid sting burned my tongue.

"This painting was drawn with ochre," I said. "My uncle has used this mineral to dye fabrics. I was coated with it when they pulled me from the mines as a child. That's why the mud on your boots has always looked familiar to me. Do you suppose your body could be elsewhere other than the grave? Perhaps underground— thus the darkness? The ochre mine from my past is in close proximity, though I cannot recall the town's name.

My uncle knows its whereabouts. I can ask him in the morn."

Hawk turned to me. Desolation masked his features. "What kind of man must I have turned out to be? Even the most powerful tree can be whittled down to a splinter, should the knife be sharp enough. Surely that's the equivalent of heaven ... the bliss of not knowing my history."

I glanced down at my own dirty boots.

"Thank you for all you've done," he continued. "But please, take off the locket. Send me to my death in peace."

The threat of him leaving shook the pulse in my neck to a menacing knock. Snatching up the parchment, I rounded on him as he settled like a defeated shadow in the corner. "You will not give up." My logic screamed that one day he might *have* to leave; but for the moment, I would barter any extra time with his wit, and intellect, and voice, no matter how fleeting.

"What does it matter, Juliet? What difference can any of it make? I am dead. Do you not comprehend the finality of that? *Death stands between us.*"

I clenched the paper tighter. Although his voice had given me unspeakable joy over the past twenty-four hours, *this* I was unwilling to hear. "You say you want peace. Now that you've had a glimpse of what might have been, you'll never have peace until you learn the whole truth. You must make amends with the past."

Hawk's gaze lifted toward my bed and the journal beneath my quilt. "There are so many more entries."

"And I am here to read them alongside you." I sat next

to my pillow and covered my lap with the book. When Hawk's ethereal form dented the mattress, I exhaled a relieved breath.

I'd given him a reason to stay. But I couldn't shake the premonition that each page turned would be another ribbon snipped free from Pandora's beautiful box of misery.

CHAPTER 8

Black as hell, strong as death, sweet as love.
Turkish proverb

It took three weeks to sort through Chaine's journal. The child was a savant. He painted words with the same deftness and intelligence portrayed in the multitude of black and white sketches which filled the pages.

We had to break often for fear of being drawn too deep into his dark torments. He suffered everything from fleas and repulsive skin infestations brought on by rat bites, to hunger so severe he had to scavenge for food. One gruesome entry detailed a doe's rancid carcass he found in the woods being shred to pieces by three vultures; he managed to ward off the enormous birds with a torch and dragged the meat several yards where he held his nose against its stench and ate it raw. As a result, he fell feverish for almost a month and suffered intense hallucinations immortalized in drawings. The illness seemed to change something in his mind, for thereafter, all of his sketches paid tribute to things broken or captured. Though disturbing, they were breathtaking and lovely in their gloom.

Six pages in, we discovered Chaine's mother had died during his earliest years, and the "monster" so often spoke of was in fact Chaine's father on a tangent. The boy believed, in his innocence, that his papa lived as two distinct entities. A semi-tolerant man and a vile beast. When one reared its head, the other disappeared for a time.

Perhaps this gave Chaine strength to survive, by holding onto threads of hope that one day his papa would conquer the monster and free them both.

In the beginning, it made it easier for Hawk to refer to the journal's author as Chaine, putting distance between himself and the tortured child. But halfway through the journal, one particular entry shattered the masquerade. Chaine wrote of his visit to a candy store, an event as rare as an eclipse judging by his excitement. He detailed the candies' shapes and sizes, but complained he couldn't see the glistening colors, even when his father's sister described them.

"A waste of Aunt Bitti's breath," he wrote. "Since I have never seen yellow, blue, red, or green, how can I know anything other than variants of gray?"

Chaine was color blind. That, along with the engraved watch, ochre stained boots, and rat painting, convinced us both that Hawk he was indeed this broken little boy.

I almost choked on the tragedy. That the one part of Hawk's identity he had carried into his death was an intense longing for color, never attained.

We drifted through our remaining journal sessions with all the desperate abandon of storm-tossed ships— alternately buoyant on waves of curiosity then sinking beneath the brutal despair of discovery.

Three pages had been ripped from the back just before Chaine's last two entries. Something life-altering happened upon them, considering in the next to last entry, Chaine spoke of finding peace—that it was brought into his world by an unexpected angel who had fallen from the sky. Though cryptic, his words were steeped in hope, wherein up to that point each entry had grown ever more despondent. The leap in mood and faith was jarring without the event to account for it.

Upon the final page, Chaine detailed his fourteenth birthday and two incomparable gifts: a black wolf pup that he named Naldi, and a successful escape with his Aunt Bitti into a city far removed from his papa—where his aunt swore to keep him hidden until he was old enough to fight back.

Hawk and I finished reading just before sunrise on the twenty-second day of November. We were expecting Lord Thornton by the end of the week, though were still no closer to understanding his part in this mystery.

I sat in the midst of my bed, covers drawn up to my waist and the journal in my lap. Hawk lounged alongside me, providing the glow we read by. His elbow was propped on the mattress so his palm cradled his chin. I had just closed the pages for the last time.

We gazed at one another, basking in our relief for Chaine's successful escape.

"So. It is plausible that I became stronger for it," Hawk murmured. "That I lived a decent life thereafter—however short it was."

I stroked my lower lip. "I would go so far as to say it's

probable, judging by the man you are now."

Hawk watched my finger's antics along my lip with such rapt intensity I dropped my hand.

"If only we'd been able to talk to my aunt before she left," he said quietly, still looking at my mouth. "I would've liked to thank her, and asked about the angel in the missing pages."

I smiled at his sentiment. Although we didn't know who his "angel from the sky" was, we at least knew the gypsy woman we had brought here was his Aunt Bitti, due to her age and the wolf named Naldi in her keeping. But the discovery was both happy and frustrating. For the old woman was long gone.

She had disappeared in the night at the physician's house weeks earlier, stealing into our shed to take back her pet. Hawk suggested that a nomadic spirit such as hers would no longer be staying at the same camp now that she'd been discovered. And we both knew there would be no sneaking away to confirm it.

My uncle had not left me alone since the last time I'd escaped. He deemed my actions and choices unpredictable due to my grief. So he gathered his dyeing equipment, stationed it within the greenhouse, and he and Chloe came to stay. This had made for some interesting days until the spaniel finally adjusted to Hawk's presence.

Anytime Uncle had an errand, he always ensured Enya was with me. To make matters worse, he refused to discuss anything about my accident in the ochre mines, claiming I shouldn't dwell upon the past.

I was a nightingale with a damaged wing, trapped within a cage.

Hawk sighed. "I cannot fault your uncle for worrying about you. You do have a way of winding around one's heart."

His lovely words warmed me, like rich, golden light. There was a genuineness there that I didn't question. Yes, he had only been in my life less than a month. But it was impossible not to become attached to someone who you were with, every moment of every day. Who could read your thoughts and know your every fear and hope without you speaking them. And, even more binding, someone who had shared the torments of their past so intimately and openly. It might've only been words on a page, but the emotions Hawk and I dredged as we read the journal had been as real and tangible as if we'd walked through each scene together—hand in hand.

"Enough about the past," Hawk said. "Let us talk about the present, and how pretty you look drenched in sunrise." He raked his free hand along my quilt where the first rays of pinkish light poured in from the window and climbed across the fabric. The padded muslin furrowed beneath his movements, tugging along my abdomen and waist. I clutched it in place and clenched my thigh muscles against their quivers.

Though we still could not touch in any traditional sense—Hawk could only make contact with an isolated shove atop my clothes, nothing gentle or soothing—he'd recently discovered the ability to manipulate fabrics when he put all of his energy into the effort. We had yet to fully explore this new development and my ghostly companion was reaching the end of his patience.

"Hawk," I scolded, face flushed. "I must put on the proper attire. It's stir-up Sunday. Enya and her entire family will arrive within the hour. I need to bring your flower up here out of the way of the children." I had been so tired the night before that I'd left it downstairs in the picture window.

"Tell me of this 'Stir-up Sunday.'" Hawk strummed his fingers, a taunting smirk on his face. "Is it a game?" The rising sun bathed his outline in primrose light.

Smoothing the blankets around me, I clasped my hands over the journal. "A tradition. Four weeks before Christmas, we invite our friends to help prepare the Christmas pudding. Each of us takes a turn stirring the batter while we make a silent wish. After that, the mixture is wrapped and steamed in a pudding cloth then hung from a hook to dry. On Christmas day we share it, which frees our wishes so they might come true."

"Ah. And what are you to wish for?" Hawk skimmed his hand along my shin, the covers dragging with a slight ripple.

I caught a breath and he met my gaze with a seductive glint in his eye.

"I-I plan to wish for you to become flesh again. To live again. I am asking for a miracle."

After a thoughtful pause, Hawk laid his head on his outstretched arm. "'Tis a waste of a wish, Juliet. You should ask something for yourself."

"It *is* for me. To walk alongside you, holding your hand

in mine. To dance with you. To ..." I leafed through the journal pages absently, frustrated. "It is all that fills my being."

He rolled to his back. A tortured expression crossed his face. "How reliable is this tradition for granting wishes?"

"In all of my nineteen years, it's only failed once. When I asked to hear again."

A bemused grin quirked his lips. "Yet here I am speaking to you, and being heard."

I gasped.

Hawk propped up on his elbows. "Well, what're you waiting for? You need to make that wish!"

Of course he was simply playing along, but my fingers shuffled the pages faster to match my rising pulse. "I'm waiting for you. Turn away. Look out the window as you always do."

He made no move other than to sit up beside me, denting the pillow which supported my shoulders and neck. "What say we dispense with the formalities at last? After all, I already saw your immaculate breasts on the night we first met."

Tantalized by his proposition and the masculine, grinding edge to his voice, I tensed, slicing my forefinger on a journal page, deep enough to bleed. I plunged the cut into my mouth, sucking away the sting. "Now see what you made me do."

"I am sorry." The apology was palpable, as was the heat of his gaze. "You know I would never hurt you purposely. You, who've walked through hell with me and back again; you, who drew me out of the abyss when I thought to jump in." He angled his head, his face so close that were he flesh, his nose would brush my temple. "I simply wish to thank you for that, *China Rose*."

After all these years, to hear Mama's pet name for me spoken aloud, soothed and comforted. Hawk was one of only three people who knew it.

"But only I know how much you miss her," he added.

I closed my eyes, Mama's face a beacon in the darkness. Though I often hid my grief from Uncle and Enya, afraid to stoke their pain, I could hide nothing from Hawk.

"No hiding. Yet no touching. Who would ever have known caring for someone could be so maddening," Hawk whispered. "But perhaps it doesn't have to be. There's something I've been dying to give you." His voice echoed within my ear, hot and affecting as any breath. It made my blood race—anticipant for sensations I'd never experienced, things so far out of my reach, they might as well have been stars in the cosmos.

The paper cut's sting was nothing to the words he'd said, teasing or not. "I-I don't find that the least funny, Hawk. *Dying* to give me ..."

In one graceful move, he straddled me, legs bent at the knee on either side of my thighs, hands braced against my pillow to trap my head. I could escape at any moment just by slipping through him, but I had no such desire. What I wanted was to learn everything he had to teach me. But it was impossible ... *we* were impossible.

I leaned against the pillow and lifted my chin, frayed and unraveled by the gnawing need within that was become more agonizing each day. "Hawk ..."

"Hush now," he said, his mouth only inches from mine. "Hush, and let me thank you properly."

I imagined his breath on my face, his scent as I'd dreamt it so many times. I imagined us dancing—my hand snug in his masculine palm, my ear pressed to his bare chest and tickled by his hairs, my flesh bared and hot enough to solder spirit to blood and bones.

"That's perfect, Juliet. Now close your eyes. Close them, and *feel*."

Blocking out my doubt, I squeezed my lashes shut—so not even a seam of sunrise bled through. I waited, anticipant and yearning, yet dreading that cool rush of air that would signal our failure to make contact once again.

Instead, the slightest flutter stirred at my lips, like the pulse from a butterfly's wings, fading to an innervation unlike anything I'd ever felt. Not pressure ... not warmth ... but a flourish beneath my flesh which washed through my face, tingling all the way into my tongue and throat.

I opened my eyes and Hawk's mouth was fading into mine—much like his lips had dipped into my hand at the cemetery.

I froze, lost to his ethereal beauty—absorbing it. My shoulders relaxed; I arched my back, lifted from the pillow, deeper into him. He opened his eyes, his pupils a dark swirl. His lashes drifted down again, and dizziness blotted my vision, as if I spun in circles until the world folded to shadows and light. Hawk became a vortex of gauzy color and sensation, channeling through my mind and body.

Internally, he touched every part of me—a shuddering,

thrumming, surge of life that shook the blood from my toe-tips to the top of my head—as our spirits connected.

My heart raced and my cheeks flushed, awakened with a new energy.

His energy.

A sudden tug leapt from my lips, and I almost cried out, not ready for the euphoria to end. The pillow dropped from behind me and my eyes snapped open. A blur resolved to Hawk standing at the foot of my bed, staring at me. Behind him, Enya teetered at the opened door, her hand clutched at her neck.

"She saw us," Hawk said, his face as flushed as mine felt.

I struggled to get out of bed, my body riding waves of pleasure—the residue of Hawk's spiritual fusion.

She could not have seen us ... I managed to reply with my mind, although my limbs weren't cooperating at all.

Hawk shot me a stunning smile. "That was glorious." His intense regard made me want to kiss him again. But there was Enya ...

When I at last shoved aside my covers, I realized my finger—earlier throbbing and itchy—suffered no more pain. The paper cut was gone. Healed without a scar or a line, as if it had never been there. Had I been on the cusp of death, I would surely have been resurrected.

Before I could register the magnitude of this discovery, Enya moved in my peripheral vision.

"Enya ... I—"

"Your pillow. It was floating against the wall. Alone." Enya's lips moved so fast that Hawk had to translate for me. "You leaned forward. So how did the pillow ...?" Enya pointed to the wall with a quivering finger. "Stayed there alone. As if ... as if something held it up."

I juggled two or three explanations in my mind and Hawk laughed at each one. "Tell her the truth. Tell her you kissed a ghost."

Enya scrambled out, no doubt to apprise Uncle of the queer event.

I glared at Hawk, only to find him fading. He said something else, but his words muffled. His face held an aura of apprehension as it vanished.

My heart dropped.

"No, no, no." Desperate, I fumbled for my locket, my fingers slow and awkward in contrast to my erratic pulse. The moment I opened the lid, Hawk's petal fluttered to my bedspread—withered and black as death.

CHAPTER 9

No rose without a thorn, or love without a rival.
Turkish Proverb

Chloe wagged her tail upon my entrance into the dining room. Normally, I would've knelt to scratch her soft fur. Normally, the potpourri of holiday gatherings—cinnamon, nutmeg, vanilla, and brandy—would have filled me with comfort and nostalgia.

But my life had not been *normal* for weeks. And today was no exception.

Christmas would not be the same without Mama this year, and a part of me dreaded the holiday. If not for Hawk. He wanted to experience all of the holiday vicariously through me, having no memories of his own to draw from.

Upon that thought I had to temper my footsteps, for I wanted to run toward the picture windows, pluck a petal from his flower, and rescue him. But such actions would cast me in suspicious light, and I anticipated already being in trouble enough, which was why I had forced myself to get dressed in the proper attire before coming down.

I passed the fireplace where Enya's four younger

sisters sat in a circle of chairs with their crinolines and bustles bubbling around them as they stitched costumes for their brothers. Each of the boys had a part in the upcoming Christmas mummer's play next month.

Enya puttered at the table with her mother, adding dried fruits to a bowl: sultanas, raisins, and currants, all glistening in a frost of sugar as the ladies raked them with knives from the cutting board. I couldn't help imprinting myself and Mama in their place, which triggered a pang of sadness and envy.

Swiping at some hairs sticking out from her head-scarf, Enya didn't even notice me. She was intent on her observation of my uncle and her brothers playing Pope Joan at a trestle table in the furthest corner. The eldest boy jumped up and danced after his handful of cards won.

My uncle grinned. He was the closest thing to a father they'd had since their own ran out. As if sensing my thoughts, Uncle looked up at me and winked. With everyone so caught up in common tasks, it appeared Enya must've kept her strange sighting to herself. Perhaps she thought it too far-fetched. That she imagined it all. Still, things would be awkward until I offered some explanation.

I turned toward the windows to seek Hawk's flower. Both box seats were barren, other than the stacks of pillows strewn here and there. I looked about the room in a futile search for the pot, accidentally backing into Aria's cage. Her wings fluttered and gusts of wind swept around me. Uncle came to my side, seating me.

He knelt down so I would see his mouth. "Why are your

cheeks so red? Are you feverish?"

I clasped the black lace at my neck in hopes to hide my desperation. "The flower ... the pot. Where are they?"

Uncle turned to Enya and they had an exchange I couldn't read. Hawk always made certain I knew what everyone said, whether I could see their mouths or not. In our short time together, I had become dependent upon his help ... forgotten how isolating silence could be.

Uncle faced me and patted my hand. "Enya moved the pot to the sitting room. She feared her siblings might topple it. She took care not to touch the petals, just as you instructed."

I willed away the panicked tears welling in my eyes, then nodded.

A pair of white, fluffy hands appeared upon my knee. Enya's littlest brother puffed out his dimpled cheeks within his white rabbit's hood. "D'ye like my costume, Julie?"

Uncle and I both smiled.

I patted his wooly head. "Splendid ears. You look well and ready to plunder a whole village of cabbages."

The boy beamed and bounced away.

If only Hawk was here. He'd developed a fondness for watching Enya's siblings interact. It made him feel as if he had a family of his own.

Enya beckoned us to the table for the ritual stir of the pudding.

Squeezing the elbow Uncle offered, I smoothed my paramatta train where it gathered at the back of my waist and cascaded down from a black velvet bow to sweep behind me in a pool of silk and wool. On my turn to stir with the wooden spoon, I closed my eyes tight, and silently wished the wish I had promised to Hawk.

Afterwards, Enya and her mother scraped the batter into a cloth to steam it. Her sisters returned to their sewing, the eldest kneeling in front of Ian to pin up the hems at his ankles.

I rushed into the sitting room. Just around the corner the flower came into view—silver and shimmering on the table next to the door. Uncle trailed me. I reached out in hopes to pluck a petal but he caught my wrist.

"Why are you hiding things from me, tiny sparrow?"

I bit my cheek. Perhaps I had been premature in my assumption of Enya's silence. "Whatever do you mean, Uncle?"

He guided me to the velvet settee. I watched the flower grow smaller—missing Hawk miserably as my petticoats bunched in stiff tangles upon sitting. What was my ghost doing now? Singing his enthralling lullabies with his hands over his ears? Did he worry I would never call him back?

Sitting close, Uncle lifted my chin. "It is more than sadness that clouds your countenance of late." He tucked some strands fallen from my chignon behind my ear. "You are anxious. You are searching for truths."

Yes, for Hawk's truth. How I wished I could tell Uncle. A wall stood between us which had never been there before. A wall I had constructed with lies and machinations.

Catching his brocade jacket lapels between his fingers,

he frowned. "It is my fault. I should never have reminded you of the accident from your childhood. And all these weeks, I refused to answer your questions. That was unfair." His chin trembled. "The reason I've been hesitant to tell you about the quarry's location is ... well, because Viscount Nicolas Thornton owns it now."

My chin dropped as I read the name upon his lips.

Uncle continued, his gaze avoiding mine. "It is in fact something we realized upon our first meeting. The subject of your accident came up. The details rang familiar to him. The prior owners kept records of mining incidents, for judicial purposes. The viscount found a copy of your interview—a written one. It didn't have any names ... it just outlined 'a little girl's experience'. The date on the record confirmed it was yours."

I frowned, feeling betrayed in some way, though I couldn't pinpoint exactly how. "Why did you never tell me this?"

His brown lashes slanted on a glance to his polished, button-top shoes. "I dreaded remembering that day. I was selfish for that. Perchance, to relive the account, it would fill the gaps in your memory, so you could move past all this. I've handled things badly." He glanced over my head at Hawk's flower. "People often resort to actions out of their character, to ease the chafing of things they feel guilty for." He had the strangest expression, a mingling of suspicion and pity. "When the physician was carrying the gypsy to his house ... she roused enough to attempt speaking in English ... she seemed to think you'd stolen something from her."

I froze in place. Did he know of the journal? How could he? Had he found it in my room?

"When I was seeking you at the cemetery on the day you were missing," he continued, "I went behind the hedgerows where you'd spent time alone after your mother's interim. I saw the enclosed grave and footprints around the gate—your size. Then I noticed the dirt turned up around the headstone within."

Blood rushed into my neck as he flicked another glance at the flower—this one meaningful and accusatory. I didn't care. Let him think the gypsy referred to only the flower. Better that, than he know the full scope of my thievery.

Uncle's brows knitted at my silence. "I've wronged you all of your life. Supporting your efforts to hide from society. And what kind of example was I? You've known nothing but lies and envy through me. Coveting not only Anston's bride for my own, but his child as well. I wanted everything my brother had. And you, in your perception, knew it. Yet you never breathed a word. Always kept my secret. I suppose to build such a fortress is much easier than to break it down."

I wanted to tell Uncle how wrong he was. How I had learned something other than guile at his knee. That the secret I kept of his sadness made me even more attuned to the value of being honest about your feelings—however society might frown upon them. And though I often hid my deafness from strangers, I faced and conquered it daily via family and clientele. But before I could speak, Uncle's attention snapped to the door.

Chloe hobbled into the room, her tail suspended as if considering whether or not to wag. Enya sauntered in behind her, slanting a sidelong glance at Uncle on her way to answer the door.

I started to stand.

"No, sit Juliet," Uncle pressed. "As lady of the manor, you must stay seated to receive guests."

Guests? All I wanted was to gather Hawk's flower and hole up in my room for the rest of the afternoon with my ghost. I didn't wish to welcome any unexpected company.

The door opened and a chill morning breeze ushered in a masculine aroma—rich and seductive—like almonds simmering in sweet liquor. Enya backed up to allow the visitor across the threshold.

I squinted against the sunlight beaming through the door. A man's powerful frame towered in the opening, the shadow of his hat's brim hiding his eyes and nose from my view.

Chloe's reaction to our guest was unprecedented. Her entire body wagged and she licked his boots. Upon bending to pet the rapturous ball of fur, the man stood and offered Enya his hat and cloak.

His back still faced me, a sturdy line of musculature beneath a gray frock coat and matching trousers. A hint of burgundy peeked out at his neckline, indicative of a notch-collar vest. His clothes seemed carefully chosen, short of one splash of color which clashed where the cuffs of his wing tip shirt dipped out at his wrists in a periwinkle blue.

The instant Enya closed the door against the bright

sun, his profile resolved to bold relief against the sapphire wall hangings.

My spine went to jelly. The angle of his clean-shaved jaw, his dark brows and exotic nose—a familiarity so startling it would've knocked me to my knees had I been standing.

I clutched the locket beneath my décolleté, fingers molded around the hollow, hard metal until it bit into my flesh. I didn't notice Uncle rising to his feet, hardly felt the chill of his body's withdrawal from my side.

It had to be my lack of sleep from all the nights spent reading the journal. How else could my eyes deceive me so?

My uncle stepped between us to shake our guest's hand. His hair became all that was visible with Uncle blocking him. Burnt chocolate, vivid with variants of ebony and auburn—color come to life. I fondled the lace at my sleeve's band, aching for a better glimpse.

Enya passed me on her way to the kitchen with Chloe in tow, yet didn't even give a sidelong glance. Her brow was furrowed in either confusion or suspicion.

My focus snapped back to Uncle as he took a step to the left, at last exposing our guest in full. His gaze swept down to meet mine and I gasped, any residue of logic fading away. Only heaven could have granted a wish of such mortal magnitude.

For standing there in the doorway was Hawk—my ghost—come to life.

CHAPTER 10

Be not deceived with the first appearance of things,
for show is not substance.
English Proverb

I leapt up and pushed Uncle aside, needing to touch our guest, to test if he was real. I stroked his face, felt the solid warmth of his cheek beneath my trembling fingertips.

He widened his eyes and removed my hand, an attempt to honor propriety. I pressed my palm instead to his chest, seeking his pulse. Upon finding it, I grew weak and my knees buckled.

He caught me against him and I clung to his shirt. His chest muscles tensed beneath my fingers. Uncle Owen was behind me, first a tap then an insistent tug, but I would not release my captive. I rested against him so the heartbeat beneath his sternum kicked hard at my jaw. His warmth and scent surrounded me, wrapped me in a moment of taste, smell, and touch so gratifying I dared not question its reality.

Uncle shook me in earnest now. Of course he couldn't understand. *I* didn't understand. I knew this could not be Hawk. But logic didn't matter, for this was the closest I had ever come to touching him.

Our guest stretched me to arm's length. His mouth became my focal point, bringing to mind the kiss I'd shared with my ghost just moments earlier—a transcendental exchange so powerful it healed me. My pulse fluttered. What would it be like, to kiss those lips in reality?

Uncle's face intruded upon my fantasy. He used his handkerchief to wipe my tears. "Please forgive her. As I said, she's not been herself of late." His expression shifted from reproach to compassion. "Juliet, allow me to introduce the viscount, Lord Thornton. Here to bring us the interview of your accident in the mines, so you might read it for yourself."

Movement at the kitchen doorway claimed my attention. Enya's siblings stood there, giggling. The fog of delusion evaporated and an ice cold rush of reality crashed me back into the present.

I had just thrown myself at a nobleman.

The very nobleman who was bent on claiming my home.

I glared at Uncle. Color crept into his face, either spurred by his shame for my actions, or his shame for deceiving me. He had invited Lord Thornton two days early, encouraged him to impose upon our family gathering, without even warning me.

Feeling woozy, I stumbled backward. The viscount transferred his walking stick to his right side so he could help Uncle guide me to the settee.

Uncle lifted my legs, propped my lower back with a pillow, and draped the woolen throw to cover my ankles and shins. He caught my wrist where I still gripped the viscount's forearm. I tightened my fingers, unable to relax the muscles. Regardless of the threat he presented, this man was my lifeline to Hawk. The most tangible one I'd ever had.

The viscount nodded to my uncle, handed off his walking stick, then knelt down beside me, peeling my hand free before clasping it in his own.

Up close, I noticed minor differences: miniscule smile lines around his eyes and streaks of sun-bleached auburn tipping his dark hair ... exactly how my ghost would look had he aged a few years and spent time outdoors. A breathtaking figure of Hawk mellowed to another level of beauty.

I marveled at his eye color ... not a winter-sky gray, but a dusky liquid gray, like shadows atop the surface of a pond—mysterious and hypnotic. A distinction in shade so minute, it might have been rendered by the periwinkle sheen of his mismatched shirt.

"It is all right, Miss Emerline," his full lips shaped the unexpected pardon. "I understand you've been battling a demon."

"Hawk ...?" The name slipped out in spite of my screaming rationale.

Shock strained his face. "On my life. You knew my brother?"

I clamped my inner cheek between my teeth. *Brothers.* Of course. Twins, judging by the flesh and bone facsimile kneeling beside me. So the rumors of the viscount being an only child were mistaken.

The olive tone in his complexion was evident in the

light of reality. He was a half-caste. The sole way a gypsy could come by nobility was through a father of noble English blood. But how did that pair with Hawk's journal, and their monster of a father who tortured him in a gypsy camp each day?

The viscount's mouth fluttered again, and I concentrated on the movement.

"Did you know him ... my brother?"

I had no answer. Considering that the viscount was twenty-seven, my ghostly companion had died years ago. I would have been a youth when he passed this life. Uncle knew each and every acquaintance I'd ever made, and would've taken grave notice of a boy eight years my senior, sitting on the fence of my innocence.

In a desperate bid to save myself, I feigned a hacking cough that I hoped sounded enough like "Hawk" to convince our grand guest that the name had been a tickle in my throat.

My tactic proved so persuasive, Enya came rushing in with a cup of water, held up my chin, and spilled the liquid down my throat until my strangles became quite real. Fortunately, upon my recovery, the subject shifted to an invitation to our guest to break his fast with us.

From that point on, the viscount proved gracious to a fault, having the same enchanting effect on everyone as he'd earlier had on the dog. Aria fluttered up to the cage bars and pecked his finger affectionately as he fussed over her beauty. Enya's brothers and sisters flocked around him as if he were the Pied Piper of Hamelin and they his orphaned rats.

The man even encouraged Enya's family to sit with us at the table, a most unheard of gesture for one of his status. He obviously had a cunning perception, and intuited they were more than domestic servants in our home. The youngest children sat at the game table, while the rest of us gathered around the dining table.

Enya's cider cakes were one of my uncle's favorite dishes, and mine as well. No one else could coax the tiny loaves of flour, sugar, butter, cider, and pearlash to such golden perfection. Each bite, each crumb, melted in the mouth like warm, buttered brandy. Still, even with the tantalizing steam curling around my chin, I couldn't get past the lump of embarrassment in my throat to taste anything.

I'd caressed a complete stranger's face, a viscount's no less. Even worse, *I had nuzzled his chest.* I was a disgrace, confirmed by Uncle's effort not to meet my gaze as he sipped coffee and nodded at the viscount's words—words I couldn't bring myself to try to read. I couldn't look at our guest at all. I could hardly stay seated in my chair.

I wanted to be with Hawk, sharing my discovery. If I had managed to snag a petal earlier, he would be bearing witness to this momentous occasion.

I nudged my spoon into a dish of custard to scrape nutmeg freckles off the surface. From beneath my lashes, I chanced a glance and found our guest laughing with Uncle. The men were hitting it off as if they were old acquaintances.

The viscount caught me gawking and offered a charming, confident smile. My wrist jerked and the custard plopped from my spoon into my coffee. Enya frowned, mopping coffee driblets from her forehead.

Biting my lip, I dipped a chunk of cake into the small, black puddle swirling in my saucer. I wished Hawk were here, filling me in on everyone's conversations.

I missed him. I missed his chuckle. The way he clicked his teeth together when he pondered something deeply. The way I always felt at ease and accepted around him. I missed his teasing touches along my blankets and skirt hems. But most of all, I missed his songs.

A sharp jab in my ribs jolted me back to the present. I glared at Enya and her bony elbow. Grimacing, she gestured toward my uncle.

"Are you finished, Juliet?" he asked. The color in his cheeks indicated he had been trying to get my attention for some minutes.

I nodded, though made sure he felt the heat of my anger. He had sprung the viscount on me, and was as much to blame for the earlier fiasco as me.

He offered an apologetic smile. "All right. Let us retire to the parlor to read the interview."

My empty stomach flipped at the thought of facing the childhood memory I'd suppressed for so long. Yet another uncomfortable challenge to face on this day of farcical fate.

Uncle wiped his mouth and stood. The viscount did the same, bragging over the quality of Enya's meal until her face deepened to the shade of a radish.

After Uncle offered his elbow to me, the viscount followed us back to the sitting room.

Uncle seated me at the settee. Our guest took a winged chair across the room and regarded Hawk's flower on the table next to him. My heart bounced into my throat. He must know by now I was the woman spying upon him at the grave, and that I'd stolen the flower.

How could he not, as unusual as it was?

He looked away, reposed elegance with his cane propped between his knees, then said something to Uncle who nodded and retreated to the kitchen once more.

Casting a fleeting glance my direction, the viscount drew out a graphite stick wrapped in a handkerchief from his jacket's flap, along with a rectangle of parchment. Deep in thought, he scribbled for an interminable span of minutes. Being an architect, I assumed inspiration hit him at inopportune moments so he kept writing tools on hand.

Upon folding the paper, he tucked it and the graphite into his jacket then draped his fingers over the cane's knob. Sun filtered from the window behind the table and the brass handle winked as if forged of flame. I squinted to focus on his mouth.

"Your uncle mentioned you read lips."

A flash of heat surged through my neck. I nodded, too embarrassed to answer aloud. I wanted to look at my shoes, the polished floor, anything but this dashing, cryptic man who mirrored my ghost. But there would be more humiliation in missing his words and having him repeat them, so I met his gaze head on.

"You do quite well. I would never have known you were deaf."

Of course you wouldn't, had Uncle not told you. I scowled.

Our guest resituated his cane's handle. "Feel no discomfort on my behalf. I can relate." The cane's tip gestured toward his right foot, twisted on an unnatural slant. "I've been burdened with this since birth."

I ventured a small smile, surprised by his kindness. Surely it was all an act to get in my good graces so I'd hand over the deed to the estate.

"In fact," he continued, "you don't seem limited in the least. I'm astounded by your many talents."

My brow arched. What other talents had he seen?

"That was a stunning performance earlier." He straightened the tie-pin in his celery green cravat, then tapped his finger against his sternum, as if remembering my cheek pressed against him there.

My spine withered, just to imagine us sharing the same thoughts. "Performance?" I ventured the word to save face, though worried how my voice must sound to him. It was the first time I'd been brave enough to speak in his presence. But since he already knew of my deafness, what did I have to hide ... other than his brother's ghost?

"I don't believe I've ever seen a cough come upon anyone with such vicious spontaneity," he answered. "Do such fits run through your bloodline, or is it exclusive to you?"

"Oh." I forced out another "Hawk" induced cough for good measure, then gripped the lace at my collarbones with my left hand. "I fear the burden is mine to bear alone."

His attention settled on my naked ring finger. "Ah. A shame. That flair for theatrics would be a fine trait to pass along to any future offspring you might have." He'd seen right through my act. His white-toothed roguish grin favored Hawk's so much my pulse broke into a gallop.

Chloe tottered in with Uncle behind her. He tipped his chin to the viscount and handed off a cup of tea with rosemary-scented clouds swirling at the brim. Taking the cup and setting it next to Hawk's flower, the viscount held an envelope out to Uncle, pulled from the pocket opposite of the paper he earlier scrawled upon.

Uncle sat next to me and nudged the envelope my direction. I took it and frowned at him, an unspoken reproach for telling our guest of my infirmity. In all my years, he'd always left it up to me to tell people on my own terms, once I deemed them worthy of trust.

Uncle glanced down at his hands like a reprimanded child.

I opened the envelope and, spreading the document on my lap, read the words silently—an itinerary of the dreaded day's events from the ochre mine's previous owner, Lord Larson. There was nothing more than my age, the date, the time, and the location: ochre mine #34. The lack of details left me an anonymous bystander to my own tragedy.

I glanced up at the viscount and saw compassion in his eyes.

"Please, Miss Emerline. I would like to have a more thorough account of the incident for my own files. Is there anything else you can offer?"

I focused on Uncle, my annoyance softening. Was it

possible he hadn't betrayed me after all? Perhaps Uncle thought that if Lord Thornton knew of my tragedy, of my deafness, he might feel sympathy for me and stop pressing for my estate.

"I remember only bits of that day." Setting the opened parchment aside, I twisted my hands on my lap. "Nothing fits together or makes sense. Can you help me with the pieces, Uncle? I'd been climbing a tree. It had ... it had a witch's face."

Uncle crossed his ankles, catching my hem with the movement. For years, he'd stifled my efforts to remember. It was to protect me; but it was also to protect him.

Sighing, he nodded. "Yes. The bark formed something of a face. A hideous image. In fact, for months thereafter, you had nightmares about old women." He kept his head turned to me, but addressed the viscount. "Her father, Anston, and I were visiting the ochre mines that day, to ascertain if they'd be a profitable investment for our cloth dying business. Juliet's mother had been ill all morning so we took the child with us, to give Emilia some rest." His mouth quirked to a grin. "Juliet was quite adventuresome as a six-year-old."

I suppressed a smile, thinking upon stories I'd been told.

"Lord Larson offered a tour of the place. We became preoccupied," Uncle continued. "We failed to notice Juliet had slipped away. The moment I looked down and saw her gone ..." His eyes pinched.

My hand grasped his.

He laced our fingers and the story became an apology.

"We looked everywhere for you. For hours. Your father was desperate to tears. Finally, just when dark came, one of Larson's men stumbled upon an abandoned shaft where the scaffolding had buckled. Up above was the tree with several broken branches. The worker surmised what had happened and called us over." Uncle's lips tightened to cords of white. "We feared the worst."

He'd always blamed himself. Even when he and Papa returned me to Mama with nothing more than a few scratches. Even when she assured them it was no one's fault. Uncle still couldn't make peace with it. From that day forward, he became my staunchest protector.

Uncle's gaze shifted from me and I realized our guest had said something. My attention centered on Lord Thornton.

"How did you find your way out of the wreckage after you fell?" he asked. "As the victim, you can offer insights no one else can."

I turned to Uncle, seeking his assistance.

"She did mention a boy helping her," Uncle said. "A boy made of dirt."

I felt a whimper escape my throat. I had forgotten that detail.

The viscount's face paled and he leaned forward, knees on elbows, as if Uncle's words had tugged him down. "There was someone else there with you? In the mines?"

Although his question was directed at me, I turned to Uncle, waiting for him to explain. My voice stayed trapped within.

Uncle ruffled his white hair. "We were never sure. It

was all she would talk of for weeks thereafter. How a mud prince had saved her. Her fantasy champion." He looked fully at me. "We decided it was someone your mind had conjured."

"I *imagined* him?" I asked, because a part of me was starting to see it as truth. Because now that I'd allowed details to surface, I could envision the boy's youthful features—masked in mud and sculpted of pain—with such precision, he must have been real.

"A dream perhaps," Uncle answered. "Your father and I wished to explore the collapsed mine to be sure, but Lord Larson said it was too dangerous for a layman. He had a staff of gypsies that mined for him ... said they would better know the tunnels. He sent us home, promising to have his men search. We later received news that they found no one else. Just red dust, broken rocks, and splintered scaffolding that blocked any other tunnels in sight."

Something began to tap at that fragile, unreachable moment within me, causing hairline fissures in the shell surrounding it. All this time, a vague sense of foreboding had shaded its birth, like a raven's wing spread possessively over her nest. Now, I tried to lift away the black feathery shadow, determined to remember it all.

My face must have revealed my inner turmoil because my uncle patted my hand and leaned closer.

"This is why I never encouraged the memory. The trauma still affects you. That was my mistake. I've kept your fears static, not allowing you to face them. My thought is, since Lord Thornton's manor sits atop the quarry, if we take his offer to work for him, you can get a glimpse of your past. With all of the changes he's incorporated at the mines, it will put things in perspective as to time's passage. You and I can move forward ... bury the memory for good."

My attempt at remembering fell stillborn, unable to compete with Uncle's bizarre announcement. Had I read his lips right?

I shot to my feet, forcing both of the men to stand.

"Me, work for *him*? In his mines?" I glared at the viscount. "Have you both gone stark-raving mad?"

CHAPTER 11

It is a long road that has no turning.
Irish Proverb

"Juliet, you'll not be expected to work in a mine shaft. Heavens." Uncle gestured to the viscount. "Lord Thornton and I have found we share some business interests. Now, I'm to fetch samples of my fabrics. Keep our guest company until I return."

As my uncle started toward the stairs, he threw a meaningful frown in my direction—*be on your best behavior.* Though my cheeks burned, I responded with a slight nod. Uncle vanished behind the banister. I stood with my back to the viscount, two steps away from plucking a petal from the flower to revive Hawk.

Chloe sniffed at my ankle as our guest came up behind—close enough that my entire body surged with awareness. I forced myself to turn and face him. He loomed over me, holding me in his long-lashed stare. An immeasurable darkness shifted through his eyes like moving clouds.

I was too intent on that mysterious gaze to notice him reaching into his pocket until he held out the folded parchment he wrote upon earlier. On the front, in lovely curving script, were the words: *To help you make peace with your past.*

Blood thrumming in my neck, I caught the opposite end of the paper. He clasped it tighter. I watched his mouth.

"Read it when you are alone." Though his words seemed a command, the way he looked at me, almost pleading, drained any defiance. I nodded and he released his clasp. Then his attention strayed to the stairway.

I tucked the letter inside my bodice as my uncle came around the banister.

Had I managed to eat anything earlier, I would've been sick upon seeing the three dress forms he carried. He had draped his fabrics over their shoulders, yes. But he failed to mention he'd be showcasing my newest creations atop each of the figures' heads.

"Did I not tell you?" He addressed our guest while beaming with pride. "The finest hats in all of England."

Numb, I watched the viscount take his place beside my uncle and run his fingers across the bonnets, measuring my work. I grimaced at Uncle. Thrice in one day he had brought my insecurities to float atop the froth of my mortification, never to sink again.

"His Lordship has already hired a seamstress," Uncle explained. "And he has a boutique ready to accommodate a linen-draper and a milliner. You and I can work side by side. I'll sell dyed fabrics and trimmings for gowns, and you can provide hats to match them."

The viscount glanced up from his appraisal of my bonnets. "I need a bright and charming young lady to attend to my female patrons, Miss Emerline. They will be the cream of society." He acted as if nothing had taken place between us in Uncle's absence. As if he hadn't passed me a secret note. As if his improper proximity hadn't made my pulse race.

Uncle's face brimmed with excitement. "You have your mother's touch, Juliet. Do not let it fade away to waste. Make her proud."

Eyes burning, I glanced at my feet, knowing he referred to more than my perfect pick-stitches. He wanted me to step outside my safe haven and forge new relationships, just as Mama had always done.

But I was satisfied here in Claringwell with the few clients I had made. I never intended to reach beyond them. I had no desire to fraternize with the snobbery and tout-abouts of an aristocracy I did not belong to.

I'd been to enough showings over the years. I saw how Mama's more elite customers looked down on me. How they treated me like a rare porcelain toy with minuscule cracks, lovely to look at, yet sad and fragile. Untouchable. Better to be seated on a shelf where I wouldn't break.

I couldn't relate to them, much less befriend them. I lacked the status ... I lacked the finesse. How could a deaf woman sit safely upon the throne of the elite, when she couldn't hear the whine of slanderous arrows in time to stop them from pricking her exposed heart?

Catching a hooded glance between my uncle and our guest, I pondered how many missives had passed between them in the last few months. How long had they been planning this?

A gritty dryness tightened my windpipe.

The viscount stepped in front of my uncle, holding one of my fall bonnets formed of spruce crape upon a foundation of straw. "Exquisite work, Miss Emerline. The finest Trianon hat I've ever set eyes on." He traced the gold bow at the crown where brown foliage gave way to peach and maroon flowers. "These blossoms are immaculate. So lifelike."

Despite my discomfort, I couldn't help but be impressed by his knowledge of the design. "Strawflowers," I mumbled, making little effort with my vocal cords. "Immortelles bred for their vividness and shape retention. Few things are more persuasive to a person's mood than color."

A thoughtful expression curved his brows. "I concur wholeheartedly."

I studied his apparel—his periwinkle shirt clashing with his burgundy vest like a black rose stands out in a vase filled with poppies. The rumors of his architectural prowess, the outlandishness of his artistic schemes, appeared to be true. If I were guessing, I would say he used color in brash and stunning ways to unbalance people. To give him power over them.

"And how do you get these to hold their form?" he asked, referring to the strawflowers again.

"It is all in the way you dry them. Bundle them in twine and hang them upside down. If the buds are facing the ground, the petals will retain their beauty. Takes little talent. Only knowledge and patience."

He secured the bonnet on its holder and smoothed the

crape as if petting a child's head. "Ah. But such patience is a talent in and of itself. And this garden hat is superb." He tweaked the round, broad brim lined with violet muslin. "Who supplies the plumage?" His breath bent three long feathers of jade and slate green, tucked within a cluster of navy roses. "I understand such embellishments are lavishly priced."

I shoved away another unwanted niggle of admiration for his knowledge of my craft. Wiggling my feet beneath my hem, I attempted to look bored. "My lord, such flattery is fruitless. I'm satisfied with the customers I have—"

Uncle caught my elbow and I pieced enough of his words together to surmise he was telling the viscount that I raised my own birds and flowers.

With an admiring nod, the viscount turned his attention on me again. "So, I venture you support the recent practice of mounting whole, stuffed birds upon hats?"

I clenched my teeth. "Absolutely not. Better to wait for them to molt and gather the feathers like leaves." Uncle squeezed my elbow gently, but I eased my arm away. "I do not condone the killing of animals for ornamentation or sport. Lest their meat be dressed for a banquet, it is vanity at its most debase."

Our guest appeared amused. "Yet you hold the birds in cages, so they can't fly as their instincts entail. Is this not cruel vanity as well?"

Hot prickles tightened my cheeks. I studied his forehead, hoping to find a bruise from anymore head-banging episodes at the cemetery. Finding no such flaw, I mentally berated how his shirt clashed with his vest and cravat. "Do you have a more suitable solution for containing them, *sir*?"

"I do. And I'll share it with you, Miss Emerline. Please." He pointed his cane's tip toward the settee and I took my seat again, staring miserably at Hawk's flower.

Uncle stood beside me and the viscount perched on the settee's arm opposite us, capturing my attention. "Seven years ago, I acquired the Larson Estate in Worthington."

Intent on the viscount's face, I noticed a taut tension between his brows upon the mention of the Larson name—a transformation so minute, anyone not attuned to reading faces would've missed it.

The viscount tilted his head and the sun highlighted the auburn brushstrokes in his hair. "The mines had been scraped hollow," he continued. "For three years beneath my watch, the estate grew stagnant. Other than ornamental gardens, I was unable to establish any worthwhile sowing or harvesting. The abandoned mines have compromised the soil's nutrients. And there are an abundance of hot springs that hinder tilling the lands. But four summers ago, I braved a new vision for the property. Along with the funds of several investors, I've put all of my assets into constructing a place where men can play, bringing their ladies along for jollies. It's called, 'The Manor of Diversions'."

I gaped just to imagine the moral misconduct such a venue could encourage, though secretly, couldn't deny being intrigued.

His hand raised in a reassuring motion. "'It is nothing

unseemly. Whereas, in the past, men have had their gaming sports and ladies their shopping haunts, I've brought it all together in one place—shops, billiard halls and clubs, banqueting halls, and lodging, all within one castle. Thus, everyone might be entertained throughout the day, yet not have to brave dark backstreets in the evenings to attend banquets and galas. No highwaymen or gangs, no gaming hells. Each separate edifice is joined to the other by enclosed corridors with gas lights and guards posted throughout for security. I've hired lady's maids, so no guest will be left wanting for a chaperone. There's entertainment aplenty indoors, which means people can winter there as well."

As Lord Thornton continued to speak, his face glowed with an almost boyish quality reminiscent of little Ian in his rabbit costume earlier. From what I could gather—aside from times the viscount spoke too fast to be read—his estate, surrounded by a forest on all sides, was immense at ninety acres. The front façade itself measured over one-hundred-and-twenty-three meters, and boasted a star tower reaching to the clouds.

Out of everything he described, the glass-roofed winter garden piqued my imagining most, for it was there the viscount proposed—that should I work for him—I could house my birds. It spanned a full ten acres and had an ingenious entrance. Two glass doors, one to enter first, then the other to provide passage to the gardens after the first door sealed shut. This prevented the escape of the butterflies and bees which already occupied the enclosure. There, my birds would be safe to fly free.

By the time he finished his spiel, a new hunger swam in my belly—an unsettling yet enthralling curiosity about what it might be like to visit such a majestic palace. Mama's pets would love to flutter within the winter garden and nosh upon fresh bugs. And my flowers would thrive there, as well.

"Would this be a permanent arrangement?" I asked, still adrift upon the viscount's amazing descriptions.

"I am suggesting a trial basis of one month," the viscount answered as he glanced at Uncle. "That should give us time to determine if we're compatible."

I looked at Uncle Owen. Could he not see this man's deception? This was an obvious ruse to win my estate, to have me settled elsewhere so I'd no longer care what became of my childhood home. The viscount underestimated me. I would never be so calloused with my loyalties.

As if sensing my mental vertigo, Uncle thanked the viscount for coming by, and asked that I be given time to consider the proposition.

"Please let me know by the first of December," Lord Thornton requested. "I plan to open the Manor the third week of the same month. I'd like you present before the guests arrive, so we might set up your boutique. I do hope you'll come." He kissed the back of my hand with warm, soft lips. I half expected his mouth to disappear like his brother's.

Instead, the soft density of his touch shocked me—like a raindrop falling upon the skin from out of nowhere, when there's not a cloud in the sky. And not only could I feel him, but I could *taste* his nearness, his almond essence sweetening my tongue.

The shadowy storm I noticed earlier played again within his eyes. I couldn't decide if it originated from greed, desire ... or danger.

Without another word, he turned, gathered his hat and cloak, and nodded a goodbye. A covetous ache weighed upon the back of my hand where his mouth had left an imprint—my traitorous skin pining for another touch.

Uncle escorted him to his black Phaeton outside, leaving me to watch from the window. Four stallions, white as spun sugar, were harnessed to the rigging which added to the fairytale illusion already awhirl in my mind.

After mounting the squab, the viscount wedged his cane between his knees, wriggled his hands into black gloves, and took the reins. He glanced at the house to catch me watching at the window. I ducked behind the safety of the drapes.

As he pulled away, the clouds from his eyes seemed to fill the sky and a heavy rain rolled in. I grabbed Hawk's flower, gathered my skirts, and fled upstairs, desperate to hear my ghost's voice once more.

An irrational fear had crept over me, that now that I'd touched the living embodiment of him, his spirit would be lost to me forever.

CHAPTER 12

The palest ink is better than the best memory.
Chinese proverb

Hawk practiced no restraint upon his reappearance. He cornered me until my shoulder blades pressed the wall, then he swept through my blood again. This time, as he broke our spiritual kiss with a tug at my lips, he kept his palms on the wall at either side of my head and drank me in with his eyes.

"Say something," I managed to plead as my body rocked from within, awash with the pleasure of rejuvenation.

"You are a beauty and a wonder," he said, "within and without."

His baritone drizzled in my eardrums like warm honey. The pleasure lasted only an instant before he started to fade again. I tripped over my skirts to pluck another fresh petal from the flower sitting on the desk. Opening my locket, I found the petal I had put in moments ago was as black and crinkled as the one before it.

It confirmed my worst dread. That just as each spirit-kiss made me feel more alive—even had the benefit of healing my wounds—it killed a small part of the blossom.

And since I had yet to see the flower sprout any new petals, we would have to be frugal with such intimacies.

Once I had the freshly filled locket in place against my skin, and Hawk had materialized, I held the evidence in my upturned palm. "We must choose our moments with care, at least until new buds form." The crinkled petal trembled beneath my breath.

Comprehension creased his forehead, and I marveled again at the incredible likeness he shared with our earlier guest.

"What guest?" Hawk turned with me toward the desk.

Skirts gathered beneath me, I sat in the chair.

"Did someone come with Enya's family?" He perched on the desk's edge. His long legs stretched out next to me so my left elbow should have raked his right thigh.

Opening the deepest drawer of my desk, I took out a black velvet toque perfect for a mourning traveler, and nestled it in my lap. "No. Lord Thornton visited today. He came early." I fished through the drawer's contents, pushing aside rolls of various colored ribbons, spools of thread, and stray laces in search of a cluster of burgundy ribbon roses to embellish the cap's crown. Finding this, I pinned it above the hat's mourning veil and threaded a needle.

Hawk's expression grew somber. "To buy your estate?"

"No. He's using a new tactic. He wishes to distract me from my home. Make me forget it."

"How?" Hawk's fingers kneaded wrinkles in the knees of his breeches.

"Uncle and I have been offered couturier positions at

his holiday establishment in another town."

"So, we are to move?"

I paused, mid stitch. "I-I don't wish to. I have no desire to be the clay pigeon for the upper class's insult shooting. I do not belong in society."

"Shush." Frowning, Hawk rushed a fingertip across my lips—a silken wisp of air. "They would all be stunned by your acumen and talent. You might find they are not as judgmental as you deem." He paused then. "And just think of it ... we could finally uncover the viscount's link to me."

"I already have." I paused, then *He's your brother* echoed in my mind as an afterthought.

Hawk's mouth gaped. "I-I have a *brother*?"

Studying his pocket watch, my ghost sat wordless as I sewed the roses and told him of the morning's experience while we were apart—leaving out the more indecorous details of my behavior upon his brother's arrival. When I had finished my spiel along with my stitching, Hawk's shoulders slumped.

"My twin. Age twenty-seven. Which means I've been dead for six or so years."

I paused mid-stitch, wanting to get back that time for him. If only I could.

He gripped his hands on his knees. "How is it that someone so young owns the quarry where you had your accident? Do I come from great wealth?"

"You appear to, but ..." I sat the velvet toque atop the desk, snipping leftover strings. "There's something amiss. To all of society, the viscount is known as an only child."

"He'll give us our answers. I'll make sure of it." Hawk stood in front of his potted plant. "Take the offer. Immediately."

I glared at him. "Oh, of course. Now that it holds something of gain for you, I should pack up all of my belongings into a trunk without a thought. I should gather up all of my misgivings and shut them away, for apparently, my feelings matter naught. To you or my uncle." I scooted the chair back and strode to my bed, plopping onto my belly atop the quilt.

Hawk joined me. "Why, Miss Emerline. I believe I've ruffled you. I do apologize."

"Don't patronize me. And do not call me Miss Emerline. It is what *he* calls me."

"My brother?"

I buried my face in the quilt.

"Look at me, Juliet."

I rolled over, sighing.

"You're flushed." Hawk frowned. "What did he do to you?"

I refused to answer. Refused to even think. Made my mind a swimming, black void.

A slow-burning flame sparked my ghost's eyes, and I thought for a moment he might press me. Then he looked at his watch again and clicked his teeth together. "You're right. Your future rides the tide. It is your decision to make. Perhaps there is another way we can uncover my past. Without any outside help."

His reciprocal tone soothed the burn in my cheeks. "Such as?"

"I didn't plug my ears this time," he blurted out the unexpected answer. "Nor did I sing. I listened to the voices in the dark. All of them."

Lying on my side, I stared at him, dazed by his courage. "And what did they say?"

Hawk sat, his phantom fingers tracing the alternate pink and blue floral prints along the quilt. "I think they're miners. They were shouting instructions down to one another ... as if constructing something. I heard hammering."

"You say *down*?"

"I believe it is a hole wherein I reside."

"A mine shaft."

His head drooped lower.

I knew it couldn't be easy, acknowledging where his body lay. I wanted to hold his hand, but instead was forced to watch his fingertips tread the quilt's stitches, envious of the fabric's response to him.

Hawk closed his eyes and moaned. "This is such torment." His hands plowed tunnels through his hair. "But we must be grateful we can make contact at all—on any level."

We both glanced at the flower.

"Even if it's to be doled out in portions," I grumbled.

Hawk leaned back on his elbows, his tousled hair making him appear almost boyish. "There's more to my discovery. While I sat there in my purgatory, hearing the yells from above—I had a vision. It came upon me soft and blurred, like a lost remembrance. A child ... a girl. Little slip of a thing. No more than six, fallen within a similar deep hole, looking around, trying to find a way out; frightened as a wren in a cat's lair. When her cries mounted to screams, a boy slipped from the shadows to comfort her. He was older—fourteen perhaps—his bony body and ragged clothes so coated with dust he looked to be formed of mud. He told her a fairytale, prompting her to smile—though I can't remember the story's details. Then he held her in his lap with a gentle hand. Wiped her tears, tended her scrapes with mud, took care of her ... until voices called from above. 'Juliet', they said, panicked yet hopeful. The boy left then. Vanished from whence he came." Hawk frowned.

A dark tremor rattled within my soul as the shell harboring my unborn memory shattered open. It was all exactly as he said ...

How did he portray the details with such vivid accuracy, when only at this moment had I remembered them myself?

I rubbed my temples, trying to alleviate the queer sickness I felt.

He moved nearer. "I believe it a result of our fusion. When I kissed you the first time, I retained a part of you within me. Your memories. And I'm hoping perhaps you did me as well. And in turn can tell me more of my life. Maybe even of my death."

The raven's wing of earlier that had shielded my mind whisked away, taking flight. The pieces were fitting together—what Uncle said about the mud prince, combined with what we learned in the journal of Hawk's time in some tunnels as a child, and the gypsies that worked for Larson ...

Hawk hedged closer. "I can't keep up with all your thoughts ... they're too, discombobulated. Slow down."

I fisted my hand at my mouth, holding in my shuddering breaths. If only Larson's handwritten account of my accident had been more descriptive, we could know for sure. Ink was more reliable than memory.

"*Handwritten.*" I gasped, dragging my fist away. "The note." I drew it out from my décolleté.

"What is that?" Hawk sat up as I did.

"Your brother said this would give me *peace* in dealing with my past. Perhaps it can do the same for you." I unfolded it and held it open.

Hawk studied me, confused, then leaned forward to read. "Dearest Miss Emerline, though your coughing fit was well played ..." He raised his brow in question.

I rolled my eyes, assuring him he didn't wish to know.

Frowning, he resumed. "Though your coughing fit was well played, I suspect you knew my brother Chaine, and for some reason wish to hide this from your uncle. Only his closest friends called him by his sobriquet, *Hawk*."

Hawk's ghostly gaze met mine.

Taking a shaky breath, I urged him to keep reading while watching his reaction, waiting for the epiphany to hit him at last, as it had me.

"Chaine and I were separated at birth," Hawk's fingertip followed the script. "I'd only just learned of him eight years ago and was trying to forge a relationship when he died." Hawk paused.

I sat there, awash in sympathy that they hadn't grown up together. Had the viscount been taken in by an English family? That would explain why they had different fathers, and such different lives.

A grimace tugged at Hawk's mouth. "It is for my brother I purchased the quarry," he continued Lord Thornton's explanation. "Chaine suffered unspeakable evils in his childhood while living amongst the gypsies. My intent was to ensure such atrocities never took place within those tunnels again."

Hawk choked on the words.

Determination to give him his truth—*our* truth—drove me to read the rest.

I knew—the moment I read your interview and saw the date—that you were the girl my brother had told me of. You may not remember, but he was with you in those tunnels. You gave him hope that day; you gave him something other than his own pain to think of. To care for another helpless soul furnished him with a sense of purpose, redemption, and light. He always believed that meeting you was the turning point. He considered you his sky-fallen angel.

I turned my eyes to Hawk, but he couldn't look up from the paper.

"Keep reading," he whispered.

Somehow, I found the strength to comply:

I'm only shocked he didn't apprise me of his success, as he'd been looking for many years—seeking the delicate little girl in the mine. He wanted, above all else, to thank her. It gives my soul tranquility to know he realized that goal before his death. Let this give you peace, as well.

I folded the note and tucked it beneath my pillow, unable to read his signature for the tears blinding me. I looked up at my ghost—my mud prince—to find his face every bit as wet as my own.

"It was my memory," Hawk whispered. "*Our* memory. That's what drew you to my flower. Our souls have been entwined since we met in the mines as children." He dropped to his knees on the floor in front of me. He tried to embrace my legs, only to watch himself blow out like a candle before materializing once more. He groaned—a loud, gut-wrenching sound.

It hurt. It hurt because I wanted to feel his palms curling around my calves, to feel his head upon my lap. I wanted to hold him and share the emotions that purled in my chest on a deep and winding burn.

Instead, our eyes locked in the only embrace we could share. The intensity of my need to touch him threatened to combust my body to flame. Hawk started to lean in and I knew he was going to touch his lips to mine, immerse himself within me again, that this time it would be more powerful and binding than any spiritual fusion thus far.

He bolted back at the last minute, his attention at the base of my closed door where a hanky slid into view. I kept my eyes averted from Hawk's, the only way I could tame my erratic heartbeat, and walked on weakened legs to open the door.

Uncle crouched on the opposite side. Throughout my youth, he'd always notified me of his presence thusly, because I couldn't hear him knock. He usually used a swatch of dyed fabric. But there were times, such as on birthdays or holidays, he would use a pressed flower to amuse me.

"I wanted to assure you're feeling well. You disappeared so quickly after the viscount left." Uncle clenched the door frame to pull himself up. He looked over my shoulder at my desk and the traveling mourning cap I'd been working on. "Were you sewing that for the trip?" His smile was hopeful.

Glancing at Hawk's matching hopeful expression, I knew I had no choice. The two men who meant most to me in the world needed me to make this journey to Worthington. But surely I didn't have to say goodbye to my house for a full month to seek closure for them. "Uncle ... might I speak to you of the viscount's offer?"

"Of course." He gestured to the bed and I settled on the edge. Drawing out the chair from my desk, he sat and faced me while clasping our hands.

Kneeling on the floor, Hawk waited for me to decide on my words.

"Uncle, I prefer we accomplish this with a simple visit. One week at the most. Why must we live and work there to put this to rest, when I don't wish to be away from home for that long?"

Uncle broke the clasp of our hands and shoved back the chair to stand. Shocked by his mood change, I regarded the wooden legs sticking up in the air before looking at his face again.

He rubbed his reddening neck. "For heaven's sake. I have tried to be subtle. To be patient. It's time to branch out, Juliet. Stop hiding within the dusk of your soundless world, letting light and life pass you by. Do you wish to become some senile old spinster? You spend all of your time sulking in a dark house with a nightingale and a stolen flower as your closest confidantes. I've heard you talking to the blossom. I'm worried for you. For your sanity."

Moisture scalded my lashes. I had no idea he'd been watching me with such a keen eye. Had no idea he'd misconstrued my actions to such a morose level.

Hawk looked on in speechless empathy. My emotions were still raw and frayed by our discovery. How humiliating, that he of all people would bear witness to this private scourging.

My fingers wound within my skirt. The combination of silk and wool felt stiff and harsh to my touch, and it occurred to me the whole world was bereft of the velvety underpinning which had once cushioned my days and nights. If this was how it felt to walk among the living, I wanted no part of it.

Tears pooled in my eyes, preventing me from reading Uncle's next words. Hawk—still in shock over our earlier epiphany—failed to interpret.

Uncle tilted my chin and blotted the moisture with his handkerchief. "Forgive me." Tender lines replaced the firm pleats at the corners of his lips. "I'm at my wit's end. You have a great capacity for living, tiny sparrow. T'would be a tragic waste for you to stay locked away merely subsisting, and never find someone to share life with."

"I share it with *you*, father bear." I mouthed my pet name for him, suspecting I failed to sustain it with my vocal cords.

Uncle knelt down, wincing until he found stability on his knees, the soles of his shoes facing upward. Hawk stood to look out the window beside my desk, hands clenched behind his back.

"I treasure our time together." Uncle tugged on a loose lock at my temple. "But I want you to find a young man for a companion, one who can care for you and share your interests." He hesitated. "The viscount, as I told you earlier, has a business acquaintance in Claringwell. To accommodate their transactions, Lord Thornton has been seeking property here—somewhere outside of the hustle of town, yet close enough to ease his travels. And ... well ... he has offered for your hand in marriage, if I give him this house and land as your dowry."

The bottom dropped out of my world. My face burned—a stinging torture of sensation—as if he had slapped me with his bare palm. "My home is not for sale. *Nor am I.*"

A penitent haze dulled his eyes, but his determined expression didn't falter. "Perhaps not, Juliet. But the land is. I was far too busy caring for your mother those last few months. I lost many customers ... spent more funds on her medications and treatment than I brought in. The bank foreclosed on my business weeks ago and the estate is soon to follow. We've been in financial straits for some time now. I should've told you from the beginning. I thought I could fix it. But ... even by taking this job in Worthington, we'll still be indebted. We have no choice but to sell. The only way for you to hold onto this house and the memories, is to build new memories here. With a husband."

From over Uncle's head, Hawk turned around. The slant of his strong jaw told me this turn of events did not meet his approval. Hips reclined against my desk, he stroked my mourning hat, so like the one I wore at Mama's funeral.

My stomach rolled into a fist as an ugly awakening tainted her memory. "Those missives you received from the viscount during Mama's last months. They were addressed to both you *and* her."

The downward sweep of Uncle's eyes validated my worst dread. Together, the three of them had mapped out my entire future behind my back.

Uncle's lips fluttered. "Two months ago, when I took your mother to that special appointment and you stayed home to tend a customer ... we were meeting Lord Thornton. She wanted to see him for herself. She'd always hoped you would find someone kind, noble, and wise. He impressed us both as all of these things and more. I promised her on her deathbed, that I would see you married and safe."

I gritted my teeth. "That is why he wanted the trial basis. To assure we're *compatible* as husband and wife."

"The offer is above generous."

"Generous?" I hissed.

"Surely you see how advantageous this would be for you. We have no title; you haven't the training or status required for a social debut. Yet the viscount is willing to overlook all of this."

"How benevolent of him. Nothing predicates generosity and refinement more than a thoroughbred stallion hitched to a milk cow."

Uncle frowned. "I haven't accepted his offer. It is yours to decide. I simply want you to know all of the details. To consider it. Allow him to court you when we're in Worthington. See where it might lead."

"We have nothing in common!" I knew by the strain of my vocal cords that I yelled. I only hoped it wasn't loud enough to bring Enya's entire family upstairs.

"You are wrong, Juliet," my uncle continued, oblivious to the grimacing, ghostly silhouette which loomed just behind. "The viscount has a deformity in his foot. Such a thing tenders him to your own infirmity."

Infirmity. I shoved a knuckle into my mouth to stop from sobbing. Tears built behind my eyes. Within a fortnight, my life could take an alternate path—overgrown with anxieties I feared would never be weeded-out.

Uncle coaxed me to read his lips. "You must admit Lord Thornton is being quite affable, considering you threw yourself into his arms before you'd even been introduced properly. He would have had every right to be offended, or to deem you a trollop, but he handled it with grace, not mentioning it again. A tribute to his character, do you not agree?"

Hawk glared from over Uncle's head, eyes ablaze with a threatening light. Some unnamed, intense emotion curdled his usual calm demeanor and he appeared to grow, the broadness of his frame more foreboding than ever before.

"My brother held you in his arms, and you precipitated it?" His phantom voice sliced through my heart—a frosted accusatory quality I had not heard since our first encounter when he thought me a thief.

I pled with him to be rational, to let me explain, but he was beyond reason.

"How could you let him *touch* you? Knowing I never can?" Hawk pounded his chest. "Knowing how I burn to!" With an earth-shattering growl and a well-aimed slap of his hand, he sent my hat soaring through the air, veil flapping behind it, until it landed atop the upturned heel of my uncle's left shoe.

CHAPTER 13

Where there is love, there is pain.
Spanish Proverb

Uncle started to turn, as if feeling the hat's weight upon his foot.

I moaned aloud, clutched his wrist, and feigned a dizzy spell. He scrambled up to support me, accidentally raking the hat several inches toward the toppled chair.

He started to look over his shoulder again, so I pretended to faint. Patting my cheek, he pressed my hand to his lips and I felt his anxious words: "Juliet? Juliet!"

Yelling inside my head, I demanded Hawk fix his mess. With one eye squinted, I watched as he swished his foot behind the hat and coaxed it beneath the bed.

I sat up with Uncle's help while inwardly I scolded Hawk for his blatant disregard of the lies I had to weave daily to hide him. He frowned at me, the flame of betrayal still hot behind his eyes.

After I assured Uncle I'd fainted due to hunger, he agreed to go downstairs and return with tea and toast. He scanned the floor behind him as he left, a fruitless search for the elusive object he'd felt on his heel minutes earlier.

Once he pulled the door closed behind him, Hawk and

I glared at each other in scalding silence.

I offered an olive branch. "I was so taken aback by your brother's likeness to you. Everything felt out of sorts ... surreal almost."

"Of course. He held you in some sort of trance. Is that it?"

"It was the first I'd ever seen of his face. The resemblance was—"

"Resemblance be damned." Hawk trampled my explanation. "There is one irrefutable difference between us, for future reference." He drifted through the fallen chair from one side to the other, his form as insubstantial as the tracings of a cloud. The muscles in his neck twitched. "Ghost, remember?"

Teeth clenched, I cast a grimace up at him. "I made a wish. Stir-up Sunday, remember?"

Looming over me, Hawk chuckled. For the first time, the sound rattled in my head, discordant and venomous. "A childish game. Were you an empty-headed wren, I might believe such an excuse. But you're bright and perceptive. And ripe for the plucking, it would seem."

Heat spread from my chest to my neck and cheeks. "Perception loses clarity when diluted by emotions. As proven by how I've been blinded to your more loathsome aspects up to now by my loneliness and grief."

His jaw muscle clenched. "Is that so?"

"Augh! No, it isn't," I retracted, at a loss for how to salvage this. "I only embraced Lord Thornton because I wanted him to be you with such fervor, I convinced myself it was possible. That somehow, heaven had heard my plea.

It was not his arms holding me. In my mind, it was yours."

"Ah." He turned his back, shoulders rigid, as if to resist knocking more things off my desk. "That makes it all the better. At last you've found an earthly vessel of me, to pour all of your unmet desires into. And he's wealthy to boot!"

My heart twisted in agony. I sat on the bed's edge clenching my temples, as exasperated as him. "Please stop. You saved me when I was a child. Then you came again on my darkest eve when Mama died, an answered prayer. To hear the sound of a voice. To have music in my soul night after night. And your laughter like rain. Heaven sent you. Each time I awake in the morning to find you sitting by the window, I'm assured of it. Why would I want an ordinary viscount, when I have my guardian angel with me always?"

Hawk looked down, engrossed in a keen study of his eternally muddied boots.

I slapped at the moisture gathering on my lashes. "Do you truly think me a scarlet strumpet who constantly craves the touch of any man?" I waited an interminable few minutes for a response. His silence pierced me through.

I stood, suppressing my tears, and worked at the necklace that draped my collar bones, determined to draw the locket out from beneath my corset and cast it across the room.

"Enough, Juliet." Hawk turned on me in a blink and nudged my shoulder, knocking me off balance. I plummeted to the mattress on my back. He leaned over me, one knee propped on the bed's edge. "Enough ..." His voice softened to silk.

I imagined his shirt raking my collar bones as he propped his elbows on either side of my head, his chest mere inches from mine.

His handsome face—a pearl against the thick, dark strands which framed him like a mane—held intense concentration as his hand opened across my décolleté. The pressure upon my bodice flattened the locket until the hard, warm metal indented the flesh above my sternum. My breath hung.

"You are no strumpet," he whispered, so close I could breathe him in if I but tried. "You're the purest, most compassionate and courageous lady ever to grace the earth. At my behest, you faced your mother's grave the day after you buried her. You nigh fell to your death descending an icy tree. And you braved a gypsy camp to steal a book. You were even willing to go to another town and face a castle full of snodderies for me. Dare say, not another person in this world would go to such lengths for a lost spirit." His glowing gaze encompassed me, from my hair tangled in a knotted, itchy mass beneath my nape, to my bodice where his hand still wrinkled the fabric. "God grant me pardon for needing you so. You deserve more than I can ever offer in return."

His outstretched fingers twitched—a shift in position that furrowed the fabric so it bunched around my breasts and ribcage like a passionate embrace. I gasped at the sensation.

I could *feel* him ... or at least feel my clothes responding to his touch.

Mesmerized by my response, his gaze grew potent—determined. He moved the bodice again, maneuvering the wrinkles so they clustered around the curve of my right breast, pinching and binding with delicious friction.

I arched into the forbidden sensation. Wonder and fascination lit his face with every response he evoked.

"Can you feel me?" I asked, though it felt more like a plea.

His lashes lowered. "No. I feel only the fabric's resistance—and even that is illusory."

My eyes stung. How unfair, that he could give me such pleasure, yet glean none for himself.

"But Juliet, I delight in pleasing you." His other hand tugged a trail of pleats across my ribs. "You, brimming with life, and me, the residue of a life gone by. I suppose, to never experience how you would feel beneath me is my penance for loving a lady beyond my station."

My heart leapt. After all these years of silence, I had resigned I would never hear those words spoken by a man. "You ... *love* me?"

"I would pledge it body and soul, but ..." His forefinger glided through the back of my hand. "I suppose one has to take a phantom at his word."

At a loss for any words of my own, I sorted through my myriad feelings. Did my heart belong to a ghost?

We shared all the characteristics of secret lovers.

Our worlds revolved around one another, yet we lived on separate planes. We planned for stolen interludes—relished any intimacy, however fleeting. Each morn, his was the first face I longed to see; and each night we were together in my dreams. His words both guided and cut me to bleed, yet his songs healed my soul.

And his kisses ... purest magic.

He was kind, witty, and brave. More than anyone I'd ever met. A miracle, considering all he'd endured as a child.

Yes. I loved him—as a ghost, as a friend, and as a man. So much that it lit a fire in my heart.

Hawk eased to the mattress beside me and I turned toward him. His face held an arrested expression, as if stunned by my confession.

I would've thought you would know before me.

"How?" he answered my unspoken observance. "When you didn't know yourself until this moment?" His brilliant smile could've blinded the sun.

I reached out, fingers passing through his face. He blurred like a reflection in a puddle. When he resolved to perfect, youthful clarity, I dropped my arm back to the bed.

Unlike his brother, Hawk would never age. If he somehow remained with me and I lived to become an old maid in the eyes of the world, he would be forever beautiful and young while I became wrinkled and frail. I shook my head, overwhelmed by the differences between us, differences I didn't wish to confront.

In that moment, I missed the complacency of make-believe.

Hawk clucked his tongue. "Sweet Juliet, have you not heard of the China rose's most fascinating characteristic? Surely your mother told you." He coaxed me to lie on my back again. His face hovered over mine, hands denting the quilt on either side of my head. "Your kind is the only rose that grows more vivid and fair with each passing year. Ask any botanist."

Caught between a smile and a sob, I yearned to welcome him into my blood.

His attention shifted to the locket beneath my neckline. "Spurn the petal, Hawk. Kiss me ... *inhabit me*."

He moaned, a raw and hungry sound. Then our lips melted together, and our spirits fused once more.

~ ᮂ • ᮂ ~

December dawned—glistening with snow and ice—and our move to Worthington was well underway.

I had lied again to Uncle, allowing him to contact Lord Thornton of my interest in his marriage proposition. After the trial period, if the viscount or I decided we weren't suited for marriage, he would give me a full six months to move out of the house that he would then own.

I wasn't going to make any effort toward the relationship, and had already made peace with losing my parent's estate—though it broke my heart, and deepened my disdain for the viscount. But my priorities had shifted. My ghost was more important than any material possession would ever be.

This trip was a means to an end. To allow Hawk a chance to meet his brother and to find out more about the gypsies who worked for Lord Larson, so he might face the monster who had tortured him in his past. Most importantly, to give him closure per his body's final resting place.

"You don't have to be a martyr for me." Hawk said one afternoon as our departure crept ever closer. "I've decided I don't wish to know. Any of it."

He was lying. For although he was a spirit, he was first and foremost a man—plagued with the inability to come forward physically as a rival for my hand.

"Hawk, my heart is devoted to you. This arrangement is fiction tantamount to any play. And it's only for a month. Remember that."

"Only one month," Hawk grumbled. "It will be the longest four weeks of my death."

During the final days, preparations consumed every waking hour. We spent mornings washing, folding, and packing, while afternoons entailed moving Enya's family into my estate. This had been my idea, as it seemed absurd for them to remain in their drafty shack during winter when my house would be standing empty and unused.

It was also my way of thanking Enya for agreeing to come to the manor as my lady's maid.

In the evenings, Uncle and I refined the merchandise which would soon line the shelves of our lavish boutique. As we worked side by side, he would glance over with a look of contentment and pride I hadn't seen since Mama's death. Guilt consumed me—knowing how temporal and false its foundation was.

After such frenetic days, everyone fell into their beds to let sleep swallow them. Everyone but me. For nights belonged to my ghost.

No longer satisfied to sit by the window while I slept, Hawk snuggled next to me atop my quilt. We conversed for hours—crafting intricate fairytales in lieu of the marriage and future we could never attain.

"Three children," I teased, well knowing he wanted five. "Three and no more."

"No. Two sons, and a trio of girls with their mother's beauty and compassionate nature."

"I'm afraid that will never do. For our sons will look and act just like their father. Strapping lads with laughing gray eyes who tease their sisters mercilessly. It would be difficult for any girl to maintain compassion while being tortured thusly."

"Oh, ha. If the girls are anything like their mother, they'll be well equipped to hold their own in a war of pranks."

Our musings always ended on those bittersweet notes ... Hawk and I imagining the lively capers of our children. Then laughing until we cried.

On cloudless nights, moonbeams reflected off the snow outside and filtered through the curtains to gild Hawk's form in silver-blue light. His soft-glowing stare resonated within me, so intense and ardent, that I swore I could fall into *him*, skim his blood. Our emotional connection had never been stronger; but I coveted the physical touches deprived us ... ached to feel his flesh against mine—man to woman. To experience sensations I had never known.

When my soul grew heavy with need, Hawk would hum a seductive tune while binding my gown to friction in sensual and forbidden places. He taught me the things I craved to learn of pleasure. Yet his ethereal body suffered in absence of the same.

I could not even offer the spirit-kisses that would grant him bliss. Fearing his flower might lose some petals in the move, I held tight to the fifteen we had left.

Departure arrived on the wings of a wintry Monday morning. Fog blotted the dawn to a dank, pinkish-gray while a moderate snowfall clustered the tree branches and frosted the grass.

Lord Thornton stepped into the parlor to greet us all. He wore a double breasted vest and pants the same metallic silver as Hawk's petals. A tombstone shirt—such a bold lime green it burned the eyes—peered out from the buttoned neck of a bright red cape. In the few weeks since his visit to my home, he had grown a soft bur over his mouth and chin once more. The whiskers complimented his olive complexion with an austere sensuality, though I put such thoughts from my mind, feeling Hawk's possessive glare on my back.

Before Lord Thornton retreated outside to help load the wagons, Hawk paused beside his brother, measuring himself against him. There they stood, head to head, the nobleman and his gypsy doppelganger, fascinating me with their likenesses and differences.

The viscount had brought his finest carriages teamed with high stepping strawberry roans, black-stockinged bays, and dappled mares to ensure our portage would be stylish and comfortable. Bundled in our coats and caps, Enya and I were led to an exquisite berline.

A lemon-yellow gilded the carriage's frame and doors while its trim and spindled axels shimmered with a lilac hue. Complete with crimson velvet squabs, lilac damask curtains, and navy pin-striped paper on the interior compartment, it reminded me of the viscount's own style ... elegant and polished, yet jarring in its tonal severity.

Once Enya and I were settled inside with furs draped from our waists to our feet, Hawk took the seat across from me. His broad shoulders slumped, forearms propped on his thighs so the ruffled sleeve cuffs hung down to the top of his shins. He studied his muddy boots, quieter than I'd ever seen him.

I clutched his flower's pot in my lap and silently bade him not to doubt my love. A mere viscount could not replace the man whose voice had illuminated two of the darkest events in my life.

Hawk attempted a smile.

I lifted the mourning veil to the back of my cap. Forehead pressed to the chilled window, I watched the six tigers load trunks onto a covered fourgon, tucking as much of our cargo within the servants' seat box as possible to save room for the crates of potted plants used in Uncle's dyes and my hats.

After fastening extra canvas sheets in place to shield the plants, the bird cages were loaded—with utmost care under Uncle's supervision—into a long and spacious britschka converted to a sleeping carriage with raised sides and full coverage hood. The viscount wrapped furs around each cage, providing my pets added insulation for the six hour journey.

Upon completion of the loading, Uncle climbed into the berline with us.

The viscount headed the caravan, perched on the

fourgon. With one flick of the reins, the horses tromped over my past and pressed hoof prints into the blank, white landscape of my future.

CHAPTER 14

Nothing is as burdensome as a secret.
French Proverbs

What should have been a half-day trip stretched into late afternoon due to snow-packed byways. We stopped several times so the tigers could warm up in the cabs and so the horses' half-frozen hooves could be scraped clean with knives.

Toward the end of our journey, one of the strawberry roans lost a shoe. We pulled up to a tavern and stable—an ivy-wreathed oasis that cut through the fog along our route. The swinging sign above the door touted: *Swindler's Tavern.* Lord Thornton, none too pleased with the location, stepped inside to ensure there were tables to spare for an early supper while the blacksmith tended the roan.

As we shivered on the porch, Uncle asked the coachmen about the safety of the establishment, but no one knew who owned it; for years the tavern had been run by an anonymous proprietor who'd never been seen. Before the viscount returned from inside, a crowd of rowdy men gathered behind and rushed us through the door.

Within the establishment's stone walls, a mingling of licorice, maple, and fruit flavored smoke tightened my throat and blurred the lit sconces beneath each high, dusty window. I could no longer see anyone's faces clearly. Were Hawk not at my side offering insights, I would have been lost once more to isolation.

The group of coachmen separated to search for the viscount as Uncle, Enya, and I waited next to the bar. Two drunken nobles seated on tall chairs cast furtive glances our way. Between smoking a cheroot and flirting with the serving matrons, one of them said something unreadable to Enya and me. My uncle looped both of our arms tight and Hawk stepped in front of me, his jaw clenched in rage.

Uncle said something back to the man who started to stand, unsteady in his drunkenness. My uncle was still at a disadvantage with his crotchety back. I searched in desperation for our coachmen.

I had just captured the eye of one and waved my arm when Hawk shoved Uncle's would-be opponent. The man slipped backward and dropped his cheroot into his companion's mug of ale. The glowing end stifled to a thin trail of muddied ash. Both men stepped up to Uncle, their faces twisted and red. I tried to intervene, but the taller one grabbed me around the waist and held me tight against him—a manhandling so intimate my skin crawled. His hot breath slithered down the nape of my neck, reeking of liquor.

Hawk shouted in anger, thrusting forward. At that moment, the viscount appeared, his silver ensemble and red cape cutting through the smoke like a bloodied blade.

In a flash, he broke the man's grasp on me. Using his cane, Lord Thornton knocked my attacker off balance and pinned him to the floor beneath the heel of his twisted foot. He yelled something unreadable and the veins in his temples bulged and throbbed—an echo of his violent outburst at the cemetery played out in full color.

Chaos erupted. The other drunk launched a fist at Uncle, but Hawk shoved his arm aside. A third nobleman jumped into the mix and a bar fight ensued with Hawk afloat between participants. The stench of spilled ale and testosterone-laced perspiration made me choke. Enya and I joined hands and ducked through the flailing fists and arms with Uncle in tow. Lord Thornton appeared and grasped my elbow. I strained my neck to find Hawk, but he was lost amidst the brawl. The viscount escorted us to some tables in the far corner where the smoke thinned to a soft haze.

My entire body trembled on the aftershock.

Lord Thornton knelt down and resituated my skewed hat—a gentle, attendant gesture. "Did that man hurt you?" he mouthed, his countenance dark with fury.

I shook my head, dazed. After assuring that Enya was all right, the viscount stepped away. Uncle informed me our host went out to the stables to see to his horse. A clammy sweat enveloped my skin and Uncle held my hand as I trembled. Hawk wandered to our table—hair tousled and shirt rumpled.

There you are. I scolded him. *Do not frighten me like that again!*

His head cocked. "That cad begged a lesson in civility,

Juliet. No man speaks such filth to a lady—whether she can hear him or not." Straightening his shirt lapels, he gestured to Uncle. "He was right to stand up for you. I just wanted to give him a little help."

My heart swelled on a strange mix of emotions. To think my mud prince had defended Uncle Owen as well as my and Enya's honor. But he wasn't the only one who'd stepped in.

Hawk scowled. "What, my brother? Ha. He had no business leaving you alone at the bar to begin with. And he should be tending you now that you've been traumatized, yet he's too busy seeing to his prized roan."

I glanced down at my fingers where they nestled in Uncle's hand, wishing there were some way to show Hawk my appreciation.

"A lady traditionally repays her knight with a kiss." His eyes held a teasing glint. "But since that's out of the question, I've another idea. When next you bathe," his gaze roved the faces of our returning coachmen, "which, after such a taxing journey, will no doubt be tonight ... what say you allow me to watch?"

I kneaded my hands in my lap. *You're asking me to make myself vulnerable, in a way you never will be to me.*

Hawk trailed a fingertip along his shirt placket. "Well, if you'd like me to strip down, too, I'll be happy to oblige. You're the one who will have to see me naked every moment of every day thereafter. Though I suppose it would give me a new place to hang my pocket watch."

I emitted a shocked snort and Uncle pinned a glance

on me. To resist Hawk's infectious laugh, I busied myself studying the room. My attention landed on the entrance where Lord Thornton was helping the burly bartender escort the troublemakers through the door. It appeared he hadn't yet made it to the stables, and something told me he had never intended to go there in the first place.

A plump matron intruded on my line of sight. Shifting from one foot to the other, she sputtered the choice of fare. Her lips moved too fast to read.

Uncle repeated the options, beating Hawk by a blink. I ordered the stewed beef and a steamed chocolate to soothe my stomach.

When our drinks arrived, the chocolate's sweet, creamy aroma curled through me. Enya nursed her tea and avoided my glance. She had spoken little to me since the pillow incident and I missed our closeness, especially now.

Uncle had his back turned to talk to the coachman next to him, no doubt discussing the remainder of the trip. My attention settled on our bar matron who delivered drinks to the tigers at the far end of the table. Her mouth shaped Lord Thornton's name, but I couldn't make out what she said. Frustrated, I asked Hawk to listen in.

Standing beside me, he scanned the room, oblivious to my thoughts for once. "Several men just slipped into an alcove in back. The entrance is tucked behind that stone antechamber and guarded by a watchman. I believe it's a gambling hall."

I glanced over my shoulder, wondering why it would need to be guarded.

His teeth gnawed his bottom lip. "There must be a great amount of money at stake. Juliet, this place ... feels familiar."

He had my full attention. The other time he'd said that, we found the journal in a gypsy camp. *Have you had a memory?*

The ropelike muscles along his neck corded. "Nothing quite as substantial as a memory. More of a ... moment. Something to do with a paneled glass humidor and a deck of cards."

I frowned.

Hawk raked a hand through his hair to smooth it. "Perhaps I gave someone a card dukkerin here, and they paid me with a humidor."

I'd learned bits of the gypsy language while he'd read his journal to me. *Dukkerin* meant a fortune telling.

Taking another sip of chocolate, I asked if I should help him explore the secret room.

"No. There's a door and a wall. We would get separated and spurn a petal. Besides, you require my help hearing something?"

With a grateful smile, I gestured toward the matron.

Hawk moved closer to her captive audience. "She just told the tigers that my brother used to frequent this place. According to her, Nicolas had a weakness for liquor which made him loose with his money ... and his bed. It appears he'll chase anything in a skirt. And she says he has a past history of going into rages—almost killed a man once. This is his first appearance back in some years, and he still brought trouble to their doorstep." Hawk pursed his lips, somber and suspicious. "My brother's been ostracized from high society. No doubt to the point he no longer has the option of capturing a debutante bride. Perhaps that is where you come in."

A queasy knot roiled in my stomach. It angered me, to know the viscount was pretending to take pity on a deaf girl to win favor with the elite, to secure success for his beloved manor's debut. Preying upon a physical shortcoming he had claimed to empathize with due to his own gimp leg. At least now I knew this attempted betrothal was a farce from every side.

The food arrived, but I couldn't swallow much of the stew.

Hawk moved closer to the conversation on the other end. "It's rumored Nicolas had a weakness for gambling. He frequented the gaming hells quite often. Lost much of our father's wealth. Some seven years ago." Hawk narrowed his eyes just as I realized what he was thinking. That was right around the time Lord Thornton acquired the Larson estate and the ochre mines. How could he have afforded such a purchase, if he had already lost his money?

"Interesting," Hawk answered, watching one of the viscount's drivers answer the matron. "According to the tiger, Nicolas has been squandering money left and right for that manor ever since. He sold his family's stables and estate from under his father's nose for funding. And no one has seen the eldest Thornton for some time."

Hawk's gaze met mine and I gulped a half-chewed bite. I watched the matron leave to tend other patrons. The tigers still spoke among themselves, and Hawk seemed captivated by their words.

What happened to the eldest viscount? Do they know where he lives now?

"Perhaps the question we should be asking is if he lives at all," Hawk said. "For a nobleman to inherit his father's title and estate without the predecessor first dying is nigh unheard of. Maybe the elder viscount's body is buried alongside me. Somewhere in the mines."

My sip of chocolate soured on my tongue.

"Or perhaps he's in the castle at my brother's lofty estate," Hawk continued, his attention still on the tigers. "They speak of a secret room in the dungeon. They've seen boxes opened after they're carried down, all of them containing disturbing and monstrous oddities. Medieval torture devices, mutated animal fetuses in jars of formaldehyde, creaturely skeletons wired together in mismatched masterpieces—fused and mounted for display, like scientific experiments gone awry. He has a proclivity for the macabre and demented, Juliet." Hawk moved back next to me. "I fear what you are going to encounter at this manor of nightmares."

My skin prickled beneath my clothes, not only for Hawk's formidable insinuations, but because right at that moment, Lord Thornton returned.

He took a seat on the other side of Uncle, his hair messy and his clothes torn. Slashes of fresh blood shimmered on his knuckles and smeared his shirt—belonging either to him, or to the man he'd escorted out.

The viscount caught me staring and wiped his hand on

a napkin, then drew his cape across his disheveled shirt, his eyes hooded in darkness once more.

When at last we crossed into Worthington, a violet sunset struggled to break through low-hanging clouds. My eyelids grew heavy with weariness, and my heart with fear. I couldn't tell Uncle of the unsavory rumors surrounding the viscount. In much the same as I couldn't tell him of Lord Thornton's familial connection to the gypsy woman we rescued. For somehow, though Hawk and I had yet to unravel the mystery behind their birth-parting, these men shared Romani blood.

How would I explain knowledge of such things?

During the final two hours of our trip, Hawk and I secretly spoke of his brother until I became overwrought. He put a stop to the mental dialogue, vowing to protect me by any means necessary. And he'd proven with the wolf and the inebriates at the tavern he could do just that.

From the top of a tall hill the estate appeared, nestled within a valley of snow-capped trees meshed together like crocheted lace. We took a steep, cobbled roadway, sanded in preparation, and wound through the forest toward a set of wrought iron gates. On the other side was a clearing surrounded by a wall of stone. In the center, the castle loomed over two smaller edifices.

Twilight moved across the glistening snow. I had hoped to look upon the manor in the light of day. Seeing it in darkness tightened the shackles of mystery and apprehension already locked around me.

Our berline swayed as the head tiger descended to open the black barred gates. Two slivers of wood hung on the stone walls at either side, bearing strange markings painted in ochre-red and glazed by moonlight.

"Gypsy rune-signs," Hawk informed me.

I didn't question why the viscount would have such symbols upon entrance to his Manor. I wanted to assume, per his earlier handwritten note, that just as he purchased the mines, he did this in honor of Chaine and his heritage. But after learning of Lord Thornton's darker tendencies, I wasn't so sure of the motives behind anything he did.

"The one on the left is the pentacle of Solomon," Hawk explained. "It attracts prosperity. It's harmless enough. Though I can't decipher the one on the right."

Hawk's memory had sharpened with each step closer to the quarry. In the hours since supper, he'd experienced several images from his past: a table cluttered with mechanical drawings; the same old man who read him fairytales, working over a jumbled array of gears; and the scent of ink, coal-oil, and feathers. Although none made any sense, it encouraged Hawk to have them.

As we rolled through the gates, I concentrated on the unsolved rune and memorized the symbol so I might draw it later in my chamber. Surely Hawk would recognize it in time, if he could study it.

I didn't notice the other carriages parting ways with us, taking the viscount with them, until we came to a stop and Uncle patted my hand from the seat opposite me.

He took Hawk's flower as the carriage door opened to reveal two footmen in scarlet waistcoats and pumpkin orange breeches waiting at the bottom of the step. I staunched the fear within, and pasted a false smile over my suspicions, as I reached for their hands and stepped down into the viscount's world of shadows and lies.

CHAPTER 15

The night rinses what the day has soaped.
Swiss Proverb

My legs gave out upon my descent from the carriage, atrophied from sitting in one position too long. The viscount must have apprised his servants of my deafness, for neither footman spoke a word as they supported me.

"Oh, they are speaking," Hawk assured me. "Albeit furtively. They consider you an upstart for aspiring to marry their master, a man above your class."

I hadn't considered what the viscount's servants would feel towards me for trying rise above them. An awkward shame flickered within my chest.

"No, Juliet," Hawk scolded. "They should be ashamed for judging you when it's my brother beneath your station. With a history like his, he doesn't deserve even a passing glance from such a lady."

Uncle Owen handed me the flower pot and climbed out behind me. After assisting Enya, he turned his attention to the footmen. Their mouths moved but I made no attempt to read them in the darkness. Only our steps were lit by the torches. I trusted Hawk to relay anything of importance.

Behind us, the star tower rose to the sky. A giant clock nestled at the top, with a face as square as Hawk's pocket watch—so similar in fact, it appeared to have been made by the same craftsman. Hawk heard my silent observation, and we shared a curious glance.

The snow-crisped air carried the underlying scent of ochre. The *Rat King* picture danced in my mind's eye along with a memory, solely belonging to me and Hawk: a young girl in the belly of a tunnel with her mud prince.

"The castle is being prepared for the patrons." Hawk's voice drifted to me, offering a reprieve from my macabre musings. "We're to stay in the Viscount's townhouse with the rest of his staff." The spacious three-story edifice sported two-tones of paint. Morning would reveal what extravagant and discordant color scheme the viscount had chosen, but even at night one could discern the exquisite design and unusual ric-rac paneling which ran the length of the townhouse and tipped the coned and spiked turrets.

Uncle guided me behind the footmen bearing our personal luggage. On our way to the door, I noted a circular balcony on the third floor at the left corner of the home's front, arranged along a turret with picture windows on each of the two lower stories.

There was movement from behind the window on the first floor, and I wondered if we would have to face the viscount again tonight.

"He's busy overseeing the placement of your birds and plants in the enclosed garden," Hawk answered. "But, he has arranged baths for all of you in anticipation of your weary bones. How fortuitous." He grinned and held his pocket watch up. "Time to try this on for size."

I bit my lip to hide a smirk, but heat flared through my neck and face, knowing he was only half-teasing.

We followed Uncle and Enya into the house, led by a middle-aged, lantern-bearing housemaid dressed in an orange frock, scarlet apron, and a mossy-green snood over her hair. I wondered upon the staff's outrageous uniforms, how similar their vivid color schemes and fabric designs were to the items in the trunk that had belonged to Hawk's gypsy aunt. Perhaps everything here was meant to honor the viscount's gypsy heritage.

The head housekeeper, introducing herself as Miss Abbot, asked for our coats and gloves. She then brought us to an expanded hallway along marble floors polished to such perfection I felt as if I skated on ice.

Arched pilasters guided the eye to two sets of stairs on opposite ends. Evergreen and berry garlands ornamented the walls in honor of the upcoming Christmas holiday, and a citrus tang—reminiscent of the special wassail Enya made each year—tickled my nose as we passed dwarfish orange trees trimmed with red and green bows.

A house steward came to lead Uncle in the opposite direction, explaining that the ladies' south-side quarters were isolated from the men's on the north wing. Uncle hugged me and bid me goodnight, though he glanced over his shoulder several times as we parted.

We ascended our staircase with Enya and Miss Abbot almost nose to nose in conversation and tossing glances my direction. I hugged Hawk's potted flower, clenching the cold wrought-iron rails with my other hand. As we passed the second story, curiosity got the best of me and I broke down to ask Hawk what the maids spoke of.

But he didn't hear, too intent on the high stucco ceiling.

"What hell is this," he mumbled and I paused mid step, slanting my gaze upward.

A line of macabre rats was sketched within the white plaster by an artist's tool. The design ran amuck along the ceiling to taint what otherwise would have been an architectural masterpiece.

"Do you think it's true?" Hawk perched next to me. "That he had all of this done for me? Some form of ... brotherly penance ... to make amends for his better life? Or was it a sadistic barb at my expense?"

I had no response. I'd realized tonight that this man—who wore my beloved ghost's features like a mask—could be any number of things: A murderer, a rogue, an architectural genius, a sadist, a loving brother, a kind guest and host.

I had no idea which was his true face.

The maids waited on the staircase four steps ahead for me to follow. At the top of the stairs, we walked a long corridor with closed doors running both sides. Coming to the end, Miss Abbot wriggled a key within a brass knob and swept us into a spacious corner chamber where cheerful flames danced inside a white brick fireplace. Tall ceramic vases filled with lotuses and lilies released a stale wine scent from either side of the hearth.

"This is the Water-Lily Room. My brother insisted you have it." Distrust edged Hawk's voice as he translated the maid's explanation. His attention stalled on the larger than life-sized portrait of a Romani beauty—in a colorful dress and long, brown braids interwoven with red ribbons—taking up most of one wall.

"Her eyes ... I know those eyes." Hawk's ghostly whisper was so reverently quiet, I almost didn't hear him. He stopped before the painting, and I didn't respond, giving him privacy in hopes it might spark the memory he was struggling to reach.

It wasn't difficult to give him his distance, for I was enthralled with my surroundings. I stepped inside, my feet springing atop an imperial carpet of delicate fleurons staggered upon a rich salmon background. Turquoise wall paper—with flying birds and ivy-covered trellises hand-blocked in aqueous tones—stretched around the room to meet in the center of the domed ceiling. It gave the illusion of standing within a globe with water pressed against the surrounding glass walls. A reverse aquarium.

White molding paneled the lower halves of the wall, and a four poster bed of the same color sat in the corner. Layers of silk draped the bedposts in shades of salmon and turquoise with matching sheets, blankets, and pillows.

The room had little other furniture; a wardrobe, a mirrored dressing bureau with wing-backed chair, and a Secretaire—all painted white like the wall's panels.

Miss Abbot strode past the fireplace where a tub of steaming water waited for my bath. To the left of the bureau, she opened a door, revealing the adjoining servant's alcove in which Enya would stay. Enya ducked inside and I used the opportunity to get the housemaid's attention.

"Did the viscount decorate this room?" I asked.

As if shocked that I could speak, the maid stammered. "Of course. As he did all of them." She elaborated on her answer while turning her head to see about Enya. I lost my connection to her lips and Hawk turned away from the portrait to help me, to fill in missing words. I asked him stop. The staff of a household often knew more about their master than he wished them to know. For that reason I needed to gain their trust.

I set the flower pot on the bureau and patted Miss Abbot's wrist to urge her to look at me. "I must see your mouth to read your words." I pointed at my lips. "Can you repeat what you said?"

Twisting her apron's hem, she nodded. There was a pinched quality to her cheeks which made her appear to be sucking something bitter. But she made an effort to speak slowly, a compassion contradictory to her sour expression. "His lordship designed this entire estate." She glanced at the gypsy portrait on the opposite wall beside Hawk. "Also painted the artwork." An odd expression passed through her face before she continued. "Even as a lad he was creative. A designer of sorts. Had the plans for this estate drawn up many years before he bought this land. Been his dream since childhood." At the confession, she brought her fingers to her mouth, as if she'd said too much.

So, Lord Thornton was not only an architect, but he shared his brother's artistic skills.

Hawk's expression darkened.

The room's color scheme surprised me. In this case the viscount's dramatic and slapdash disregard for conventional palettes reaped a reward, for it was beautiful beyond words. Considering how his clothes often clashed, along with the garish berline we had arrived in, I was all the more curious as to what the remaining rooms in the house and castle looked like.

"Personally, I'm most curious about the décor in the dungeon." Hawk's growling voice shattered through me. He was obviously done hearing about his brother's many talents. He waited at the opposite side of the room, tense and alert as he glanced out over the grounds through the salmon, blue, and clear glass blockings of a French door. "You need to bathe, and we need to talk. Get them out. Or I will."

He purposely brushed his fingertips along the gauzy drapes to swish them. Enya returned in time to see the movement. Her mouth gaped and she backed into her room, closing the door behind her.

Miss Abbot noticed the curtains and rushed over to check the double-doors, assuming one stood ajar. Casting Hawk a scalding glare, I followed the housemaid and pretended to help check the latches.

Pleased with himself, my ghost stepped aside. I looked through the glass to find that I had the room with the rounded balcony I'd earlier admired. "Doesn't this face east?" I could only imagine how lovely dawn must be, pouring in through the multi-colored panels.

Miss Abbot frowned. "We can order heavier drapes

should you wish to sleep in."

"No. I've always liked the dawn." I shifted my attention to Hawk, imagining him in the morning, gilded by a prismatic spread of light. He arched a brow and smiled.

Miss Abbot drew the thin drapes closed. "All right then. The cooks are preparing browned tomatoes and cheese on toast, on the chance anyone needs sustenance. Ring the bell there," she motioned to a long cord draped from the ceiling, "and I'll bring it up."

Miss Abbot's attention jerked to the door. She rushed to open it. Two footmen carried in our luggage and left. The head housemaid started to follow, but paused, then came close enough so I could see her face in the firelight.

"Tomorrow you'll break your fast with His lordship. He wishes to discuss new gowns for you." Her gaze ran the length of me in obvious disapproval of our courtship. "He'll be your escort to each party and gala upon the Manor's opening." With a curt nod, she offered the room key and closed the door on her way out.

I locked it behind her and faced Hawk.

My ghost leaned against the hearth and grimaced, arms crossed over his chest.

"You are jealous," I stated.

"I am worried." A wry frown belied his calculated answer.

"Worrying is fruitless. There is no turning back now." I sat the key on the Secretaire then rummaged through my baggage, checking for Hawk's journal within a hidden pocket in the trunk's lining. Finding it safe in its hiding place, I shut the lid and trailed my fingertips through the bath water, my bones hungry to soak up the steamy warmth. "Beginning tomorrow, we will solve the mystery of what happened to you. Then we will leave. Simple as that."

After dragging the wingback chair to the French doors, I positioned it to face the glass and opened the drapes a crack so Hawk could look outside. I motioned for him to take the seat.

He refused to budge. "Simple, aye? We've no idea how dangerous my brother is. At the very least he's a randy and volatile spoiled prig. I may remember little about myself. But be sure, given the same opportunity as him, I would bed you within a fortnight and leave you with child to bind you to me forever. We're twins. So who's to say he won't do the same?" Hawk stepped up next to the tub. He bowed in a dramatic sweep, beckoning me to the water.

Face burning, I didn't budge. "The viscount and I aren't even acquainted. He won't have such politics ruling his heart. This entire charade is to earn his way back to society's good graces. It is enough for him to offer me a pity proposal. When I turn him down, I will be left looking like an idiot, and he a charitable man."

"He will not *let* you turn him down." Hawk clenched a fist next to the edge of the tub.

"Of course he will. I'm beneath him." I gestured to the chair, more insistent this time.

A muscle jumped in Hawk's jaw as he tightened his stance ... immoveable. "That's precisely where he wants you. Beneath him and naked. Lord knows what else is on his agenda with his demented pastimes and hobbies.

Throughout his life he's been given everything I haven't. A kind father ... money ... power. I refuse to let him desecrate the one thing that can better all of it. I refuse to let him seduce you right under my nose." He tilted his head toward the tub in a less than subtle command, eyes aglow with mystical light.

I remained rooted to the floor. "You envy every aspect of his life—from his riches to his childhood. Even if I weren't involved, even if you hadn't heard the rumors, you would despise him."

"But you *are* involved. And I did hear the rumors, much too clearly for my liking."

"You think me a dimwitted country maiden."

"I said no such thing. You're too compassionate, and innocent to the ways of a man and a woman. He can use that to his advantage."

"I have more wisdom than to let a stranger lure me into his bed, or into any sort of danger."

Hawk frowned. "In a few weeks, he'll no longer be a stranger."

"Not so. I've known you for over a month, yet at this moment you're acting as if I'm a stranger to you. As if you know nothing of me."

A cloud of frustration extinguished the light in his eyes, but quickly passed. "Take your bath my lady, before your water ices over."

"At your leisure, my lord." I curtsied and pointed to his waiting chair. "If you'll but take your place."

"You can't keep me from watching. It isn't as if you can blindfold me."

"Ah. But I can remove my locket."

He raised an eyebrow—a dare.

"Or perhaps I shan't bathe any while I'm here," I demurred. "All the better. If I stink, the viscount will keep his distance and you won't have to worry for my inability to resist his charms."

"Dammit, Juliet!" Hawk slapped his hand atop the water in emphasis. The liquid sprayed across the floor and flecked my forehead. "Is it so much to ask for this one intimacy? I cannot even kiss you, for God's sake. Yet he can tempt you into his arms any time he deems fit, simply by resembling me."

I didn't respond with the sharp-edged response he deserved. I couldn't. Because where the water trickled from Hawk's palm, he had become flesh.

We gasped simultaneously as he heard my thoughts.

Brow furrowed, he rolled up his sleeve and dunked his entire hand beneath the surface. He lifted his palm above his head. We both watched as the droplets drizzled from his fingertips to his palm to his wrist, coating him, coloring that part of him to life, making him solid where he was once transparent.

Holding my gaze, he moved toward me, dripping water along the way. Within moments we stood face to face. I propped my shoulders against the chair's tall back.

"Your hand." His husky demand prompted me to heed without question.

I held up my palm. His met mine with a warm, firm resistance.

He moaned.

I sobbed.

Staring at my face to gauge my reaction, he tugged his hand in a sensuous tour down my inner wrist, glazing me with wetness.

The pull along my skin was substantial and real ... a joining of flesh to flesh. Man to woman. ... so different from our first kiss. Nothing healing or invigorating like the merging of our spirits. I didn't have to ask. I knew by the severity of his expression he could feel me as well.

At last, we were touching.

Tears blazed down my cheeks. *We are touching.*

In rapt silence, Hawk retraced the watery path, his fingertip following the veins in my wrist, probing the intricate lines in my palm and the delicate skin between my fingers, waking places I never knew were dormant. Taking a deep breath, he laced our fingers.

I squeezed his hand.

Caught so off guard by the sensation, we laughed: the secret laughter of children who have discovered they can fly—despite that every adult swore it impossible.

The water formed a seal between us ... a link between our worlds. But it was fleeting, for in each place it dried, Hawk became translucent again and our connection faded. A desperate wrinkle crossed his forehead as he pried our fingers apart to swipe the remainder of water across his lips. The wet glaze sparkled in the moonlight.

In dreamlike astonishment, he leaned over me. A droplet trickled down his chin and plopped on mine—so unexpected and gratifying it burned like steam.

In that glorious moment of suspension, one breath

away from a kiss, he jerked back and glared over his shoulder.

Struggling to contain my pounding heartbeat, I shoved myself upright as Enya's door opened.

She stepped into the firelight, an odd expression on her face. "I thought I heard you laughing." Her gaze followed the droplets on the floor leading from the tub to me. "Oh, were you testing the water for your bath? I will assist. And when you're done, I would have a turn."

She hadn't offered such help in weeks. This was her way of reaching out, an effort to mend the bridge between us.

"Get rid of her, Juliet." Hawk's voice was demanding, but his face full of supplication.

I didn't know what to do—torn between my estranged friend and this amazing discovery. Now that Hawk and I had found a link to one another, so many more intimacies could be shared between us this night were we submerged together in the tub. The mere thought heated my entire body as if my blood had caught fire.

Enya frowned—either at my hesitation or my flushed skin. "Do you wish me to leave?"

If I told her yes, there would be no salvaging the closeness we once shared. In that moment, the limits of my mortal frailties swallowed me whole. My bones ached, my skin drained of the heat that had consumed it, and my mind thickened with exhaustion. The warm bath looked more inviting by the minute. And I could no longer stave off my stomach's bid for food. Yet I knew once Enya and I both had a turn, the tub would be taken away ... the water emptied.

So the decision would not be mine. In fairness, I couldn't make it. Instead, I left it for Hawk to decide.

His gaze roved my body before settling on my mouth. He cursed, then, with a pained grimace, rolled down his sleeve. He slipped into the chair—so reluctant, his muscles coiled in resistance beneath his clothes.

He propped his elbows on the arms and stared out the window at the moonlit landscape ... my silent, stoic phantom, locked in the chains of a gentleman.

CHAPTER 16

The wise adapt themselves to circumstances,
as water molds itself to the pitcher.
Chinese Proverb

I slept, adrift in dreams filled with light and hope, though strangely devoid of music. When I awoke to the dawn, my ghost still sat by the glass doors, elbows on the chair's arms, head tilted so I could see his profile. It looked as if he hadn't budged for hours.

I nestled beneath the warm, lavender scented covers, and watched—captivated—as iridescent colors glided along his crystalized silhouette in the way a sunrise torches a serene lake. Our contact from the night before came back in a delightful rush, how he touched me, how close we came to kissing. Anticipation sluiced through my veins for our next such moment together, and all that it might entail. I planned to ask for a bath to be drawn every night. Perhaps even in the mornings.

"Seven petals—withered and fallen." Hawk mumbled the words, breaking up my fantasies. "We are down to eight."

The chill of morning clamped my shoulders as I shoved off my blankets, forcing my gaze to the bureau where seven brown petals spattered the white surface beneath Hawk's flower.

I groaned. "No. How? I watered her last night."

Hawk didn't answer.

For a moment, I considered planting her in the winter garden to see if she might blossom anew. But once the patrons arrived, the possibility loomed that someone might pluck her remaining petals. "All she needs is some fresh soil and a larger pot. That will encourage her to bloom." So difficult to portray a hopefulness I didn't feel. "She'll be fine soon enough. The journey was too much. It shocked her."

He sat, unmoving. "The journey? Or our physical contact?"

I opened my locket and found the petal within still fresh and silver. Shutting it, I settled the locket back in its place against my skin. "The one in my necklace is safe. It was the transfer here. It had to be."

"Or my interaction with the water. Each time I touch you, whether flesh to flesh or spirit to spirit, we pay a penalty. If we lose another seven, we'll be left with but one. Are you willing to risk it, Juliet?"

His logic frayed to splinters and bruised my heart. I fell back onto the mattress, drew the covers over my head, and wept.

$\backsim \cdot \frown$

"The viscount cannot see you like this." Enya had been scolding me since she came in and caught me with my face stuffed in the pillow, the locket clenched in my hand. My crying had awakened her.

Bewildered, Hawk sat on the edge of the bed where he'd perched after his observation about the petals brought me to tears. He had tried to apologize, tried to comfort, but I was inconsolable.

To wake in this strange place and encounter yet another barrier between us after such a glorious taste of hope; to anticipate breakfast with a man who embodied all of my beloved ghost's features, behind which he harbored enough dark secrets to out-bluff the devil in a game of poker—it was too much. I was emotionally spent, and wanted nothing more than to crawl back to the gods of sleep and find my way to the dreams of death and music that brought me such comfort.

Enya clutched my elbow and steadied me to standing. "We'll dress you, and find a way to hide the puffiness." She patted the skin around my eyes, then moved the chair from the window and seated me before the mirrored bureau. I refused to look at the dead petals. Instead, I focused on my maid's heart-shaped mouth in the reflection.

"We will call for a pitcher of water and make a compress." She cinched her shawl around her chemise and rang the bell pull.

At the mention of water, Hawk growled in frustration and I bit back a new rush of sobs. My reflection didn't help things—frizzed tangles and swollen eyes—the chaotic result of convulsing beneath the covers like a landed fish.

Finding a brush on a silver tray, I dragged it through my hair, wincing as the bristles snagged. I gave up and let the brush hang there in the knotted strands—a leech of wood and hog's quills—sucking away every remaining ounce of my dignity.

Hawk stared out the window, silent as death.

"Tell his lordship I am ill," I said to Enya when she returned to stand behind me. "I'm going back to bed."

The maid clamped my shoulders and spun me along with the chair to face her. The brush, still attached by tangles, swung around and thumped my cheekbone. I winced at the resulting ache.

"You will do no such thing." The freckles on Enya's nose bounced as her face twitched. "You are to attend this breakfast. You are to be charming and demure. You will win the viscount's heart and give your uncle the peace of mind and solitude he so richly deserves."

Her command leveled me to awe. "*Solitude?* You want Uncle to be alone?"

Enya turned me around again and looked down so I couldn't see her mouth. Had Hawk not been there to translate, I would have missed her response. "He will not be alone. He shall have me. Only me. At last."

Hawk and I exchanged glances.

Enya tugged on the brush stuck in my hair, oblivious that I knew her heart's deepest secret. I hardly noticed the pain at my scalp now. The gravity of her confession numbed all other sensations.

"I've suspected for some time," Hawk said from beside the glass doors.

Why had I not seen the signs? A sidelong glance, a lingering pat on the back, the appearance of Uncle's favorite food at each meal ...

Enya and I had stayed up after our baths last night and ate together. First, she spoke of the weather, then of the mourning dresses I'd be wearing during our stay. But gradually, she opened up about Miss Abbot, how the head maid had been with the Thornton family since the viscount's childhood. How she'd worked for his father before moving, along with several other familial servants, to the Larson estate under the young Lord Thornton's request.

After that, all of our conversation centered around Uncle.

There was only one mention of the incident in my room in Claringwell. I explained that the pillow had been tucked behind my bed's head frame making it appear to float— that Enya couldn't see the wrought iron bars since they were the same white as the pillow dressing. She accepted the excuse too hastily, because she was eager to shift the subject back to her heart's dearest obsession.

"On my mother's grave," I said aloud. "You love Uncle Owen."

The tangled brush slipped from Enya's hand and cracked my cheek again. Cringing, I patted what was sure to be a striking bruise to offset my puffy eyes.

Enya stumbled over to my bed's edge and sat, burying her face in her hands. Hawk leaned against the double doors, looking on with interest.

I settled beside Enya. The mattress sunk beneath our combined weight.

She met my gaze, a lovely pink coloring her damp

cheeks. She looked terrified, as if she feared I would level her life to ashes.

"Enya." I took her hand in mine. "I love you like a sister. Your secret is safe with me."

Her eyes filled with fresh tears. "He thinks I am a child."

I stroked her hand, not knowing what to say.

"But with your mother gone," Enya continued, "and were you to leave as well ... I hoped he might turn to me, lean on me. He may never come to love me, but, to be needed would be salve enough to ease the burn."

No sooner had she spoken than she shot to her feet and clambered for the chamber door. She unlocked the latch and Miss Abbot entered with a pitcher of water. The older maid's face turned sour the moment she looked at me.

I stretched my arms over my head as if just waking, letting the brush dangle from my hair for effect. I padded to the glass doors, watching in the reflection as Miss Abbot spoke to Enya then left.

My maid found my merino-wool mourning gown and laid it out on the bed before digging through the trunks in search of my crinoline. Without the cage beneath my gown, the skirt length would trip me. That was precisely why I had slipped the contraption from the luggage before we left. By leaving it on my bed at home, I had successfully limited my daily options to my princess panel and walking mourning gowns. Though less posh and elaborate, they were form-fitting and easy to move about in. I had decided if I was to be forced into this trip, I could at least be comfortable in my misery.

"Wicked girl," Hawk said with a smug grin, joining me at the curtains.

Silently, I watched Enya's busy reflection in the glass, lost in her confession.

Hawk shook his head. "It would appear we aren't the only ones ensnared in cupid's insidious barbed web."

Yet it's just as impossible a romance. She's too young for him. Too young to know her own heart.

"She's older than you, China Rose." Hawk smiled sympathetically. "And you know your heart well enough. Besides, she was the age you are now when she first met your uncle. And he's a mere eight years her senior."

Neither of us said what we were both thinking: it was the same age difference as between me and Lord Thornton. In our society, women often married men twelve or more years their senior and had families.

Enya's reflection moved to another trunk. Pinpricks of nausea rushed through my stomach. Not because I was about to be scolded severely for leaving behind my crinoline, but because I didn't want either of my loved ones to get hurt.

Uncle is still grieving Mama. What if Enya is confused? He's been her father figure for so long. What if she's mistaking feelings of gratitude for something more?

"I suspect he was never a father figure in her eyes." Hawk glanced out at the snow-dusted courtyard—rich with vine-covered arbors, flowing streams, pebbled pathways, and yellowed grassy slopes.

I lifted a gauzy drape to hide myself beneath it,

following his line of sight through a block of clear glass in the midst of the tinted ones.

"Love is inside each of us ... a dormant seed." Hawk's voice resonated within me. "Once it has been planted, whether in the soils or the fallows"—he pointed to a stony path in the distance where winter heath burst through the rocks to dot the snow with splashes of purple—"it will take root and either flourish to something beautiful and dramatic, or grow dormant, content in its stasis. But there's no right or wrong season for it to bloom."

His poeticism didn't surprise me. I'd already seen his knack for emotive sentiments and dramatic visuals on every page of his tragic childhood journal.

What amazed me was that although his colorblindness kept him from fully appreciating the beauty within the scene outside—the way the frosted ground contrasted yet complemented the flower's vivid stir to life—he still retained that spark of wisdom.

Didn't Uncle's heart—so giving, so loyal and kind—merit a keeper, someone that would fill his colorless days with happiness and life? A blossoming young woman, with eyes only for him? Were they to marry, he could one day be a father in truth.

The right thing to do was allow nature to take its course.

Hawk grinned and his attention settled on my hair. "Speaking of nature, it appears a rare breed of bristle bird has taken up residence in your tangles."

I snorted and tried once more to wrestle the brush free. With a mischievous glint in his eye, Hawk twirled the drapes, winding me within the thin fabric. I laughed so hard, I forgot anyone else was in the room until my ghost shushed me.

On the other side of my curtained fog stood not only Enya, but Lord Thornton and Uncle Owen as well, all three staring. And there I was, wrapped up like a demented caterpillar. I strained my arms within the curtains, unable to budge.

I said the first thing that came to my mind to save face. "Enya was showing me how to dust using the curtains ..." I wriggled my backside from one panel to the other—letting the drapes swipe the glass clean.

Both Uncle and the viscount gawked in stunned wonder. A slight tremor played at the corner of the viscount's mouth. Whether an amused smirk or a disgusted convulsion, I couldn't be sure.

"I-I don't understand ..." Hawk translated Uncle's words since I couldn't read his lips for the hazy film over my eyes.

Enya tapped her foot. "Ladies often discuss cleaning tips first thing in the morn. We're too busy the rest of the day to prattle about such things. If it bothers you, then perchance you should knock next time before opening the door of a lady's room, whether it be ajar or no. It is highly improper for either of you to be looking upon us in our bed gowns."

Uncle's face reddened as if he'd just noticed Enya's sparse attire. She shooed the duo out, shutting the door behind them.

The instant she freed me of the curtains, I hugged her,

tighter than ever before. At last, I had my dear friend back, and a flesh and bone accomplice. I knew she would be loyal, no matter how eccentric any request or scheme, as long as I kept her secret.

And who better to honor silence, than a deaf girl?

CHAPTER 17

It is a bold mouse that nestles in the cat's ear.
English Proverb

While Enya prepared me for breakfast, Hawk sat quietly, running his fingertip along my dress where it waited on the bed.

My lady's maid pinned a peak of glossy gold curls atop my head, then allowed the rest of my hair to cascade along my nape in straight tendrils. Hawk whistled at the finished product.

When it came time for me to change, he strolled to the double doors, keeping his back turned. But as Enya laced up my corset, I watched him intently trace my hazy reflection in the glass with his fingertip. I wondered if he felt as I did ... if this unmet need to touch one another swarmed in his stomach like a thousand humming birds aflutter.

After finding out about my missing crinoline, Miss Abbot brought five petticoats, borrowed from the ample supply the viscount kept on hand for his servants.

I was forced to step into each one so the fullness would fill out my merino gown and my hems wouldn't trip me up. I had escaped wearing a cage, only to be imprisoned beneath ten pounds of extra weight.

The maids stood back and smiled, pleased with their ingenuity. Out of spite, I dragged my veiled mourning hat from my trunk and shoved it atop my shimmering hair, crushing Enya's painstaking curls.

Unfazed, she agreed that I should cover my face, since the brush had left a bruise on my cheek the size of a trampled cherry.

All the while Hawk stood beside the glass doors—chuckling at the spectacle.

A simmering bouquet of spicy and salty aromas greeted us when we stepped into the grand dining hall. Uncle stood at the hearth with the viscount—cane propped against the bricks—deep in conversation. Lord Thornton clashed as always: a purple frock coat paired with a yellow and red plaid vest over trousers of black. His black cravat, secured with a sapphire pin, topped off the outfit. How he managed to still look dignified remained a mystery in itself.

The room, however, was perfectly arranged. Crimson velvet hangings draped the walls. The molding and pilasters held a tinge of gray, adding a sober, masculine tone. A sage green upholstered the table chairs, pulled from the design of the paisley Turkish carpet beneath our feet—a combination of all three colors.

So fascinating: that this man's instincts for decorating a home didn't transfer to his own apparel or his staff's uniforms. The servants hustled about, each of them suited in a maelstrom of reds, greens, and oranges, like bloodied pumpkins.

The sun shone through picture windows located on the north and east walls, softened to bluish warmth by translucent draperies, the same color gray as Hawk's eyes. There were no heavy drapes anywhere in the room. Perhaps the viscount preferred light to darkness ... a contradiction to his shadowy and elusive reputation.

"Dare not let your guard down." Hawk's voice took on a gruff tone. "You should ask him what is located above your balcony porch."

Hawk had sworn he'd heard shuffling sounds in my ceiling throughout the night, and suspected there was a fourth floor attic apartment. I was unconvinced. It hadn't looked as if there was a fourth level when we first arrived and viewed the townhouse from the outside.

"Juliet ..." Having wandered toward a sideboard of dishes at the south end of the room, Hawk pointed to a glass paneled humidor. "This is it! The one from the memory I had at the tavern."

My mouth gaped. Miss Abbot walked by with a tray in hand. I lifted my veil to ask of the humidor's history.

"His Lordship won it in a game of chance."

I quickly dropped my veil again as the viscount noticed me and strode over with that fluid gait, as if the cane and his body were one. With a cordial nod, he led me to the table, pulling out chairs for everyone. Place settings—marked with polished silverware, linen napkins, and bone china plates and teacups—lined one quarter of the table, leaving the remainder a shrine to silver tureens, berry-colored doilies, and swan-shaped crystal bowls filled with food: devilled kidneys, sausage and mashed potatoes, egg soufflé, baked apples, cinnamon fritters, and pink grapefruit glazed with sugar.

Enya and Uncle found places across from me. I sat on the right-hand of Lord Thornton's spot at the table's head.

I kept my veil pulled down. I needed to remain hidden, to be exempt from conversation, so I might work out a plan. Somehow, I had to question the viscount about the humidor. I also wanted to learn what he knew of his brother's death. I'd have to be alone with him to broach such subjects.

"I forbid it." Hawk's words floated from the sideboard where he still studied the humidor. "Remember the rumors we heard? You yourself saw him at my graveside in a rage. And his fascination with the grotesque. He is emotionally unpredictable. You shouldn't be alone with him at any time."

The logic of his concerns iced the blood in my veins. I still didn't know how many secrets the viscount kept—where his father was, how many innocent maidens he'd spoiled, and why he kept a secret room in his dungeon filled with gruesome and violent objects.

But I was here to get answers. I could read faces, measure how a person's words contrasted their expression with something as small as an eye twitch or a wrinkled brow. If asked him questions outright and caught him off-guard, I'd catch him in any lies.

We could talk somewhere in the open, where there would be servants aplenty in the background. Lord

Thornton had promised to show me the winter gardens, so I might see Mama's birds safe in their new habitat. Uncle would insist on chaperoning, but Enya could distract him somehow. She would leap at the chance to spend time with the man she loved.

I glanced over at my ghost for his opinion, but he was oblivious.

"There's a sealed envelope," he muttered to himself. "There, beneath the cigars. It appears to be from a legal office." He attempted to slide his fingertips through the humidor's glass panels, cursing when he failed.

My heart pinched for him and the frustration he faced each day.

The servants filled our plates and the viscount took his seat at the head, his leg brushing my skirts. Just as I lifted my veil to sample a cinnamon fritter, the viscount—putting on a show of speaking to Uncle—raised my skirt hems with his foot beneath the table. The pressure was soft as it brushed my stocking. He must've taken off his boot for more intimate contact.

I gasped. All eyes turned to me. Lord Thornton looked on in bold, wide-eyed innocence, all while he continued to caress my leg.

My face flamed.

Hawk, still preoccupied with the humidor, was oblivious. I nudged Lord Thornton's foot away with my toe and shot my attention to Enya. She watched her spoon make a line through her baked apples—every bit as distracted as my ghost.

Before I could even sip my tea, the viscount's foot

found me again, rubbing my shin. Jaw clenched, I sat my tea cup on my saucer, drew back my boot, and shoved the leg of his chair with such force it tipped over.

Sprawled on the floor, Lord Thornton stared up at me, having the nerve to appear shocked. Uncle leapt from his seat to help our host stand, handing him his cane. Enya, aghast, sat like a statue. Hawk loitered at my side, curious as to what happened, but I couldn't answer. For as the viscount dusted off his trousers with a linen napkin, I noticed he still wore both boots upon his feet. Not only that, but the stroking continued beneath my skirt and petticoats.

I jumped up with a screech and a silvery-orange tabby cat shot out from beneath me, fluffy and irate. I slapped my veil away and met the viscount's eyes, expecting another glimpse of his famous temper.

Instead, he glanced the direction of the runaway feline and then back at me. An infectious stir of white teeth broke through his whiskers.

He threw his head back and laughed.

Enya, Hawk, and Uncle looked on, bewildered, while I broke into laughter, too.

It appeared the dark Lord Thornton had a sense of humor—the one secret I had never expected to uncover.

After breakfast, Enya and I retreated upstairs with Miss Abbot in search of our shawls so we could tour the grounds. I filled Miss Abbot in on the frailty of my flower.

Pointing to the withered petals on the bureau as proof,

I claimed the trip had strained it and I planned to gather new soil and find a roomier pot. I insisted no one touch or move it under any circumstances, and that my room would remain locked in our absence.

A pitying glance passed between the two maids and I understood. *That* was the discussion they'd shared last night as they led me up the stairs. My odd obsession with a flower.

Well, I didn't care. As long as Hawk was safe, I would bear the stigma of an unbalanced, heart-broken daughter.

I spent the rest of the morning in the company of Enya, Hawk, Uncle, and the viscount, winding around the estate. Hawk walked on one side of me, a foot or so in front of Uncle, clenching his jaw as Lord Thornton offered me his free elbow.

I wrapped my fingers around his velvet sleeve for appearances and kept my veil drawn back so I could witness his architectural genius.

Cats roamed the grounds freely—oftentimes sneaking into the townhouse and castle, which explained the one that earlier violated me. Lord Thornton pointed out that his pets kept the estate vermin-free. Then, as if reading my mind, he assured me the cats were never allowed access to the winter garden, so I needn't worry for my birds.

Each of the Manor's three separate buildings connected to one another via tunnels jutting off from their back doors. The viscount's investors were generous indeed, for no expense had been spared in the construction of these passages. The arched ceilings joined the walls seamlessly, covered with arabesque wallpaper rich in taupe and sienna. A running carpet spanned one end to the other to cushion footfalls, complemented by an occasional plush chair or tufted fainting couch.

Gas lights offered illumination in the evenings. The bulbs remained unlit during the day, as sunshine streamed through an abundance of round windows that allowed a breeze inside like portholes on a passenger ship.

For added security, guards stood at each passage's end.

The front entrances to the townhouse, the castle, and the stables served as the only three outlets into the courtyard. The winter garden's double doors linked to the castle with no other way in or out.

Before leading us into the garden, the viscount showed us the six floors of the castle. He cupped my arm, supporting me and my heavily layered skirts on the winding staircases in spite of his limp. Each level held a theme and fluttered with activity as carpenters and servants employed last minute tasks.

Upon the ground floor were the boutiques and cafés. We did not stop to look—even at mine and Uncle's—as the viscount assured us we would have time to arrange our goods within the next few days.

Giant halls, equipped with billiard and card tables, filled the second flight. Upon the third, a grand and glorious ballroom remained under construction, with an antechamber off to the side to serve as a fainting room. We moved on to the fourth floor for a quick glance at the eighty-some guest apartments—each one simple yet elegant with two beds, a wardrobe and bureau.

The fifth level supplied sunrooms for sitting and visiting, along with two libraries and a map gallery with smoking appurtenances for the men. We stopped at the sixth floor where a spiraling staircase led to the star tower. The viscount promised to take us some evening when the stars were out. Refractors and telescopes had been arranged within the open-roofed, walled-in turret, for guests to view the night sky.

Winded, we took the stairs down again, the viscount bypassing the locked dungeon without even a word. I shot a sidelong glance to Hawk and he responded with a concerned frown.

At last, the tour ended. My legs ached from carrying the weight of my petticoats up and down five flights of stairs, and even my enthusiasm to check upon the flowers and see my birds in the garden paled to my weariness.

Once we arrived at the double glass-doors, my energy renewed. I glanced at Enya and she nodded.

"Juliet," Hawk scolded. "You should not be alone with him. Stop this plan at once."

It's the only way to get the answers we need, I reasoned with him silently. *The sooner we learn the truth, the sooner we get on with our lives away from this place.*

I stalled, realizing that I'd used the word "lives", when truly—painfully—I was the only one who lived.

"For the moment, at least," Hawk said, and the hardened edge to his voice made my skin chill. "Having a handful of servants about will not protect you. They will do whatever their master commands. If you go through with this, I'll upset all your birds and cut the morning short."

Realizing that Hawk's protectiveness and jealousy would prove too much an obstacle during the interrogation, I did the one thing I promised I'd never do. I sent him to his purgatory by removing my locket from beneath my bodice and placing it away from my skin.

His expression blurred to anguished accusation as he faded from my sight, banished to the isolation he despised, by the person he loved and trusted most in the world.

CHAPTER 18

To know the mind of a man, listen to his words;
to know his heart, listen to his silences.
Chinese Proverb

The moment we stepped into the sunlit garden, Enya stumbled over a loose stone and sprained her ankle—the pain so intense she almost fainted. I would have smiled at her performance, had I not felt so guilty and worried for Hawk.

Falling into my role, I suggested Uncle help her into the townhouse so she might prop up her leg. The viscount unknowingly contributed, vowing my reputation would be safe with all the servants, gardeners, and maids milling about. We would not be left alone.

He assured my uncle he'd send me back to the townhouse with the kitchen maids upon their completion of gathering spices, then gestured to them working not five yards away.

Watching our chaperones retreat through the double doors, Lord Thornton and I stood, an invisible barrier of three feet between us. Warm beneath my layers of petticoats, I dropped my shawl from my shoulders.

My heart stuttered as I considered what I'd sent Hawk to face ... that thing he feared most. And why? His concerns were valid. The viscount harbored an eccentric genius, morbid diversions, and violent temper. I myself had seen indications of each. And he had stolen money from his father who was now missing.

However, I had a plan to play on my host's ego by feigning interest in his estate. Hawk was determined to be the albatross around my neck—around his very own neck. I did what had to be done. The justification was weak, but gave me the ability to move forward.

Walking beside me, the viscount took a path within sight of the kitchen maids.

I squinted. Sunlight glistened off of every leaf, petal, and pebble. Shadows of my birds fluttered overhead, comforting and familiar.

The title of *Winter Garden* seemed out of place for the seven acre expanse. It was more like a world of spring and summer, captured within glass panes. It could have been paradise, but for one minor discomfort: the humidity caused by the warm geysers springing up from fountains everywhere. Porthole windows, much like the ones in the corridors—screened-in to confine the bugs and birds— allowed a breeze to whisk through. Otherwise, the balmy heat would've been stifling.

Some fountains were staircases where water cascaded in silvery streams; others were waist-high pedestals specked black and white with bird droppings. In the distance, a life-sized Greek statue released sparkling droplets from its flowing marble robes.

Lord Thornton had told us of the Manor's access to warm water all year round due to the hot springs abundant upon the estate. Beneath the mines, the water percolated deep enough to come into contact with hot rocks. When it gurgled up from the ground, it provided gushes of steamy water.

The viscount, in his ingenuity, had arranged for underground piping to merge the flows with cooler streams, providing a constant source of warm water for the garden fountains, the town house, and the castle.

There would be no shortage of baths for any of us, which taunted more than comforted. The reminder of Hawk's tragic discovery this morning drained the blood from my cheeks. I stroked my necklace's chain, careful to keep it atop my dress.

The viscount handed me a handkerchief.

Grateful, I dabbed my forehead and neck—avoiding my bruised cheekbone and trying not to notice his almond-liqueur scent embedded in the cloth.

He led me to stand beside a wrought iron bench within a honeysuckle copse. The fragrant shade cooled my shoulders. All of the plants from my greenhouse at home surrounded us: sea holly, hydrangea, strawflowers, bachelor's buttons, lavender, and pygmy roses, each nestled in freshly dug soil.

"Did your gardeners plant these last night?" I asked, leaning over to stroke a hydrangea before turning to read his response.

Working his buttons free, the viscount shrugged out of his frock coat and smoothed it on the ground beside the flowers. "I did. Though I planted some a few weeks ago, so you might be able to harvest them today." He slipped off his vest next, leaving him in a linen shirt that clung to his broad shoulders.

"How did you know what kind to plant?" I asked in an effort to distract myself as he rolled up his sleeves, revealing dark hairs on his sturdy forearms.

"I asked your uncle at my last visit," he answered. "Now, I would like you to lead me through your routine. Which flowers should we cut and dry for your hats today?"

His request surprised me. I'd never had any man other than Uncle interested in helping me with my craft.

After assisting me to sit atop his discarded jacket on the ground, my host knelt in the dirt across from me, seemingly unconcerned for his fine tailored clothes. He looped his cane over the bench's arm and offered a basket from beneath the seat. A set of gardening shears and a spool of twine were tucked within.

He had arranged all of this for me.

I'd assumed we would stroll the many paths so he might showcase his own plants, flowers, and innovations. But without seeing his face, I would've had no hopes to communicate. Now, I could read his lips without worrying of tripping over my feet. We were on even ground, as it were.

Thoughtful, I silently snipped perfect blooms from a shrub of lavender and laid them in the basket. The viscount gathered the stems into bundles and tied them with twine to prepare them for hanging.

"Wait." I reached for a loosely tied bundle and rearranged the twine. "Wind each bundle several times near the base of the stems. Make the knot tight enough that the flowers won't slip when hung upside down, but not so tight you crush them. It is the only way to retain their natural form."

Watching intently, and without complaint, he retied every bundle he'd already done, his masculine hands careful yet precise.

As we worked, a trio of Mama's bluebirds fluttered overhead, each trying to claim the closest pedestal fountain. The winner celebrated by preening its feathers beneath the trickling water. Lord Thornton watched and grinned—a smile turned inward, personal and private— then returned to helping me.

He looked so at home, sitting in silence, gardening, and contemplating nature. Characteristics I never expected to see in a spoiled, arrogant, worldly nobleman.

I mopped my neck again, refusing to be charmed. It was time to get answers so I could return to my room and rescue Hawk. I cleared my throat. "I want to assure you ... I do not have a nervous affliction of the brain."

My host looked up from bundling a cluster of sea holly, his lips curving to a smile in the midst of dark whiskers. "All right then. Assure me."

"As to what you saw this morn ... my game in the curtains, when I was 'dusting.'" I pressed my lips together to appear sincere. "The incident with the cat."

"Ah. Not to mention the coughing spell upon our first meeting at your home."

I glanced down at my lap. The rush of blood returned to my cheeks, causing the bruise from my brush to throb. I rubbed it before looking at him again. "Please believe me."

"Oh I do. I believe that you believe it." He waved at a passing gardener, gestured to a patch of herbs north of us, then turned back to me. "Still, one must wonder if an afflicted mind can truly know whether or not they are afflicted."

His sharp wit struck a giddy note and I laughed in spite of myself. His face brightened with a merry smile.

The gardener reappeared and tipped his hat to me before offering the viscount a handful of long, thin, gray-green leaves with woody scallion-like stalks.

Lemongrass.

Upon the gardener's retreat, Lord Thornton pinched the plant. I watched, one part wary, one part mesmerized, as he rubbed the oily residue on his fingertips then raised them to me.

"Might I tend your bruise, Miss Emerline?" Long, black lashes fanned shadows beneath his eyes. Due to his resemblance to his brother, I couldn't help but imagine his every word drizzled with Hawk's velvety baritone.

Touching my cheek absently, I tried to find the maids in the herb garden, but the honeysuckle vines blocked my view.

My host waited. A dark lock of hair fell across his forehead, exposing a sun-kissed auburn streak at the roots, reminding me this was not my ghost. This was his experienced twin brother, trying to win over the affections of a naïve woman who'd been upon the shelf for too long.

But I wasn't as naïve as he thought, nor was I on a shelf.

"Would you like to apply it yourself?" he asked upon my hesitation. "I assumed it would be hard for you to see, and I shouldn't want you to get any in your eyes."

To lull him into a false sense of trust, I leaned forward. His warm fingertip made contact and eased the lemon-scented oil over my cheek in one soothing motion.

I shut my eyes. His touch was light, but his skin surprisingly rough. I would have assumed one of his status would have soft hands, having no hard labor to callous them.

Once he'd finished, I opened my eyes again.

Still on his knees, he studied me, his expression one of troubled enchantment. The look of a man who had not touched a woman in some time. Not of an unquenchable rogue.

Quiet and solemn, he swiped his hand on the handkerchief still between my fingers, then took his place on the bench. He clenched the wrought iron frame beneath him until his knuckles went white.

After tucking a batch of hydrangea into the basket, I sat on the other end.

"Thank you," I said, my hand splayed close to his on the bench's seat. "For caring for my flowers and birds. And for tending my wound."

Although he didn't look my way, his pinkie lifted and touched my wrist, almost as if by accident. My body reacted, awhirl with confusion.

He seemed ... storm-tossed. Struggling with something. I wanted to help him.

Hawk's words from last night echoed in my head: *"You're too compassionate, and innocent to the ways of a man and a woman. He can use that to his advantage."*

I stiffened on the bench and placed both of my hands in my lap.

The viscount's shoulders slumped, a movement so slight I almost thought it an illusion inspired by the wintry clouds swirling above the glass roof.

At last, he turned to me. "The kitchen maids will be done soon. We should discuss your ball gowns. Fabrics must be chosen. I'm unsure which are best suited for a lady in mourning."

My spirit plummeted at the reminder of Mama's absence. I could only imagine what styles of dress a man of his class would prefer for his charity bride: restrictive corsetry that would bend even the most rigid spine ... crinoline and bustles so wide a pregnant donkey could take refuge beneath them. I was fortunate to still be wearing black or I might've fallen victim to his deviant artist's brush, prancing about in experimental rainbows like his servants.

Wadding his handkerchief within my fist, I noticed a heron's feather skim by on the ground, the ideal color for a beaded Catalane I'd been working on. I pinned it beneath my boot before scooping it up and securing it in my fist.

The viscount's strong hand found mine, startling me. He flipped my palm upward. I didn't realize how hard I had been clenching the feather until he pried my fingers free to reveal the imprints of my fingernails in my flesh.

He tucked the feather into the pocket of his plaid vest draped across the bench's arm. "Miss Emerline, you may instruct my personal tailor however you deem fit. She's adept at women's fashion as well. Your uncle tells me you're a follower of The Rational Dress Society."

I was surprised at his compliance. The society was formed two years ago, but their ideas of fashion reformation—boneless stays and less restrictive patterns—had been frowned upon by the upper class.

The viscount's gaze lingered on my features. "I'm not personally familiar with the founders—neither the Viscountess Harberton or Mrs. King—but I encourage you to employ their comfort standards. I'll arrange a consultation with Miss Hunny tomorrow. I should like her to make you some riding dresses, as well."

My mouth gaped. Why was he doing this? He'd already won the deed to my home whether we married or not.

"I don't ride," I said once I found my voice. I pulled his handkerchief between my thumb and forefinger, a childish amusement to settle my unease. "Uncle never ... that is to say, I've never had the opportunity to learn."

"I know your uncle has some reservations." The soft crinkles at his eyes turned upward in an earnest smile. "But would you like to learn?"

I tugged the handkerchief through my fingers a second time. If I were to become adept at riding, Hawk and I could explore the grounds outside the Manor walls while we were here. Possibly even find his mine. "Yes." Then I wondered how far this man was willing to go to win my favor. "But I should like to sit astride the horse. Side saddle is impractical."

I expected him to be put off by my boldness, but he nodded in agreement.

"And ..." I bit my lip to appear coquettish, but there was no humility in my heart. "Let it be a surprise for my uncle."

The viscount shook his head. "I'd rather discuss it with him. I do not wish to go behind his back, or fall from his favor."

"What of my favor, my lord? Do you wish to fall from it?"

His fingers tapped the bench between us. "Ah. That would be a much more perilous climb to regain footing." His teasing grin boosted my confidence.

"You would teach me then, in secret?"

His gaze shifted to the clouds above. "I will teach you," he said simply. "You seem very eager to learn. Why is that?"

I couldn't tell him about searching for his brother's body. But there was the other reason: I had always wanted the freedom of flying atop a horse's back. And since I couldn't float through tables and drift in place like Hawk, I believed that would be the closest thing to having wings. "There are many things to accomplish on this side of death. Riding is merely one of them."

"And why would a lady, so young as you, be entertaining thoughts of death?"

I clamped my lips tight.

He stroked the feather in his vest's pocket. "I understand. The loss of a mother does change one's vision of the world. Brings to light one's own mortality—often with nightmarish clarity." The shadows returned to his eyes.

"How old were you when you lost yours?" I asked, for his remark was personal and intimate. Hawk needed details of their elusive mother, and how his gypsy heritage came to be.

The meditative mask over my host's face crumbled away, as if someone woke him from a dream. "That, Miss Emerline, is a story for another time. Some afternoon when you're cozied by the fire, drinking the chocolate you're so fond of." A boyish grin lit his features, shattering any residue of melancholy.

With that, the viscount stood, leaving me unsettled in the wake of his growing awareness of my likes and dislikes. I still knew so little of his.

He picked up my basket of flowers and craned his neck to see over the honeysuckle copse. "It appears the kitchen maids are gathering up their things. They'll take you by the shed before you leave. You may hang your flowers there. And you mentioned wanting to find a pot and some soil." He offered his free palm.

I accepted his help and stood, marveling at how small my hand looked in his. The sun beat down upon my shoulders as we left the shade. I resituated my shawl.

"I will see you later today." He lifted the back of my hand to press it to his lips.

His facial hair brushed me, a prickle so real it titillated my skin.

I quelled the desire to feel it again, remembering I had yet to ask of Hawk's humidor. "Lord Thornton?"

"Yes." His dark hair curled where it grazed his shoulder, making him look almost innocent, as if he were a rumpled little boy.

"Something caught my eye this morn," I continued. "In the dining hall. A humidor ... upon your sideboard. I've never seen one quite like it. Where did you get it?"

His features pooled to the unreadable mask once more. "A Thornton heirloom."

A bold-faced lie. "Indeed? For I understood you won it in a bet. Possibly at the Swindler's Tavern? A certain ... secret room." I was using Hawk's disjointed memories too flippantly, but they were the only bluff I had.

The viscount's jaw clenched and he set the basket on the bench. "How would you know of such a room?"

"I know more than of the room," I snapped. "I know of your reputation there." That he chased women. That he nearly killed a man. That he'd used up his father's funds.

Something new billowed in his eyes: ice and smoke intertwined. He unclipped the pin from his cravat, loosened the tie, and hurled it toward his coat, startling a white butterfly perched on the purple velvet. The neck of his shirt fell open, revealing a line of chest hair similar to his brother's—though these glistened with tiny beads of sweat. "My reputation?"

I wrung my hands together, winding the viscount's handkerchief between them, distracted as the butterfly lit beside my foot on the castoff lemongrass. "I eavesdropped on a matron. Heard her speak of your misconduct with women, among other discrepancies."

Lord Thornton's eyes narrowed. "You heard her? You mean you read her lips. As smoky as that tavern was, I would think it difficult to cipher one's words with any certainty."

The tables were turning on me. "S-someone relayed me what she said."

The viscount nodded. "Ah." He crouched to capture the butterfly at my feet with all the grace and deftness of a hungry wasp. He stood and held the insect to his cheek by its fragile legs—careful and studious—letting its wings whisper over his skin. I feared he was going to crush the helpless creature.

His lips moved again, stealing my attention. "Your translator wouldn't have something to gain by spoiling your image of me, would he?"

"No. He—"

"He," the viscount interrupted. "So, it was a man. A rival."

My knees locked beneath my heavy petticoats. I'd been caught in my own trap.

Lifting his hand, my host set the butterfly free. It fluttered away, dancing on the breeze. His expression was pure smugness. "I don't tolerate sharing, Miss Emerline. Your uncle mentioned no affiliations with other suitors."

The crass assumption burned my ego like a brand. "You mean to say, that because I am deaf, you imagined no one else could ever want me."

The viscount regarded my features. "Not at all. In your sixteenth year, you caught the attention of two men. One retracted his interest the moment he realized you were deaf. He feared you would taint your offspring. He was unworthy of you. I hope you know that."

Again, my host confounded me; not only with this intimate knowledge, but by the empathy emanating from those silent words.

"And the other man?" Lord Thornton pressed. "Your uncle never told me what happened with him."

I wanted to lie. But something about Lord Thornton's tender expression, something about the way he had patiently helped bundle my flowers and watched Mama's bluebirds in quiet thought and retrospect, coaxed the truth from my lips. "I managed for four months to sustain the illusion I could hear. He became besotted with me and offered his hand in marriage. Wanted me even after I confessed the truth. But I turned away the proposal."

"Why?"

How could I tell this stranger that the thought of being intimate with a man without the ability to hear our shared breaths, the rhythm of his heart pounding inside my ear, or the moans of our pleasure, both frightened and embittered me?

My tongue ran across the back of my teeth. "I ended our courtship without any explanation. If I refused him a reason, why would I offer you one?"

The viscount's demeanor changed from sympathetic to resolved. "Your secret beau—this cad who speaks ill of me—would do well to be warned. I've no intention of losing the battle for your hand."

"You mean the battle for my dowry."

He scowled. "Stop telling me what I mean. You read lips, not minds."

I struggled for the upper hand. "If I'm to uphold this farce as your intended, I would like to meet your father. Where is he? It is rumored he went missing when you sold his estate to buy this one."

Paling to a white that rivaled the honeysuckle petals around us, the viscount took two steps back and slumped onto the bench, barely avoiding the basket of flowers we'd gathered.

I almost pitied him, to be so defeated by my accusation.

"I didn't buy this estate with my family's funds," he said at last. "Father went away on holiday to escape debtor's prison. To save our family's name, I challenged the prior owner of the mines, Larson, to a game of cards at the tavern." His teeth clenched. "The humidor was one part of the wager. But there was a deed within. The land that you're standing upon ... this Manor of Diversions ... it is my winnings."

CHAPTER 19

To whom you tell your secrets,
to him you resign your liberty.
Spanish Proverb

As I stood staring at the viscount's lips, wondering if I'd misread them, Hawk's observation from earlier resurfaced in my mind. He had mentioned a sealed envelope beneath the cigars in the humidor.

It was the deed to this land.

The maids were leaving the herb enclosure. Their timing annoyed me. I wasn't ready to go. The viscount wanted me to believe he was a hero ... that he had saved his absent father's reputation with a game of cards. Yet there was more to this story.

"You had nothing to ante," I baited. "You said your father was bankrupt. And from what I understand, your gambling had a hand in that."

His jaw, a blurred haze beneath the honeysuckle's canopy, appeared to spasm. He stood and my heart hammered a staccato rhythm at how large he appeared. "Enough of this dance. My past conduct is none of your concern, Miss Emerline. Unless you wish to divulge your past to me as well."

"I am a deaf milliner. What part of my past could possibly interest a grand viscount such as you?" I blinked against the glare of sun behind his solid form, knowing I fanned a flame, but somehow unable to stop myself.

He leaned in, his shadow imprisoning mine. "Let us start with the time that you spent with my brother."

I licked my lips, my tongue turned to sandpaper. From the corner of my eye, the maids paused on their trek toward us to talk to the gardeners. A rash change of heart overtook, a plea that they would hurry and rescue me. I had no explanation as to how I would possess intimate details about a Romani man who would've been eight years my senior. "Why do you presume I spent time with him?" I stalled.

Lord Thornton's hands twitched at his sides, as if he thought me some enigma whose meaning was just at his fingertips. Either that, or he wished to strangle me. "You called out the name Hawk. To acquaintances he was Chaine Hawkings. Only his closest friends shortened his surname thusly."

I knotted the handkerchief in my hand, wondering upon the discrepancies. In Hawk's journal, his name was Chaine Kaldera. So, he must've changed it to Hawkings upon his escape from his father. That could explain his tombstone. And the weathering of eight years could've worn away most of the letters. Unless his nickname had been used.

Did Lord Thornton bury him? Or, perchance their Aunt Bitti helped arrange the burial. But the viscount didn't know her. If he did, then why had he been locked out of his brother's grave that day in the cemetery?

Curiosity made me bold. "I want to know how Chaine died."

An annoyed wrinkle formed above Lord Thornton's brow. "And why should I tell you?"

"As the little girl in the mine ... as the child he saved. He would want me to know."

The viscount's defensive scowl softened at my words. "He died out here. In the mines. An accident."

My heartbeat leapt into my throat to have my and Hawk's suspicions validated at last. It was unbearable, to think of him dying in the same place he'd endured such torments as a child. "So ... where are his remains?"

Lord Thornton glanced at his palms. "His body was never found. Some servants saw him fall through a decayed scaffolding."

"I should like to interview them."

"They were employed by Larson. They no longer work here."

"Could you offer their names?"

"I have none to give you." That hardness in his brow returned, impenetrable.

The maids resumed their stroll in the distance. A suffocating weight heaved upon me—either the humidity, the sun, or my emotional turmoil—and I turned on my heels, determined to meet up with them and escape.

I inhaled sharply as Lord Thornton snagged my elbow. He coaxed me back into the copse's obscuring depths, standing behind me, close enough the wool of my skirt clung to his trousers. His warm palm glided down to my wrist—his thumb heavy against my pulse point.

I struggled to breathe, as helpless as the butterfly that he earlier pinched between his fingertips. I couldn't face him, unnerved by the feel of his breath at my ear, his lips whispering unreadable words.

My wrist chilled as his hand moved to my chin. He slanted my head, leveling my eyes to his mouth.

"What did I just say?" he asked.

His insensitivity stung like a slap. My eyes burned as I refused to answer.

"Only in this is your infirmity a downfall," his lips said. "For you become a victim when you must rely upon another's paraphrasing of unreadable conversations. Trust no one but yourself. Even the most honorable man might lie to gain advantage over another."

Was he speaking of himself? Or his assumed rival?

He began to release my chin but I shifted my body around to face him and spread his fingers to cup my cheek, holding him there, not yet ready to give up the reality of his touch.

His lips tightened, a reaction so slight, I almost missed it.

"I will tell you what I can," he resigned, and I realized my precarious grasp for tangibility had coaxed him into answering my question.

I held my breath, waiting.

"Larson wanted a rare clock my family owned. I used it as my ante. As for my"—he cringed— "past reputation, I've abandoned that lifestyle. I have interest in only one woman. And your dowry has nothing to do with that."

Hawk's earlier warnings shook me from my trance. The grand Lord Thornton had almost seduced me with his pretty words. Pushing his palm from my face, I stepped back, nearly toppling as the petticoats gathered around my shins. He reached out to steady me, but drew back at my angry scowl.

The maids approached, no less than a yard away now.

"I know what I am to you," I whispered, careful not to use my vocal cords. "Kind Lord Thornton and his charity bride. What but a saint would overlook her deafness and want her despite it? I must wonder, will you display me in your dungeon alongside your mutant exhibits?"

His face paled again, but only for an instant. An angry blush replaced it, spurred by his hot Romani blood, darkening his skin so that the storm-cast quality to his eyes brightened in contrast to a steel, glossy gray. "What I do in that dungeon is no concern of yours." He leaned closer. "Least not yet."

I feigned a laugh, though inwardly, the subtle threat rattled me to the bone. "Do you not see the folly of your plan? I've experienced society's prejudices. I've worn their chains most of my life. They will not embrace you as a saint for marrying me. They will deem you a fool."

The expression on his face flickered between anger and frustration. "My brother was obsessed with finding a maiden he met once when she was a child; in all of his twenty years, he'd never been with another. He was saving himself for her, waiting for when she came of age. Many thought him a fool for such blind fidelity." His long lashes lowered, as if it vexed him to speak of Hawk. "But the girl shared a piece of his past," he continued. "She provided light in the midst of an inconceivably evil darkness. It burned her image into his brain ... and altered his future. I could never have imagined a woman worthy of such reverence. Yet I've found you to be captivating and courageous, worthy of all that and more. Not despite your deafness, but because of it. If that makes me a fool, I will proudly wear the title."

The beautiful sentiment spun webs of contrition around my heart. I glanced over my shoulder. The maids were a few feet away, coming up the path.

After pausing to gather my wits, I turned back to the viscount, but he, his clothes, and his cane had vanished somewhere beyond the honeysuckle copse, leaving nothing except the basket of flowers as a reminder of our time together. Trembling, I placed his handkerchief upon the bench and pondered over the mysterious man who owned it.

The sense of being watched unsettled me. I pulled down my veil, picked up the basket, and fell into step with the maids, clutching my abdomen to disentangle the knots of confusion inside and lock them away. For once I arrived in my chamber I would be with Hawk again—the broken child who rescued me in his youth, the man who saved himself for me in his adulthood, and the ghost who had grown so possessive he would leave no thought unturned regarding the long hour we'd spent apart.

I removed my hat as I stepped into my room, and set the new pot and the bucket of soil on my floor. There was no fire in the fireplace, nothing at all that resembled warmth—an iciness accentuated by Hawk's absence. Yet I procrastinated reviving him. I needed to be alone for once. To work out my thoughts without anyone else in my head.

What had Lord Thornton meant, when he said the dungeon wasn't my concern—*yet*? Were those medieval torture devices mere pieces in a collection, or tools for some twisted sense of sadistic pleasure he liked to use upon the women he bedded? My gut clenched.

The man who sat with me, patiently and gently wrapping flowers so as not to break their stems or crumple their petals ... the man who seemed to have an affinity for animals and nature and children ... was he capable of such demented cruelties?

I patted the bruise on my cheek, remembering how tender he was when he soothed it. How full of wonder he looked after we touched.

He baffled me. On the one hand, I felt a connection with him, an inexplicable kinship. I felt as if I *knew* him— understood him on some deep level. Perhaps due to the physical hindrances we had in common, or to our shared affinity for creating things with color and texture. But on the other hand, he frightened and infuriated me.

A desperate, thudding sensation awoke behind my sternum, and I reminded myself none of this mattered. I was still in control. I wasn't going to wed him. I would never have to know who he truly was.

So why did I *ache* to know? Why did I want to feel his touch again?

A chill seeped into my bones. In the soft afternoon light, my turquoise ceiling swelled overhead, a rolling ocean of gloom waiting to crash down upon me. Craving the security Hawk's presence always provided, I tucked the locket beneath my bodice so it touched my flesh.

He didn't appear.

Hawk? I called to him in my mind. Was he so angry and hurt he refused to return? Was that even possible?

Tears sprung to my eyes. I surveyed my surroundings through the blur. Nothing seemed to be disturbed. The spiced aroma of his flower still filled the room. It sat on the Secretaire, all eight petals shimmering in place. In fact, it appeared to have flourished since I last saw it. No new petals, but the ones remaining seemed perkier.

Then I noticed that something *had* been disturbed. The dead petals I'd left sprinkled upon the bureau were gone.

"She must've taken them with her."

My pulse leapt at hearing Hawk's voice. "Where are you?"

"Hiding." With a rustle beneath my bed, my ghost rolled out from under the frame. "Thanks to your Judas kiss, I was forced to perfect a new trick today." He stood, dusting himself, though nothing clung to him. It was all for show.

Unable to face his wounded frown, I focused on his muddied boots as they tracked toward me. At the last moment, he spun and appeared beside the double doors across the room—this burst of speed another new trick he had learned.

"You cut me, Juliet." The betrayal in his voice grated

within my ears, like a fork digging away at the tenderness. "You know how I hate the darkness."

Tears burned behind my eyes, but I wouldn't let them fall. I was tired. Tired of apologizing. Tired of having my every thought measured and scrutinized. "You are in my head. Always in my head. It is unfair. I can't read *your* mind. We are unequally yoked. There shall be times when I need to think or act separate from you. Please understand."

"I understand. I understand my brother is weeding his way into your sympathies."

I stared at Hawk's hand where he swung his pocket watch. Before I could stop it, the image of Lord Thornton's rough palm touching my cheek flashed through my mind. My attention slid back to Hawk's feet, but it was already too late.

"What happened between the two of you today?"

I kept my eyes averted. My mind blank.

"He may be able to touch you," Hawk growled, "but he can't put a dent in the cold silence that once encompassed every minute of your life. Despite that he's an architect, he cannot build a bridge of sound for you. Only I can."

I snapped my chin up. "I know that!"

"Then why are you falling beneath his spell?"

I clamped my teeth, my hands working at the pleats in my dress. I couldn't even explain to myself what sort of hypnotic power the viscount held over me. I moaned, wishing to change the subject.

"I can help with a subject change." Hawk wore a new expression, edged with cruelty. "I looked this time, while in my hell. And there was a sliver of light, just enough to see a skeleton. Every bit of skin eaten away by rats. Its bones pitted with holes; its clothing consumed by worms. It was me, Juliet. Me, in a state of decay."

A sob stung in my throat like a swarm of hornets, just to imagine such horror. I clutched my neck. "Dear Lord. I-I'm so sorry!"

"You are correct. Our love is indeed unbalanced. For how can a woman respect a man she has so much power over? At the drop of a petal, you can castrate me. Cut me out of your life and leave me helpless on my knees in the throes of Purgatory." He studied me, his voice pinched with agony. "I understand you need time alone. But for me, being alone is nothing but darkness and disorientation. If I could but remember what it's like to live and crave a peaceful solitude." His eyes saddened. "If I could but *remember*."

Sympathy rushed through me. Even should he remember what it was like to live, he might still have this fear of solitude after all the loneliness and terror he had suffered in his childhood—a facet of a personality molded and shaped by a tortured past.

Hawk regarded the floor. "You think me repulsive and needy."

Every part of me longed to touch him, hold him. "I think you brave, beautiful, and broken." How could I not, after he saved me during his fractured childhood? After how, as a man, he had searched for me? After all he had sacrificed to find me?

At last, the familiar light ignited in Hawk's eyes, a

scintillation of curiosity. "What sacrifice? What did you learn today? Was it about the humidor?"

I paused to glance in the mirror, considering how to present all that his brother had told me. "Your name is Hawkings. Chaine Hawkings. Hawk is a sobriquet."

He moved to the bed and sat. "Go on."

"Wait." My hand swept across the bureau's smooth surface. "*She* who?"

His brow furrowed. "Pardon?"

"When you first reappeared, you said *she* took the petals."

He stretched his legs out and crossed them at the ankles. "That would be the gypsy. My aunt. She was in your room."

CHAPTER 20

Better the devil you know, than the devil you don't.
English Proverb

Aunt Bitti ... here on the estate?

I wavered, my legs as insubstantial as softened butter.

Hawk pointed to the bureau's chair, insisting I sit. "So what do you think of your sainted Lord Thornton now?"

Trying to settle my stomach, I smoothed my skirts around me on the cushion. "I never thought him a saint. Far from it."

Hawk leaned on his elbows. His expression was haughty.

"Why would your aunt be here? Your brother met you after you were adults. I assumed he didn't know of her since he couldn't access your grave."

"Apparently he knows her quite well."

"How did she get into my chambers? Miss Abbot gave me the key."

Upon this, Hawk sat up again. "I'm sure your viscount has an extra key, which he gave to Aunt Bitti. What I wonder, is *why* she was in your room."

"The journal!" I leapt to my feet and tumbled over my petticoats to get the trunk. Pushing aside some clothes, I found the book in its secret compartment, safe. Relieved, I glanced up at Hawk where he sat on the mattress, still balanced on my knees and the balls of my feet. "So, you saw her?"

"She evoked me when she touched the flower," he said. "Before she could see me, I dove beneath the bed, watched her from there as she stroked the petals."

"The withered ones?"

"No. The flower itself, on the Secretaire. I read her thoughts. She remembered the plant from my grave and wanted to take it back. So I coughed. It must have startled her, for the darkness banished me when she released the flower. Upon my return, you stood at the bureau, and the withered petals were gone."

I shook my head. What purpose would Lord Thornton have for bringing the old woman here? Unless, since she was his aunt, too, he felt responsible for her somehow. Otherwise, why would he hide her in this holiday escape where a plethora of upper-crusts would soon be hob-knobbing and gaming? Were she discovered, it wouldn't bode well for his reputation, or his Manor's success.

Perhaps Hawk had been mistaken who the visitor was. Or perhaps ...

My thoughts shifted to the viscount's earlier advice of trusting only myself. It occurred to me that Hawk was a gypsy—descended from a long line of master story-tellers.

"You're calling me a liar now?"

No sooner had Hawk flung the accusation, than he rushed toward me. His speed toppled me from my crouched position. I sprawled on my back as he levitated parallel to my body, inches above me, a diaphanous vapor with eyes of mist and fire.

"One morning with my bastard brother," Hawk growled—the potency of the sound at odds with his delicate, transient form, "and you are doubting every word I say. You don't want to accept it. Because it means the viscount is in league with our aunt, the woman who guarded my grave. Which means he knows what you've stolen—both the flower and the journal—and he's baiting you."

"Hawk, please. I am simply confused. He seemed so thoughtful, so introspective and gentle in the gardens. The opposite of all I expected him to be. And I am a master of reading faces and sincerity. It has left me at odds with myself. With my judgment on any matter."

He lowered himself, careful only to touch my clothing. Had he been flesh, his heaviness would have imprinted my form into the cushion of carpet beneath. And I would have welcomed the itch of the weave at my nape, the burn of the nap between my shoulder blades. Just to *feel* him cover me.

"If the world would turn on a different axis ... just for one day." Hawk's anger and hurt culminated to a hungry knell—a din of longing which echoed in his voice. "Hell, even one hour. One hour to make love to you, China Rose. I vow, you would never again be confused as to who my brother and I are, or to whom is the better man for you."

Seeing the love in his eyes, I wanted to forget everything that had transpired this morning. Hawk deserved my loyalty and my trust. I knew him better than

I did the viscount. And I had already caught my host in several lies.

"Juliet," Hawk whispered my name sweetly. Furrowing the fabric of my sleeves, he urged me to lift my hands over my head. I knew what came next, and craved it. Craved any contact, no matter how ambiguous or fleeting.

His touch shifted my dress until my corset wrinkled and clenched my right breast tight, like an eager hand. Arching toward him, I begged for more. He dragged the fabric, rippled it along my abdomen, then stopped atop my skirts between my thighs where layers of petticoats formed a barrier no amount of ghostly concentration could manipulate.

Sunlight streamed through the French doors in multiple colors, illuminating our differences. A whisper of vulnerability shuddered through me. Our games had always been played beneath the veil of darkness and shadow. To enact the fantasies in broad daylight left us exposed—bared to the limitations of reality.

I tilted my spine to increase the pressure of Hawk's fabric manipulation. "Do you not know how much I long to be with you?" I wrung out the words, squeezing them from my weary heart. "I would spurn all the wonders of this place, everything that calls to me in this world, if it would bring you into my arms. I would embrace *death* for you, Hawk."

I'd never allowed myself to think it, and I couldn't ignore the mortified turn to his features—the obvious concern. He started to answer, then lifted away and gestured to the door.

I had time to push to my knees, smooth my skirts, and feign searching through my trunk before Miss Abbot entered carrying a tray of steaming chocolate and Shrewsbury cakes. After setting the food atop my bureau, she dumped a basket of coke into my fireplace.

She motioned to an envelope on the serving tray, with Lord Thornton's seal affixed. "His lordship requests you read that."

I stood to take it. The viscount's scent radiated from the parchment.

Upon starting a fire, Miss Abbot started to leave. She paused. "Do you require anything else?"

I frowned, flipping the envelope's crisp edge between my fingers. "I did not ask for the chocolate, nor the cakes."

The maid shrugged. "Lord Thornton was insistent. Said you would want to drink it while you read." She turned toward the door but I caught her arm.

"Miss Abbot, did I not make it clear that my door remained locked this morn while I toured the grounds?"

Her thoughtful expression brightened to a yellow glow as flames shook the turquoise walls in tremors—like sun refracted off of water. "You did. And I abided."

I glanced at Hawk. We needed to be sure his aunt had been responsible, since he didn't see her take the petals with his own eyes.

Chewing my lip, I met the maid's gaze again. "Does the viscount have a key of his own?"

Miss Abbot appeared befuddled. "He gave me his extra one." She patted her apron's pocket. "I know of no other."

My attention shifted to the bureau then back again.

"Did you come in ... did you straighten my room in my absence?"

"No." Shadows of distress settled in Miss Abbot's hollowed cheeks. "Is there something amiss?"

I shook my head, convinced by the honest confusion in her face.

Hawk sighed. "That leaves *only* my aunt."

"Everything is in order," I assured the maid. "Thank you. Oh, might I ask you one last thing?"

Her hem fluttered where she tapped a foot, either eager to leave or annoyed with the questions.

"You've known Lord Thornton for some years ... came with the viscount from his father's estate, correct?"

"Yes. I've known him since his childhood."

"Did you know his brother at all?"

She seemed hesitant, but responded. "I knew of him. He died before any of us could meet him."

"What can you tell me of his death? It seems to have affected Lord Thornton quite deeply."

The maid's tiny lips grew even tinier, as if they might vanish from her face completely.

"Miss Abbot, bear in mind I'm soon to be viscountess of this estate. I shall be deciding which help is extraneous, and which is necessary. The relationship we forge today will surely have a bearing on my decision."

A worried line crossed her brow. "Lord Larson wouldn't give my master any details of his brother's death. It has haunted him."

"I see." I offered a nod. "That will be all for now."

As soon as the door closed behind her, Hawk propped

himself against the bureau. "Look at you, pulling rank."

I frowned, refusing to feel guilty. "At least she substantiated your brother's claim. I wonder if perchance your aunt is here to help him make peace with the loss of you?"

"Or to get revenge. It's possible he doesn't know she's here. She could've picked the lock. Remember the blood on my brother's fist yesterday at the tavern. He is violent. Prone to rages. And he knows more than he's admitting about the circumstances surrounding my untimely demise. That much is loud and clear, however you refuse to hear it."

His pointed reference to my deafness on another level than physical did not go unnoticed. Awhirl in confusion and gloom again, I sat at the bureau and poured some chocolate. Balancing a cake on my palm, I took a bite. The velvety texture melted to a zest of brandy and coriander on my tongue. As I chewed, I pried off the seal from the viscount's letter.

Hawk crouched beside me, his head level with my shoulder. "Why do you think he wished you to drink chocolate as you read this?" he asked. "Seems an odd request."

Holding my cup at my lips, I sucked in a breath as realization struck. "In the garden, he promised to tell me of his mother some afternoon when I sat in front of the fireplace, drinking a cup of chocolate."

Hawk and I both looked at the cheery fire.

"His mother?" Hawk said. "That means ..."

"*Your* mother." I set down my cup. It was time to meet her, at last.

CHAPTER 21

A drink precedes a story.
Irish Proverb

"Hurry! Open it."

Hawk's enthusiasm spread through me like a contagion, but I unfolded the note with utmost care, afraid on some irrational level the script might slip off the page along with its precious secrets. After I'd nudged the serving tray aside, I spread the parchment on the bureau.

Hawk and I read the first sentence together:

"Dearest Miss Emerline, our time in the garden left me bewildered. For too long, I've erected walls around my heart. But as I hope to one day win your hand and share a family with you, I must brave tearing them down."

"What the hell?" Hawk glared at the words. "He already has you married and plump with his seed. Bloody assuming."

The viscount's next line left us both aghast. *"If you would like a visual of my heritage, consider the portrait on the wall. It is my mother, Gitana Kaldera—a gypsy queen. My brother painted it before his death."*

Hawk gaped as we both stared over our shoulders. So Miss Abbot had been mistaken. Lord Thornton didn't paint the portrait, his brother did. And upon closer inspection, I could not believe I'd missed the resemblance. The almond-shaped eyes cloaked by limitless lashes, the high cheekbones and full lips—both sons hailed these gifts from their mother. No wonder she'd looked familiar to Hawk upon our arrival.

I turned back in my chair, finding my place again in the note.

"Chaine and I were born to royalty. Our mother married Tobar Kaldera, the Romani Roi—king of the gypsies. Understand, there is little prestige in the gypsy hierarchy. A king is exclusive to the camp in which he resides. The title is self-appointed and allows it bearer to put on airs to impress outsiders. The other Romies of the camp assent to the charade as it protects them from reaping dues for any crimes they commit. Only the most vain and power hungry of the gypsies take the Roi title, for when outside authorities come to seek retribution, the king becomes the scapegoat. Tobar Kaldera was just such an ambitious fool."

I paused to consider the noble profile and strong physique of my phantom companion. "You are a prince."

As if the force of discovery had nailed them in place, Hawk's eyes refused to stray from the parchment again.

"There is no delicate way to put this, Miss Emerline. So I shall be blunt. Tobar was not our blood father. Our mother seduced an English clockmaker from Worthington who had a temporary assignment for Lord Larson here at this estate. My mother's gypsy clan worked the ochre mines. The clockmaker's name was

Merril—whom you know as the elderly Viscount Thornton, my father. Before you judge my mother harshly, you must understand. By gypsy law, a marriage is not valid until the wife conceives. Gitana loved Tobar. She had grown up alongside him, wanted no other man but him. Yet after he tried to conceive a child with her for two years, he threatened to marry another woman should my mother not give him an heir."

Prying my gaze from the letter, I glanced at the portrait again. The flickering glow from the fireplace highlighted her dark eyes, giving them a poignant depth. What unusual beliefs they had. Then again, what would they think of the English model of sexuality with all its hypocrisies and areas of gray? It appeared it was all a matter of perspective.

Hawk took over reading as I continued to regard his mother's portrait.

"For a month, Gitana had a secret tryst with the young clockmaker. Then one morning, the gypsies left for the season and Gitana went with them, offering not a word to Merril. He never saw her again. Brokenhearted, he finished up his business with Larson and went back to Worthington. Gitana's deception reaped a reward, for she conceived. The first seven months of her pregnancy were blissful. Until Tobar's sister learned of Gitana's betrayal while reading cards, and told her brother everything. He became violent, attempted to beat the truth out of my mother as to who fathered the unborn child."

Hawk clamped his mouth shut. The firelight filtered

through him and his face reflected a fierce stirring of emotions. Though I couldn't read his mind, I knew we shared the same thoughts. Could this be Aunt Bitti? The woman Hawk had grown so fond of for her part in his escape from Tobar?

"Perhaps we should not read the rest, Juliet. You're too sensitive for such violence."

I sensed it was Hawk feeling vulnerable, but I also knew he needed to know everything. "Lord Thornton is expecting me to read it. He's entrusting his secrets to me. This gives me power over him. Do you not agree?"

Hawk sighed and nodded. *"Gitana refused to admit our father's name, infuriating Tobar. Upon seeing the extent of her brother's rage, our aunt feared for the unborn child in her sister-in-law's womb. She laced her brother's food with a sleeping dram then helped Gitana escape the gypsy camp into a cottage hidden away in the hills. After two months in hiding, my mother bore twin boys and named them Nicolae and Chaine. When we were six weeks old, she prepared to carry us to Merril. But Tobar found her. As she held the door against his entry, my mother begged our aunt to hide one babe in the cellar, choosing to save the one with the deformed foot. In her wisdom, she anticipated Tobar's wrath upon another man's offspring and knew the weaker child would have no chance of survival. After Tobar forced our mother and Chaine back to the gypsy camp, our aunt escaped with me, leaving me on Merril's doorstep with the note our mother had prepared. The missive did not specify two babes, so Merril never knew of Chaine's existence ... never knew to search for him."*

My heart sunk. To think, all of this had been brought about by Hawk's aunt. It must be the same woman. It would explain why she kept watch over his grave. Why she had helped him escape. All these years, such a weight of guilt to bear—such a penance to fulfill.

I could no longer look at the painting on the wall, or the woman's sad gaze.

"It says here,"—Hawk's baritone soothed my aching spirit—"that Tobar never knew his wife bore two sons. Nicolas writes that on our fifth birthday, the grief of giving up one of her babies along with that bastard's relentless abuse, killed our mother. Bitti became my only solace at the gypsy camp. As I grew, the lighter turn of my skin and my unusual eye color reminded Tobar of Mother's infidelity. I became the object of his hatred until my aunt could no longer stand by and watch. She helped me run away." Hawk met my gaze, the light gone from his eyes— having slipped somewhere deep within him. "In the gypsy tongue, 'hawking' is the term for selling homemade goods. Apparently, that had been my mother's livelihood. According to the last lines of this note, she was a gifted artisan. That must be why I chose the surname. To honor her."

There was strength in my ghost's voice, despite the pain filling his eyes. He strode toward the portrait on the wall. His boot's toe touched the bottom of the frame where it met the floor's baseboards. He stood face to face with her, the woman who died to give him life, and ran a finger along the delicate turn of her jaw.

The intimacy of the moment moved me, to witness the tender side of such a powerfully built man. It reminded me of the viscount in the winter garden, when he released the butterfly from his grasp.

I couldn't help but envision Lord Thornton in Hawk's place now, paying homage to this missing thread in the tapestry of his past. He must have stood before this portrait countless times once he learned of her part in his salvation—her excruciating sacrifice which bought him a better life than his brother. No wonder he carried such remorse for his ideal upbringing. Could that be what I had seen in him that day at the cemetery? Not anger, but unbearable regret and sorrow for his brother's broken childhood?

I rose from the cushioned chair and went to Hawk. I would have given anything to nestle my head beneath his chin, press my heart to his, and weep with him. Instead, I could do no more than stand beside him.

He didn't look at me. To honor his introspections, I occupied myself by studying every intricate line and brushstroke of Gitana's likeness. When I came to the etchings on her bodice's neckline, something in the artistic styling struck me as familiar.

I strained to look beyond the flowers embroidered of colorful threads on her dress, allowing my eyes to glaze. Covert images blurred to life within the embellishments. Rats, clocks, and human faces—each of them strangers to me, yet vivid in detail. Indeed, I had seen such hidden pictures before.

Rushing to my trunk, I dug out Chaine's journal, my

fingers tingling with excitement.

I sorted through the pages until I came upon Chaine's drawings. Standing, I held up the book for Hawk. "There ... in this sketch of a vulture, the feathers are a labyrinth of camouflaged images. Just like in the portrait on the wall. There's a face that matches your mother's. Here, in the bird's chest. Do you see it?"

In a blink, Hawk stood before me. He regarded the journal then returned to his mother's portrait. "Juliet ... you're bashing brilliant!"

I couldn't stop my smile from spreading. "You're the brilliant one. You drew them."

From across the room, he frowned in thought. "I've heard you comment on the colors of this painting. How would I have known what scheme to use?"

"Perhaps you had some help. From someone who thrives in color. Could it be you drew the lines and Nicolas filled them with paint, in homage to your mother? Perhaps that was what caused Miss Abbot's confusion as to whose hand gave it life."

A dreamy satisfaction softened his features. The theory seemed to please him. "Did you see this one? This image here, in this cluster of fruit in the background."

Upon returning the journal to my trunk, I hurried over, my boots stirring a wave of petticoats around my ankles.

His translucent finger tapped at a symbol. "Do you recognize it? The rune on the plaque of wood beside the iron gate—the one I couldn't decipher when we first arrived here."

I nodded in disbelief. In all of our settling in, I'd

forgotten to draw it for him so he might study it. "Do you think it has some significance?"

"I do. I believe it might be the key to everything." He smiled down on me.

"So ...?" My pulse quickened. "Do you remember what it means?"

"No."

I frowned. "Then why the dotty smirk?"

"Because you have captured my brother's attention and trust, China Rose. Nicolas must know the meaning of the symbol to have placed it upon his gates. Tonight at supper, you will charm it out of him, my alluring little spy."

CHAPTER 22

The girl who can't dance says the band can't play.
Yiddish Proverb

I was hard pressed to find a moment alone with the viscount—for spying or anything else—due to unexpected visitors.

Lord Thornton's five investors and their wives arrived early to oversee the final touches on the Manor, and from the moment they entered the townhouse, the viscount had his hands full giving tours and directing the servants in preparation of guest chambers. He didn't even make it to supper.

After our meal, Enya, Uncle, Hawk, and I retired to the drawing room.

Several candles flickered on tall, twisted sconces. Light danced upon walls hung in cotton damask the same color as moss beneath a tree. Enya settled in front of the fireplace with a book. Uncle pulled up an ottoman where she could rest her ankle and sat beside her on the couch.

Mama had been helping Enya learn to read just before she took sick. After she hurt her ankle today, Uncle had offered to continue her lessons. They passed the entire afternoon with the activity which worked out nicely since

Enya could do little else without casting suspicion upon her *injury*.

Seated on a divan in the corner, I busied myself with a pink garden hood of dotted Swiss muslin, intending to finish the pleated ruffle trim so I could put it on display in the boutique once we opened for business. Pausing, I watched my uncle and his pupil.

In the soft glow of the fire, something wonderful was taking place—a prolonged meeting of the eyes, an accidental brush of the hand upon turning a page, a shy smile hopping like a restless bird from one flushed face to the other. I searched out Hawk and his delighted smirk mirrored the one hidden within me.

"By the look of things," he said, "Enya has made great strides in her transformation from a child to a lady today."

I agreed silently. Once out of the element of sameness, in an environment foreign to us all, Enya's intellect and wit took center stage. Uncle appeared beguiled by this other side to the often stoic and productive young woman.

"Amazing what a difference in perspective can make," Hawk's voice teased.

I pressed my lips to stifle a grin, thinking upon the truth of the statement, of the tolerance Hawk now felt toward his brother after realizing their true history this afternoon. And though still discomforted by the dungeon's secrets, a part of me had come to trust the viscount more, as well.

I slipped a needle through a pleat to baste it in place on the hood. Tomorrow morning, Uncle and I planned to arrange our shop's displays. An influx of customers were expected to arrive this weekend—only five days away—and we would be open for business come Monday. With ball gown and riding habit fittings scheduled in Worthington, not to mention the riding lessons Lord Thornton had promised, I'd have little time for sewing after tonight.

So absorbed in my stitches, I almost missed the stir of activity at the door. Hawk nudged me mentally just as Lord Thornton entered the room with his investors close behind, each carrying a cigar and a snifter of brandy. Smoke curled through the air on a mix of cloves, cocoa, and vanilla. The wives followed, all five of them dressed in frills and bustles so wide their posteriors almost didn't fit through the door.

I felt not only inadequate for my status, but underdressed—having not changed out of my wrinkled merino gown all day. Even the viscount had freshened up. He wore a long-tailed coat of celery brocade, a silver vest with navy pinstripes, and a silk puff tie one shade lighter than his orchid fitted trousers. As always, in spite of his clashing attire, twisted foot, and cane, he made a striking entrance—far more elegant and tasteful than the entourage behind him.

Tonight, he looked every bit the Romani prince with firelight glazing his olive complexion. His thick hair was parted down the middle, and the shoulder-length waves knotted at the back of his nape. The style laid bare his hooded eyes—painting him both vulnerable and virile in one sweep.

Our gazes met and something darkened his features, as

if he bore a heavy weight. I wondered if he regretted sharing the secrets in his note, exposing his heart to me. If he could read my thoughts as his brother did, he would know he had nothing to fear. For where I assumed it would give me power over him, somehow I was now at his mercy.

"Careful, Juliet." Hawk's voice drifted in beneath my musings. "He's still harboring secrets, and could yet be a dangerous man."

I agreed inwardly.

My uncle stood to greet the investors and their wives. After introductions, Lord Thornton patted Uncle's back, set his half-drank brandy on a passing servant's tray, and made his way to me. Hawk followed the investors on the other side of the room to see if he could pick up any information while they were free to speak outside of the viscount's earshot.

I forced my attention to the hat in my hands as my host settled himself on the other end of the seat. His scent surrounded me. It was becoming entirely too familiar.

Noticing the rhythmic tap of his cane against the floor a few inches from my foot, I turned my attention to his lips.

"A bit ragged around the edges, I see." He offered the unexpected observation, propping the cane between his knees.

Heat prickled from my neck to my cheeks as I pulled a shawl tight around my shoulders. "I-I was not aware we were to be in full-feather tonight."

Tucking wayward strands of hair behind my ears, I

regretted my decision to leave it down for the evening. I'd brushed it smooth, but had I known there would be other guests, I would've had Enya make me more presentable. I pressed my palm over my bruised cheek and sunk deeper into the cushion.

The garden hood waited in my lap with the needle still attached by a thread. The viscount lifted the hat, forcing me to face him.

He grinned. "I did not refer to you, Miss Emerline." He gently pulled my hand from my face. "That paltry bruise cannot mar your beauty. I referred to the hat. I noticed you were trimming it. 'Ragged around the edges.' It was meant to be a joke." He held up the hood and drew the thread tight so I could cut the needle free and tie a knot.

Afterwards, I perched the hat next to the sewing basket at my feet and tucked away the scissors, needles, and pins.

Lord Thornton's cane tapped the floor next to my foot again and I looked up, intrigued. It appeared he'd developed this subtle trick to claim my attention without making my deafness a spectacle for his guests. He was honoring my privacy without my even asking.

"I shall introduce you to them, when you're ready." The viscount gestured his cane toward the investors. All of the men gathered around the fireplace with Uncle, laughing at something he said. "I didn't wish to spring them on you after your reaction to my initial invitation to work here."

Chagrined, I considered how I'd cowered weeks ago when he first invited us to open a shop. Looking at the ladies now, they seemed so cordial. They sat, three on a fainting couch in the corner opposite me and two next to

Enya, inviting her—a lower class maid—into their conversation.

Could it be, all these years, I'd misjudged them? Could it be that they had treated me like a fragile doll because I acted like one ... introverted and inadequate?

As I pondered this, one investor strayed from the others. Hawk stuck close to him. The man appeared to be Uncle's age—gangly, with hair so black that when combined with his beakish nose, gave him the semblance of a crow. He seemed very interested in the viscount's possessions. His mouth moved with each step, as if speaking to himself as he wrote upon a small square of paper.

"Who is he?" I asked my host.

Disdain flashed across the viscount's face, so fleeting I barely caught it. "Lord Larson." He cringed on the name—like he tasted something unpleasant. The same reaction I noted at our parlor in Claringwell that day, when he spoke of his manor.

Miss Abbot had said Larson was secretive about Hawk's death at the mines. No wonder Lord Thornton didn't like the man.

"He appears rather ... sluglike," I said.

The viscount grinned. "Sluglike? You mean sluggish?"

"No. I mean there is slime trailing his every move. He is not trustworthy."

The viscount propped his hands on his cane and watched me, openly fascinated. "How can one so unworldly, know so much of the world?"

A rush of pride filled me. "I'm simply observant."

"Observant indeed. But there is nothing simple about you."

His compliment made me smile. "I wonder, how wise is it, to invite the previous owner to invest in the manor's opening? Larson lost the mine's deed in a gamble to you. He must be harboring ill will."

The viscount's expression closed, an indication that the subject closed, as well. Perhaps he hoped that by being generous to Larson, he might gain more details of Hawk's death. I could respect that.

He twirled his cane on the floor. "So, what do you think of the others?"

I shrugged. "What matters is what you think. They are your business partners, your guests."

"Bah. I don't like playing host."

"Why would you have a dream to open such an establishment, if you dislike sharing your company?"

"This is nothing of what I dreamed." The moment the words slipped from his mouth, he looked as if he wished to gobble them up again. He stared at his black silk slippers, jaw clenched.

I frowned. "But Miss Abbot alluded that you have wanted this since childhood, planned such an establishment since your youth."

He faced me. "Miss Emerline, as I'm sure you surmised from my earlier note, I was once a very different man. Spoiled. Selfish. Meeting my brother, learning of his broken past ... being faced with his death—it changed me. I now crave a quiet routine. A happy home with gardens to tend. A wife and children. Tranquility."

Tranquility? How did the dungeon's torture chamber fit into such a life? Knowing I couldn't possibly ask that, I asked a more obvious question. "So, why go to all this trouble if you don't want any of it?"

"To uphold the family name. I made a promise."

I narrowed my eyes. "To your father? He should be here, sharing in your successes. A family should stand beside one another in happy times, just as in tragedies. It is what they do."

"Is it?" Lord Thornton shook his head, as if he truly didn't know.

Within me, a hundred questions begged for answers. There was more to his father's absence than he let on, not to mention his aunt's clandestine presence. But this was not the place to broach such subjects. Not with so many guests puttering about.

"Have you eaten?" The question bubbled up before I could stop it. He seemed so lost and alone. I felt a tug at my heart to imagine him in any discomfort. "You missed supper. A good host must maintain his stamina."

An attractive flush dusted his cheeks—the first I'd seen of such a trait. I rather liked it.

"I had some tea and toast earlier," he answered. "It will suffice until the servants bring out cake for the guests. Thank you for your concern."

I dropped my focus to the hat at my feet. "It was just an observation."

He grasped my hand and cradled it in his palm, a warm and genuine gesture. I looked up. "Whatever the case, it is nice to have someone tending me."

"But haven't you always had that?" I asked, thinking of his privileged life in contrast to Hawk's. "A man of your status has servants to tend his every whim."

His demeanor saddened. "It is not the same as a woman's caring touch."

I regretted my careless words. As of this afternoon, I knew he'd never had a mother. Could this be why he'd sought solace in so many women's arms and beds? Seeking the love of a mother he'd never had? On some level, I could empathize with his emptiness, after losing my own.

My fingers curled around his hand. "I intend to see that you eat two slices of cake to make up for your missed meal."

His stunning smile flashed then faded to an intense study of my own mouth. Several seconds flitted by. My lips *felt* the attention, as if he traced them with his fingertip instead of his eyes.

The moment shattered as the viscount's attention shifted to the door. Three men stepped in carrying instruments: two violins, one flute. My host stood and said something unreadable to everyone. All of the guests clapped, the silent applause mocking my deafness in the same as wind mocks the most capable vision.

The instrumentalists set up to play in the corner where the ladies sat. Lord Thornton turned back to me and held out a palm.

"Might I introduce you to my guests, Miss Emerline? Then perhaps you might honor me with a quadrille. These men are from the orchestra I've hired. As the others have yet to arrive, I thought we might grant the trio a rehearsal."

A handful of servants moved the furniture, opening up the floor for dancing. Four of the married couples whisked into place and formed a square.

The musicians warmed up their instruments—though it was all lost on me.

"I-I have not danced in years, my lord."

Lord Thornton didn't withdraw his hand. "Then tonight, we practice."

"I don't wish to."

"Why ever not?"

"It is a quadrille. I cannot hear the calls, so I wouldn't know which position to take."

"So we forfeit the quadrille and dance a waltz instead. Thus there are no promptings from the orchestra to hear."

I winced. "Ever since I've lost my hearing, I've been ... inept at rhythm."

The viscount's fingers curled and opened alternately, beckoning me. "Follow my lead. I shall provide the rhythm."

Something in that suggestion brought my pulse to race. I used to dance with Papa and Uncle as a tiny child. Standing on their toes as we floated to the music. But to be in this man's sturdy arms, held close enough to vanish inside his scent and warmth—it would be a sensual awakening. One of which Hawk would not approve. I searched for my ghost and found him still preoccupied with Lord Larson across the room.

"I would be awkward and graceless," I said to the viscount.

Lord Thornton dropped his hand. Behind him, the dancers drifted across the floor—a rainbow of muted laughter and adroitness. How I coveted all of the things they took for granted. How I wanted to glide on a river of music. So much, my ears and limbs itched with envy.

My host studied me. "Graceless? Can you imagine how graceful I am, with a bum foot and a cane to boot?" His expression gentled to a smile, and I knew in that moment we would be perfect dancing partners.

Still, I couldn't get past my fear of being the object of ridicule. I shook my head.

"You are to attend the galas with me, Miss Emerline. To this we agreed."

"Attend, yes. I never said I would dance, my lord."

Pinned by his frown, I squirmed in my seat. The resulting scrape of petticoats against my legs reminded me of my rumpled appearance. "I am inadequately dressed to even greet your visitors, much less to attempt dancing among them." I bent to gather my basket and hat.

The viscount cupped my elbow and helped me stand.

Hawk, having lost Lord Larson to his wife, appeared at his brother's side. I sensed by the anxious turn to his brow that he had something to report.

"Your lordship," I pleaded. "If you could retrieve Enya, I should like to retire for the night."

The viscount released my elbow and nodded. "As you wish. I'll find a servant to escort you and your lady's maid up the stairs. We wouldn't want her hurting her ankle again." A perceptive glint pierced his gray eyes.

Of course he'd seen through my and Enya's scheme.

His perceptiveness never ceased to amaze me. Yet he had allowed our ruse to play out to preserve my dignity.

Touched by his graciousness, I smiled. "Remember," I said, grasping his palm. "Two slices of cake."

Lifting my hand, he kissed it. "And you remember ... we shall have our dance. You'll find I don't give up so easily. Neither should you."

CHAPTER 23

A woman has the form of an angel,
the heart of a serpent, and the mind of an ass.
German Proverb

"You are far too stubborn for your own good." Enya stepped into my chambers from the hallway, holding a wriggling broadcloth bag. A spread of tiny claws punctured the weave.

"Did anyone see you?" Nervous, I stroked my princess panel dress to feel my locket's chain beneath—the black crape slick against my fingers.

Enya shook her head and shut the door.

"And did it give you any trouble?" I asked.

She held up one of her cotton sleeves to display the shredded cuffs, her face as pink as the early morning sun which splayed through the salmon tinted glass from the other side of the room.

Opening a linen napkin from breakfast, I took out a large slice of ham. Its salted aroma hung on the air as I smiled. "I shall see that you get a new dress. I'm glad you took my advice and wore gloves."

As she settled the moving bag on the bed, Enya glared at me. "Taking your advice ..." She loosened the tie and the bag fell open, revealing our befuddled hostage's head. "Is sure to cost me more than a dress. I'm going to change before we enact the next phase of your ludicrous scheme."

Enya retreated into her room.

A fluffed out tabby cat, little more than a kitten, scrambled out of the bag and off the bed to vanish underneath.

I dropped to my knees and lifted the bedcover. Two glassy eyes reflected back at me from the darkness.

"She's hissing at you." Hawk's voice stirred in my ears.

"Rather obvious. Even to a deaf girl."

"Shall I rush her out?'

I glanced over my shoulder where he stood. "I wish to befriend her, not mortify her. You stay by the Secretaire and protect your flower in the chance she runs rampant." The blossom perked happily in its new pot. I didn't want anything to upset the balance.

Tearing off a bit of the ham, I tossed it toward my bristled captive beneath the bed. She inched from the shadows to sniff the meat, then her pink tongue lapped at the peace offering.

I formed a trail of ham, scooting several feet from the bed, keeping the biggest piece of meat in my hand. "She'll be out shortly for the rest."

Hawk leaned against the Secretaire, grinning. "Simple as that, you think?"

I smoothed my dress so it shimmered around me like a puddle of ink. "I have a way with animals."

My ghost's smile broadened as he swung his pocket watch in his hand. "Too bad the envelope was no longer in the humidor this morn. Would've been much easier to filch the deed from the dining hall. You're sure this distraction tactic will work?"

"Enya said all of the servants have been instructed to chase out any cat they find in the house this morn since it's cleaning day. And as the viscount is preoccupied with his investors, the maids will be tidying his bedchambers now. His door will be unlocked, making it the perfect opportunity. But we must be swift ... I have one hour before I'm to meet Uncle in our boutique."

"You think Enya will keep your secret?"

"I gave her no details to why I'm going inside the viscount's room. She prefers it that way." I pointed to the bed where the kitten's head poked out from the bedcovers. A quiver shook her whiskers as she licked her lips. My gaze slid up to Hawk. "The question is, are you sure of what you heard last night?"

"I listened to Larson's words myself."

"But you said he was mumbling beneath his breath." I furrowed my brows. "For me to sneak into the viscount's room and try to find where he hides his legal papers ... you must be sure beyond a doubt." The kitten tumbled out from her hiding spot and stood rooted in place, staring at me with round eyes and a twitching tail.

Hawk watched the cat with an amused grin. "I practically stood on the investor's toes. I heard every muttered word; saw what he wrote on the paper. Each time he passed a possession, he calculated its value. Said he didn't give a fig what the other investors expected to make, his intake would be eighty percent or he'd parlay all of Nicolas's equity. It would appear he still harbors a grudge toward my brother for winning their card game; and he seems to think he has a chance to gain everything back."

"It would *appear* you care about your brother and wish to help him more than you let on." I clicked my tongue at the kitten, dangling the ham in an effort to coax her closer. Her yellow eyes widened and her mouth opened on a silent mew, baring needle-like teeth.

Hawk snorted from beside the flower. "I simply want to study that deed for myself. See if my brother has a foot to stand on ... other than the twisted excuse of one he's always using as a link to your sympathies."

My shoulders stiffened. "Hawk. That is a beastly accusation. He understands what it's like to be different. He empathizes in a way few others could." Before I could tear my focus from Hawk's annoyed frown, I felt movement along my skirts and then a tug on the ham in my hand where my furry captive's tiny teeth gnawed at the meat. I stroked her lush fur with my free hand as she ate. A roll of vibrations greeted me beneath her ribcage.

Wearing a smug grin, I met Hawk's gaze. He couldn't hold back a chuckle.

"You see?" I laughed. "I do have a way with the beasts. Even you can't resist me."

"As if there was ever any doubt." His eyes smoldered with a sensual light that, had he been flesh, would surely have led to a fiery kiss.

In spite of a rash of nerves, my plan worked beautifully. Enya, still feigning a limp, accompanied me to the third floor of the north wing, having told Miss Abbot I wished to visit my uncle in his chambers. Hawk followed behind us. All the while I had the kitten tucked within my emptied sewing basket where she munched on the remainder of ham. I hung the handle around my lower arm and smiled innocently as we passed two investors going in the opposite direction toward the stairs.

When we came upon the viscount's room and found the door ajar, Enya assured me with a nod that the maids were inside. She kept watch in the hall as I tilted the basket to empty its furry contents inside, then eased the door closed to prevent the kitten from escaping. On Enya's signal, I stepped back so she could throw open the door at the last minute. In a flurry of orange and white fur, the cat darted out with three flustered maids chasing her.

Taking the basket from my hand, Enya hobbled after them as if to help. She had insisted she would not stand guard for such nonsense. Little did she know I had a phantom accomplice fit for such a task.

Hawk and I slipped within. I shut the door behind me and leaned against the frame, in awe of the surroundings.

Some say a man's abode is a mirror of his soul. Were this true, then the viscount was a very direct and honest man with a fair sense of right and wrong, for everything was laid out in black and white. Literally.

Black velvet coverings draped his canopy bed. The pillows and sheets shimmered white as satin clouds. The walls were white-washed with a mottled affect, like the foam of a turbulent sea. The curtains—black and opulent—had been drawn open to allow sunlight to stream through the picture window. An avalanche of pillows with tassels in pristine blacks and whites peppered the cushioned window seat. No grays anywhere to be seen.

On the floor stretched a plush rug, the pile woven in a checked pattern. Not one picture graced the wall. Instead, flat backed baskets—formed of the same black wrought iron as the bed frame—hung upon nails. Each one housed sprays of fresh flowers in welcome splashes of color. The bouquets released a delicate potpourri, and when I closed my eyes, I could almost envision myself in the winter garden.

"Juliet ..." Hawk's voice snapped me back to the present. He stood beside the bed. "You said we had little time."

I nodded and took stock of the room. A tall wardrobe, a writing desk with two drawers, and a nightstand with a hinged cabinet—all constructed of polished black oak—provided possible housing for legal papers.

First, I pored over the contents of the nightstand's cabinet and found several scientific, architectural, and legal tomes. Leafing through each one resulted in nothing more than a paper cut on my thumb.

Inside the wardrobe's drawers, I found the viscount's underthings. Despite my best efforts, my skin flashed hot to imagine them clinging to his well-built form, a thought which won me a scalding grimace from my partner in crime.

I threw open the doors and an array of prismatic jackets, trousers, and vests danced on wooden hangers as if delighted to be freed from their dark prison. It looked like the entrance to some rainbow netherworld, far removed from the land of black in white in which I stood.

Leaving the wardrobe doors ajar, I checked the writing desk, surprised to stumble upon a small stack of charcoal sketches drawn by Chaine: captured moths, featherless birds, broken-stemmed flowers. I could find nothing significant about them, other than his keen insight for flawed beauty. More proof that the viscount had taken great pains to honor his brother's memory. At this point, I suspected even the room itself might be a tribute to Hawk's color-blindness.

"Would you stop finding reasons to like him, for saint's sake?" Hawk glared at me. "His legal papers must be here somewhere. Look again."

Frustrated, I made another run of everything ... dragged my palms along every nook and cranny, even on the underside of the furniture and beneath the bed's mattress, in search of some secret compartment. But the only thing I managed to find was a splinter in my pinky to compliment the paper cut on my thumb.

I threw up my arms, defeated.

"You're not giving up are you?" Hawk asked.

I tried to suck away the splinter. "There's nowhere left to look ... and I'm running out of good fingers." I held up my reddened pinky to the sunlight. "With the crowd of people now running amok through this house, it makes sense the viscount would send any important papers to his solicitor." I started for the door to leave before someone caught us.

Hawk tilted his head. "Wait. There ... there at the window seat. At the cushion's base."

Following his line of sight, I noticed the corner of a quilt sticking out.

Hawk was there before I could blink, tapping the fabric. "The cushion is a lid to a hidden compartment."

I stepped up and raked the accent pillows to the floor, then hoisted the hinged cushion open. The scent of stale wax, dust, and ochre filled my nose. Moving the quilt aside uncovered a pocket-sized pistol—brown, silver, and sleek—staring at me from a nest of used candles like a snake ready to strike. Next to it was a box of black powder and some lead balls for loading the weapon.

I stepped back, shivers skimming my spine.

"A single-shot derringer." Hawk's composure calmed me. "Most gentlemen keep those handy, in the case they're challenged to a duel. Just be wary."

I cautiously lifted the pistol and dropped it on the quilt. Next, I shoved aside the box of ammunition, feeling the roll of balls as I exposed some papers beneath.

"That's it!" Hawk pointed. "The envelope. The left corner is still curled from being pressed against the humidor's glass."

Grabbing the envelope, I started to open it. But my eye caught on some blueprints a little deeper within the compartment. I dragged them free and gasped upon seeing descriptions alongside the designs. One was called a *Judas Chair*, an iron throne of sorts, with spikes on every surface and tight straps to restrain its victim. The other was called a *Malay boot*, also formed of iron to fit upon a victim's leg. Like the other device, it was armed with spikes that squeezed the foot, ankle, and leg. As if that wasn't enough, the metal could be heated to red hot temperatures.

"Juliet," Hawk's voice grounded me—brought me out of my dark introspections.

My fingers tightened around the pages. "Are you going to tell me most gentlemen keep these handy, too?" I asked.

His face reflected my own trepidation. "They must be for his dungeon."

My lips trembled. Each time I started to see some light in the viscount, shadows swarmed in to suck the breath from me. "What does he *do* down there?"

"I'm not sure ... but look. There's more of my artwork."

Sure enough, underneath an empty ink well and some broken quills, there were drawings painted in red ochre like the Rat King picture.

Balancing the deed and the blueprints on the compartment's ledge, I explored the depths of the compartment. The drawings were leading me to something else. Something toward the bottom—a trio of handwritten pages, identical to the ones in Hawk's journal. It was the missing entries that we had been so curious to find. The ones that spoke of Chaine's sky-fallen angel.

Hawk's chin fell. "My brother *is* after the journal. He tore out those pages and wants the rest of it now. That must be why he sent our aunt to your room."

The thought sent anxious pulses through me. I squinted at him. "But why would he have torn these out? Is it possible you tore them out and gave them to him before you died?"

Hawk's only response was his hand motioning toward the door. "Someone's coming."

For a split second, I considered diving into the window compartment. But I'd never fit. I rolled up the journal pages, tucked them between my cleavage, then put everything else in place, panting as the air thinned around me.

No sooner had I propped the accent pillows on the seat than I twirled to see Lord Thornton in the doorway—hair unruly and damp shirt clinging to his muscles. He held a basket in one hand, the other clutched around his cane. He took one look at his opened wardrobe and exposed desk drawers, then snapped his gaze to me. Sparks of distrust rained from his stormy eyes like brimstone.

Without a word, he stepped across the threshold, shut his door, and locked it, trapping me alone with his silent rage.

CHAPTER 24

Every garden must have some weeds.
English Proverb

I gulped my heartbeat from my throat. It fell into my chest and hammered the journal entries rolled within my bodice.

I'd been caught again like the white butterfly of earlier, and this time I had no doubt my wings were to be crushed. What would he do? Take the pistol from beneath the seat and shoot me? Flog me with his cane? Lock me in his dungeon of horrors?

Lord Thornton wore his usual discordant attire—lavender shirt, crimson trousers—yet I was the one conspicuous against the room's backdrop of black and white, even in my mourning weeds. Though the sunlight reflecting off of the snow outside warmed my shoulders, I sat upon the seat, stiff as a statue of ice, with an accent pillow cradled in my lap.

"Find what you were looking for?" The viscount's lips formed the silent accusation with such exaggerated restraint, my ears burned as if he'd yelled it.

Hawk gravitated to my side, speechless for the first time since I'd met him.

A lot of help you are, I snarled inwardly.

He found his voice. "You're alone, here for the taking. And you've turned his room upside down. You must think of an excuse lily-white, or you'll be bedded before the hour's out. You're already compromised. Should anyone find you together, you will *have* to marry him."

Of its own accord, my imagination supplied a detailed fantasy of what being bedded by Lord Thornton might entail. My breath twisted within me, hot and frantic, like a vagabond flame. A sensation not entirely disagreeable.

Hawk growled. "Damnit Juliet. That wasn't meant to entice you. Have you lost all reasoning? Need I remind you of the torture chamber blueprints? Now fix this before your uncle comes looking and finds you here."

That sobered me. If by some chance there was a logical explanation for the viscount's torture chamber, Uncle would never forgive a violation of our host's privacy. Especially knowing how I'd stolen the flower.

"A kitten," I blurted with such fervor the journal entries between my breasts shifted.

The viscount's shadowed chin twitched. "A ... kitten."

Hawk slipped to the corner adjacent from where his brother leaned against the door—cane tapping in silent rhythm as he awaited my answer.

"Yes, my lord." I dropped from the window seat, still clutching the pillow like a shield. "I-I found her running about the house. Befriended her. With a piece of ham."

Lord Thornton lifted an eyebrow—a glimmer of interest breaking through the clouds of his gaze. He nodded for me to continue while thumping the closed basket against his thigh.

Splotches of dirt muddied the damp shimmer of his forearms and palms—indicative of spending time in the garden. What might he have in the basket?

"No doubt the bones of the last person that crossed him," Hawk offered. "Perhaps they're our father's. You did ask to meet him, after all."

My stomach balled to a knot. "I-I tried to keep the kitten in a basket," I addressed my captor again. "So she would be out of the way ... but she escaped. The maids were chasing her up and down the stairs. I thought I saw her come in here." I exhaled, squeezing the pillow between my fingers.

Hawk grinned at me from his corner and I felt a rush of pride. I'd managed to conjure an excuse with very little lying. Most of what I said was an accurate account of the morning's events. Events that could be substantiated if our host questioned his servants.

The viscount's lip turned on a half-grin, amused. "And you closed the door ... why?"

The rolled up pages itched between my breasts as if ants crawled along them. "To keep her in one place, until I could capture her."

The other side of his lip drew up slightly. "Ah."

Hawk applauded as the viscount appraised the messy room again.

"So. Where is the basket?" Lord Thornton asked, skepticism creeping back into his brow.

"Um ... right there." I pointed to the one he held.

"No. Yours. You said you had a basket for the kitten."

"Oh. I dropped it when she first escaped. I intended to carry the kitten out wrapped in a swatch of fabric." I gestured to the disheveled room. "I was looking for something that would suffice when you came in."

There. Perfect. I'd explained the opened drawers and the wardrobe. What could possibly be left?

"The kitten." The viscount limped forward a step. "You found her, I assume. You wouldn't have been so foolish as to open up an abundance of new hiding places unless you had her contained."

Waving his hands to get my attention, Hawk motioned toward the window seat behind me.

I swallowed. "Contained, yes. She's inside the window seat."

Hawk shook his head fervently, appearing beside me. "No, Juliet. The deed. *I can see the bloody deed hanging out.*"

No sooner had he said it then the viscount's eyes settled on the white envelope bent between the closed lid and the compartment's rim. His jaw clenched and his whiskers reflected light from the window behind me, rippling like velvet caught on a breeze. Still holding the basket, he started forward, his cane beating out a muted cadence beside him.

I dropped the pillow and planted myself between the viscount and the envelope, my skirt blocking it. We stood face to face, my head tipped up to meet his gaze.

"My lord, perhaps we could use your basket for our prisoner." I covered his hand where he clenched the handle. He became solid where I was not, his muscles hardening to a spasm beneath my touch.

He set the basket at my feet. The musk of his sweat wafted in place where he'd stood.

He laid down his cane, opened the basket lid, and rose. "For your hats. I planned to seek your approval before I bundled them to dry."

The whicker container overflowed with a vivid array of feathers and strawflowers. He'd spent the morning gathering them. For me. The same morning I'd spent making a mockery of his privacy. The rolled papers began a burning torture between my cleavage tantamount to poison ivy.

I shot a guilty glance to Hawk.

He studied the basket's contents. "Ulterior motive. I guarantee it."

I searched the viscount's features for tell-tale signs of his true intentions, but found nothing but openness ... openness and a streak of dirt upon his forehead where he must have wiped off some sweat while toiling in the garden.

He rubbed his forehead. "I must look a mess."

"You're above perfect." The statement leapt from my mouth before I could stop it. I slapped my fingers across my lips.

A boyish grin stirred the viscount's whiskers, a stark contrast from the disgruntled snarl on Hawk's face.

"I-I mean *they* are perfect," I said, looking at the floor. "The flowers, the feathers. Thank you."

Lord Thornton flipped the basket's lid shut to get my attention. "Do you think me an imbecile, Miss Emerline?"

Prickles of heat mushroomed in my cheeks. "On the contrary, my lord. I find you to be a clever and capable adversary."

"Adversary? I wasn't aware we were on opposing sides. This is a game, then. A cat chase, as you said. And you, the delectable mouse, that for all her prowling and probing has found herself well and duly trapped" —he lifted a hand, his pinky grazing my temple—"beneath the cat's clever and capable claw."

The delicate press of his finger and the warm rush of his breath spun me into a panicked dream state where everything fell away in a blur of black and white. He was the only color I could see—crimson and lavender, a painting brought to life—all the more hypnotic for his erratic state of dishevelment.

"Best dig your way out, Juliet." Hawk's husky mumble shook me awake. "He's about to bury you."

I took a quivering breath, keeping my host's strange and dangerous secrets foremost in my mind. "I misspoke, your lordship. I meant, rather, that you're an efficient *escort*."

Using his bad foot, Lord Thornton swept aside the basket and closed the space between us so my skirt hem caught on his shoes. "Try again."

I gave it one last woeful attempt. "An ... apt companion?"

He paused to consider, wearing a gypsy smile. "I was thinking more along the lines of a masterful paramour." He caught my wrists and pressed my palms to his chest.

Faced with the hard turn of his muscles, my body

betrayed me instantly—fingers curling into the fabric. I struggled to maintain my poise. "A lover? Ha ... *indeed.*"

"Indeed." Sobering, he skimmed his fingers up my arms to my shoulders. Flutters danced through my stomach.

Hawk cursed from the farthest end of the window seat where several pillows were piled, threatening to topple them. But he didn't have the chance before Lord Thornton captured my necklace between his fingers and tugged the locket from under my gown. The journal pages within my bodice moved infinitesimally before the charm popped free.

Hawk was no longer in view. He was back in his purgatory. Yet I couldn't help but think he was better off there than witnessing what was taking place here.

Suspended by the chain in Lord Thornton's hand, my silver heart glimmered in the sunlight. The viscount held the locket against his lips, kissing the embossed rose, then gently pressed the metal to my mouth where his had been. Some lascivious demon possessed me to touch the silver with my tongue, to savor the metallic tang mingled with his taste.

Hawk flashed into my peripheral then was gone. I barely heard his grumblings, too caught up in my other senses to pay attention to my ears. Lord Thornton was watching my every move, desire drifting over his features like a slow gathering storm.

Somewhere in my attempt to outmaneuver my host, he had trumped me with the ultimate weapon ... tangibility and touch.

The viscount dropped my necklace in place atop my dress. Hawk was gone now—my clothes and the journal entries forming a barrier he could not breech. The viscount drew me close, our bodies pressed together—a real and solid resistance. His lips brushed across the bridge of my nose on a prickle of whiskers, and my lips ached to share the sensation.

To feel, just once.

His warm breath brushed my mouth, mere inches away. At the last minute, his gaze drifted down to the window seat. He nudged me aside and cool air replaced the press of his body. Intent on the envelope's exposed corner, he dragged the deed free.

Looking from me to the paper, Lord Thornton threw open the lid, seeking the kitten we both knew wouldn't be there.

My lips grew heavy—craving the kiss that lingered on my locket, neglected and dying. A new emotion sliced through me—fear—as the viscount shoved the blueprints aside in the seat, as if to cover the pistol.

He then turned and tapped the deed against the seat's lid. "It would appear my rival has been putting doubts in your head again. What has he accused me of now? It had to be monumental for you to scavenge through my room."

"This has nothing to do with your assumed rival." *A lie.*

"Why then?" he seethed.

I couldn't think of any response, tongue-tied over my gullibility. The teasing grin, the witty banter, the impassioned embrace—all of it had been a trick to distract me so he could get to the envelope.

He had been going through the motions, laughing to himself as I let his fingers play me like a mindless mandolin. And now he was staring at me, an accusation hanging between us.

Why he'd asked ... an empty-ended word, oh so volatile for its vacancy. "I wanted to explore your assets. Imagine my shock, to see the caliber of toys you waste your lucre upon." I laced my explanation with all of the contempt I felt for myself, forgetting the caution I should have sense enough to employ.

He looked back at the blueprints, anger receding to a bewildered frown. Then he faced me again, so I could read his response. "I assure you. I have the means to keep you well cared for. I will spare nothing when it comes to your happiness."

"Happiness? Am I to be treated as a queen, then? Seated upon a throne of nails? Or perhaps I'll be kept as a broken trophy on a shelf, taken down and dusted when your guests come to visit, so they might pity my cracks and rusted veneer. Where's the happiness in that?"

His chin tightened. "I would see myself drawn and quartered before my 'toys' would ever be used upon you." Fierce resolve darkened his eyes. "And as for being a trophy ... when will you understand that you are worthy of being cherished for who you are? Of being valued."

"The only thing you value is collecting instruments of torment, gambling away your father's funds, and deflowering maidens. Take off your mask, my lord. For I see right through it."

He winced as if I'd slapped him, then shook his head

almost sadly. "It is you who wears a mask. One you've hidden behind for so long you cannot even remember the spirited girl underneath, begging to come out. The girl who allows her feet to dance, instead of folding them beneath her in the corner; the girl who stands up for what she believes—defiant—instead of hiding her crinoline in lieu of packing it; the girl who has no desire to read lips, but longs instead to read what's in the heart." He tucked his deed back into the window seat and slammed it shut, leaving the pistol and blueprints there as well. "Until you learn to live life fully—embrace every facet of who you are, strengths and weaknesses alike—I fear no man will ever bring you happiness."

Shame burned my cheeks, for his words were truer than any I'd ever seen spoken, and they scalded like a splash of boiling grease.

"I would've been willing to overlook concerned curiosities—for the taste of your kiss, for the feel of you in my arms." His teeth ground so tight his jaw looked like it might splinter. "I would've bared all my secrets, bettered this anonymous rival in any duel of his choosing for your hand. Had you but offered me the benefit of the doubt just once. Instead, you accuse me at every turn. I will not battle skeletons from a closet long closed, to appease a lady who has no respect for herself or the man I strive to be today. Get out."

I saw the command on his mouth. But I couldn't move for the injury marring his handsome face ... injury and resentment.

His desire had been real, his tender smiles sincere.

"I said leave me." He grabbed my elbow, not hard enough to bruise, but enough to make a point. Cane in tow, he escorted me across the room. The swiftness of our pace whisked several tendrils of my hair free and they stuck to my lashes.

I expected fury. I expected rage. Instead, what he did next shook my insides like a blast from a cannon.

He opened the door and ducked his head out, assuring my reputation remained safe, still guarding my well-being after all I'd done.

He guided me across the threshold then released me—in every meaning of the word.

"I will send the basket of flowers to your room. You may finish your month in the boutique while I find a replacement. And you'll receive the payment we agreed upon." He paused, lifting a hand as if to sweep the strands of hair from my eyes. Instead, his fist slammed the door jamb. The silent vibration shuddered through me. "Rest assured. You'll no longer be expected to uphold this farce of a betrothal. I shall withdraw the proposal from your uncle today."

Instead of feeling liberated, I felt ensnared. Ensnared within a net of my own making. I reached for his palm, the one that had almost stroked my hair, the one that now flashed red where it gripped his cane.

He pulled back—too incensed to even make eye contact.

The door closed on a puff of almond-scented air. Unable to move, I clutched the journal pages between my cleavage, every bit as blind as I was deaf.

CHAPTER 25

*A wise man makes his own decisions;
an ignorant man follows public opinion.*
Chinese Proverb

Emptiness chilled my sternum, but the void had nothing to do with the absence of the journal pages in my bodice. I hadn't stopped to read the stolen entries when I stashed them in my bedchamber. I was in too much of hurry to find Uncle in our boutique and confess what happened with the viscount before he heard it elsewhere.

Uncle's lack of response disturbed me more than an angry explosion would have. Expression blank and void of emotion, he continued to stack bolts of fabric on a shelf—categorizing them by their color families. He didn't spare even a frown my direction as he and Enya emptied the two trunks of dyed cottons, velvets, and muslins. After they finished, my maid left for the townhouse. She shot me a grateful glance on her way out, for my omission of her part, and for the first time in my life, I envied her. She was still in Uncle Owen's good graces.

Tears pricked my eyes. It made no sense; I should've been basking in relief. I had managed to break the betrothal that had plagued me since my arrival, and it had no effect upon the real reason I came to begin with. Yes, I would lose my parent's beautiful home, but I came into this knowing that all along. I would still be here for a month. I could still use that time to learn of Hawk's life and death. The servants would be more receptive now that I was no longer an upstart.

So why was I drowning in dread and grief? Because my uncle had been my lifeline for over eleven years and I'd severed our bond with my careless plotting and lies. There was a distance between us. An ocean which had never been there before.

Without him, I struggled to stay afloat.

"Is it so difficult to understand that I wished to make sense of the man?" I attempted to pull him back to me. "For heaven's sake! Our host is hiding his gypsy aunt somewhere in the townhouse. You didn't know *that* about him, did you?"

Uncle wasn't shocked by the news. He already knew. Which meant he most likely knew about everything: the viscount's gypsy blood, his tragic mother, and his dead twin.

But there was one thing he couldn't possibly know. "He has dark and frightening fascinations, Uncle. I've seen blueprints for torture devices. There is a room in his dungeon where—"

"He calls it *The Museum of Oddities*." The movement of Uncle's lips stopped my accusation cold. "He took me there the first night we arrived. It's for the men's amusement. For those who are drawn to horror or a walk along the deformed and macabre. It is not for ladies or their delicate sensibilities. He didn't like hiding the display from you, but I personally requested he not show it during our tour."

My mouth gaped. To think, all along, Uncle held the answers I'd been seeking about the viscount. And never once had I thought to ask him.

"You had no inkling how to broach the subject." From across the room, Hawk tried to comfort me, but his efforts only served to widen the chasm between my mixed emotions.

Gulping back a sob, I turned from Uncle and busied myself setting out hats. Even that activity stabbed me with irony. I had expected dreariness and dankness in our boutique, with the shop being set inside a castle and the room being a twenty-by-twenty foot enclosure with a domed ceiling.

Instead, a chandelier of pink crystal shimmered with candlelight. Upon the walls, pasted strips of paper alternated in almond-blossom pink and white, accented by portraits of meadows and flowers. Daylight streamed through the six gable-end windows and glazed the white marble floor with a liquid sheen.

The intimate details captivated me most: the copper-wired dress forms—glimmering and new—waiting to be draped by Uncle's fabrics; the wooden hat forms set upon shelves that ascended like winding staircases from the floor up to the top quarter of the wall; the four cheval mirrors, adorned with fragrant roses, peonies, and daffodils, where ladies could model their pending purchases. Last of all, the ribbon and lace trimmed hat boxes—stacked upon a table draped in sheer silver sarcenet—every bit as beautiful as the merchandise which would be carried out in them. It was as if the viscount knew the secret desires of the little girl within me ... as if he had stepped into my fairytale fantasies and breathed life into them.

Setting out my last bonnet, I dropped into a floral settee behind me, overcome with remorse. Hawk paused in front of a window to gaze out. I looked through him, my soul raw and dazed, so much like the frozen landscape outside.

A brush of heat warmed my right thigh as Uncle came to rest on the settee. He turned to me. "It is the spirit, Juliet."

My heart thumped. "The spirit?" I asked, my throat catching like the tumblers of a rusted lock. Did he sense Hawk's presence?

My ghost spun at the window, his head tilted curiously.

"That is why Nicolas—Lord Thornton—wants his aunt here," Uncle continued. "Why he wears the flamboyant colors, why there are gypsy runes and symbols throughout this place. Because the spirit is in his blood. I know he has told you of his mother. Of his dead brother. Surely you can understand his loyalty to his aunt. And surely you can understand his need to keep her hidden, for her own safety and his reputation. You must stop being so suspicious of him. If you wanted to learn more, you should've asked him yourself. Or come to me."

Nicolas. Uncle called our host by his first name. How had I missed the depth of the bond these two had forged?

He obviously had been Lord Thornton's direct line to my likes and dislikes.

My fingers twisted in the lace at my wrist. "I know so little of him, yet he knows so much of me. It left me desperate for information."

The severe turn to Uncle's mouth softened, and in that moment I knew I was forgiven. "I would've told you anything you wished to learn. But now ... oh, Juliet. What have you done?"

I reached for the hand on his knee. "I've learned things of his past. Unsettling things. I have caught him in lies."

His chest rose on a sigh. "I know of his dealings with women and gambling. I know of his alleged temper and weakness for liquor. Do you not think I visited the rumor mills before allowing him to court you? But he assures me those days are behind him. And as for lies? It isn't as if you've been entirely honest with him." He squeezed my fingers. "How long have you known the gypsy woman was his aunt? Yet have you mentioned how you helped her? He told me he saw you at the cemetery when he visited his brother's grave. Yet have you ever explained to him why you stole his brother's flower?"

Heat flashed through my face, a bristling surge of nerves. There it was. Confirmation that Lord Thornton had known it was me all along. Why hadn't *he* said anything?

"He didn't wish to tell you," Hawk grumbled. His voice startled me and I looked up to find him gazing again out the window. "Otherwise he'd have to explain his actions at my grave. His hostility towards a dead brother. His knowledge of the journal."

Uncle's hand moved within mine and recouped my attention. "There's something real between you and Nicolas. Anyone can see it. In the way you look at one another, in the way you connect so often without words. It could be your shared physical encumbrances. It could be because he grieves for a lost loved one just as you do. Grief can bridge to friendship, even to something much more powerful. Whatever the case, there's a reason you act irrationally around him. A reason why you snuck into his chamber this morning ... a reason you stole the flower from his brother's grave." He paused, cocking an eyebrow. "Why you keep watch over it so judiciously."

Yes. But that reason was so much more complicated than Uncle could ever conceive.

"There are times a woman has no explanation for her actions," I mumbled. "There are times her emotions rule her, and she knows not why or in what direction they will lead. All she can do is follow, and hope her heart proves a reliable compass. Mine has failed me, of late."

Uncle's eyes glazed, as if he was somewhere far away. "Enya shall be disappointed when we leave. She's grown rather fond of this place. I believe she hoped we might stay. Did you know her favorite poet, Lord Byron, lived in a castle much like this one?"

I strained to read his lips—they moved so minutely now. Hawk filled in the words that I missed.

"She can recite the sonnet, 'She walks in beauty, like the night'. Makes it sound like a song ... never missing one rhyme or rhythm." Coming back to the present, Uncle's grasp on my hand withdrew, as if he were embarrassed.

I couldn't help smiling. "Enya is quite remarkable."

As if a bee stung him, Uncle leapt to his feet, kneading his hands. "I love your mother. I always will."

Rising, I stopped his nervous fingers. "Mama shall always be in your heart. But if there's room for another, you should bear no guilt for filling that vacancy."

He shook his head. "It's wrong. Enya is ... is yet so young. What could I offer her?"

"Warm arms and a loyal heart. Children."

So shocked by my suggestion, Uncle sputtered an unreadable scolding. Then, regaining his composure, he slowed his lips. "What would others say of such a pairing?"

Hawk observed us from across the room as he rested his pocket watch on his palm.

"That there can be beauty in a winter-spring love, father bear." I patted my uncle's cheek. "Just look at the purple heath upon the snow outside." I felt Hawk's gaze on me and thanked him silently for wisdom imparted.

Uncle's confused frown deepened. "Snow and heath?"

I straightened the cravat at his neck. "Never you mind. Just know that I support whatever you decide. You deserve to be happy."

Tapping my nose with a fingertip, Uncle smiled sadly. "As do you, tiny sparrow. We'd all do well to disregard the opinion of others. Had Nicolas not been so desperate to maintain his reputation so this Manor might be a success, perchance I wouldn't have conceived of such a ruse as the 'dowry' to sanction his desire to court you. After all, at that point he'd already said he would buy your parent's estate, keep it in your name, and let us stay there indefinitely, so long as he could have my cottage to use when he ventures into Claringwell."

My chin dropped. "You mean to say, I was never to lose the estate? I thought it was his *requirement* in order to marry me."

"I came up with that. Deemed it the best way to ensure you traversed here, to get to know him. You can be so stubborn at times, Juliet. But had I told you the truth, perhaps you wouldn't have been so suspicious of his intentions. This disastrous morning could've been avoided."

I couldn't fathom it. "He wanted to court me even without the property? Why?" Then it dawned on me: the interview he found in Lord Larson's mining files. Perhaps he felt obligated to help us financially out of respect for his brother's memory.

"Wait," Hawk said. "From what your uncle said, my brother didn't find the interview about your accident until your uncle told him of it." His words were logical, yet my heart still couldn't make sense of it. "He was bidding for your estate long before that."

"Juliet." Uncle's hands cupped my shoulders, his white shirt and brown vest wrinkling. "Those follow-up missives we exchanged all those months ... they were about you. Not the property. The viscount is drawn to you, just the way the good Lord intended. That visit when your mother and I met him in person, she took a portrait of you. I watched him as he studied it; he was captivated—

enamored. As you said earlier, there are times a woman's emotions rule her and she knows not why. The same holds true for a man. But it's ever more difficult for him to act upon rash feelings in our society. Everything he does must be treated as a furtherance of his career. Even courtship involves negotiations and—" Uncle's mouth clamped as his gaze drifted over my shoulder.

I turned to see the viscount stepping into the shop. Just as he promised, he was here to retract his marriage proposal. A pinched sensation tweaked behind my sternum.

I inclined my head in greeting.

He tipped his top hat in response, his free hand squeezing a linen bag tied with a bow. Dressed in a purple frock coat, a canary yellow double-breasted vest, and a tombstone shirt one shade browner than the mossy green of his trousers, he appeared to be on his way out for the day.

Then I remembered. This afternoon he had planned to take me for my dress fittings in Worthington while he ran some errands. A sinking perception pooled at the base of my throat. He would be going alone now, just as he would to all of the upcoming galas. He would be unattached and available to fill other women's dance cards. Having fresh insight into how it felt to be touched by him, and learning all I had of his generosity toward me and my uncle, I didn't like the thought of that. Not even a little.

Utilizing his cane in that graceful manner, the viscount paused to stand beside us and nodded to my uncle. With an answering nod, Uncle shook his hand.

Lord Thornton removed his hat and smoothed his thick hair.

Before he could speak, I stepped up. "Might you give us a moment, Uncle?" I directed the plea to him while keeping my gaze on the viscount's troubled features.

My uncle excused himself and returned to his bolts of fabric on the other side of the room.

"How's your arm?" Lord Thornton studied my sleeve. "Do you think it will bruise?" He looked almost green, as though sickened by the possibility he harmed me.

I wiggled the elbow he had used to escort me from his room. "I am fine. You were not as rough as you assume."

"Thank God. I never meant to ..." His eyes closed. When they opened again, he had regained his composure. His cane gestured all around the room. "So, does it suit? We can change anything you wish."

I made a point to look nowhere but him. "I see nothing I would change, my lord."

His eyes dropped to the bag in his hand. He held it out. "I brought this for you."

Hawk appeared at my side in a blink, as curious as me.

I took the linen bag. My hand brushed Lord Thornton's and warmth radiated from my arm to my chest, reminding me of our embrace in his room. I balanced the gift upon the settee to untie its bow.

The bag fell away to reveal a dome of spun glass— porous like crystallized mesh—seated upon a wooden base. The dome was a removable lid with a lock set into the front. Given its size and shape, it reminded me of a case waiting to house a large mantle clock.

Confused, I looked up.

"I had Mr. Diefendorf make it," Lord Thornton explained. "He's the German gentleman who runs the glass shop next door to your boutique." Untangling a small chain from his pinky, the viscount handed me the key for the lock. "His expertise is glass-blown ornaments and jewelry. But this is a terrarium. To house that special flower you're so fond of." The viscount studied me with a deadened gaze, as if a wall of opaque glass dropped into place between us. "This will keep guests from touching it if you wish to have it with you in the boutique; yet it still allows the plant to breathe and receive light." Thick lashes smudged his cheeks as he ran a long finger over his top hat where it balanced topsy-turvy on his can's handle. "On the night of your arrival, your lady's maid told Miss Abbot of the flower's importance to you. Of its ... frailties."

All this time, he'd known it was the flower from his brother's grave, and still he was pretending *not* to know. Even after my despicable behavior this morning, even after our parting of ways, he was still sanctioning my lies, allowing me to keep the plant because he thought I needed it—emotionally.

I held my breath, feeling utterly unworthy of such a gesture.

Hawk cleared his throat. "He's hoarding it over you ... to remind you that he has the upper hand." His theory pierced the swell of air from my lungs. "Don't forget he still harbors secrets. Why was our aunt in your room? And there's more behind our father's absence than he's letting on."

Yes. I could not deny that the viscount was keeping things from me. But I doubted it could be any worse than all of the truths I'd been hiding from him.

"*I stole it,*" I said.

The viscount's brow twitched. "Pardon?"

I strained my vocal cords on my next attempt, in case I had mumbled. "I stole the flower from your brother's grave." Judging by the size of the viscount's widened eyes, I must have yelled the confession.

Across the room, my uncle's head popped up from his folding. He quickly turned his back to give us privacy.

"Juliet, *shush.*" Hawk's voice hissed in my ear.

The viscount's dulled gaze shattered to an inquisitive light. "You stole it."

"Yes. I was grief stricken over the loss of my—"

The viscount lifted one of my hands to his mouth. "Shhhh." His breath warmed the pads of my fingers. He released me to reveal a most beautiful smile. "That's all I need to hear. Thank you for your honesty." Then his countenance sobered. "I should talk to your uncle now."

"There's more," I said, trying to speak quieter this time.

Hawk stood behind his brother. "He'll think you're mad if you tell him everything. You'll be locked away in a bedlam somewhere."

Not if I show him you exist …

"I will leave," Hawk threatened, making his way toward the door. "I'll disappear on the other side and assure he never sees me. And you'll spurn a petal in the process."

A gouging fist twisted in my stomach.

The viscount waited for me to continue, patient.

I sighed, surrendering to Hawk's pressure, but undefeated in my effort to gain ground. "I should like to beg your forgiveness, my lord," I said to my host. "For my conduct this morning, for all of my offences thus far. And to assure you,"—my fingers locked hard in front of my waist— "that from this moment forward, I'll leave your past where it belongs. I *do* respect you ... for your patience and gentility, for your intellect and wit. For your generosity toward me and my family. But most of all, for your acknowledgement of your flaws, which has helped me embrace my own. If the offer yet stands, I should like to accompany you today for my fittings. You're the only man with whom I wish to attend the galas—*only you.*"

Lord Thornton's features softened to an expression of fragile astonishment.

Hawk cursed from across the room, having settled where Uncle smoothed out his fabric. The glow of pride upon Uncle's dear face was well worth the awkwardness of stepping outside my dignity. I awaited the viscount's response.

At last, Lord Thornton frowned. "No. This will never do." His answer was a punch aimed at my stomach.

"I understand." Biting back a humiliated sob, I started to back away.

He captured my fingers. "Wait. Yes. I covet your company. But you're not the only one who should make amends. I have been lying to you, too." A tremor shook his jaw. "My father isn't on holiday. He's in Worthington, in a sanatorium. He is the errand I was to attend while you were being fitted. Do you wish to accompany me still?"

My fingers squeezed the viscount's. "Yes. On one condition. I would like to meet your father."

"Are you sure?" The viscount asked, rubbing my knuckles gently. "It is a rather severe setting for a woman's constitution."

I almost rolled my eyes. If he only knew how strong I was. How strong all the women I'd ever known were, in fact. We were so often underestimated.

Hawk frowned, moving closer. "This is different than spending time with a dead man, Juliet. Have you ever attended one of those places? I venture it would make my brother's dungeon look like a child's carnival."

I fidgeted. Imagining the inside of a sanatorium was unsettling. But for Hawk's sake, I would brave the trip. He needed to meet his true father, to rinse his mind of the monster who raised him ... tortured him.

"I am sure." I answered both of the brothers at once.

"Fair enough." Lord Thornton smiled before turning me loose. He plopped his hat on his head but forgot to tuck in his bangs. My fingers clenched around the settee's arm, itching to touch the auburn streaks that spanned the hat's brim.

"Well then ..." He reluctantly stepped back. "I should allow you time to prepare. Of course, your lady's maid will accompany us. And I'll ask your uncle along, as well."

I nodded.

The viscount tipped his hat and limped across the room, meeting Uncle's pleased smile with one of his own.

Relief rushed over me in a balmy wave.

"You should never have acted on your guilt." Hawk's

husky baritone battered my happiness. "Nicolas is no saint. He locked our father in a bedlam ... that is how he managed to get his inheritance to spurn as he pleased. Had he changed as he claims, he would've brought our father here by now. To let him share in this privileged life he's built."

I paid no mind to Hawk's accusations regarding the viscount, too busy tripping over his observation of my own motives. For guilt alone could never have resulted in laying my pride at Lord Thornton's feet. Something more—something deep, real, and unexpected—was taking root within me ...

Something neither me nor Hawk could bear to face.

I traced the terrarium's dome, captivated by its intricacies. The glassy mesh felt like icicles beneath my fingertips.

"A fitting gift for you, Juliet," Hawk muttered from over my shoulder. "A cage of ice. The perfect size to hold a dead man's broken heart."

I could not contain a sob.

CHAPTER 26

A new broom sweeps clean,
but the old brush knows all the corners.
Irish Proverb

Lord Thornton's colorful berline offered warm transport, cutting through the heavy winter mist and snow-powdered roads. We arrived in Worthington around one of the clock.

First, we stopped at the haberdasher for my dress-fittings. After listening to my opinions of dress reformation, the seamstress, Miss Hunny (who true to her name had silvery-gold hair scented with honey-water), showed me an array of mourning fabrics: bombazines, satins, and crapes, even some silks. After I chose several, she adjusted her spectacles, took measurements, and promised to have at least one new gown prepared in time for Monday night's opening gala.

When Lord Thornton mentioned a riding habit, I feared Uncle would be anxious. But it appeared they'd already settled the matter. Hawk, having been silent up to that point, stressed that the viscount had betrayed my trust. But in truth, Lord Thornton never once agreed *not* to tell my uncle. His ability to get my stand-in father to comply was a testament to the bond of respect between them.

Miss Hunny brought out a riding habit that another customer similar to my build had ordered a month earlier but never purchased. Made of fawn-colored brushed cotton, it featured a tailored jacket with an attached bustle of soft netting, puff sleeves, and long tapered cuffs. Its crowning glory was an ankle-length split skirt with a double row of filigreed buttons that pinned back the fullness for ease in riding.

I tiptoed into the display room to model it for the viscount. So tickled to be wearing the equivalent of men's trousers, I beamed in the mirror. Behind my reflection, Lord Thornton's image beamed right back.

The waist required a few alterations which I was capable of doing myself. Lord Thornton purchased the matching suede gloves, then led us next door to a cobbler to order a pair of leather lace-up riding boots, insisting I pick the color. I chose a deep chocolate that favored the viscount's hair. He assured me he'd send a footman to fetch them Friday so I could have my first riding lesson on Saturday before the guests arrived.

We stopped for lunch in a small chophouse set within a pink stone cottage, rumored to serve the best cuts of meat in town. Upon tasting my braised fillet of mutton, I had to agree.

At half past four, we took the winding road to the sanatorium. The building loomed on a high hill. Scarlet bricks, wearing webs of tenuous ivy, stood dark and foreboding against the wintry backdrop. On the upper levels, every window had black bars welded across the panes.

At lunch, Lord Thornton had explained his father didn't stay at a typical bedlam but more of a maison house: a four story composite of small apartments. The patients on the ground floor—most of whom were wealthy and self-diagnosed with little more than exhaustion or a lust for gambling and gin—were free to roam about the enclosed courtyard and ornamental gardens.

Seven physicians and twelve nurses occupied the second-floor apartments, each owning a set of keys which opened the padlocked staircases to the third and fourth levels. There the morbid and incurable cases of mental unrest resided, locked within their rooms.

The elderly Lord Thornton lived upon the third floor due to his failure to grasp reality. With the addition of his blindness, he became easily excited. Since his physician insisted he receive only two visitors at a time, Enya and Uncle opted to wait in the courtyard.

Uncle squeezed my hand. "I intend to find some blooms of heath to share with Enya," he mimed the words and winked. I smiled, squeezing his palm in return.

Lord Thornton waited for me at the gate. A nurse unlocked the entrance, and led us up to the third floor where the bars over each window pane threw shadowy lines along our path, daring us to cross them.

Lord Thornton offered his free arm and I took it gratefully. Trudging through the sterile corridor to his father's room made me feel like a pathogen—a menacing intruder bent on disrupting the poor man's solitude.

"There's nothing of solitude here." Hawk said from the opposite side of me. "Be thankful for your deafness, Juliet. There are sounds in this place which could unnerve the dead."

I didn't need working ears to sense the wilderness of dementia we entered. I could see it: in the onslaught of fingernail scratches along the walls; I could taste and smell it, in the stench of urine and feces diluted by splashes of ammonia; and I could feel it ... in the icy slap beneath my shoes upon tiles scuffed from patients being dragged to their rooms.

I shuddered. The viscount noticed my reaction and drew me closer, his muscle firming where I tightened my clamp on his arm. He assured me with a nod that all would be well.

By the time the nurse reached the end of the long hall and unlocked the elderly viscount's door, I had myself prepared for the worst. Yet as I stepped into the room behind the viscount, where only a bed, table, and chair testified to a human occupant, I found an orderly, peaceful scene instead.

The nurse nodded toward an old man seated in front of the table beside a lone window, back turned to us. He tilted his head as if hearing us, all the while tapping his fingers across the shiny trinkets spread out on his table top.

His hair, shoulder length and yellowy-white, sprung up in thick knots. The viscount mentioned his father wouldn't let anyone but family brush his hair or shave his face. So Lord Thornton made weekly trips to tend him.

"What does my father smell like, Juliet?" Hawk stood behind the elderly viscount's willowy, hunched shoulders. Emotion broke over his voice like a wave crashing on the rocks. It was the first time he'd met his real father—at least that he could remember—and he had nothing tangible to grasp onto.

I weighed the scent against the stench in the halls still clinging to my nostrils. *Oil perhaps. And feathers, unmistakably.* I studied the table's contents and the memory Hawk shared upon our journey to the Manor of Diversions rebounded in my mind. Copper glinted on the table, gears of some sort, along with a vial of oil and several feathers used to lubricate the copper teeth. Lord Thornton had mentioned his father being a watchmaker during our talk in the winter garden.

Hawk inched closer. "'It is him. The same old man from my memory. And the one who read to me."

Time-wise, it made no sense that his father would've known him as a child. Had Hawk been a man when his father read to him? We assumed him a youth because the telling of Hansel and Gretel. Could we have been wrong? Perhaps it had been *after* he met his brother.

Hawk's trembling hand reached up as if to pat the elderly viscount's hair. It hurt to watch him try to make contact. I pressed my fingers to my lips, in an effort not to cry.

The gesture caught Lord Thornton's attention. Assuming me overwhelmed or mortified, he pointed his cane, indicating I should sit on the mattress's edge. As I settled, the bed springs groaned—a vibrating sensation beneath my hips. The nurse handed Lord Thornton a brush and razor then left the room with a promise of water.

I watched, astonished, as the viscount propped his cane against the table then took his place next to his phantom brother. For an instant, they were the family they should've been. The three Thorntons, all together, side by side. An obscure past that never had the chance to see the light of a future star.

The viscount stroked his father's hair to sooth him as he brushed through the knots. I wondered how many times in Nicolas's past Miss Abbot had combed his boyish tangles, and if she used the same tenderness.

If only he'd known his mother.

Hawk observed the poignant exchange—unmoving and contemplative. I knew he, too, would've given anything to have experienced such love. Either from a father or a mother.

A conversation began between the two viscounts—the young, industrious architect and the waning elder.

"Our father tells Nicolas that all the music is gone from his world." Hawk relayed the exchange. "He asks why Nicolas never sings him songs anymore. Says it was money well-spent, all those years of voice lessons." Hawk's gaze fell to the floor. "I wish I could sing my lullabies to him."

Sympathy clenched my throat like a vicious talon, making it impossible to swallow. My ghost scooted closer to the table, palms propped on the edge, so intent on relaying the conversation it was as if I listened to the two viscounts myself.

"Father, my heart has lost the will to sing."

"But I venture you still dress like a dandy clown. You know when I started going blind? T'was that first year when you began sporting circus tents in lieu of nobler trappings." The old man tilted his head back on a laugh.

Lord Thornton smiled gently. "It is much worse now. You should count yourself lucky you no longer have to view me."

"A waste." The old man felt around the table and found a gear—spindled like a miniature wagon wheel. His fingers tapped each tooth, as if forming a mental picture before sandwiching it atop the watch's base on a screw-shaped piece. "We've so little money to spare. For you to buy unnecessary things."

"The clothes were necessary for me to honor mother's heritage. Besides, we've plenty of money, Father. Everything is fine now."

"Yet instead of using our newfound wealth to get me out of here, you buy more doctors. Bring them to my room to poke and prod." The old fellow turned in his seat toward me, staring blindly through Hawk with filmy, white eyes. He had sensed my presence all along. "Sorry doctor. You're wasting your time. Nothing ails me that a good roll with a whore won't fix."

Lord Thornton paled and threw an apologetic glance my way. He turned the old man around in his chair. "Please, Father ... there are no doctors. I brought a lady. A special lady. You must be civil. Make her feel welcome."

"Ah. Should've known your bout with celibacy wouldn't last." He fitted a solid gear then several other pieces in place, using his sense of touch to guide him.

Flushed, Lord Thornton held out his palm to coax me over. Hawk looked over his shoulder, waiting.

I rose and smoothed my dress. Senseless really, since the old man had no chance of seeing it. Then I took the viscount's hand.

"Father,"—my host ensured I could see his lips—"I should like to introduce you to Miss Juliet Emerline. Miss Emerline, meet Lord Merril Thornton."

The viscount secured my hand within his father's cool and wrinkled counterpart.

Before I could say a word, Merril squashed my palm to his nose, snorting hot moistness over my flesh like a horse seeking out a snack. "Hmmm, this one's soft ... smells of gardenias and fresh snow. Found you a young innocent, aye? Take care not to spoil her. Don't make her like your mother. That woman reeks of gin and myrrh. Don't you find it so?"

"Of course Father." Lord Thornton patted the old man's shoulder, pity curving his lips downward.

"Gypsy whore." The old man dropped my hand and scrounged around the table once more. "Leave me with one son when I have two. Have you found him yet? Poor baby child. You must find him so I can raise him proper."

Lord Thornton closed his eyes and raked a hand through his hair. "He is my age, Father."

As if not hearing him, Merril snatched a feather and dusted off his developing watch. "I wish to hold him snuggled in a blanket. To tell him stories ... as I did you. Find him, Son."

Lord Thornton raised his broad shoulders on a sigh. "I shall try." When he opened his eyes again, he looked like a man drowning.

I eased two steps back, out of respect for the intimacy of the conversation. I used my deafness to restore Lord Thornton's dignity. He did not need to know I could hear every word between them via Hawk's voice.

"Bring him to me." Merril turned the gears of his creation with a fingertip, testing his progress. "Your mother will follow. We shall be reunited as a family. Then I'll kill that Romani king. Yes. That's what I'll do. Kill him. Dead." Agitated, the old man slapped both hands on the table and trifled through the remaining metal forms, desperate in his search for something specific.

Lord Thornton caught his father's wrists, his features sharp with annoyance, and I wondered if was about to witness his temper firsthand once more. "Father. You mustn't let the nurses hear you say such things. And if you aren't careful, you'll cut yourself. Then they'll take away your materials. If they perceive you dangerous to yourself or anyone else, they won't allow you to make your watches." He released the elderly viscount.

Lips pursed, Merrill nudged a square-shaped base with his thumb. It reminded me of Hawk's geometric watch and the giant clock in the star tower. Too similar and unique to be coincidences. Had Hawk's father made the watch in the tower, and the one for him that said Rat King? This same man that thought Hawk was still a baby? It was all so confusing.

Reading my thoughts, Hawk swung the watch at the

waist of his trousers, every bit as puzzled as I.

The viscount knelt down to gaze up into his father's face. He shielded his mouth from my view with Merril's head, thinking me blind to their discussion. "As I've told you. Tobar has already been dealt with. Be at peace with it."

"I cannot be at peace! Not until I find the blasted click spring!" His hands went wild over the table.

Lord Thornton rose to pick through gears and bits of misshapen metal. His brow crimped as he searched for the key to the clock's inner workings and his father's tranquility.

In a clumsy sweep, Merril's thrashing hands tipped the vial of oil. Inky liquid drizzled from the table's edge onto Lord Thornton's elegant leather boots, saturating the tassels.

Irritation tightened the younger viscount's jaw. He drew out a handkerchief and crouched to dab at the floor and his boots.

His father—oblivious to what he'd done—continued seeking the spring. Without a word to me, Hawk inched forward and stretched out his hand. Chin tight with intense concentration, he moved a tiny wire, shaped like a shepherd's crook, within his father's reach.

Merril held it up, beaming. "There it is! Ah yes. There it is." His milky, white eyes tilted in Hawk's direction. "Thank you, Sir."

My chin dropped and Hawk mirrored my surprise.

Lord Thornton looked up from his ministrations, puzzled as he noted my distance from the old man. "To whom are you speaking, Father?"

"The other guest you brought. The one I mistook for a doctor. The gentleman that moves like mist. He found my spring for me."

The nurse returned just in time to hear Merril's answer. She exchanged a worried glance with Lord Thornton.

"He knows I'm here ..." Hawk's statement startled me from my shocked stasis. "My father senses me. He bloody-well senses me."

My breath stalled. *No. It is impossible.*

Hawk smiled, his hope impermeable. "My father knows I'm here. He feels it, the way the animals do."

How can it be? The old man is as blind as I am deaf.

"Your point being?" Hawk's voice resonated within my dysfunctional ears, more of an awakening than if he'd slapped my face with a cold fish.

CHAPTER 27

The man who does not love a horse cannot love a woman.
Spanish Proverb

Back at the Manor that evening, I couldn't relax for all of the questions rattling in my brain. As soon as Enya helped me into my bed gown and retired to her own room, I curled up in the chair by the glass French doors with Hawk sitting on the arm next to me, both of us anxious to examine the pages I'd earlier stolen from the viscount's window seat.

Using nothing more than moonlight and Hawk's glow, I matched the torn edges to the journal's spine and found them the perfect fit. They were indeed the missing entries. My ghost deciphered the date and we realized it was the account of my fall into the mines—through Chaine's eyes. That explained why his brother had it in his possession. Chaine ... *Hawk* ... must've offered it as explanation to why he searched for me. This also proved that the viscount knew all along, even before buying the mines and reading Larson's accident files, of my existence. Now I knew why he came seeking me, and why he offered to buy my parent's estate, yet let me stay.

He was carrying out his brother's wishes.

This knowledge touched me deeply, and instilled a change in Hawk as we settled in to read, his words tender toward his brother now. Accepting and grateful.

"Today," Hawk deciphered the foreign script, *"I hid up in a tree while Father spoke to young Master Larson about the arsenic supply. I always thought it a stroke of bad fortune Tobar had been given the task as rat catcher on the estate. Never did I realize the two men had arranged it as part of a pact."*

Hawk's chin stiffened as he leaned closer to the page. The writing took a messy turn, as if Chaine pressed too hard with the quill. *"Larson has known all along about the monster and his practices. Larson has condoned my father and his sickness. He kept the monster's secret in exchange that as gypsy king, Father would arrange for the cheap labor of my people, and the promise of our return each spring and summer to work these mines for the same paltry dues—"*

Hawk slumped against the chair. All of the light had drained from his eyes. "They had a bloody business arrangement with my misery as collateral." He sat so close that could I have hugged him, my cheek would've pressed his sternum where his shirt hung open.

I covered the page with a shaky hand, unable to bear another word. Weeks earlier, I shared this child's humiliation and abuse through entries now as elucidative as any fossil, with traces of emotion so powerful I experienced Chaine's state of mind as if they were my own. Most indelible was the crown of living rats writhing on his head for hours until his savage step-father deemed fit to lift him out of the pit.

Never would I have imagined that a partnership between two grown men had enabled this unthinkable crime. It made sense now as to why Lord Thornton invited Larson back as an investor—even why he appeared to hate him so.

He was planning revenge.

"Yes," Hawk murmured. "My brother has something in mind for Larson ... something sinister." Hawk's quivering timbre made my stomach twist. "I told you what he said to our father about Tobar being 'already dealt with'? Perhaps I went after Tobar and something went awry. Nicolas must be planning to avenge my death. That must be why my aunt is here as well. Perhaps even the dungeon plays a role. Listen to the rest of the entry."

His finger floated over the erratic script. *"Let them laugh. Let them plot. Aunt Bitti says that to die frees your spirit. You can be places no man can be ... do things no man can do. So I'll let the monster send me to the tunnel today. But I'm taking his arsenic with me. Shouldn't be so hard to swallow. I'll close my eyes and pretend it's garlic. After I'm dead, Aunt Bitti can bring me back to settle everything. Better this way. I want to see the other side ... I want to be free. The pit is so dark. So cold. I need proof of light. Any light. There's none in life, so it must wait for me in death. It must."*

Hawk's voice broke and tears scorched my cheeks. Perhaps Lord Thornton's quest was not simply to avenge his brother's death, but his brother's stolen childhood as well. And, oh, how I wanted to help.

My thoughts ran rampant with a poison which both boiled and chilled my blood. I burned to leave my room ... to storm the dark halls of this house ... to find Larson's chambers and suffocate the greedy pig beneath a wave of rats and mud and arsenic. I'd almost worked up enough senseless rage to rise to my feet and let them take me where they would, when Hawk spoke again.

"Wait." His composure had returned, so strong and unwavering it gave me pause. "Hear this." He pointed to the final short paragraph, written later the same day with lilting curves and loops as if Chaine's entire demeanor had changed. *"I chose to live today, with the help of a sky-fallen angel. I thought to swallow the arsenic, truly I did. I held it up to my lips when a tiny slip of a girl fell upon my shoulders and into the pit. I lost the arsenic in an effort to dig us out from under the debris. When I found her, she hugged my neck and wept. I've never felt such warmth ... to be needed. I never knew that to help another is what gives us light. I made up a fairytale in rhyme to stop her tears, and she giggled with the laughter of a meadow lark. When her family came for her, I had to hide ... else they would fish me out and I would suffer the wrath of the monster for being found. But I have a plan now. I'm going to leave ... escape this place. And one day, I'll find the girl again—look upon her in the light—and thank her for saving me."*

Hawk met my gaze, his luminescent face a portrait of gratitude and awe. "No wonder my brother sought to find you after reading this. He's taking care of you, to make up for my suffering. Juliet, he does love me."

Fresh tears welled in my eyes as there in our solitude we silently pondered the power of a brother's devotion and loyalty, and the unbreakable bond of gypsy blood.

Saturday arrived on snowy wings, and along with it, my first riding lesson.

Hawk insisted I go alone, worried that his presence would spook the horses. I was so proud of his bravery, going to his purgatory even knowing his corpse awaited him. I chose to hide the locket in my trunk so that if I fell, I wouldn't risk breaking the chain. But as I walked with Enya to the stables, I found myself yearning to run back up to my chamber and put the necklace on again, just so I could see him ... assure he was all right.

Over the past two days, amidst the busy preparation of the boutique for the guests who were arriving tonight, I had witnessed a change in my ghost. The only way I could define it was growth.

He no longer questioned his brother's good intentions. Somewhere between the reading of the entry and our summation that Lord Thornton held a strong loyalty to his lost twin, Hawk had made peace with Nicolas ... even liked him. Though he still struggled with jealousy when the viscount lingered too long with a glance in my direction, or touched my hand in passing.

Despite those insecurities, Hawk had forged new depths of amenability, proven by his willingness to send me off today with Enya to chaperone. But I needed time alone with the viscount. To work out the confusion in my own heart. For every moment I spent with him fueled my hunger to know him more, inasmuch as he baffled and mystified me.

He was a conundrum: a master of the Manor, a friend to butterflies and birds, a study of thoughtful and quiet patience when dealing with his father, despite all I'd heard of his violent and selfish past.

So unbeknownst to Hawk, I had sweet-talked my lady's maid into making herself scarce when the opportunity might surface.

Enya was a very adept equestrienne with an excellent sense of direction. She agreed to go off alone once we reached our destination, so I might have time with the viscount. She asked no details, only that I vowed to remain chaste.

Upon our arrival at the stable, the viscount hand-picked our mounts. Enya received a dappled mare named Dancer. For me, Lord Thornton chose a gelding with a gentle nature. At thirteen hands, the Hanoverian Cream stood shorter than most horses.

"Miss Emerline, meet Little Napoleon." Lord Thornton patted the horse's shimmery neck and I couldn't suppress a giggle.

"Is that a barb against his stature?" I asked, smirking.

Grinning back, Lord Thornton placed a finger at his lip as if to shush me. "Now, you don't wish to offend royalty, do you? This fellow is descended from one of the very Hanoverian Creams responsible for drawing Napoleon's coach upon his coronation in 1804, during a cold December day much like this one."

"Ah." I performed a regal curtsy. "Please forgive my insolence, your majesty."

There was a lively twinkle in the viscount's eyes that I had never seen as he took my hand and urged me to pet the horse's sleek neck. "Hanoverians are bred to hold balance in slickness and snow. It's why I chose him for you."

Winter had settled at the Manor to stay. A foot of snow covered the grounds and wilted plants in a glittery, velvet blanket. Barren trees sparkled with icicles frozen mid-drip. A beautiful but less than ideal environ for a riding lesson. To know my mount was bred to be sure-footed put a feather in my cap of relief.

A stable hand kept Enya and me company while the viscount prepared Little Napoleon and Dancer for riding. The boy showed us a map on the wall of the one-hundred-and-twelve mines once located on the land. I searched out the one significant to me and Hawk, #34, remembering it from Larson's accident interview. I'd just found it when I was distracted by the boy stepping in front of me, his lips flapping through the condensation.

"Six years I've worked here," he said, ears and nose as red as his bushy hair, chafed from the cold. "Ne'er once have I met an animal—horse or otherwise—that the master cannot befriend." The lad gestured toward a magnificent black Arabian with a white mane, already saddled and tied to a post. "Lord Thornton tamed that stallion three summers ago. He'd just mounted the wild beast when a thunderstorm hit out of nowhere. A streak of lightning sliced the sky and struck the horse, sending him a-gallop through trees and brush, yet still the master stayed astride and rode him back, both of them unharmed." The stable boy pointed to a white streak in the stallion's muzzle where the lightning had left its mark. "After that stormy ride, he named the stallion *Draba*. It means 'magic charm.'"

I marveled again at my host's innate ken with nature.

As the stable hand helped Enya onto the mounting block so she could climb into her sidesaddle, the viscount took my gloved hand to catch my attention.

"Two rules I want you to remember above all else. One, never walk up behind a horse. Two, never stoop beneath them. They must always be able to see where you are so they won't be spooked."

I nodded.

He propped his cane against a post and instructed me on how to mount. "You don't wish to hold the saddle. It will wobble and slide. Hold the withers, here." Lord Thornton towered over me, one gloved hand a warm pressure on my waist, the other resting atop my own as he centered my palm above Little Napoleon's shoulders where the white mane ended and the creamy-gold hide began.

Patiently, the viscount steadied the horse by his bridle until I was in place. He checked my stirrups to ensure they hung at my ankles.

"Are you settled in?" he asked upon tightening the saddle's girth.

I nodded. For the first time since we'd met, I was taller than my host. I felt shy with my legs straddled over the animal's broad back—thrilled to be wearing the split skirt, but at the same time unaccustomed to how seductive such a pose seemed. Lord Thornton resituated my cloak over my legs for modesty, as if reading my mind. He took Little Napoleon's bridle and led us the full length of the corral and back, acclimating me to the feel of the horse's gait.

Enya followed astride her mount, looking rather bored. After my short lesson, Lord Thornton stopped next to Draba and swung gracefully into the saddle. As he slipped his cane through a loop behind the stirrup bar, nervousness burbled within my chest and my fingers clenched the reins.

Draba's elegant head lifted as mist puffed from his nostrils. Lord Thornton took control of the stallion and turned him onto a heavily powdered trail to the left woven through some ash trees. The viscount, with his black coat and hat, blended into his horse's movements—a singular impression against the white backdrop—like a charcoal painting come to life. I squeezed my knees into Little Napoleon's ribs, as the viscount had warned that kicking with my heels would numb the horse to my commands.

My ride lurched forward and Enya nudged Dancer to take up behind me. Once I mastered steering with my knees and the reins, we accelerated to a trot. I settled into the rocking rhythm, chill wind rushing around my riding hat.

The trees thickened and branches twined overhead. We ducked through a curtain of withered ivy. The dried leaves raked my shoulders and tugged bits of hair loose from my braid.

A gazebo came into view beneath an archway of ash

trees, sizeable enough to house twenty people or more. White wrought iron formed the frame along with a roof evolving to a pattern of ivy and flowers. On both sides of the entrance, two Cherubic water fountains spouted steaming water. Within the structure, curved benches squatted at the north and south ends.

Following Lord Thornton's lead, I stopped my horse and looked over my shoulder to find Enya gone. The viscount turned Draba to search for her, but I grasped his arm as he started around me. He pulled back on the reins.

"I asked my lady's maid to grant me some time alone with you."

He studied me, his whiskered chin twitching. My heart stuttered, worried he might misinterpret my reason for seeking solitude.

Before I had time to clarify, he stood beneath me, helping me dismount. With my hand in his, he led me to the steaming fountains and the shadowy depths of the gazebo.

CHAPTER 28

Silence was never written down.
Italian Proverb

I stopped at the gazebo's entrance beneath a cloud of steam, intent on the symbol etched within the archway's frame: the self-same symbol that was on the Manor's gate, and the one upon the portrait in my room.

I pointed to it, glancing up at the viscount with a question tugging my brows.

His gloved finger reached out to trace it. "It represents a mystical portal. An entrance to a secret world."

That explained its presence on the gate and here on the gazebo's opening. But why would such a symbol be on a portrait of his dead mother? The viscount's fingers laced through mine and lured me through the archway.

He turned me to face him. "You owe me something, Miss Emerline. Shall we tally up here in the gazebo?"

Steam from the fountains warmed my right side. Was he referring to the journal? Or perhaps he'd discovered that I'd taken the entries from his room the other day ... that I dug through his things and, like a demented pack rat, hoarded my findings with everything else I had stolen from him and his kin.

His hat's brim shaded his eyes, and his handsome face was poised between amusement and insistence. Removing his glove, he lifted a roughened finger to my chin. "Well, what say you?"

His touch warmed my chin, neck and cheeks. I had always prided myself on reading other's thoughts through their expressions. But now I felt emotionally deaf—so much more unsettling than the physical equivalent. "I-I am unsure to what you refer, my lord."

Replacing his glove, he paused as if rethinking his strategy. "The dance you owe me. Is this not why you wished to be alone? So we might practice privately before Monday's ball?"

Relief coaxed my lips to a smile. "Yes. I am nervous for the ball."

His answering half-smile made me wonder if he had just given me a reprieve. Perhaps he knew all of my secrets ... perhaps I was the one being read. I wasn't sure I liked being sprawled upon the slide of a microscope, after spending so many years bent over the lens.

The iron vines overhead drew shadows in tender blue relief upon the snow beneath my feet. I traced one with my toe. After laying his cane on a bench, the viscount led me toward the center of the platform. He positioned me to stand in front of him.

Taking two paces back, he scored a square in the white powder between us with his boot heel. "We will only partake in the waltzes. Do you know the box step?"

I once knew it ... but eleven years had blurred the memory. "As I said. I no longer have any scope for rhythm."

The viscount took off his hat, his dark hair tied at his nape. He cast the hat onto the bench, sending snow flying until it stopped next to his cane. "Bah. Rhythm. They try to write it on paper for the maestro. But any instrumentalist knows. Rhythm cannot be captured in ink any more than silence can. And it has nothing to do with your ears. It is something you feel and see all around you."

I frowned. "Easy for you to philosophize."

He laughed. "Oh, believe me, you make nothing easy." His chin cocked to one side, teasing. "When you are outside and it begins to rain, how do you know it's raining? You cannot hear the patter on the leaves overhead."

My jaw clenched. "Are you poking fun at me?"

Any trace of amusement faded from his expression. "Never. But you can feel the droplets, yes? They have a rhythm. You can see the spread of them on the ground, darkening the dirt to mud. Rhythm. Have you ever been to a pond in summer, and watched the frogs sing?"

In my mind, I envisioned bulbous chins swelling with air then deflating, keeping time with one another. "Ah, rhythm." I smirked.

He grinned back. "Yes. So, when we dance, if you never take your eyes off me, I'll not let you falter. I shall provide the rhythm." Palm on my waist, he lined me up at one corner of the square and pointed to his sensuous lips. "Watch here." My hands in his, he guided our footsteps with his counting. "One ... two ... three ... one ... two ... three ..." Together, we traced the square's lines until our footprints erased them, until we broke loose and twirled around the gazebo from one end to the other—his coat and my cloak spinning fans around our feet. Soon, we were laughing with the thrill of it.

I fell into his flow—easier than I had imagined. Similar to riding the horse, a grace so natural it became my own, transforming me from the inside out until I was no longer a separate entity but joined with another. Two becoming one in the matrimony of movement.

My partner amazed me, his ability to waltz even with a damaged foot—as if he lost his limp when he danced. And me? I could *feel* the music. Both physically and mentally. For the first time since I'd gone deaf, I didn't need to hear the chords to know the song. This architect, in his wisdom, had built a bridge so I could dance—uninhibited and completely at ease.

So intent on the freedom of our fusion, I didn't notice the change in my partner's mood until his counting slowed and he stopped dancing altogether.

Finishing out the step I'd started, I tripped over his boot and slipped in the snow. He reached to catch me but my momentum dragged him down, and we ended up seated on the ground together.

I laughed and rubbed my hips, the netted bustle doing little to ease the pain. A gust of wind caught several tendrils of hair, tugged loose from my braid by our dancing, and lifted them across my forehead, half blinding me.

Lord Thornton removed my off-kilter hat and pitched it to the bench opposite the one holding his cane and cap. The moment had taken a serious turn. I watched him from behind the golden screen of my hair, afraid to move. Afraid to even breathe.

I didn't wish to break the spell or risk losing the expression on his face—the same one he exhibited at the garden—troubled enchantment, head tilted to the side like a tamed wolf trying to make sense of its master's desires.

I paid no mind that we sat alone and unsupervised in the wilds of a forest.

I clenched my hands within my cloak, feeling anticipation more than fear. Clamping a gloved finger in his teeth, Lord Thornton unsheathed one hand and, with as much care as he took tending my wound days before, his fingertips gathered the hair stretched over my eyes and tucked it behind my ear.

His touch almost burned my half-frozen earlobe. Startled by the sensation, I sucked in a breath of icy air. This brought him to focus on my mouth with those irises of shade and ice ... of liquid and smoke ... a paradox, so much like the man who owned them.

His lips moved then, such a slight flux I had to strain to read. "Sky-fallen angel."

The words made me think of Hawk, and pricked my conscience. But I didn't have time to wrestle guilt. The viscount's gloved hand cupped the braid at my nape and drew me close. His mouth stopped mere inches from mine—an excruciating restraint—and I tasted his scent.

Our breaths formed a cloud, enclosing us in our own world ... a world of mist, and wonder, and unexplored expectations.

Surprising me, he tilted my head down so his lips would brush my brow—a pressure so delicate it could have been the rasp of a butterfly's wing if not for his whiskers scraping me.

He kissed my eyelids, leaving each one tattooed with heat. Even when I opened my lashes, I still felt his mouth there—firm, yet so, so soft.

But it was an illusion, for his mouth was elsewhere, trailing my chin to my cheek. I made a startled sound—a lump that climbed my throat. His lips covered mine and swallowed the cry along with my breath. A prickly warmth replaced the air in my lungs as both of his hands tangled in my braid and slanted my head to deepen the kiss. My own hands opened haplessly beneath my cloak, unable to reach him for the cloth binding them.

He savored me, devoured me, gently sucking my lower lip into his sweet, hot mouth. Somewhere, in the darkest throes of my mind, I imagined that I was lying beneath him, twisting like wildfire, losing myself to his touch as the snow melted to puddles all around us.

The thought slapped me awake.

I jerked back. A string of spittle, sylphlike as spider's thread, joined us for an instant before breaking.

Motionless, he stared at me, lips shiny and swollen. His panting breath rose between us, shrouding us in white vapor.

"Forgive me." His dilated pupils showcased an intense state of arousal that mirrored my own. "It is ... this place. It's magic."

Magic. No question. I was nothing if not spellbound.

He stood and lifted me to my feet. Using his discarded glove, he slapped white powder from my cloak and skirt as if I were a mussed child in need of preening. I couldn't control my erratic breath, relieved yet disappointed that he hadn't sought to lay me out in the snow, to touch me in hungry, secret places.

I hated myself for the fantasy, for betraying Hawk, even if for a moment. Without him here to force my thoughts into seclusion, the desires I'd been suppressing broke loose, as if a thousand wind-blown leaves danced in my blood and skittered through my chest.

My host's jaw muscle twitched as he led me to sit at the bench where my hat waited. The feathered plume bowed in the chill breeze when he returned it to my head.

He knelt before me. "I used to come here as a boy." He gestured to the gazebo and slipped into his glove. "Alone, seeking solitude. I would lie on this very bench and look through the roof at the trees overhead. Then I would ask the wind questions of my future, and wait for her to answer through the rustling leaves."

His face opened on the childish rumination, an expression so rare and lovely I paused to admire him. "This gazebo was here so long ago? Did you not have it built after you acquired the land?"

"No. It's always been here. Though I carved the symbol on the entrance and added the fountains."

"So you came with your father? Merril? During your childhood? I thought he had just one job for Lord Larson. The one where he first met your mother, before you were born?" My stomach jittered to brook such an intimate subject. "Might I ask, how is it that he never ran across her again?"

The viscount's face closed to me then, as if I'd drawn the shutters with my brazenness. He pressed a fist to his lips and I scolded myself, remembering how sweet and tender they felt upon mine. How could I have used my mouth for so insensitive a question?

He dropped his hand. "My father received a letter of Gitana's death from Aunt Bitti upon my mother's passing. Lord Larson commissioned him for a project thereafter. My father's talents as a clockmaker were becoming well-renowned, and he was in high demand. Larson had a special request. He wanted a geometric clock to set upon the turret of his country house—wanted it to be the first of its kind, the largest one in all of England; he was willing to pay Father ten times what he made on his mantle clocks in a year. So we came throughout my youth to work upon it. Larson invited us only in the fall. Made it easier for my father to agree to it, as he knew the gypsies mined only in spring and summer, and he couldn't bear to see them—to be reminded of her."

I fought the tears burning my eyes. "You mean to say, you and your father missed Chaine by a mere turn of the season ... year after year after year?" The profound tragedy pierced my heart. Hawk would be devastated.

I could never tell him.

The shadows had returned to the viscount's eyes tenfold, so intense and dark they seemed to bleed from his pupils and infiltrate his irises. He took a place beside me on the bench, propped his elbows on his knees, and looked up into the sky.

We sat silent for a while, as I couldn't bear to hurt him anymore than I already had with my questions. He harbored such obvious guilt for Hawk's mistreatment. But try as I might, I had too many other questions that would not be contained.

"How did you ever find your brother?"

Lord Thornton faced me. "Our aunt. She confessed everything to Chaine after they escaped Tobar. Chaine was fourteen then. He spent the next five years searching for us with only our surname to go by. Unfortunately, we were abroad for some time for Father's health. But finally, Chaine found us ... just after Father and I settled at an inn in Worthington."

I leaned forward, filled with hope. "So ... Chaine and Merril met before his mind went lapse?" I thrilled at the thought of having something positive to relay to Hawk.

Jaw clenched, the viscount skated a finger along his thigh then let it drop to the bench between us so he could etch something in the dust of snow. I couldn't watch his doodling for fear I'd miss the answer to my question.

"No. I met Chaine first, and was so shocked upon seeing him—upon our likenesses—we both worried how it would affect Father, for he had already begun to slip. My brother and I spent half a year getting to know one another in secret. I helped him refine his English and learn the ways of nobility, and he taught me Romani and how to read the lines of an open hand. By the seventh month, we came up with a plan to give Father the news. Together, we painted the portrait of mother hung upon the wall in your chamber—I filled in the colors, and Chaine used his memory for the lines, since I had never seen her. Then we brought the portrait up to Father's room in the inn, to give him the gift from both of us. But Father's vision and mind were already too frail. He at first thought the portrait was Gitana's ghost, sitting before him. Then to see Chaine and me standing side by side next to it, he assumed the oddities a result of his failing eyes. Our voices, speaking to him simultaneously, well ... it merely confused him more. He was convinced he was seeing double. He couldn't grasp it. So, to keep from upsetting him, we hid the portrait and visited him one at a time from that day on. We allowed him to think we were the same man."

The heaviness in my chest sucked the breath from me. "So ... he never accepted he had another son?" I worded my question with care so the viscount wouldn't know I had overheard the conversation in the sanatorium.

"Only by making up a fantasy in his head ... that he had married Gitana and they had two boys. Me, and a younger one. A baby he had never seen. In his delusional world, Gitana and he were married for years. She broke their vows while pregnant with their second son, and went back to Tobar, leaving Father heartsick for his child. A child he wants me to find."

I swiped away tears with my glove. Now Merril's erratic rants made perfect sense. Why he called Gitana a whore ... why he thought she would come back to him to reunite their family. Poor, confused old man. I wished to ask Lord Thornton why he didn't sing to his father anymore, as it seemed it might make Merril happy. But I could never explain how I knew such a conversation had taken place.

Lord Thornton stopped drawing in the snow and caught my hand as I brought it away from my eyes. "Thank you for your compassion. I apologize for Father's behavior the other afternoon. You need never go with me to see him again. I know how unsettling it must be for a lady, to visit a place like that."

"But I should like to go with you again."

His lips parted slightly, as if awed by my words. "Truly?"

I squeezed his hand. "Yes. I very much like your father. And I like spending time with you ... no matter where we are." I smiled at the confession. At last I could admit how fond I'd grown of his company over the past few days.

The man seated beside me was generous to his servants, a caring and responsible son to his father, a kind and witty friend to my uncle, and attentive to me. Even when busy with Manor or money matters, he always made time to take me on a pleasant walk through the gardens, or sit with me in the drawing room as I stitched a hat, or visit my boutique and help with the placement of our merchandise. Not to mention his wit and often profound insights. For the life of me, I could not see this great flaw of his—the erratic temper.

The viscount nudged his knee against mine to recoup my attention. I glanced up at him.

"I'm not sure what's to become of Father now." He studied our entwined fingers. "He appears to be getting worse."

I'd seen the look he gave the nurse when the old man

spoke of the "other" guest. Guilt resonated within me, a gnawing desire to tell Lord Thornton his father had indeed sensed someone there. That he wasn't crazier than they thought. But I had no proof; and I would do nothing but risk losing Lord Thornton's faith in my own sanity, unless I could convince Hawk to reveal himself to his brother. Perhaps their gypsy aunt would help me, if I could garner a moment with her.

I curled my fingers tighter around the viscount's hand, tried to gather the courage to ask him why his aunt was here and if had to do with Larson, when he stood abruptly. "I think I hear Enya approaching."

He limped to the other side of the gazebo and gathered his cane, dropping his hat to his head. Then he held out an open palm. "Even if I'm mistaken, we should seek her out. She mustn't go beyond the walls of the Manor. The horses all know their way, even in the forest. But just on the other side of that rise ..." He pointed to a hill in the distance covered with fir trees. "There are decaying mines and hidden springs she might fall into."

I thought upon Hawk's fallen corpse somewhere out there, alone and abandoned, and my heart ached.

As we started away from the bench, my hand in Lord Thornton's, I glanced over my shoulder once more to imprint the image of the gazebo in my mind, so I might never forget my first tangible kiss—flesh to flesh.

From the corner of my eye, I caught sight of the picture the viscount had etched in the snow on the seat, drawn with precision and mastery.

It was a bird with a broken wing.

CHAPTER 29

Truth is the safest lie.
Jewish Proverb

"You are sure a sound came from up there?"

I stood on my bed in my chambers—half-dressed in my sleeveless chemise and pantlets—staring at the domed ceiling alongside Hawk. Once more, my ghost was insistent that the townhouse had an attic. I still thought it impossible, due to the shape of the plaster above us.

His eyes grew round and he pointed toward his mother's painting. "I hear it again. Over there this time. Almost as if it's in the wall." Sunset had fallen, and being on the east side of the house, my room grew dark. To compensate, the servants always had a fire burning in my fireplace by mid-afternoon.

The flames reflected along the walls and Gitana's image in shimmering slices of light. My attention caught on the symbol camouflaged in the portrait's background. The symbol it shared with the gate. I rubbed the locket beneath my chemise's low ruffled neck, considering what the viscount had told me of the rune's meaning.

An entrance to another world.

Hawk frowned at me from our perch atop my bed.

"Why did you not tell me he said that?"

"You were too busy throwing a tantrum over the kiss."

Cursing at the reminder, Hawk drifted off the mattress and stationed himself at the portrait, waiting for me to join him.

When we had first returned from horseback riding, Enya came upstairs to help me freshen up and dress for lunch. During the meal, Lord Thornton apprised me we would take supper with the investors in the evening so he might make introductions. Until then, he suggested I spend the afternoon resting in my chambers.

I had undressed and laid my gown aside to keep it fresh for another wearing, but instead of resting, spent my solitude with Hawk, relaying all I'd learned at the gazebo. Everything slipped out ... even those things I feared would hurt him most. Yet his grief over lost moments with his brother and father during his childhood paled when my mind tripped across Lord Thornton and me dancing. Hawk's temper had burst asunder upon realizing we'd been unchaperoned and shared a kiss.

He had leapt onto my bed and stirred all the pillows into a frenzied tornado. Two came within inches of the fireplace, nigh bursting into flames. One hit Hawk's flower. Thankfully, I'd locked it within its new terrarium, so it was unscathed.

I stepped over the pillow pile to join him beside the portrait, at a loss. "Why is it," I asked, "that I can't stay on the good side of one of you without offending the sensitivities of the other? Are twins always so competitive?"

Hawk glared at me. "How would I know, Juliet? I remember none of it. I respect the way he cares for Father, and the way he runs this estate. But that doesn't mean I'm going to stand back and watch him seduce you. One wink of his lashes and you become a puddle of wantonness at his feet."

I ran my hands along the right side of the frame to redirect the anger rising to rosy-hot swirls along my cheeks. "Oh, how I wish you were flesh."

Hawk's head dipped down, so close his breath would have singed the shell of my ear. "You do, aye? So you could stop using him as a substitute? So you could kiss me instead?"

"So I might slap your arrogant face."

Hawk's chin set to iron, and I worried he was about to unleash another room-rocking tantrum, when my fingers passed the left side of the frame where curved, metal ridges met the wall. I gasped.

"What?" he asked.

I blindly ran my fingertips across it again. "It ... it feels like hinges."

Our gazes met and all of his jealousy melted away. "A door. *Brilliant*, dear brother."

It impressed me as well. Such a cunning ruse. The burnished frame curved out so wide it hid this anomaly from the wary eye. Only by feeling behind could someone find it.

"So ..." Hawk backed up, expectant. "Where there's a hinge, there's an opening. Search for a latch on the right side. What are you waiting for?"

My heart knocked in my chest. *What was I waiting for*? Acknowledgement that all of this time, my chambers and privacy had been at the mercy of an old woman on the other side of a hidden doorway. I didn't want to face such a truth. Everything I'd experienced with Lord Thornton today—the admiration and trust he stirred in me, my ever growing fondness of him—it all grew ugly and withered in light of such a secret.

To think he would allow his aunt to spy upon me ...

Hawk clucked his tongue. "Are you listening to yourself? Do you forget how you spied upon her? Stole from her. From him as well?"

My cheeks flamed. "Under your advisement! Every dour turn my morality has taken has been by your urging. You were my mentor in sin and skullduggery."

He grinned, a teasing lilt to his brow. "And an excellent student you've been." His gaze ran from my sleeveless chemise to my pantlets, reminding me of our many moments of sensual play. "Come now, China Rose. All is fair in love and war. I love you to the point of pain ... and though it is at war with your nature, you've proven yourself a fine accomplice in the arts of pleasure and plundering. Some part of you must like it, to be so adept at it."

With his dark, unruly hair ... his open shirt and furred chest ... with the smug gleam blinking out at me from sable lashed eyes ... he looked like the devil himself. I had to admit, I did like it. I liked it more than was good for me.

I flushed and glanced down at the floor.

"Ah, just once, to see that blush in the full glory of

color," he whispered. His fingers rippled the ruffle at my décolleté. "My brother has no idea how fortunate he is."

Envy pocked the statement, and that familiar twinge I despised gnawed inside my belly. Unrequited, unanswerable desire for the boy who had saved me in the mines. For the man who had sought me till the day he died.

Before my despair could get the better of me, I ran my hand along the frame's right side, nudging my fingertips into the space where it met the wall. I dug deep until a cold, metal clasp met my fingers about midway down. Pressing on it, I felt a click. The frame jerked out and slapped my leg, unable to fully open for my body.

"Move over," Hawk pressed, but I stood firm, one hand banked on the wall.

A stench drifted through the cracked door—a combination of musk and old cabbage—carried in by a cold gush of air that stroked my upswept hair like a demon's caress. Chill bumps raised across my underdressed flesh.

My pulse rocked at the base of my neck. Opening the door a smidge wider to spread some light upon the surroundings, I peered within. A stone staircase wound in circular ascension, disappearing as it rounded the domed obstruction of my room's ceiling. Hawk had been right all along. The staircase led to a fourth floor on the other side of my chamber, in the part of the house where the ceilings became level.

I swallowed at the lump in my throat. "I should get dressed first."

"No time," Hawk answered. "Enya will be back soon to help you prepare for supper. I'll take the lead, assure no one is there."

I bit my lip and opened the door as wide as the frame would allow. "It's quite dark."

Of all the dreams I'd had of the afterlife, nothing compared to this. I sensed something foreboding about this darkness and the secrets it hid. Beyond even death. Something monumental waiting to be overturned, that could alter my world forever.

Hawk swept around me and stood on the first step, slathering the wall and stone with his soft, greenish glow. "I will be your light, China Rose."

Staring at the winding steps, I craved the soothing comfort of contact, like when Lord Thornton took my hand in his.

Sadness bridged my and Hawk's gazes. "I would give anything to hold your hand," he murmured. "But you're brave. And I'm here, in spirit."

I took the first step, my bared feet chilled by the stone's iciness. Each step grew easier. In short time, I found myself at the top of the flight with my ghost, standing outside a closed door. To keep myself from fleeing back down the stairs, I forced my hand to grasp the knob and turn it.

"It's unlocked," I said to my accomplice with surprise.

On Hawk's instruction, I cracked it ajar first. He slipped inside and I watched through the slight opening as he drifted around the room to assure no one hid within.

"No one's here. Come in."

The door creaked, a stutter lost on my deaf ears that rushed through my palm. As I stepped in, a glut of spices accosted my nostrils along with the scent of dog.

The windowless room was cool but not cold, and larger than I had envisioned. It appeared to take up the ceiling space of two chambers. Another door sat diagonal from where I stood. Though closed, I suspected it led to a stairway and the grounds outside.

"Do you recognize these?" Hawk stood beside two trunks, lending soft light to our surroundings.

I nodded, running a finger along the trunks from his Aunt Bitti's tent in the forest. Her pots and dishes littered the floor in one corner, along with her knife and three spoons made of bone. At another corner, her thin mattress waited, covered with the hand woven rug.

She even had the shallow three-legged iron pot, and judging by the coke within, used it as a fireplace still, just as in her tent. Why would Lord Thornton force her to live up here in such sparse conditions, when he lived below like a king?

"Not that I should wish to defend him in your eyes"— Hawk stood at the opposite wall where Bitti had piled her books—"but I imagine she *chooses* to live like this. She's accustomed to moving constantly. For anyplace to feel too much like a home would be an aversion to her lifestyle."

Hawk's explanation rang true to the man I had come to believe Lord Thornton was.

Upon a table in the room's midst, I found an opened book written in the gypsy tongue, and a small wooden box. I called Hawk over to translate the pages as I worked off the box's lid.

"It's some sort of summoning spell," he said of the script. "For a fallen spirit tied to the earth." He paused, his voice wavering. "A spirit which cannot leave."

Right at that moment, the lid popped off the box. I looked within to find the seven withered petals from Hawk's flower, along with something crinkly pressed upon a paper, like snake skin yet transparent. Shuddering, I took a step back. "What is that?"

Hawk glanced at it, then at the book again. "A caul."

A sick knot twisted my stomach. From watching the birth of Enya's youngest brother, I knew of the filmy membrane sometimes covering a newborn's head. But why would anyone save it?

"It says here," Hawk offered, "that the presence of a caul intact and unbroken upon a newborn babe is considered a sign the child will one day have wealth and power. By rubbing a sheet of paper across the baby's head and face, the caul is transferred, and upon drying, the paper is presented by a midwife to the mother as a sumadji."

Sumadji. That word had latched onto my vocabulary weeks ago when we explored the tent. So this caul was an heirloom, a keepsake.

"Yet so much more." Hawk's face held an arrested aura, as if he didn't believe his own findings. "It goes on to say that when a man dies with something yet unfinished, his spirit can be bound to the earth, so it can later be summoned up to speak or interact with those who are yet alive—so he might complete his task. One must bury the dead man's caul along with the seeds of a flower. When the flower blossoms, it shall inherit his spirit, thus holding the deceased in the world of the living."

"A ghost flower," I said. Feeling dizzy, I propped myself against the table. "She ... your aunt ... she is the one who kept you here? She enabled you to make contact with the living by using your caul. Why? All so you could find me to thank me? Surely there is more to this."

Hawk had no answer, and looked as nauseous and perplexed as I was.

I studied the box's contents again. Something was written in the corner of the caul's paper backing. Gingerly, I lifted it with my thumb and forefinger, holding it as close to my face as I dared. I scanned the word twice, unable to make out the script, then held it up so Hawk could see.

"Nicolae." His eyes widened. "Nicolae? The gypsy equivalent of *Nicolas*."

I took a trembling breath. "This caul belongs to your brother? To Lord Thornton? So why is it in a box with your petals?"

No sooner did I think this, than the door opposite us— the one leading to the grounds—opened slightly. I dropped the paper, startled as a silhouette crept within, low and stealthy.

"Juliet, get back!" Hawk's voice jostled me into movement.

I stumbled toward the wall to escape Naldi, her jagged teeth opening on a slobbery snarl. She rushed me toward the far corner, eyes aglow with icy light. I almost tripped over the pans as Hawk positioned himself between us, the one thing keeping her from attacking.

The door opened all the way to reveal the viscount and Aunt Bitti. Their lips moved in agitated calls to the wolf.

Ears lying back, the beast retired to the viscount's side. She settled next to him, not the old woman, and gazed up at Lord Thornton with her wolfish stare—a study of adoration a pet reserves for no one other than their master.

Her master.

Candlelight glazing his face, the viscount regarded me, his mouth clamped shut. Something other than anger sparked within the flames reflected in his eyes: *profound relief.*

It dawned on me that he didn't have his cane. He had taken the flight of stairs without it.

A flicker of revelation must have crossed my face, for I saw that he knew the exact moment when I realized who he was in truth ... when I realized he'd been lying to everyone all along.

My heart pounded against my sternum. I gasped for air. Dazed and overwhelmed, I turned for the door behind me, tottering the pans as I shuffled for the secret stairs leading back to my chamber.

CHAPTER 30

*In love, there is always one who kisses
and one who offers the cheek.
French Proverb*

Too shocked to follow my flight, Hawk stayed in the attic room with Bitti—numb and wrestling reality. Even he could not refute the many signs that had pointed to Lord Thornton's true identity all along; the idiosyncrasies we'd failed to acknowledge. It explained why Hawk knew all the parts of a watch, why he harbored memories of Merril reading to him in his childhood, and why his ailing father missed Nicolas's songs now—the melodies Hawk sang to me alone.

The viscount shut the door at the top of the staircase as he chased me, cutting off my contact with his brother. My ghost would be cast into the purgatory he hated—until I could bring him back with a new petal—fighting more than the demons of darkness. Now he had demons within himself.

My host entered my chamber behind me and closed the portrait as I whirled to face him. We stared at one another, winded from our race down the stairs. I felt utterly naked in my underthings, not only stripped of modesty, but of balance. With his true identity revealed, nothing stood us between us but shadows, flickering light, and a pile of pillows.

"Enya?" His lips formed the maid's name as his gaze ran the length of me from head to toe.

"Downstairs. Your limp?" My mind shook so fast I could think of nothing else to say.

The viscount's eyes darkened. "Never had one." He leaned a broad shoulder against the picture, looking vulnerable yet ominous—a pigeon with a serpent's bite.

I considered his raspberry breeches and the clashing purple shirt, at last understanding the flash of his clothes ... the black and white of his chambers. It wasn't a gypsy eccentricity. He had no concept of color, for he was color blind. The only thing that made sense as to the tasteful décor of the townhouse and castle, was to assume he had used his brother Hawk's—no, *Nicolas's*—architectural layouts, the plans Miss Abbot spoke of to Enya. He must have followed them to the letter when he stepped into Lord Thornton's life. Just as he marked his brother's headstone with his own nickname.

My host picked his way through mountains of pillows toward the door. He appraised my bed's messy covers on the way, no doubt assuming I'd been napping as he suggested.

Once he'd locked my latch, he centered his attention on me.

Feeling the room shrink two sizes, I stiffened. "You are not the architect."

"No. I am the artist."

Confusion lumped in my throat. "Everything you have told me is a lie."

"Not so." He cast a soulful glance to the beautiful portrait we'd just stepped through, then looked back at me to assure I could see his mouth. "Everything has been true. Told through my brother's eyes."

I swallowed. "Your reaction at the gravesite, your anger toward him?"

The viscount clenched his fists. "I never wanted to take his name. To live a nobleman's life. He didn't listen to me. Made a hasty decision and left me standing in the wake of his folly—alone without him once again. But I made a vow, to take care of our father. To build Nicolae's palace of dreams. It's imperative you keep my secret, and tell no one my aunt is here."

I struggled to frame my rattled thoughts. "Did you have anything to do with your brother's death?"

In contrast to his bright costume, the viscount drained of color. "Holy *Devla*, woman. Does your distrust know no bounds?"

Ashamed of the accusation, I framed a new question. "Did Larson kill Nicolas ... did he take your brother from you?"

As if avoiding a punch, my host flinched. "No. But his greed had a hand in it."

"Then who?"

He paused, studying his palms in the firelight. "Tobar."

I did not need to hear his voice. I could *feel* the repulsion snarling his lips upon his step-father's name. To think of all the things that monster had done to Chaine—

the man standing before me now—and then to have killed Nicolas as well? Rage simmered in my heart, softened only by my compassion for all Chaine had endured, both in his past and present.

Fire-sheen dusted the sculpted lines of his high-boned cheeks, glistened upon the turn of his auburn-tipped hair. His whiskered jaw clenched—a ravaged gypsy prince in a foreign land. All this time, I'd failed to notice how out of place he was ... until this very moment. But one thing I had noticed from the beginning—this man was an enigma. Even more so, now.

Gentle and steadfast, despite all of the torments of his childhood, as testified by how he cared for his family and staff, how he adored nature and animals. As testified by his loyalty to a girl he had not seen in thirteen years.

"So ... it is true? You were never after my estate?"

His expression tendered. "Lord no. I hated putting you through that. I'd found your interview in Larson's files years ago, long before I met your uncle ... long before he had me look for it. I knew it was you by the date. But there was no name, no town wherein you lived. For years, I traversed all of England, asking at local taverns if anyone knew of a child who had almost died in the Larson mines years earlier. Finally, I came to Claringwell, and someone directed me to you. The young, deaf milliner whose mother was ill. I couldn't come forward as myself, for by then I wore my brother's shoes. So I pretended to want to buy your estate to have a reason to see you."

For so long, he'd searched. Such devotion humbled me. It must have been so difficult for him not to confess the truth upon our meeting in my home. "The bird. The bird with the fractured wing. You drew it on the bench at the gazebo today. You were trying to tell me."

He nodded, a studious slant to his chin.

I should've known. So much like the sketches in the journal, and the ones in the writing desk of his chamber. My fingers clutched the puffy legs of my pantlets, twisting the cotton between them.

"I've wanted to tell you since the moment I saw you at the cemetery," he said, standing rigid in front of the door. He appeared distracted by my hands' activity.

I released my pantlets and laced my fingers in front of my waist.

He relaxed and propped his shoulder blades against the wall. "All these weeks, I waited for you to come. Then when you arrived, it was hell. Every day I walked in the shadow of my brother's sins, and you despised me for it. But I had to know you would accept me, no matter what my past entailed. I had to know I could trust you."

My mouth went dry. "So today you drew the bird ... as I'd finally made peace with your—Nicolas's—reputation."

"And now the lies shall end. At least between us."

I, too, wanted us to strive for the honesty lacking since that first day in Claringwell. Trembling, I made my way over to my trunk and fished out the journal with the stolen excerpts folded inside. I held it out.

He didn't budge—didn't even look surprised. "I don't mind that you took it. I had Aunt Bitti bury it in the grave for a reason. I wish to forget my past. All but one scene."

Our scene.

His hand raked through his hair, shoving long strands from his forehead. He penetrated my lingerie with his gaze of smoke.

From the corner of my eye, I glanced at Hawk's blossom. "And what of the flower?" I asked, defenseless beneath the intensity of his stare.

"Ah. Well, that I needed. Nicolae desired to come back. It was the last thing he said to me. It is why my aunt planted seeds with the caul, because he had something yet undone. But she's having no luck summoning him, even with the petals she gathered from your room. She believes you might have ... she believes ..."

"That his spirit has visited me?"

The viscount's jaw clenched. "She said you knew of the pocket watch he made for me, of the engraving upon the back. He had it with him when he died."

Of course. That had to be why it didn't disappear with Hawk's clothes when he dropped it our first night. Because it never belonged to him as the other things had.

My host's countenance softened. "It was his gift to me. To show me I had moved on from my past. To show me I controlled my future; that time was no longer my enemy."

This glimpse of their affection for one another made me hurt inside ... for all of their lost moments ... for the years they would never get back. More than anything, I wanted to give Chaine hope. Still, I couldn't bring myself to disclose everything. Not until I discussed it with Hawk. For now, a half-truth would have to suffice.

"Your brother *has* visited me. In dreams."

His face lit.

"Is this why you wanted to court me, why you invited me to stay at the Manor?" I asked. "So you would have access to the flower, to my thoughts?"

My host angled his head in a scolding gesture. "You know the reason."

"Yet I cannot fathom it."

"You were my"—he pounded his chest—"*desrobireja*. My emancipation from a life of slavery. You saved me from killing myself."

"I was just a blundering child ..."

"No. You were light and hope. An angel." A wrinkle formed between his brows. "Once upon a time, long, long ago, there was a young man who lived in a hole. He was the prince of mud and grime. The rats were his chancellors, the spiders his stewards, and the salamanders his jesters of rhyme."

Hand clasped to my mouth, I choked—memory surfacing at the words upon those lips. The beginning of the fairytale. The fairytale told to me in the mine so many years ago. Hawk had never been able to remember it. I hadn't either, until now.

I squeezed the journal and shivered as all the terror of the event came to dance upon my heart: plunging into a shaft that seemed to have no end; my shins and arms torn by jagged wood and tree branches; bugs and rats scraping me with their claws and spindly legs. But the boy ... he broke my fall.

He brushed the vermin away, ministered to my wounds with soothing red mud. He worked leaves and pebbles from my hair and cooed to me, comforting and calm. When my crying ebbed, he made up a fairytale rhyme so I would not fear the creatures sharing the darkness with us.

From beneath my down-turned lashes, I caught my host's movement when he took a cautious step forward, as if trying not to frighten me. I watched his mouth recite the second verse, but had no need to read it. For I was back in my memory, sitting beside him in the tunnel, hearing his beautiful young voice.

"There the prince lived, alone and unkempt, with no one to tend to his hunger and stench. Until an angel fell from the sky. She combed out his tangles, mended his trousers, and fed him plums and gingerbread pie."

My legs shook, inconstant, like sheets fluttering on a line. I tried to steady them as he took another step.

"The finest of friends, they both came to be ... this spotless angel and the prince of debris. They renounced the word goodbye. They sewed suits for his chancellors, baked moths for his stewards, and gave the salamanders wings to fly."

I stood, rooted in place, unable to speak, tears banked behind my eyelids.

"Say something." His unexpected request knocked me off kilter. "I need to hear your voice."

He needed to hear *me*? He knew nothing of need ... nothing of how I longed to hear his voice, to know if it matched the pleading turn of his brow.

"Please, Juliet." He strode toward me, kicking pillows to clear a path.

I backed up to my chair and plopped down with the

journal clutched to my breasts. "*Chaine.*"

My breath froze as he dropped to my feet.

Jerking the book from my hands, he flung it away and clasped the chair on either side of my hips. "Thank you. Thank you for saving me."

Was I dreaming? My mud prince, the boy-hero from my childhood, knelt before me as a man—flesh and blood and bones—profound gratitude etched in every minute line of his face.

Without warning, his head buried in my lap.

As if it all came back to him in a crushing blow, he wept like a child—flaming tears that saturated the cotton and singed my thighs. I wove my hands through the hair at his nape, letting the length slide through my fingers in strands of silken chocolate. I suppressed my answering sobs. It was my turn now, to be strong. To cradle and comfort.

In the absence of Hawk's presence, a profound silence roared in my ears, a lovely silence that spoke of forsaken dreams recovered, of lost moments recaptured, of a broken boy stepping up to reclaim his manhood. A silence not to be abhorred, but to be honored.

Time wrapped around us, a cocoon of minutes and seconds binding our emotions in a symbiotic exchange. His lips mimed indecipherable words against my lap, his breath heated my thighs—intimate, fragile sensations.

I lifted his head and placed my palms on his wet cheeks. He slid his fingers up my ribs over my chemise, a slow skim along the outside of my breasts which made my lips part in a tortured gasp. When he reached the nape of my neck, he drew out the pins holding my hair until it fell in a golden rush around my shoulders.

He mouthed the word, "beautiful," with such conviction, I believed it was true.

Leaning forward, he nuzzled my hair. His breath sent a shimmer of sensation through my neck and into my stomach. His abdomen—a firm press at my knees—grew corded and tense as he drew back so our noses touched and our breaths mingled.

His lips took mine—no longer cautious, but a confident, languorous pressure that awakened my body. Sampling the outline of my mouth with his tongue, he left me writhing in anguish beneath a tease of whiskers. Then sweet union again in a kiss—tangible, delicious, real.

I couldn't hear his passion, but I felt it. In the moan at his chest where my hand sought his heartbeat, in the shift to insistent exploration as he nudged his tongue to break the seal of my lips. I allowed him passage, allowed him to fill me.

I became drunk with it—the slickness of his teeth and tongue, the taste of salted tears and almond liquor. So drunk, I might've imagined his hand moving down ... down toward my neck ... across my décolleté.

I sobbed into his mouth in anticipation.

Answering my need, his palm cupped my right breast over the cotton—full contact—thumb skimming a slow circle. I arched into the resistance that met me—this man, this body afire and unyielding, meeting my every demand with acute proficiency.

I broke our kiss to catch a breath. While he nuzzled my

head, I let my mouth wander to his throat and tasted the roll of his growl with my lips.

My nose nestled in his soapy-scented hair as his kisses followed my temple, my jaw, then my necklace's chain, his beard tickling my skin on the descent. Reaching my chest, his tongue plunged beneath my chemise's neck and grazed the taut tip of one breast with velvet-heat. I cried out.

He drew back, assuring I could see him speak. "We must be quiet."

The wet fabric clung to my skin with a chill that tightened the tip of my breast—a hurt so deep it was pleasure. As if sensing my torment, he stared at his own hand as it tugged at the chemise's blousy neck in an effort to free my flesh.

Shyness overtook and I clasped his palm against the swell.

He restrained himself, a struggle taking place behind his eyes. "I don't mean to rush you." His lips trembled. "I've searched so long for my little fallen angel. Then to find her all grown up—an alluring, intelligent, brave young woman. I'm overcome by the grace of it all."

Then I remembered how he'd waited for me. Taken no other lover in his life. That this was all new to him, too.

The epiphany fanned a fire I could not contain—a smoldering blaze that laid waste any residual sense of virtue. I became the seductress: my fingertips tangled in the dark furring at his chest, skated past the coppery beads of his nipples, then raked through the trail of hair on his rippled abdomen. As I moved, he released the fastenings of his shirt to accommodate my curiosity, rapt and patient while I explored the wonder of our differences.

But his face opened to predatory delight once I stopped at the waist of his trousers. He dragged his shirt tails free, and with a flick of his wrists, sent the purple silk drifting to the floor, abandoned and unnecessary, like the lies that once stood between us.

His bared upper torso caught the firelight, each line gilded with golden flame and minute beads of sweat, taut with animal arousal. In poignant contrast, moisture streaked his cheeks, a marriage of both our tears where our faces earlier touched.

The sense of enormity overwhelmed me ... of where we would go from here ... of the changes his true identity would precipitate. Our joining would be so much more than lust. It healed me, this acknowledgement of my feelings for him, inasmuch as it cut me to bleed. For somewhere within my heart, Hawk still had residence as well.

This thought gouged behind my sternum and made my breath so shallow I grew light-headed.

Chaine lifted me into his arms. I held his nape with one hand as he stole another kiss, gliding my fingertips along his shadowed jaw. He stepped over pillows on the way to my bed then eased me down—the covers wrinkled and lumpy beneath me, my hair spanned across the blankets. His weight pressed me into the mattress, his body fitted to my curves perfectly—heat and hard potency penetrating the sparse fabrics between us.

As if fearing he was too heavy, he positioned himself

half on and off, his thigh wedged within the center of my pantlets, heavy against the part of me that ached for him. Propped on his elbows, he twirled his fingers through my hair and stared into my eyes, both of us panting.

"Marry me," he said. Simply and beautifully.

I caressed his bare back and his muscles answered with tiny twitches. I burned to say yes, to let him inside, to give him forever. But I could not forget his brother.

Chaine sensed my hesitation. "What stands between us still? This man ... my rival?"

Perceptive, as always. "It is so much more complicated than you can imagine."

"No." Chaine kissed me, a sweet and gentle bribe. He said something unreadable against my lips then drew back and repeated the words in my line of sight. "We belong together. I'll not allow him to touch you."

"You need never worry of that." My heart pinched. "It is impossible."

Perplexed, he studied my face for answers, fingernails grazing my scalp, a delicate abrasion that tingled and taunted. Tears blurred my vision as I studied his face in the firelight, his lips swollen and moist, his expression arrested between desire and worry. In my haste to *feel* ... I had complicated everything.

I wriggled out from under him and scooted to the bed's edge. Chaine stood with me.

The back of his fingers whispered across my cheek and jaw, drying the tears.

"I'm to blame for all of this," I muttered.

"Blame? There's no blame here. My feelings for you.

Yours for me. They're guileless and pure. The only things decent and true in my life." His attention flicked toward my chamber door. "The ladies are returning to their rooms." He straightened my chemise. The ruffles clung to my skin, still wet from his tongue. "No doubt to prepare for supper." His fingertip traced the outer curve of my breast over the fabric, as if he couldn't resist touching me again.

I bit my lip as tendrils of heated pleasure shot through my sternum and swarmed my belly, then lower. Raking a hand through the dark trail of hair along his abdomen, I struggled to compose myself. We could not afford to get sidetracked. "Your shirt." We both glanced around, but it was lost somewhere beneath the piles of pillows. My pulse's racing rhythm shifted from arousal to worry. "If Enya finds you here half naked—"

"We could wrap me in the curtains; say you were teaching me how to dust." He gestured to my French doors and winked.

I smothered a giddy, panicked snort.

Grinning, he tweaked my nose. "I'll leave the way I came. I can find something to wear in my aunt's room." He captured both my palms and nuzzled my knuckles with soft lips as he walked backwards, leading me toward Gitana's portrait through the path in the pillows.

He lifted his face. "I want you, Juliet."

I had to force my gaze away from his naked chest to read the words.

"I want to be more than your companion. I want to be your confidante, your lover. Your husband. I want to hold you with nothing between us. But there is much to be explained. Things you need to understand. That I need to understand. Tonight, after supper, we shall tour the star tower. It will be private, as I've yet to open it to the public. There, we'll settle everything."

He wrapped my loose hair around his wrists and drew me close, kissing my forehead. Then he released me. My hair dropped to my waist, all but some static-filled strands which reached toward him, as if grieving his departure.

Looking back once, he stepped within the portrait door and vanished into the darkness—leaving his shirt behind, but taking one half of my heart with him.

CHAPTER 31

Stars are not seen by sunshine.
Spanish Proverb

I didn't have time to reach out to Hawk before Enya came in to help me prepare for supper. She accepted that my chemise was damp from a spill I made while trying to water Hawk's flower. After I was ready, she ducked into her room to tend herself. I plucked a petal, gloom-struck upon noting that only seven remained upon the flower.

Hawk reappeared in that moment, quiet and somber. His despair went much deeper than concern over the plant's failure to bud. He had accepted he was Nicolas. I could read the resignation and shame in his eyes.

"You have nothing to be ashamed of," I assured him, seated upon my bed as I struggled to contain my own spinning thoughts and chaotic emotions.

Hawk strode to the window and looked out at the dimming sky. "I am the very pig I accused my brother of being. We both saw it, didn't we? But neither of us could admit it. My evolving tendencies toward jealous outbursts alone were indicative of a past temper."

I clenched my jaw, frustrated by his inability to see the goodness in himself. "But there is light in you, as well.

Your talent for architecture. Your beautiful gift of song. It's *your* voice your father has been missing all these years."

Hawk turned to me, a glimmer of tenderness in his eyes—though it was fleeting. "I could've spared us all of this. If only I'd thought just once to look." He drew off the boot from his right leg carefully; not all the way, only enough to show me a glaring malformation of bone beneath his ghostly skin before pulling the footwear back into place. "My lack of a limp is no different than my lack of appetite or sense of smell. I'm no longer tied to the same physical laws as those who live. My 'memory' of finding you in the tunnel, my knowledge of the gypsy tongue ... they were imprinted upon my mind by the journal entries and exchanges Chaine and I shared during our short acquaintance. And as for being color blind myself, it must be a veil dropped across my eyes as a result of my death. Fitting, how I'm experiencing the loss my brother does on a daily basis." The regret and remorse in his expression deepened with each word he spoke. "I suspect karma had a hand in that. Penance for all the times I used a woman, hurt a fellow man, or shamed my father."

The fading outdoor light stretched through the prismatic glass and painted a hazy rainbow across the floor between us. "Hawk, none of this changes the way I feel about you."

He bowed his head. "It should. Since I've been the rogue brother all along, I have no claim on your heart or your innocence. Chaine is the only one worthy of such things."

His surrender shattered within me. I would have been stunned by such humility, had he not walked in his brother's shoes for all of these past weeks. Had he not lived Chaine's abuse and torments vicariously through pages of a journal he believed to be his. His resignation stemmed from guilt for his brother's broken past, compounded by the impossibility of a pairing between the living and the dead.

An impossibility which had eaten away at my own soul for weeks.

Sharing my affections with two men was bad enough. But for one to be on another plane entirely ... to be forced to watch each and every move his rival made and not have a chance to compete physically, it was agonizing. An agony which oozed like venom from Hawk's phantom heart to mine, striking dead any hope of a happy ending.

Enya returned to the room before I could respond to Hawk's self-castigation, and Uncle arrived thereafter to lead us to supper. I accompanied them both, although I had no appetite. Like Hawk, I no longer desired food or drink. It appeared at last I had managed to become a ghost myself.

After we dined with the investors, Chaine led me, Enya, and Uncle to the star tower. It was more magical than I ever imagined. Hand-wired strings of gas-powered miniature blue light bulbs wound around pillars and were linked by lattice-work like incandescent grape vines.

Beneath our feet, an inlay of black marble—swept clear

of snow—reflected the stars from the open night-sky overhead like the smoothest pond in a midnight meadow. Tucked within tube-shaped iron vases, fresh cut sprigs of lavender and mint perfumed the air and added to the fantasy aura.

The walls rose at least eight feet high, with small, square openings cut into the stone to coax a refreshing breeze throughout. Using them, one could look down upon the Manor grounds safely without fear of falling. The turret spanned eighty feet. For privacy, canopied niches were set up in intervals against the wall, each containing a cushioned settee and two chairs, along with stacks of furs to combat the chill.

At the midst of the tower, the telescopes and refractors tilted up to the open sky, offering a view of the stars.

The viscount ... *Chaine* ... had outdone himself with the design. Or was it Hawk's original creation?

My ghost had no answer as I settled upon a cushioned settee with Enya, while Chaine and Uncle took the opposing chairs. All evening, Hawk had been forced to watch my feelings for his brother continue to manifest, however I tried to hide them. Hawk couldn't miss my blush when his brother and I exchanged glances during supper. Or that the viscount sought any reason to touch me: knees bumping beneath the table; hands searching out the same silver spoon to stir our soup; elbows turned out just enough to graze the fabric of our sleeves.

Now, my ghost stood by a square opening in the tower's wall, gazing out: a graceful silhouette of blue echoing the twinkle of lights around him. It was so unsettling, to see him defeated ... no jealous remarks, not even a frustrated scowl.

Hearing my thoughts, Hawk turned and leaned against the wall as he met my gaze. So engrossed in watching him, I didn't even attempt to read the conversation taking place between my living companions. My eyes blurred with tears and I cursed this day. I cursed this night. Along with everything that had led to this torturous predicament. More than anything, I craved Mama's presence. I longed for her advice.

My thoughts scattered when Uncle leaned forward to get my attention. Hawk turned his back again. Slanting my face out of the light, I dabbed my tears with a lacy cuff before Uncle could see them.

I studied his lips, grateful for the lantern that hung from a hook in the canopy overhead. As always, Chaine had been thinking of me when he brought the extra light, anticipating my need for illumination.

"You made me proud tonight, tiny sparrow," Uncle said while smiling. "The way you charmed the investor's wives before supper. I watched from across the room ... they were riveted to your every word. What were you speaking of? Your hats?"

A wry smirk turned my mouth. "The Rational Dress Society. No one of them had ever heard of fashion reformation. I decided to plant the seed and see what might blossom."

Uncle's grin widened. "And?"

"And it shall be interesting as to what sort of trappings line the halls upon our welcome gala on Monday. The husbands are in for a brimming good shock."

I shifted my shoes beneath me, making waves in my seven petticoats. No new gowns had yet arrived from Worthington, and as the merino-wool was my most posh ensemble, I had been forced to wear it again tonight for our visitors. I would also have to wear it on the morrow, too, as everyone planned a trip into Worthington for Sunday worship at a local parish. I dreaded it. My legs already ached from the climb up the stairs.

"And what did Lord Thornton think of your brass with his guests?" Uncle asked, his hand on mine to recoup my focus.

Chaine and Enya were discussing the constellations. Chaine pointed to the sky with his cane, but I didn't miss his sidelong glance my way.

"He seemed ... pleased." Chaine had in fact encouraged it—stood by my side with an amused smirk stirring his whiskers at the ladies' enthralled expressions. I couldn't deny his presence and support had given me the courage to attempt such a connection. The ladies turned out to be more personable and receptive than I ever anticipated, and I no longer dreaded servicing the upper crust in my and Uncle's shop.

"I am not surprised," Uncle said. "The viscount lives only to make you happy."

I nodded, though secretly disagreed. The "viscount" lived for something more. I knew that now ... just as I knew his true identity. He had an ulterior motive for inviting Larson here. He'd been harboring revenge, and it was cold and ready to be dished upon a platter.

Tonight, I would learn of his plan, however dark and twisted it might be.

⸎

"I have something for you." Chaine sat beside me on the settee after Uncle and Enya strolled over to a telescope in search of Hydras—the water snake constellation. He sat as close as propriety allowed and pulled a cylinder of paper from his coat pocket.

I hesitated to take it. "You have yet to answer my question about Larson," I reminded him.

He pressed the paper into my hand. "Just, please. Look at it. I drew it for you."

Biting my cheek, I unrolled and flattened the sketch along my thigh to reveal a black and white rose—its petals drawn to such spiraling perfection I might have plucked one off and sniffed its perfume. A broken, bloody thorn marred the stem. So beautiful in its fragility, it took my breath.

I met my host's gaze. "You always see beyond the faults and capture the loveliness. Thank you for sharing your gift, Chaine."

Grinning like a schoolboy, he traced the sketch's lines along my thigh, his gloved finger penetrating the paper and my skirts, sending a dark coil of desire from my legs into my belly.

His eyes narrowed in the shimmer of the lantern. "Sweet *Devla*. This is torture. I want to take your hair down ... to touch you again." He was making it difficult to keep our earlier rendezvous in my chambers blotted from my mind, something Hawk shouldn't be forced to see over and over.

I rolled up the picture and Chaine took it, tucking the cylinder into my shawl's knot to keep the sketch safe.

"Might I have just a kiss?" He leaned closer. "'Tis all I could think of at supper. The wine held nothing to the flavor of you."

"A kiss would hardly be appropriate here," I stalled. "Considering our present company."

Chaine craned his head around the canopy's edge where my uncle and Enya stood out of earshot in the tower's midst, looking through a telescope. He drew his head back in. "They are lost in their own besotted world."

How to tell him I referred to his phantom brother? Outside, Hawk drifted aimlessly from one window to the next, feigning distraction. Seeing his shoulders hunched in despondency severed my insides like a razor. Bad enough he had to witness the romance Chaine rained upon me. I would not add to Hawk's emotional contraband by kissing his brother in front of him.

"You are trying to distract me." I steadied my gaze on Chaine and squeezed his hands to scold him.

He responded with a roguish half-smile. "You distracted me first, by stroking my hair."

"It was falling into your eyes."

"Like I'm falling into yours?"

I couldn't refrain from laughing. "Answer my question."

He inclined his head and smiled back. "For a lady of silence, you certainly cater to noise. Has anyone ever told you this?"

"Practically everyone who knows me." I linked our fingers. "Now, indulge me with an answer."

"Oh, it will be my pleasure to indulge you." He lifted my inner wrist to his mouth, breaking his other hand free to skim up to my elbow. He nuzzled me, his whiskers snagging on my lace gloves before assuring I could see his lips again. "Once we are married, proper and true, I will carry you up the stairs wrapped in nothing but furs, and indulge every facet of your beautiful body, here beneath the stars."

Despite the dark, hungry fire racing to my core, I managed to glower at him. "You are incorrigible."

Laughing, he turned me loose. "Not even one kiss?"

I pressed a finger to his lips. "Not even one word, lest it's in answer to why you invited Larson to the Manor's opening."

He took off his gloves and rested his elbows on his knees so the splay of light illuminated his entire face. "Larson invited himself, just as he assigned himself an investor. He knows my true identity. He's blackmailing me."

This caught Hawk's attention and he came to sit in a chair opposing us.

I regarded Chaine. "How did he find out?"

Chaine tensed. "I'm not sure. Before I won this estate from him in a card game, I learned that Larson ran a gaming hell in the *Swindler's Tavern*. He's the anonymous owner of the place. If I could prove that, and that he cheated dozens of noblemen out of their purses, I would have something to barter with."

Hawk and I both leaned forward, as if connected to his

words by a towline. "So the gambling room in the tavern—" I pressed.

"Was Larson's snake pit," Chaine answered. "During the gypsies' off seasons, Larson masqueraded as a customer and used my stepfather Tobar as the card dealer and ivory turner, pretending they didn't know one another. The gypsy could turn a hand or dice to Larson's favor at the drop of a wager. Only the most affluent customers were invited to partake in the games, and the wealthy idiots never had a chance. To keep Tobar quiet, Larson gave him a percentage of the winnings each time. Part of my and Nicolae's plan was to get proof of this, so we might always have a way to keep him in line."

"Do you know how to get the proof?" I asked the question given to me by Hawk.

"No. And I could use it now, more than ever. Should Larson come forward with my identity, I'll no longer own this place. My brother's name is on the deed."

"You should be wearing Nicolas's clothes," I said, worried. "And you should bide a stricter adherence to his way of living. You are casting suspicion on yourself through obvious discrepancies."

Loosening the crimson cravat at his neck, Chaine propped an arm over the settee's back, his hand just short of touching my shoulder. "I've been living this lie for eight years, and I've managed to fool everyone but Larson. People think me eccentric, with a touch of my father's madness. In the gypsy culture, it is bad luck to wear the clothes of the dead. So upon Nicolae's death, I had to have a new wardrobe, post haste. My aunt provided the fabrics. Then I hired Miss Hunny to sew styles befitting a viscount. And as to following his lifestyle ..." Chaine's wrist moved so his thumb and forefinger could pinch the shawl where it grazed my left breast. My flesh tingled in learned anticipation. "Would you have me romancing every woman I see? Or hold true to my heart, and desire only you?"

Hawk squirmed in his chair, either uncomfortable watching his brother's advances or shamed by his own repute as a whorehound. Either way, I knew by the twitch in his jaw—so much like Chaine's—that his emotions were set to kindle.

"Don't fret," Chaine said, reading the turmoil on my face. "I intend to put a stop to Larson's threats very soon."

I caught his hand. "Assure me you aren't to kill him."

His expression shifted from concern to malevolence in an instant. "That would be a most satisfying solution. But I can't abandon my father. Were I to be put in the pillory, all of this,"—his sweeping gesture encompassed the Manor and the grounds—"would fall to commonwealth. There would be no funds left to oversee my father's care at the sanatorium, and he would be sent to some bedlam within a fortnight. I'll not have him in a place like that ... thrown into a pit of lunatics and left to fend for himself." His jaw clenched. "No. This must be handled with cunning and foresight. And a measure of gypsy magic."

Gypsy magic.

I inhaled an icy breath. "That's why your aunt is here."

Chaine grinned. "Precisely. Larson has insisted on overseeing and approving every aspect of the Manor before it can be opened to the public. It is why the star tower is still closed to the guests who've begun to arrive. He has yet to endorse it. I've supported his idiosyncrasies, as this very arrogance has provided the leverage I need to silence him once and for all. Monday night, after the ball, I will take him into the dungeon."

My stomach shuddered as I glanced at Hawk. His suspicions had been right.

"I've a room prepared there," Chaine continued, oblivious to my silent exchange with his dead brother. "It's called the Museum of Oddities. The grim theme is slated to entertain the younger men who take sport in feeding their own fears. Larson must approve of it tomorrow night, so I might open it to the public. I shall take him on a tour, alone. Within the museum—alongside several circus-macabre attractions and torture devices to set the mood—will be a gypsy fortune teller who has a penchant for conjuring ghosts."

"*Ghosts?*" Blood rushed to my face. The night at the tavern, when the tigers spoke of the viscount's macabre fetishes, the blueprints I'd seen in his room ... all along, Chaine was setting the scene to trap the man who tormented him. It was never a dark indulgence, nor an exhibit. It was a brilliant ruse.

"Paranormal subterfuge," Hawk said in my mind.

I focused on his brother. "This is why you and your aunt wish to summon Nicolas. So he might help you scare Lord Larson to silence. Because that slug played a part in his death."

Chaine watched my reaction with interest. "The dead speak louder than the living, Juliet."

I coughed, a knee-jerk reaction to the profound truth behind those words. "You are using your brother's spirit in a game."

"Game? There is nothing frivolous about this. Nicolae left me with this mess. And he asked to come back, don't forget. I believe it may be the only way his spirit can be at peace and move on to the other side."

I glanced sideways at Hawk—his expression a jumble of worried lines. In all our time together, never once had he and I discussed what would happen should his purpose for remaining be fulfilled. Such considerations boded a finality neither of us wished to face.

Chaine caught my hand, centering my attention on him again. "You say Nicolae has visited your dreams. Is there something you know that can help us make him visible for just a few moments? That's all it would take. Is there anything we can—"

"Larson is on his way over!" Hawk interrupted and I reacted instantly—leaned forward and pressed my lips to Chaine's, silencing him before the investor could hear our discussion.

Chaine stiffened. Then his mouth curved to a smile beneath mine and his arms drew me against his willing male body. I clung to his shoulders. Just as his hand trailed upward over my back so his bared fingers could nestle into the hair pinned at my nape, the edge of the canopy lifted.

Chaine broke away, the glaze of interrupted passion clouding his eyes. Lord Larson's crow-like features lengthened to shadows in front of the blue lights. He winked at me. In a flurry of movement, Chaine shoved the man back and stepped outside the canopy—locked in a protective stance between us.

He gestured to Larson with his cane then turned back after the investor strode to the other end of the turret. Offering his palm, Chaine led me outside of the canopy. I shivered from the cool rush of wind and he tightened the shawl at my neck, assuring his sketch remained safe in the knot.

He frowned. "Wait for me. I wish to escort you back to the townhouse. And perchance visit you later tonight, as well? Through our secret doorway."

I nodded, but couldn't hide my concern.

"All will be well," Chaine assured me. He glanced toward my uncle and Enya. "Perhaps you might look at the constellations with your uncle, until I finish this ... business." His lip curled on the final word. Then his expression softened and he leaned forward to kiss my forehead, smoothing my hair as he would a child's.

Without my prompting, Hawk followed Chaine to keep me apprised of their conversation. I borrowed Uncle and Enya's telescope while Hawk relayed Chaine and Larson's words from across the other side, his voice loud and resonant in my mind.

"How dare you interrupt my time with Lady Emerline." Chaine's profile stood a full head taller than the bird-like investor. I slanted my telescope in their direction and turned the dial to adjust the lens so I could watch them. The visual, when combined with Hawk's narrative, made me feel as if I stood right next to them, eavesdropping on their hushed exchange.

"I wanted a tour of the tower. So here I am." Lord Larson turned his head to scan the surroundings. "I suppose it will suffice. You may open it tomorrow."

"*Sarp.*" Chaine clenched his cane so tight his knuckles whitened.

"What did you just say? Don't start with your gypsy gibberish again."

Chaine met the investor's gaze as he put on his gloves. "Snake. You, sir, are a snake. A scale-bellied, vermin-eating, icy-blooded reptile. Clear enough for you?"

Studying his fingernails in the blue light surrounding them, Lord Larson shook his shoulders on a laugh. "Ripe talk from a migrant tramp masquerading as a viscount. You'd do well to remember I have enough dirt in my shovel to bury you ... to bury you like you did your twin."

Upon this, Hawk glanced my direction. I watched my ghost through the telescope as he shook it off and resumed relaying the argument.

"Keep your voice down, pig." Chaine's profile snarled.

"Oh please. I'm whispering, for God's sake." The investor looked toward my uncle and Enya. "Who's to hear from such a distance? Are you worried the linen-draper and his niece's maid might tell your little deaf chit about your murderous ways?"

Chaine cast an anxious gaze to me and I tilted the telescope toward the sky. When I saw him turn his back to face the investor, I resumed my spying, swallowing a knot of trepidation.

"You are never to speak of her," Chaine said—a wall of corded muscle ready to spring. "Keep her the hell out of this."

"Me? I'm not the one who involved her. And on that note, there's been a bit of a change in my demands. I want the deed to this Manor back; a percentage is no longer acceptable now that you're planning to take a common wife and have heirs with her. I refuse to let my legacy fall to the tainted bloodlines of Thornton madness."

"Oh, you want the estate back do you? Now that I've made something out of it ... how convenient, that you waited all these years." Chaine threw down his cane, caught the man by both shoulders, and propelled him against the wall. "Shame I don't negotiate with snakes."

I gasped. Enya and Uncle came to stand beside me, curious as to the emotional conversation taking place in the distance. Uncle urged me to stop spying through the lens but I refused.

"Ahh. This scene is familiar." The investor clutched Chaine's wrists where his hands gripped his jacket. "Is this not the same hold you had on your brother just before you shoved him into that open mine shaft?"

Hawk's voice broke as he turned to me. Confused tears banked behind my eyelids, but I pressed my ghost to listen ... there had to be some explanation.

Chaine's back tensed to a powerful ripple of restraint as he dropped his hands from the investor.

Lord Larson straightened his jacket lapels. "Too bad you had a witness, aye?"

"A drunken witness."

"Not too drunk to know you and your brother switched places in that card game to fool me. I've never told you what tipped me off, have I? You limped on the wrong foot at one point. Caught yourself, you did, but not before I noticed."

Chaine clenched his hands to fists, silent.

"And I also know once you cheated me out of the deed with your gypsy trickery, you decided to cut your brother out, as well, so you could live his life without sharing the lucre. And don't even think of killing me. I've written it all on parchment and sealed it in an envelope along with my will. It sits in the office of my solicitor. Should anything happen to me, all will be read. Just after midnight it was ... ochre mine #34. Wouldn't be hard to find the bones in that shaft. All someone need do is pry back the boards on the opening and have a look. Soon as they find a skeleton with a deformed right foot, they'll be no question who you are. Too bad you're so afraid to go into that tunnel yourself—after all those years you spent there as that weasley little child—else you could have hidden the body away by now, aye?"

Hawk choked on the narrative, unable to speak another word. Through a blur of tears, I watched in disbelief, wanting it all to be a lie. Wanting to wake up in bed, victim to a cruel nightmare.

I eased back from the telescope, legs sluggish beneath me, as if I'd stepped into a sinkhole of mud. Larson hadn't mentioned Tobar being there. And Chaine hadn't denied the investor's accusations.

He'd lied. He did have a hand in the death of his brother.

My Hawk.

I sought out his ghostly face. He'd propped himself

against the wall, breath heaving, as if he couldn't grasp it. "It's true." Hawk's voice carried over to me. "I remember ..."

I sobbed. Tobar and Larson had succeeded in turning Chaine into a monster. He wore his kindness and gentleness as a mask. I should've known. No child could live through years of such torment and not lose humanity in the battle.

He had fooled me so easily. All his promises that he cared for me. Lies woven into pretty pictures.

Trembling, I plucked the sketch from my shawl and let it drop to my feet. I had fallen for him, thinking at last I'd found a man of flesh who could see beyond my faults and love me despite them. No ... that he could love me *because* of them.

When all along, he'd been using me to cover up a murder.

Across the way, Hawk rose behind Chaine, levitating. Lights gilded his silhouette—a phantom of fury and blue ice, ready to toss his brother over the wall.

Only my plea stopped him—silent cries in my head no one but Hawk could hear. As my hostile ghost moved to the stairway, I begged Uncle and Enya to take me back to the townhouse, feigning a headache.

Abandoning his fight with Larson, Chaine tried to intervene as we started to leave the tower, his cane in hand.

"I've a headache," I whispered, not even attempting to use my vocal cords.

"Then I shall walk with you—help you down the stairs."

I looked away from him, fearing he'd pull me into his

spell once more. "You left to play fisticuffs with your investor when you should've been seeing to my welfare. So go back to it." Petty and insolent. Yes. And there was no ignoring the doubt within Uncle's and Enya's faces. They knew me well enough to question such a tantrum.

However, Chaine didn't. Holding a fingertip to my chin, he coaxed me to look at his face. "Please, forgive me. Let me see you to your chamber at the least."

"I don't wish to see you again, *at all*." I made sure he caught the underlying message. With that, I shoved him aside and accompanied Uncle and Enya back to the townhouse, nursing the bloody stub that was once my heart.

CHAPTER 32

He that lives on hope will die fasting.
North American Proverb

When we first arrived in my bedchambers, Hawk was calm. Too calm.

He stood before the French doors, painted by moonlight, and the words rumbled from his throat, quiet and chilling. "Chaine and I had started to suspect Larson owned the tavern, so we took turns frequenting the place, to spy on his routines. He was a degenerate, shared my weakness for bourbon and card games, so we arranged for a private set at the tavern, to cheat him out of the deed for this land. Wasn't so hard to convince him. The mines were used up. The land was useless. For my ante, I told him I would finish the giant clock my father had never completed. I offered it to Larson, free of charge."

"The clock your father was working on when you were young?" I asked from my seat in the midst of the bed, fingers gripping my quilt. "The one at the top of the tower?"

"Yes. I never had any intention of paying up. I wanted that clock for myself. I felt no guile in the deception. Larson owed Chaine. Hell, he owed my family. All those

367

years, watching my brother being tortured summer after summer ... seeing me in my contentment during the seasons when the gypsies were absent. He could have told my father. It is impossible that he missed the similarities; we were mirror images of one another. I believe it's why Larson forbade any of his servants to mingle with the gypsies ... he wanted to keep the secret for his own. He liked having Tobar in his pocket."

The investor's cruelty gouged at my sternum. Just like Chaine had said in his journal entry and the note about his mother. Larson controlled the gypsies through their king, and used Tobar to trick the English gamblers out of their money.

"On the night of our plan's execution, Larson excluded Tobar from the private game. He couldn't risk the gypsy king recognizing his son. Perhaps Larson thought he had learned enough tricks from the Romani. He never considered my brother and I might have found one another. That we knew he secretly owned the tavern. Or that my brother would be sitting in my place during the card game. Gypsy tricks are useless against a gypsy. But what I never suspected, was that when it was all over ... when Chaine had trumped him ... he would throw me into the mines, so he could have it all to himself."

"Are you absolutely sure?" I asked on a trembling breath, still wanting to believe in my mud prince, even after all he'd done.

"Dammit, yes, Juliet! I remember that moment ... Chaine and I met at the witch tree, because of its significance to his past ... to you. I only see bits and pieces after that—but we were arguing. He clenched my lapels in his hands, shaking me, and next I knew, I was falling into the mine ... then everything crashed atop my head." Hawk's face contorted on a snarl. "I cannot believe I ever pitied him. He doesn't want the goods on Larson to save the estate and Father. He wants to save his own worthless neck. To silence the one witness to my murder!"

I sensed it on the verge: the eruption of emotions he'd been holding at bay. I buried my face in my hands, bracing myself. Given all he'd just learned of his brother's ruthless betrayal, I didn't try to stop him. I allowed his fury and frustration to run its course.

He roared and scattered things about. The brush, comb, and tray from the vanity ... the pillows from the bed ... papers and quill from the Secretaire. Even the inkwell. Splotches stained the salmon carpet in blots as black as nightmares, the musky scent overpowering the wilted lilies beside a fireplace now faded to embers.

Had I not wedged Chaine's discarded shirt between the bed's frame and mattress earlier, Hawk would have cast it on the embers to revive the flames.

My ghost clenched his hands in the hair at his temples. "Damn his lying tongue and petty gifts!" He kicked aside a basket of strawflowers and feathers. The contents erupted and drifted all around me—a snowfall of petals and plumes—several catching in my hair. I didn't bother cleaning them up. I was too miserable to care.

"First he steals my life ... then he steals my love and breaks her heart. I could kill him!" The venom in Hawk's voice burned my incompetent ears. I had no idea how far he'd carry this rampage. A flicker of conflict crossed his face as he considered the flower's terrarium—his brother's most treasured gift.

"Hawk, no ... its contents are priceless." A sob gathered in my chest. "Your time with me is too precious to squander in a moment of rage."

He met my gaze then glanced at the seven fragile petals locked safe within. Groaning, he turned aside and stared out the French doors.

I scooted to the bed's edge. "There are things that make no sense. Why would Chaine wish to bring you back if you could accuse him?"

"He only wants me to materialize before Larson, the one person who already knows. I doubt I even asked to be brought back at all. Chaine just told you that, to pacify you. He and Aunt Bitti are using me. Once the investor is terrified to silence, poof, they'll send me back to my purgatory forever."

Light shifted beneath my door from the hallway.

Hawk grimaced at the locked latch. "You still have an audience. Wretched lives of the living ... so bored with reality they must glean entertainment from other people's angst and turmoil." Silver moonlight gilded his panting silhouette. His hair was mussed, his teeth clenched, an excited glint to his eyes—a portrait of enraptured misery so beguiling yet terrible my breath stalled in my lungs.

"I'm glad to be dead. Do you hear me, Juliet? I'd rather be a rotting corpse than what they are ... vultures supping upon the bloodied carnage of another's raw emotions."

I shivered, for two of those vultures were my loved

ones. I had no doubt Enya and Uncle still stood on the other side of my door where I'd left them. By now half of the servants must be gathered, drawn by the outburst. Everyone assumed the viscount and I had a lover's quarrel. That *I* was destroying my room.

If only it could be as insignificant as that.

The moon sunk beneath a cloud outside my French doors, and the growing shadows brought unexpected serenity. Hawk studied his destructive wake while leaned against the portrait of Gitana, his face awash with change as sorrow rolled over him in a dark, silent wave.

His shoulders drooped. "You may let them in now. They're jiggling the latch. Given much longer, they'll send for Miss Abbot and the other key."

Hesitant, I scanned the room, but realized I was too tired to care. I cracked the door enough to invite Enya in, telling my uncle I loved him but needed a woman's company tonight.

He surrendered under the insistence I let him check on me first thing in the morning.

Locking the door behind her, Enya stepped around the mess and lit two candles in the sconces on the wall, casting an amber glow so she might survey the damage.

Before she could ask, I spoke. "Do you know of his lordship's tawdry past with women?"

Her cheeks grew rosy with embarrassment as she shook her head.

"He's taken many lovers. I don't believe I can ever trust him ..."

Hawk frowned at me, then understanding dawned and

he nodded in encouragement.

Pillows tucked beneath her arms, Enya dropped them two at a time on the bed. Her chin tightened. "That's what it was all about—in the tower? The investor, Larson. He told you of Lord Thornton's past and it started the fight?"

I suppressed the bitter smile threatening to break. I had become quite adept at leading people to conclusions. I was starting to feel a bit like a gypsy myself.

On that thought, I crouched to retrieve the comb and brush. My eyes clenched closed, images of Chaine's betrayal an earthquake within me. Even now, some part of me refused to believe his guilt, despite the crumbling foundation of my trust.

Enya came to my side and lifted my chin. "The past is in the past. Anyone can see he desires only you now."

I answered nothing, so Enya gathered the tray for me. Together, we arranged things on the vanity. Next, she dragged the chair over and bade me sit so she could work the feathers and flowers from my hair.

Upon finishing, she picked up the brush but I caught her wrist. "Leave the tangles for tomorrow."

Her gaze toured the room once more and I feared she would insist on cleaning before we retired. Instead, she helped me out of my clothes.

For once, my ghost refused to turn away. And much as I tried to turn my back to him, I couldn't. I hurt for him, for all he had learned of his identity, of his brother's part in his unbidden death. He needed a distraction.

So I faced him, as I had wanted to for so long but was never courageous enough. I stood before him, vulnerable in my nakedness—and let his eyes drink me in. All of me.

He hissed through his teeth and watched like a predator behind a cage. When Enya finally tugged my bed gown on, and the clean, crisp fabric fluttered around my ankles to cover me, he whispered the sweetest words: "Thank you, China Rose."

Enya retreated to her chambers after she tucked me into bed and blew out the candles. Hawk settled atop the covers, a comforting weight next to me—however insubstantial he was.

"I want to hold you." I couldn't stop the agonizing admission, or the tears slicked upon my cheeks.

He met my gaze. "And I you." His fingers furrowed the covers along my ribs.

I sighed. "What would you do? Were we to have one moment, here and now?"

His focus shifted to my hair where I struggled to free a strawflower Enya had missed.

"I would pull the petals from your hair, one by one, and bury my nose in the tangles left behind." He rolled to his back. "My father said you smell of gardenias and snow." His palm rested on his chest and a cynical smile trailed his lips. "I always loved the taste of snow. So pure."

I propped up on my elbow, the covers drawn to ripples beneath his indention. "Do you truly remember ... the flavor of winter?"

He crossed his arms behind his neck and closed his eyes. "Yes. I do."

"Is there anything else you recall? Anything happy?"

A pause.

"I remember loving him. I remember loving my brother."

I awoke at dawn, sunlight warm on my face, and opened my eyes to Hawk standing in front of the glass doors. I had to squint, his radiance almost blinding.

"I have doubts."

That was all he said. But it was more than enough to give me hope. During the night, I had awakened to find Hawk seated and staring outside, oblivious to me. Reaching between the mattress and bed frame, I withdrew Chaine's purple shirt and wrapped the silk around my gown to surround myself with his scent.

When I fell asleep again, I dreamt of wingless fireflies safe within fractured glass jars, and fields upon fields of wildflowers snapped at the stem and waving like rainbow-haired puppets in the wind.

Any man who could find beauty in the spoils of life and help others see it, would not have killed his brother in cold blood. Larson's tale had another side. It had to. But I needed to do more than nurture hope.

Hawk's memory had holes that must be filled.

As often happened, morning brought fresh perspective. I threw the covers off then stood barefoot beside my ghost, still wearing his brother's shirt. Hawk made no comment. In thoughtful silence, we watched the sun rise; and as streaks of apricot and pink curled like lashes over the wide-eyed horizon, we shared our strategy.

Together, we would go to the mine I fell into as a child, the one beside the witch-faced tree. There, we would prove Chaine's innocence ... or make him pay for the unthinkable crime he'd committed over seven years ago.

Without any premeditation on my part, the groundwork fell into place for our plan.

I snuggled beneath my covers and feigned a headache while several servants cleaned Hawk's mess from the night before. After they left, Uncle visited.

The worry on his face pricked my conscience, but I stayed focused, encouraging him to accompany the viscount and everyone else—including the majority of the servants—to Worthington for Sunday morning services. I assured Uncle I would stay abed until he returned. He conceded when Enya agreed to sit with me.

Chaine didn't try to visit my chambers, but he did send up a bouquet—sunflowers, hollyhocks, and Sweet Williams from the winter garden. He'd dipped the petals in melted chocolate to fill my room with the delectable perfume. In the flower basket I found the picture he'd drawn of the flawed rose, though this time the stem pierced a bleeding heart. Upon the right-hand corner read the words: *Forgive me,* in a script now more familiar than my own.

I watched from my balcony doors as everyone loaded onto berlines, carriages, and fourgones, ducking behind the curtains when Chaine looked up at my window. Even with the distance between us, I noticed the circles beneath his eyes. A pang of guilt wracked me over his obvious sleepless night, along with an even stronger emotion I had yet to name. I shook off the feelings. Today I sought facts, and would let nothing interfere.

After the forest swallowed the travelers, I allowed Enya to brush and plait my hair into a long braid that swished at the arch of my lower back. Then I convinced her to go down and read a book in the drawing room, as I intended to sleep all morning.

Miss Abbot almost caught me putting on my riding habit when she came up with tea, biscuits, and apple jelly. But Hawk warned me before she opened the door. I dived beneath the covers, boots and all, and feigned sleeping.

It worked. The maid set the food upon my vanity and left. Upon Hawk's assurance she'd cleared the stairs, I leapt out of bed.

I folded a linen napkin around two biscuits slathered with jelly and tucked them in my jacket. Then, after gulping down the cream, as the tea was yet too hot to drink, I hesitated, fretful of how it would feel to see the mine again. But I had no time for second-thoughts.

I followed Hawk into the stairway behind the portrait, taking care to secure the picture shut. Finding Aunt Bitti gone, we used her back-steps to sneak out of the house and remained hidden in a labyrinth of icy shrubbery until we came to the stables.

The snow-clad roof glistened in the morning light. Hidden within the building's shade, I checked for the stable lads, but they had accompanied the caravan of worshippers to tend the horses upon their arrival in Worthington.

Though Hawk did not approve of my riding a horse alone, he had no choice but to talk me step-by-step through the tacking of Little Napoleon. My ghost kept his distance, so as not to make the gelding nervous. The bridle presented the greatest challenge. Napoleon kept jerking his head until I opened a biscuit and smeared apple jelly on the bit.

After Hawk and I studied the map to determine my route, I removed my locket and tucked it in the saddle's pouch. Then I mounted, and trotted through the gates of the manor with a chilly wind turning the ends of the scarf that covered my hat—not daring to look back ... looking only ahead.

CHAPTER 33

A drowning man is not troubled by rain.
Persian Proverb

Chaine did not exaggerate his horse's sense of direction. Once I guided Little Napoleon onto the appropriate trail, he never veered from the snow-covered path, slicing through frozen sedge and undergrowth. I braved eating a biscuit while the shimmering scenery brushed by, keeping one glove on the reins.

I wasn't sure how long we trekked, but when the forest thickened overhead and the scent of pine saturated the crisp air, I suspected I'd been gone an hour. Tucking my scarf's loose ends into my collar, I studied Napoleon's ears. On my first outing, I had learned that for both ears to turn back signaled annoyance, but only one signaled the horse listened to something that I could not hear. Today, neither possibility soothed my ragged nerves.

Twice I looked over my shoulder as prompted by the swivel of his ear, wondering if someone followed, if they had noticed my escape. But I saw only trees casting their willowy shadows on the snow along with the sporadic flutter of crows.

I knew the moment we arrived, for just as I

remembered, a large oak, gnarled and aged, stood in the midst of a clearing, a few feet from the mine's boarded opening. The bark's knots and ridges formed a distinctive face with a long, crooked nose that tapered to a mouth-shaped hole—cruel and dark.

An overwhelming sense of dread shaded my thoughts.

I dismounted and tied Little Napoleon's reins around an ash tree then turned toward the entrance of the mine.

My throat felt like sand. Something cold plopped on my nose—an icicle melting from a branch overhead. Balanced on my toes, I tugged it free and put half in my mouth, then gave the rest to Napoleon.

Desperate for Hawk's company, I took off my gloves to fish my locket from the saddle's pouch. As I tried to clasp the necklace around my neck under my scarf, my hands started to tremble.

It occurred to me, that I was as powerless to my circumstances as the icicles dripping from the branches all around. Alone in the middle of my childhood nightmare, in search of a skeleton belonging to one of the brothers that I loved. Depending upon what I found, I might be exposing the other brother as a murderer.

And yes, I loved Chaine. Why deny it any longer? I fell in love with the boy of the journal weeks ago. For his artistry and courage ... for the ability to see past ugliness or failings and find beauty within. Perhaps even years before that, for being the mud prince who attended and comforted me when I fell into the mine, despite his own torment. And over the past week, I had come to adore and admire the man that boy became—gentle, accepting, patient, and wise.

Better to admit it to myself before I brought Hawk back. On the other hand, as well as he read my thoughts, I suspected he already knew.

I tried again to thread the necklace's hook through the loop, my fingers still fidgety.

What would I do if Chaine were guilty?

Were I to go to the local jurisprudence, the pig Larson would win and sweet old Merril would rot away in bedlam. If I kept Chaine's secret, he would live the rest of his life as his brother, never paying the consequences of his actions, and Hawk would not receive the vengeance he deserved.

There didn't seem to be an easy answer.

At last, the clasp caught. Tucking the locket under my bodice, I scolded myself for failing to bring any rope to help me climb into the mine.

"Oh no. No. You are not to climb down, my lovely. That was never the plan." Hawk towered before me, his back turned so he could regard the decaying scaffold over the shaft. "Once you've opened the boards enough, I'll go down and call up whatever I find."

He turned to me. Anxiety sucked the light from his eyes. He wanted his brother to be innocent as much as me—for all the same reasons.

"Get a stick to pry them apart," he said. "It should be easy enough. Most of them are rotted. There are just a few new slats."

I found a fallen branch about the thickness of my arm and the length of my leg. My ghost waited as I wedged the pointed end beneath two boards nailed together.

"Careful now," he said. "Stand clear of the platform. It might give beneath you."

My time in the tunnel with Chaine resurfaced, rasping like claws up and down my spine. I ignored the memory and heaved my weight upon the thick end of the stick. A snapping crack reverberated through my arms, and three of the boards gave way.

I repositioned the branch and pried away two more. My wrists and elbows ached. Panting from exertion, I stood back to admire the hole, kneading my raw hands.

"Beautifully done." Hawk drifted to the edge. "Now say put, and don't get too close to the opening. I'll keep you apprised." With that, he dropped out of sight.

I tossed my stick aside. "Remember not to put any walls between us."

"I'm not a simpleton, Juliet," Hawk called up.

"And avoid water puddles." We had never ruled out if his contact with the water was what had killed those seven petals that night, or if it was in fact our contact with one another. We couldn't take any chances, having only eight left, including the one in my locket.

"Anymore instructions, Mum?"

"I'm trying to keep you safe."

"I'm a ghost, Juliet. It isn't as if I can die again. Wait, my nose is feeling a bit drippy. Dear me, I fear I've caught a chill!"

"Oh, hah."

His answering chortle lifted my spirit, but only a little. Running my fingers along the smooth metal buttons of my split skirt, I leaned over the hole and watched his smearing glow within the depths.

The mine was deeper than I remembered. I scooted my toes a few extra inches away from the edge. "Look for something shimmery, it might be the watch."

"Nag-nag. Leave me be. I know what I'm—" His voice broke.

"Hawk ... what is it?"

After a torturous span of silence, he answered. "I-I recognize this place. My purgatory."

His voice dragged as if weighted down. Foreboding snaked through me. If this was where his body was buried ... it further implicated Chaine. I couldn't bear to ask if he could see a skeleton.

I crouched closer with my palms on my knees, straining to hear his breath, his clicking teeth.

"Juliet ... look out!"

A shove from behind knocked the air from my lungs. My knees slammed onto the platform, my neck slung backward like a whip. The rotted scaffolding gave beneath me. Splintering boards ripped my shin as I fell through.

I was spinning, spinning in my head. Memories jumbled with reality. A child, falling. Stomach queasy with the descent into oblivion. Terror ... helplessness. And darkness.

Deaf to it all, not even my own screams to comfort me.

Broken wood floated everywhere. I grabbed blindly at each piece.

Struggling to catch a breath, I hit the ground—right side first. On impact, a shock wave rippled through my body. My teeth jarred in my head. Blood scrambled through my veins. The taste of dirt and bile coated my throat.

I groaned and torqued my neck to see a silhouette looking down from the dizzying heights, perched on the shattered opening. A shadow crept into view beside it. In a moment of horror, I recognized Aunt Bitti and Naldi, the daylight a nimbus behind them. Whimpering, I searched for my locket and found the necklace gone. It had snapped off during the fall; I wasn't sure I'd had it latched properly to begin with.

I tried to reach with my right arm in search of the locket, crying out for Hawk. Icy fire raced from my shoulder to my elbow, and I fainted dead away.

⤳•⤸

A warm, rough tongue licked my chin. The scent of musk and fur itched my nose.

The kitten. It must have eaten all of the ham and wanted more.

It hurt to open my eyes, so I kept them shut and started to lift my arm to stroke the persistent feline. Shooting needles of fire leapt through my shoulder. Nausea gushed into my head.

Disoriented, I groaned and tried the other arm. This one worked. I reached out and met a handful of wiry hair that shuddered and jerked free. A burst of kittens scrambled all across my body.

My eyelids eased open. Bright light filtered from somewhere above, dotting my surroundings with patches of illumination. The kittens didn't look right ... black with beady red eyes.

Rats!

I screamed and sat up too fast. Every part of my body ached, as if barbed wire wrapped my bones and joints. Warm wetness soaked through the left leg of my split skirt. Gingerly, I lifted the torn fabric with my left hand and saw the bleeding gash in my shin.

I shivered, cold despite the hot throb in my right shoulder. Groaning, I propped myself against a dirt wall. The sea of rats parted and vanished into the darkness, outside the light's reach.

Memory crashed over me. My fall ... the missing locket. Bitti.

Why had she pushed me?

I looked up at the opening, so high overhead I would never make it out on my own. Tears rushed my cheeks, hot and searing. I was alone, and unless someone discovered me, I would be here when night fell. There would be no sun to warm me or keep the rats at bay. No fairytale or gentle, muddied hands to provide comfort. Only utter darkness.

My insides quaked. I knew deafness, but had never been blind as well ... not literally.

I clamped my mouth with my good hand. My mind shuttered, blinking in and out of lucidity. I struggled to catch a breath, the air shallow and dank in my lungs. My past came back, images of spiders, roaches, and rats creeping in and out of my hair and clothes. The muscles in my stomach rolled.

I lurched forward and threw up my biscuit from earlier, coughing to catch a swallow of air between heaves.

Bending my knees to my chest, I slid down the wall. The friction of my spine loosened dirt to sprinkle around me. I didn't stop until the ground met my left side. There I curled up, sick and defeated.

I heard it then ... not a living voice, but a voice captured within a memory.

"Once upon a time, long, long ago, there was a young man who lived in a hole. He was the prince of mud and grime."

Chaine had been a child when the monster first tossed him into this pit. Yet he managed to survive. Taking a deep breath, I sat up again, slower this time. I forced myself to stand on trembling legs. My left shin almost gave beneath me, but I took a step to assess my injuries. My right shoulder was useless. I'd lost my hat, but my scarf remained hanging in disarray on my head. With my good hand, I tugged it free and formed a sling. Lightheaded and woozy, I pressed my back against the wall and studied the outskirts of the light for any movement.

"The rats were his chancellors, the spiders his stewards, and the salamanders his jesters of rhyme."

If a child could tame such creatures, so could I. Smacking my lips to quell the bitter bile on my tongue, I took another shaky step forward in search of the locket. The edge of my hat appeared, just outside the light in a pile of broken wood. A glint of silver glistened from underneath it.

One wary step, then another four. Wincing, I nudged the debris aside with a broken board I'd picked up along the way for a cane, and toppled my riding cap. I laughed, hysterically happy to see my locket, still closed and intact, coiled beneath it.

I bent—as careful and creaky as an old woman—to retrieve the necklace. There was no possibility of putting it around my neck with just one good hand. Instead, I wrapped the chain around my wrist that rested immobile in the sling, so the necklace wouldn't be dropped again. Then, with my right fist, I clamped the locket as tight as possible without aggravating my shoulder.

"Juliet ... thank God ..." Hawk's breathless murmur stirred before I saw him aglow in front of me. He reached out as if to embrace me, then remembered he couldn't. His hand dropped to his side. "I've never felt so damn useless. The shadow appeared behind you and then I was gone." His jaw twitched. "A part of me kept waiting for you to join me. In my purgatory." He punched his thigh. "I'm such a selfish worm, to even consider such a thing."

The remorse on his face made me long to touch him. "I've longed for the same, many times. It is only natural."

"Natural? There is nothing natural about you wanting to die. Do you hear me?" His tortured gaze swept over my body and paused at my sling before catching on my bloodied skirt. "Oh Lord, you're hurt."

"I am fine," I tried to assure him.

"Do you know who pushed you?"

"You didn't see?"

He shook his head.

Before I could respond, something in the distance distracted me ... over Hawk's shoulder, on the other side of the debris where his glow reached past the shadows.

"Look." I limped around busted boards and rusted nails, out of the warm comfort of sunshine into the dark. The collapsed platform had opened up a lower end of the tunnel leading to a steep drop and a wall of wooden slats. Several of the boards had cracked, showcasing a dingy white shape on the other side.

"Sweet heaven. That wasn't opened earlier." Hawk followed me.

I picked my way through the rubble on the slope, leaning into my makeshift cane to support my left leg. The closer we came, the faster my heartbeat and the slower my pace. A skeleton took shape through slits of broken wood.

A sob pressed against my windpipe. I wasn't sure I had the courage to see Hawk's decaying corpse.

The light around me waned and I hesitated, looking behind to find my ghost had stopped moving. Intense apprehension furrowed his brows.

I squeezed the locket in my cold fist. "You do not have to come. You need not even watch. Turn your back. I require only your light."

His shoulders stiffened along with his chin. "No. Whatever we find, we face it together."

In that moment, I understood. Like me, he would never be able to believe in Chaine's guilt lest he saw it for himself. Thus was the strength of his love for his twin ... an unsurpassable, inexplicable faith.

Choking back another bout of tears, I nodded and took the final few steps, putting me face to face with the widest crack. I peered within, inhaling the scent of mildew and rot. Hawk's glow spread across my shoulder, brightening the morbid scene beyond the wall.

The skeleton, dressed in nothing but a few threadbare rags, caked mud, and cobwebs, lay wedged beneath a heavy pillar which must have fallen upon him during a cave-in. I swallowed a whimper, determined to be strong for Hawk.

My gaze ran the length of the remains, finding the square pocket watch in a macabre pose: the chain twisted around a rib, the hinged lid open, the face cracked, and the hands frozen at half-past midnight. Now I understood why his watch did not disappear with the other things that night I met him. Aside from his ragged boots, it was the sole article that hadn't decomposed and still remained upon his person.

Upon seeing the skeleton's right leg, I covered my mouth. The leather boot had rotted enough to split, exposing his foot where bones twisted upon one another, setting the ankle at an awkward slant—an obvious deformity.

I cried behind my hand. Hot moisture streaked from my eyes. I couldn't look at my ghost. Instead, I waited for him to speak. But I never expected the words he said.

"There's another one."

"What?"

"There ... in the furthest reaches. I see a second skeleton."

Sure enough, another frame of bones lay sprawled beneath the debris where the small chamber ended against a dirt wall. I had no time to debate what this meant before Hawk shouted behind me.

"Flood!'

My feet swept up beneath me. A wave of warm water pinned me against the wall, knocking my fist open so the locket dangled from my wrist. The mine's collapse had busted a reservoir, as if a dam had opened. I struggled with both hands to grasp at slats of wood for balance. I cried out—pitch dark swallowing me in the absence of Hawk's light. Another gush smashed me against the wall, the water rising up to my waist.

The pressure became too much and the boards snapped, dragging me down into the lower level. Muddy water slithered into my throat, gagging me. The torrent twisted me to my back. Something sharp pressed against my side. *Hawk's skeleton.*

I tried to escape, but my braid snagged around his ribs. I tugged free by loosening the plaits so my hair floated in the water all around me. Blindly, I searched for his pocket watch and tucked it in my skirt's waist before another rush of water spun me around. The raging fire inside my shoulder ignited again.

The ceiling overhead began to buckle. Wave after wave sloughed over me. I tried to clamber to higher ground, but the lack of my right arm, my gouged shin, and the water's momentum proved too great a challenge.

Gasping for air, I drifted helpless in the surge. It carried me to the furthest dirt wall, slammed me against the barrier. In spite of my body's reluctance to move, I paddled my feet to stay afloat. The space between ceiling and water diminished bit by bit. I closed my eyes as warm water enveloped my head. Debris tangled in my swirling hair. I immerged to steal another breath.

I knew I faced death, yet I could think only of Chaine— a man more multi-faceted than any diamond.

A murderer. What other explanation could there be? It explained why Bitti pushed me in, so I wouldn't learn the truth and expose him. Protecting her beloved nephew ... his new way of life—so hard earned. She was repaying her debt for betraying his mother all those years ago.

I gulped another breath.

Even were I to live, I could never betray him. Yet I would never be with him. I loved him despite his evil—for his tenderness toward his father; for his fondness of nature; for his rare and extraordinary admiration for all things broken. His horrendous childhood had crippled an otherwise benevolent heart, rendering him deaf to his conscience. Could not I, of all people, understand deafness?

Now Chaine's past would haunt him always, for he would be alone without me; therein would be his punishment.

The water cocooned me again. Remorse slashed my slowing heart. Uncle would be grief stricken once they found my drowned corpse, so close to losing Mama. I prayed Enya could console him, strengthen their bond through the tragedy.

In a final, desperate plea for life, I thrashed my legs. My nose surfaced for an instant in the tiny space that remained. I sipped one breath before a wave slapped over me. My frantic movements expended the tiny taste of oxygen instantly. Cramps gouged beneath my ribs as I fought the urge to inhale water. My lungs curled and withered, like so many petals of Hawk's flower.

Hawk.

Serenity surged upon his name. Death waited, along with the strains of my ghost's sensuous baritone. A familiar and comforting retreat. He would be there when I arrived.

The water swayed my body. My pain subsided, nerves numbing. My mind clouded. Something butted against my right palm—a tiny heart-shaped thing, suspended in the water. I stretched out my fingers and clenched it tightly—strangely unafraid.

CHAPTER 34

A man need never avenge himself;
The body of his enemy will be brought to his door.
Chinese Proverb

I awoke to someone carrying me over their shoulder. Muddied walls passed by in a sickening, dizzy haze. I thought myself dead, until my lungs jerked and heaved, forcing up a mix of bile and foul-tasting water.

I clenched the locket in my hand, my wet hair hanging over my face. Bits of wood and mud had knotted in the tangles, making it difficult to see. Being placed gently on the ground, I sat, cold and disoriented. With my good arm, I supported myself, trying not to aggravate the angry throbs in my right shoulder. I couldn't be dead, since I still felt pain.

Steady fingers coaxed hair off my face, dragging out the debris from my tangles, opening my line of sight.

I watched him as he moved, in utter disbelief. My ghost—now flesh and bone with clothes dripping wet—burrowed his nose into my hair before tucking the strands behind my ears.

His eyes studied me, the striking gray of granite with a hint of sunlight. His jaw clenched, so serious and quiet, sharing in my awe.

Without a word between us, he lowered me to my back in the shallow warm water, and propped my head on a large rock sticking out from the stream. The liquid covered my body and swirled my hair on the currents, its warmth easing away my shivers and the ache in my shoulder and shin.

I held my breath as his hands, with the masterful strokes of an architect, brushed over me beneath the water, checking for other wounds from my legs to my shoulders. My body responded to his touch. For it knew him, long before this moment.

My tongue had tasted his chicory scent, my breath had savored his minty flavor—during dreams of death, dancing, and song.

We were settled at the highest point of the mineshaft where I'd first fallen through. The broken platform invited sunlight to slant in. I blinked at the brightness, at Hawk's solid form blocking the sun.

On his knees, he straddled me, tending my injuries while the water lapped around his thighs.

He had yet to speak—this man who had filled my head with glorious words and sounds over the past months, now speechless and stirring my heart all the more with his silence.

I reached for him with my left hand, arched my body toward him as he submersed himself atop me all the way up to his shoulders. The contact hurt my shoulder, but the wonder of his realness negated any pain. My fingers ran circles along his back, savoring the reality of muscles beneath his shirt.

Water sloshed around us. Sunlight reflected off the waves onto his face and hair—a flash of brilliance along golden skin and sable spikes.

"China Rose ..." His voice wavered, as if it hurt him to say it. With one hand he cushioned my nape from the rock, the other skimmed my wounded shoulder inside the water. "If I weren't wet ... our spirits could merge. I could heal you."

"No. I'd rather hold you."

His fingertip traced my jaw. Flesh to flesh. He tilted my chin up. My right fist tightened around the locket.

His drizzling fingers coated my forehead, nose, and cheeks with a mask of wetness. He chased the water with his lips, keeping his mouth against my skin, until he came to my lips. He paused there—as if fearing to step across, to make it real—then our lips met on a kiss so gentle and chaste ... the slightest palpitation as if he might break me.

His fingers tangled in my drifting hair. "You *do* taste like snow."

I tightened my clasp on his arm. "You're *here*."

He pressed his forehead to mine—eyes shut. "But for how long?"

His words gushed through me like cold mountain springs, icing my veins. So captivated by our connection, I hadn't even considered the flower at the Manor, or the seven remaining petals that must be withering even as we spoke.

My fist curled around the locket, fingernails biting my palm. If this were true, I held the last one in my hand.

He stared into me, and for once, I read his thoughts,

his desires: *I've waited forever to touch you ... all of you.*
His eyes spoke the plea, not his mouth.

To think I'd watched this moment unfold in slumber for weeks. But now, I was awake. Awake and fervent, but for another man.

Hawk rose to a crouched position, still straddling me, yet putting distance between us. "You're in love with my brother."

It wouldn't do any good to lie; I was more transparent to Hawk than any ghost.

He swore beneath his breath. "Were it any other man ..." His hand wrenched from my grasp. I tried to catch him again, to comfort him, but his wet wrist slid out of my fingers. "All along, you've been falling for him; as we read the journal; as we discovered 'our' pasts were entwined. I was wearing his shoes. What I wouldn't give to put them on again."

His agony pierced me through. I sat up and cringed when my shoulder moved. Still, I managed to clasp his fingers.

"I love you both. So many of the reasons I found myself admiring Chaine are yours. Your gift with architecture; your eye for design; your wholeness in spite of a damaged foot. Besides all of this, you have empathy, tenderness, humor—and songs that soothe my soul. My feelings for Chaine no longer matter if he killed you. How could I ever be with him if he's a murderer?"

"Yet how can you be with me, a ghost, trapped within one last flower petal?" Hawk gazed at the water surrounding us.

Hot pinpricks flushed my cheeks, a rush of self-disdain. "I'm unworthy of you Hawk. To fall for two men, what quality of lady does such a thing? You're too good for me."

"*Good*?" He laughed, a tortured sound which stung my ears and prickled my spine. He stood, water cascading from his clothes in shimmery streams. A thousand emotions played across his face, illuminated by the sun's bouncing reflections. "I remembered everything—my past, my death—the moment you revived me with the locket and I dragged you from the water. Being in the place of my death brought it all back." A muscle in his jaw clamped. "But when I realized we could touch, I decided not to tell you the truth so I could make love to you just once, so I could have you for myself. My brother's innocence be damned."

His confession froze the air in my lungs.

He wouldn't meet my gaze. "Yes, let us bask in my goodness. Once a rogue ... always a rogue, aye?"

Silent, I studied him, teetering between injury and empathy.

"Let there be no mistake, Juliet. My brother's the good one. Always has been." He turned his back, his shoulders rising on a shrug. "When we first met, Chaine and I kept our knowledge of one another a secret. We never let on to anyone but Father there were two of us. And he ... as you know ... never believed it. For twelve months, Chaine and I took turns trading places. At times, he played Lord Thornton. Borrowed my clothes. Learned to talk like me, move like me. Damndest thing. His gentle spirit enabled him to see past my deformity. The one weakness that had shamed me my whole life. The imperfection that drove me to seek validation in bourbon and strange women's arms, that made me rely on empty rage to verify my manhood. Yet Chaine took pride in emulating that very flaw. That's why I made him the pocket watch. It was my way of honoring his shame ... his broken past."

Hawk's hand fumbled for the watch that once hung upon his waist. "I lost it when I dove into the water after you."

Absently, I searched the waist of my riding skirt. Was it he or me who had lost the watch in the chaos? I supposed we would never know.

"Only one thing Chaine could not master." My ghost angled a glance over his shoulder, a half-smile dimpling his cheek. "How to sing. My brother is blasted tone deaf." Snorting softly, he turned away again and towed his boot through the water to leave ripples in its wake. "I had never met anyone like him. How can a man who cannot hear the tonality of a note, have such an affinity for the songs of birds and the aura of the wind? How can a man who was never blessed with color or beauty throughout his childhood have more appreciation for a rose's bleeding heart or a butterfly's fractured wing than a man who has had beauty and light cast at his feet all his life?"

My heart bruised upon the profound admiration in his voice ... for a brother he hardly had a chance to know.

Hawk trudged through the water then leaned against the dirt wall, facing me. "I was intrigued by my Romani blood. So each time Chaine walked in my shoes, I visited

Aunt Bitti. She taught me the language of the gypsies ... their symbols and folklore. Their songs. I suppose it was her way of making up for her mistakes. I coaxed her into moving to Claringwell, to keep her close to Chaine and me. Father had purchased a plot in the graveyard years earlier when he'd learned of Gitana's death. He couldn't bury her memory in his family plot in Worthington. His cousin's family was buried in Claringwell, and he'd always thought the graveyard peaceful and lovely. To honor Gitana, he fenced in a small parcel of his land and erected a tombstone. Left it blank out of respect. In the gypsy culture, to etch the name of the dead on a stone ... their given name ... is an insult."

I frowned as the puzzle started to fit together; I had to have been wrong about Bitti throwing me in. Perhaps someone else had done it, and she saw the aftermath. "Is this why Bitti buried your caul there years later ... and the flower? Why they engraved 'Hawk' upon the stone, in lieu of your name?"

"I assume." Hawk looked toward the darkness of the tunnel. "I was already dead by then."

"But Chaine played no part in your death?"

Hawk smoothed the wrinkles in his shirt, already fading to translucent in places where he had started to dry. "No. Only Tobar and Larson are to blame. From the beginning, Chaine and I had different reasons for tricking Larson out of his deed for this estate. We both wanted to save our father from debtor's prison. It was my responsibility, as my drinking and gambling were what put him in debt to begin with. My brother joined the cause for a second reason. He wanted access to the mine's records. He hoped to find you through them."

As Hawk spoke, my shoulder throbbed, the pain grinding beneath my flesh. I resituated my arm with the other hand, propping my lower back against a rock to quell the nausea in my stomach.

"Remember, how I told you that Tobar was excluded from Chaine and Larson's card game on that fated night?" Hawk went on, unaware of my suffering. "Well, Tobar was furious. No doubt he thought Larson was holding out on him. So while Chaine was bettering Larson in a game of cards at the tavern, Tobar visited the estate and broke into Larson's country house to steal his handwritten ledgers ... records that not only exposed Larson as the anonymous owner of the tavern, but provided a decade's worth of names ... men Larson had hoodwinked into financial ruin. Tobar planned on blackmailing Larson with the information. What he didn't plan on, was me being at the estate for the very same reason. I saw him coming out the back door. My brother never knew what transpired next. This is why I needed to return from the dead ... to tell him where to find the ledgers."

A cold sweat dotted my brow, and my surroundings became dusted with black fuzz. But I could not give in. I had to relay Hawk's message to Chaine once I was found. *If I was found ...*

"Chaine and I were to meet in this very spot beside the witch tree after he got the deed and I found the proof to blackmail Larson. Chaine had drawn pictures of Tobar, ugly and twisted as the man himself. I knew it was him the moment I saw him leave Larson's home. And he recognized me as well. Or thought he did. He came at me with a knife, intent on killing the bastard son he had abused for so many years. The one who had escaped at the age of fourteen."

My vision blurred and I couldn't swallow for the stomach acid burning my throat. I squeezed the locket and a lightning sharp pain radiated through my arm. Hot and cold raced through me. I clenched my teeth in an effort to stay conscious.

"We struggled. Tobar stabbed my chest with the knife. I'd been holding Chaine's watch within my breast pocket, until he finished cheating Larson. The blade dented it, broke the face, but protected my heart. I bent forward, feigned injury, then snapped up and cracked Tobar's chin with my cane. As he slumped to the ground in a daze, I took the ledgers filled with Larson's sins and set off on my horse for the witch tree. I had just shoved the pouch into the tree's mouth as Tobar's mare broke through the bush. When he arrived, I made it look as if I'd tossed the ledgers into the mineshaft.

"There was a rope and pulley system leading in and out of the tunnel. Tobar took the contraption down to retrieve his prize. It was the perfect opportunity to make him pay for all the years of misery my brother lived. The fitting place for the gypsy king to meet his end. I was about to follow him when Chaine came upon the scene. He tried to stop me, fearing for me, but I was so drunk and set on revenge I could think of nothing else. My brother and I argued. He clenched my jacket, trying to shake some sense into me. Then we both heard a sound behind us. Larson's spying provided just the distraction I needed. I broke free from Chaine and took the plunge, riding the rope to the bottom."

Nausea rushed through me, a roiling snarl in my stomach.

"Tobar and I fought in the tunnel," Chaine reached the ugly conclusion. "A cave-in resulted, and crushed us both. Chaine climbed down to find me, but he was too late. I was dying, and had only strength enough to make him promise to live my dream, and to bring my spirit back. I took my last breath upon those words."

I wept as the morbid scene unfolded in my mind; yet in the same instant, the weight of Chaine's guilt lifted off of my chest as if it sprouted wings and took to the sky. Shivering, I could no longer hide my pain. "My arm ..." Black speckles dotted my vision.

In a blink Hawk was at my side. He dunked his hand in the water then felt my forehead. "You're feverish. Just hold on Juliet. I hear horses in the distance." A worried wrinkle etched his brow.

I tried to smile, but groaned instead. "You're lying. There's fear behind your eyes."

Another gut-twisting jolt shot through me. The black fog swarmed me. My body fell lax, and the locket slipped through my fingers into the water below.

CHAPTER 35

Death closes all doors and pays all debts.
English Proverb

Six times I had watched dawn come into this room, but never one as dark as this. For not once in my stay here, not once in the prior weeks at my home in Claringwell since Mama's burial, had I faced a morning without my ghost.

Propped on a feather pillow, I touched my neck, devoid of the locket I'd lost forever in the mines. My gaze wandered to the terrarium on the Secretaire. Seeing the barren stem, the spattering of the last seven petals withered and black upon the wooden base—scored my insides. As if the very air I breathed sprouted thorns and raked me from within.

I'd spent the night abed, in and out of consciousness. Never lucid enough to ask any questions. This morning, I would have everything answered. Enya sat next to my bed, reading. She was to be my informant.

Unfortunately, my chamber danced with activity: maids tending my every whim, butlers carrying in bouquets of flowers from Chaine and my uncle in their absence, Miss Abbot spooning porridge into my unwilling mouth, Enya fluffing my pillows beneath me and laying compresses on my shoulder.

The Manor's physician flitted in to check my stitched shin and shovel bitter medicine down my throat. I'd already decided I spared no affection for him. The one memory I had of my arrival back to the Manor yesterday centered around the red-haired rooster-faced man and his conclusion my shoulder was out of socket. With all the tenderness of an insolent child forcing a square peg into a round hole, he popped my bone back into place.

I had screamed. I knew it was loud by the tension on my vocal cords and the startled looks on everyone's faces. Uncle and Chaine had stood in the corner, both of them holding their hats in their hands, their coloring green as algae. Tears steamed Chaine's cheeks ... just to see me suffer so.

I had the passing thought of how it would be one day when I gave birth to our children, as I imagined such pain would be tenfold.

I hadn't yet told Chaine that I would bear his sons and daughters. But I had decided it yesterday upon my rescue from the mine.

For I *remembered*.

I remembered how he lowered himself into the shaft with afternoon sunlight splaying behind him like an angel's halo; I remembered thinking of the courage it took to face his childhood nightmare—the rats, the darkness, the demons—yet he had insisted he be the one to save me.

No one told me of his insistence. No one needed to. I saw how the determination stormed in his eyes as he wrapped me in his coat and tied the rope around us both, how it throbbed in the thudding of his heart as he held tight to me, kissing the top of my head while the others lifted us out.

And I knew in that moment I would share the rest of my life with him.

Which led to the question I wished to ask Enya. Where were Chaine and my uncle now? The two men who loved me most in this world had yet to visit me this morn. It left a very unsettled feeling in my gut, compounded by the agony of Hawk's absence.

I couldn't believe I would never see my ghost again. I could not make peace with it or risk breaking down. So I chose, for today, to push aside the niggling emptiness, bury it deep, and focus only on those who lived.

As I had finally realized, after all this time, I did indeed belong among them.

At last, my chamber cleared of servants. Asking if I'd had enough of the bland white slop, Miss Abbot gathered her tray and left.

Enya and I sat in solitude.

I placed my hand atop the pages of the book she read. She looked up and turned it—open-faced—upon her lap. A tender smile lifted one corner of her mouth, but dread cowered in the circles beneath her eyes.

I asked of Lord Thornton's and Uncle's whereabouts. Instead of answering, she bent forward and pulled a small box from beneath her chair. Without a word, she placed it in my good hand, helped me lift the lid, and spread open the tissue paper. My locket and chain lay there on a swatch of red velvet.

My heart skipped a beat.

Reading my unspoken question, Enya explained.

"When Lord Thornton brought you up from the tunnel, you kept mentioning your locket. After the physician treated you, his lordship asked me about the necklace's significance. I told him you kept your parents' portraits within. He went back to the mine with a net, a lantern, and three footmen, and dragged the flooded shaft until he found it. I was told he wouldn't even let his servants help. They waited above to draw him up when he finished. He didn't return until well after supper."

Such devotion humbled me. At the same time, I worried for what else he'd found. Had he been forced to face his brother's bones ... Tobar's skeleton? Apparently everyone still believed he was Nicolas. I vaguely remembered his cane in hand while he stood watching the physician mend my arm and stitch my shin. He still maintained the masquerade. That must mean Larson hadn't come forward with his true identity.

Had they met some sort of compromise? After learning all I had of the investor, it seemed implausible he would even know the meaning of the word.

Then something else occurred to me. Had Chaine touched the silver charm when he drew it from the water? Had he seen his brother's spirit—talked with him?

With it so cold in that tunnel he had probably worn gloves ...

Enya fluttered her hand in front of my eyes to catch my attention. "I must tell you, Juliet. When the viscount handed me this box while you slept, I waited for him to leave then opened it to see if your parents' portraits had survived. Only to find a silver petal within. I didn't touch it ... I know how fragile you say they are. But when I held the locket in my palm, I had the strangest feeling ... as if someone were looking over my shoulder, watching you. I even thought I heard a groan. I placed it back in the box and glanced behind, but no one was there."

Heart aflutter, I grabbed the locket, keeping the velvet between the metal and my flesh. I held it in my right hand and worked the hinges open with my left to reveal Hawk's last petal, bright and alive. As I closed the locket again, anticipation swelled within me. It hadn't withered. I could place the chain upon my neck and revive him. We didn't have to say goodbye. I could preserve it forever within the silver, if I was careful enough.

Enya lifted my chin, centering my gaze. "What is this power the blossom wields?"

My thoughts jumbled; I could think of nothing but the truth. That it conjured a man's specter; that it could fuse your spirit to his and heal your wounds; that it could bridge him to flesh with the assistance of water.

A ghost flower. Who would ever believe such a Banbury tale?

Enya had yet to tell me where Uncle and Chaine were. I shut the necklace within the box. "Tell me where Lord Thornton is. Why hasn't Uncle been to see me? I want someone to bring them both here, post haste."

Her face flushed. "You don't remember?"

My shoulders tensed, spurring a distant ache in my wounded arm. I could move it now—a vast improvement over yesterday. "What am I to remember?"

"I tried to tell you when you awoke in the night. You must have been too groggy to read my words." She sighed, closing the book upon her lap. "Lord Thornton's aunt is here. The same gypsy that you brought in from the forest those weeks back. She saw you get pushed into the shaft. Came running into the house with her wolf, caused such an upset with all the cats running awry everyone became distracted. It didn't help that no one could make sense of anything the old woman said. Had Lord Thornton and your Uncle not come back from Worthington early ... you would have been in the mine till nightfall when the others returned."

I shifted in my bed, trying to get comfortable. "Why did they return early?"

"The moment they arrived in Worthington and unloaded, Lord Thornton realized someone was missing from the guest list. The investor, Lord Larson, had not ridden with the caravan. He'd stayed behind, here at the Manor, without any of us knowing. The viscount borrowed a fresh horse in Worthington and came back, with your uncle following behind in a borrowed carriage. When they arrived, the old gypsy told Lord Thornton everything. How Larson had followed you as you left the manor. How he'd shoved you into the mine. I suppose he thought it would look like an accident. In truth, it would have, had the old gypsy not seen."

I pondered what motive the investor could have to push me into the shaft. Perchance he wanted to lead others to the mine in their search for me and expose Chaine's true identity.

I studied Enya again and noticed her eyes tearing up. "Enya, whatever is wrong?"

"Your viscount ... he was furious."

My chest twisted to a fist. Something in her haunted expression did not bode well. "*Was*?"

My maid dabbed at her lashes with her sleeve cuff.

Sitting rigid in the bed, I threw off my covers. "Tell me."

She shook her head. "Your uncle says you're too weak. We must wait until this evening ... perhaps ... perhaps you'll be strong enough to visit him then."

Bile burned my throat. "Visit who? My uncle? What's wrong with him?"

She shook her head. "No. Lord Thornton. He challenged the investor to a pistol duel. The man hurt you, yet would not admit to any wrong doing. No one could prove his part. Larson claimed the old gypsy was lying, that she pushed you in. But your viscount was bent on justice—on defending you. So they met at midnight in torchlight. Your uncle served as the viscount's second. They were to use single-shot derringers. It was to be one shot fired ... those were the terms."

"No. No." I slung my legs over the bed's edge, shoved aside Enya's hand when she tried to stop me. How had it come to a duel? Why would the investor not have told everyone the truth about Chaine when he was being accused ... to take the heat off himself and stoke the flames beneath another? "Did Lord Thornton win?"

Upon Enya's nod, I felt a flash of hope, but the cloud over her face shattered it. She reached out her hand to steady mine, as it was now shaking. "They both fired their shots. His lordship's bullet grounded Larson. But when your viscount turned to walk away," her eyes filled again, "the investor dragged out another gun he'd hidden in his coat, and shot Lord Thornton. A lead ball lodged in his back. The doctor is performing surgery."

The room swam around me, a cold sweat forming on my brow. I tried to stand.

Enya stood first, holding me back. "There is nothing you can do. You must wait until we are summoned; your uncle is with him, as is the physician. We simply must pray they can successfully remove the ball and save him."

I perched on my bed's edge, holding the locket's box to my aching chest. "I have the only means whereby to save him. Either you help me dress and accompany me, or I will traipse through this townhouse in my chemise until I find someone willing to be my lady's maid ... even if I have to settle for a cat."

⌒ ᴐ•ᴄ ⌒

The black curtains drawn across Chaine's windows blocked out the sun, adding an aura of gloom to the already foreboding circumstances. Throughout the chamber, lit candles in sconces flickered dancing patterns along the white, frothy walls.

He had done all he could, the rooster-faced physician told me. He had removed the ammunition, he said. He'd stitched the incision. But the bleeding wouldn't abate.

I tried to pretend to be grateful, to not despise him for his cynicism. His red hair stood against Chaine's black and white chambers like a bush aflame. His breath smelled too similar to the antiseptic which overpowered the flowers in the hanging baskets.

He expected the viscount would not outlast the night. And even if by some miracle Lord Thornton did survive, the rooster predicted he would be paralyzed. And what sort of life would that be for such an active, strong young man who'd once held such promise?

What did the physician know? I knew more of life and death than him. I would not let Chaine fade away like his brother without a fight. The man I had come to love could accept being paralyzed, as he had always embraced imperfections, but I wasn't willing to accept such an end for him. He deserved so much more after the childhood he had endured.

I sat in the white chair next to the black bed and studied his stubbled chin, how it quivered with each shallow breath. With his thick mane so dark, and his olive complexion faded to a wan opacity, he blended into the achromatic décor. Holding his hand, I felt like a watercolor portrait—unmoving, observing, serene within the throes of silent chaos.

Other colors trickled in and out: butlers in their outrageous oranges and greens, loyal to their kind master, wanting to keep him comfortable; maids sporting vivid crimson aprons and purple frocks, acting as nurses, changing the dressings on Chaine's muscled back to keep his sheets clean; several of the investors came in to pay respects wearing gray suits—a small reprieve from the parade of concerned rainbows.

I waited, quiet and demure. No one expected

otherwise. The deaf, lovelorn girl from Claringwell, watching her future slide away like sands through an open hand. What would become of her now?

Let them ponder. I had other things to think upon, such as Chaine's face. The stormy eyes which harbored so much love and angst now veiled by sable lashes—shutters drawn over the mind of a child savant within a man's consummate form; the high cheekbones that twitched with pain as he slept fitfully—the ones which captured me in the magic of his smile; his mouth stuttering with unheard groans—full lips that had brought me so much pleasure and wonder through witty discussions and interludes of passion barely tapped.

My heart would have broken to see him so fragile, this powerful gypsy prince, were it not for one shining hope. I grasped the locket's box in my lap and with my good hand, lifted Chaine's wrist to run my lips across his blue veins, breathing his scent, feeling his pulse.

I bided my time in such a way until Uncle returned from the hall where he'd been speaking with Enya. All I needed was solitude with Chaine. My uncle would ensure that I had it.

CHAPTER 36

Keep a green tree in your heart,
and perhaps a singing bird will come.
Chinese Proverb

Uncle stood within the doorway, his eagle-like features gilded in grief and firelight. Reading my expression, he sent the servants away. Several of them glanced over their shoulders as they left, sympathy and respect in their eyes. They thought different of me now, for we had shared vigil over their master's listless form.

Once the room cleared, Uncle knelt by the bedside, wincing as he strained his lower back. He looked up at me with such deep sorrow, the dam holding my tears almost cracked wide open.

Laying Chaine's hand upon the covers, I cupped Uncle's chin.

"Be strong," I told him, half-speaking to myself. "Have faith."

"I should be telling you that, tiny sparrow." He tried to smile, but ended up sobbing. The shudder in his throat shook my palm. "I was his second; I should've warned him. But I never saw it coming. Larson had another pistol hidden in his jacket."

I stroked his white hair. "No one blames you, father bear."

He glanced down. "At least that investor met his comeuppance. Nicolas can take heart in that."

I squirmed. It was little consolation to know Larson died before dawn this morning. The investor's death would cause a dire chain reaction. Once his will was read, Chaine would be exposed as a fraud and murderer.

Uncle lifted to sit on the bed's edge, but kept my hand. "I don't know what happened between that investor and Nicolas. I think it had to do with that pouch over there. Nicolas brought it back from the mines when he returned with your locket." Uncle motioned to the writing desk where a leather bag sat, its flap buckled tight. It startled me to see the square pocket watch lying next to it, turned up so the inscription could be seen. *Rat King*.

Chaine must've found it when he searched for my necklace.

I frowned. "What is in the bag?" I had my suspicions, and it would explain why Lord Larson didn't follow through with his threats when Chaine confronted him about my fall. By the looks of the leather, it was very old. Yet it withstood the years. Which meant that the books within—which could expose Lord Larson's embezzlements—might've withstood, too, and would still be legible.

Uncle shrugged, eyes misting again. "It is not my place to look through Nicolas's things. Rumor has it he was involved in some sort of blackmailing scheme. I only wish I knew what side he was on. I'd like to believe he was innocent. Otherwise, I battle this rage that he pulled you into it and nearly got you killed." His gaze fell to Chaine's listless form. "I hate to think ill thoughts of anyone in such a bad way. Even more so of this lad. He's become like a son to me. I thought he was worthy of you."

"He is. And he's innocent."

"You know that, do you?" Uncle's eyes narrowed.

"I love him."

Uncle's eyes reflected tenderness and pride. He'd waited so long to hear me admit such a thing. "Love can be blind."

"Love can also be discerning. It can find goodness where others see only evil."

Uncle shook his head. "If he comes out of this—"

"*When*," I corrected, my jaw tightening.

"When ... he's likely to have a scandal on his hands. If you stand by him, you shall be in the midst of it all. People will talk."

I stiffened my shoulders. "What has a deaf girl to fear of talk?"

Uncle's forehead relaxed along with his grasp on my hand. "You've changed. This man has made you strong."

"The experience has strengthened me. All of it." I studied Chaine. "Uncle, might I have some time alone with him? Please."

He nodded, patting my hand. "Of course. I'll keep watch in the hall so no one disturbs you."

The moment the door latched shut, I jumped up, clenched my teeth against the shooting pain in my shin and shoulder, and opened the box.

I held the locket up to the candlelight, watched the silver glisten ... remembering Hawk's and my first night together. How helpless he seemed. But it was me all along who needed his help. For only by walking with the dead could I see how precious life was—and rekindle my desire to live it.

Knelt beside the bed, elbows propped on the mattress, I opened the necklace's clasp. Sweeping Chaine's silky hair aside, I secured the chain around his neck but kept the locket tight within my fist, away from his skin.

"What happened?" Hawk appeared on the other side of the bed. He glanced down at his brother then up at me. "Juliet?"

"He was shot in a duel. Trying to defend my honor."

My ghost cursed. "No. I was just with him ..."

"A full day has passed since then. So, you saw him in the tunnel?"

Hawk nodded. "He was rubbing muck off of the locket between his fingers. I couldn't believe it. To look up and find him instead of you. And then he saw me." His lips pressed tight. "We stood there staring at one another for what felt like an eternity. I-I can't even remember who spoke first. But once we started talking, we couldn't stop. It was as if ... as if we'd never been apart. At first he was angry at me, for dying. But we were so happy to be together again, he forgave me." He gave me a sad smile. "We spoke of everything. I told him of my time with you."

My mouth gaped.

Hawk smiled. "Of course I left out some details. I'm not a complete rogue. But he knows I love you." Hawk's fingertip traced the quilt under his brother's arm and wrinkled the fabric. "He told me I couldn't have you. That he'd waited too long. And if that's what I came for, well, I might as well go back to being dead." Hawk winced against a pain I could only imagine. "I don't blame him. I mean, the shock of it, to know his rival all along had been a ghost? His brother's ghost, no less." Hawk's attention caught on the pouch at the desk. "Good. He found them. I was hoping it was still in the witch tree. Those ledgers should help in silencing Larson."

"Larson is dead. Perhaps they can help in the aftermath." Keeping the locket cradled in my palm, I sat upon the mattress's edge. Pressing my empty hand to Chaine's sternum, I felt his heartbeat in irregular palpitations where the covers grazed a line of hair on his bared chest. "Chaine is dying. Unless you step in."

Fear crept over Hawk's face—the dawning of a dark realization. "I saw you in your room when your maid summoned me. I looked upon my flower. You have the last petal."

I squeezed the locket so hard its edges bit into my flesh. "Yes." Tears flooded my eyes. I could no longer keep the emotions at bay. "If you could heal my paper cut ... surely you can heal your brother. You once shared a womb. You're already portions of one spirit."

Hawk regarded his brother's helpless form. He rubbed his temples. "How can I say goodbye to you, now that I've held you in my arms?"

His question sliced deep—a knife's edge to the core of my being.

"Where will I go?" His voice wavered. Dread crossed his features.

I couldn't block out my own memory of being in that mine alone—much less imagine an eternity there.

A sob snagged in my throat, almost strangling. "I don't know. I don't know what happens now." The cry burst free; I muffled it so Uncle wouldn't hear. Hot, slick tears and saliva coated my palm where I clutched my mouth so hard it pinched my lips. "I cannot send you into the darkness forever. But ... I don't know what else to do ..."

Weak and weary, I curled my legs upon the bed and snuggled next to Chaine. My face buried into his neck. The warmth of his body radiated around me and soothed my sore shoulder.

Hawk moved behind me.

Looking up into his face, I sniffled. "I cannot have you both dead and untouchable to me."

Hawk's jaw ground so tight, the imprint of his gums appeared beneath his skin. "My brother saved himself for you, his whole life ... after meeting you once as a child. I was one of the dogs that called him a fool for that. But he knew you were special. Me? Had I met you when I was living, you would just have been another conquest. It took me dying to learn how to love a woman with such devotion. He always was the wiser one."

I closed my eyes, unable to look at him. At either of them. I nestled into Chaine's neck again, letting the sound of Hawk's clicking teeth pulse through me. "I love you, Hawk."

His phantom touch stroked my back, furrowing ripples

along my silken walking dress. "I never doubted it. We both knew from the beginning, we had no future. You brought me back to my brother. You helped me finish what I'd left undone. So be with him. Give him the happiness and family he never had as a boy." My ghost rippled my dress once more then pulled away, leaving me cold in his wake. I turned to watch him roll up his sleeves. "Do it now ... before I change my mind."

My body tensed as I shoved the covers down to Chaine's waist. I placed the locket over his heart between a spattering of hair and covered the charm with my palm, holding back the cries dammed behind my sternum.

Hawk drifted to the other side of the bed.

Wait! I screamed in my mind. *Oh, wait ...*

Hovering over his brother, Hawk met my gaze, his eyes aglow and teary.

My throat swelled on a thousand unspoken words. Even all of them together would not be enough. How could I live without him in my life?

"You'll never truly be without me, China Rose. I will leave my music. That I vow to you." He nodded toward Chaine's chest. "Keep your hand over the locket. Keep it sealed until the end."

I pressed my palm tighter atop the heart-shaped charm, the silver warmed by Chaine's and my body heat combined.

Averting his gaze, Hawk placed his naked palms on his brother's chest, and as if Chaine were a pond, he faded into him, bit by bit, until he ceased to be.

In that moment, I understood his final request and

promise, for I absorbed part of him, too. A rush of warmth shot from the locket to my hand, evoking a change in my shoulder and shin. The throbs and aches eased away. Then my ghost's voice, his songs, hummed within me ... melodies I not only heard but felt in my very soul.

A spiritual serenade.

Numb, I stared at where he had been. After all of our time together, after his dramatic entry into my life—so filled with sound and bravura—that he would leave so quiet and swift ... like morning mist fallen on a desert, evaporated in an instant by the sun. But so much like the mist, a remnant of him remained, far beneath the surface, nurturing a seed which would flourish to fond memories, long after the agony of his absence was gone.

Tangled in emotion, I opened the locket to find nothing left of the petal but dust. Snuggling beneath Chaine's chin, I wept. I wept for his tortured childhood, for his brother's tragic death; but most of all, I wept for the sacrifices both men had made for me.

All around, the world spun as if nothing had changed. Throughout the castle, preparations proceeded for the ball tonight, in spite of Chaine's condition. Before his duel, he insisted everything go on as scheduled no matter the outcome, so his investors wouldn't pay the penalty of his personal issues.

"Come back, Chaine." I breathed the words against his flesh, my lips trailing his neck to taste him. "I need my dance partner. I'll not attend a single ball, not without your rhythm."

As I lay there, lost in my grief, I felt a slight tug on the mattress. I nuzzled deeper into Chaine and gripped my hands around his pillow. If Uncle thought he could make me leave, take me back to my room so I could rest, he was sorely mistaken. I would not abandon Chaine. They couldn't drag me away. I had yet to tell him what he meant to me.

The movement stirred against my side this time, and a hand—with a touch so familiar for its calluses and compassion—lifted my chin.

Face to face with my gypsy prince, our noses touched. So grateful to be looking in his open eyes, my heart took wing.

"Chaine ... I love you."

A smile of genuine surprise parted his whiskers. "And I love you." Wrapping me in his arms, he dragged his lips over my chin, my cheeks, my temples—whispering unheard words. It didn't matter that I couldn't hear them. For in their silence, there was a melody, sweet and pure.

I tried to kiss his lips, but he stiffened. He moved so I could see his face as he stroked my shoulder. "What are you doing in here? Aren't you to be mending in your chamber? Your arm ..."

I almost laughed at that. "You're the one who almost died. Should I get the physician?"

"Surely you jest. I've never felt more alive." He circled my waist and drew me atop him with just the blankets and my clothes separating us. My breasts pushed flush against his muscular chest, sealing the locket between our heartbeats. I stretched in perfect alignment with his beautiful maleness. His gaze held me—eyes overcast with those shadows I had come to understand were catalysts to profound emotion.

He cupped both sides of my face, thumbs stroking wet hairs off of my temples. "Am I in heaven? Your eyes ... your skin ... your hair ..." He took strands in his fingers and splayed out the length, letting it fall in a golden curtain around us. "What is this?" His gaze scanned the room, stopping at each spray of flowers on the wall. "Something's wrong. Or ... no, it cannot be. Is it ... can this be *color*?"

I had a passing curiosity. "Chaine? It is you, isn't it?"

He winced as he resituated his back under my weight. Fearing I might be hurting him, I shifted. He tightened his hold on my waist to put me back in place atop him, surprising me with his strength.

"Of course it's me. Who else would I be?" Perception furrowed his brow as he noticed the locket wedged between us. "Is Nicolae here with us?" He asked, his fingertips tracing my spine. A thousand tingling torches ignited beneath each vertebra.

I tried to concentrate in spite of the sensations. "I want to know that myself. You say there's color? You're color blind."

"Yes. I-I am. The room looks like it always has, save the wildflowers, and you. What is happening? Did I get shot in the head?" He released me to rub his temples.

I repositioned his hands on my body and told him everything about the flower. And how his brother saved him with the last petal.

Remorse darkened Chaine's features. "You had to

choose me ... over him?"

The question gouged my heart for an instant, until the truth became clear: I didn't choose one brother over the other. I chose something much more monumental. And Hawk made that choice possible.

"I chose life over death, Chaine. I chose to *live,* with you by my side. It is the same choice you made in the mines, all those years ago."

He closed his eyes and pressed my forehead to his, motionless.

At last, his lashes opened again, coated with tears. An almost-smile twitched his lips. "So, you thought, when I mentioned color, that I was Nicolae, having a jolly in my brother's body?"

"Yes." I narrowed my eyes. "In fact, tell me our fairytale. He never knew it. I want to watch you recite the last verse."

The olive tone returned to his complexion in a dark blush. "Here we are lying in my bed, having confessed our undying love, both of us healed up right and true by my brother's generous spirit." He glanced all around. "No chaperon in sight. And all you can think of for celebration is to jabber about a ghost story and a fairytale?" His eyes lingered on the spread of my breasts against him and I felt the change in his body in response. The chance of paralysis no longer concerned me.

I traced his lips with my fingertip. "Indulge me."

"Oh, I plan to." He bit my finger gently, sending tendrils of desire uncoiling through every inch of my body. "The finest of friends, they both came to be," he mouthed the words, "this spotless angel and the prince of debris. They renounced the word goodbye. They sewed suits for his chancellors, baked moths for his stewards, and gave the salamanders wings—"

I didn't let him finish, too hungry for his lips. If his telling of the rhyme hadn't convinced me, the passionate heat of his kisses did. So lost in one another, neither of us noticed Uncle's entry until some unheard sound caused Chaine to break contact. I looked up to see Uncle flushed and beaming in the doorway. Behind him, Enya giggled alongside a line of maids.

"What?" Chaine looked at me and ran his fingers through my hair as he addressed our audience, eyes alight with joy. "Have none of you ever seen a man kiss his betrothed?"

CHAPTER 37

A hard beginning maketh a good ending.
The Proverbs of John Heywood (1546)

Chaine amazed the physician with his swift recovery. The first afternoon upon my visit to his sickbed, his back stopped bleeding. Two days later, the incision had already begun to scar. Within a week, he was waltzing with me at the Christmas gala.

Once he fully healed, Chaine arranged for the mine shaft to be closed up again with new slats. The busted reservoir caused the entire lower tunnel to cave, leaving nothing but a solid barrier of mud; so even had anyone wished to search for bones of any kind, they would have had to dig for years.

As to Lord Larson's accusations, read on the opening of his will, it raised not even an eyebrow. All it took was one look at Chaine's twisted and gnarled right foot—yet another odd consequence of his spirit melding with his brother's—and anyone could see by the birth defect that my betrothed was who he claimed to be: Lord Nicolas Thornton. And that the deed to the manor belonged, incontrovertibly and undeniably, to him and no other.

Holding true to his noble character, Chaine burned all

of the damning ledgers he had on Lord Larson, so as not to drag the dead man's family through the mud. He buried the past along with the sins of everyone who had ever wronged him.

And I loved him all the more for it.

Chaine had dreams during his recovery—dreams of his brother in heaven, spending time with Gitana. In the most vivid one, Hawk and Gitana sat beside a glistening waterfall with doves swooping in and out of the spray. Two other people joined them. A man who shared my lips, and a woman with long, golden hair and fawn-soft brown eyes, so much like mine. They asked Hawk of their daughter, China Rose. He told them she had found true love and abiding happiness.

I might have thought it some form of delirium, some residual malaise upon Chaine's mind inflicted by the medication or the pain of healing. I might have thought that, had it not been for two anomalies: never once had Hawk seen my father; and never had I, Uncle, or Enya ever mentioned the pet name my mother gave me to Chaine.

The first week after Chaine's full recovery, we retrieved the elderly viscount Merril from the sanatorium and brought him to the Manor to stay. In the mornings, we took him into the winter garden with us as we weeded and planted, so he might hear the birds and smell the flowers. During the afternoons, I was the old man's caregiver. Enya helped Uncle run the boutique as it had become quite busy—so many women sporting new fashions brought about by The Rational Dress Society, and me providing custom ordered bonnets to match every gown.

Father Merril and I got along famously. I would sit up in his room day after day, working on my hats as he built his watches. We would talk about his stolen son and his gypsy bride, or even sit unspeaking, absorbed in our own contemplations. I respected him despite his mental unbalance. He was a kindred spirit. We both had what other people considered physical limitations, yet those prejudices did not prevent us from accomplishing what our hearts desired. In fact, it seemed we were made stronger for having such flaws.

At times, Chaine joined us in his father's chamber to sketch when his schedule would allow. Inevitably, he would tease me with a flutter of breath at my temple, or a fingertip trailed along my nose in gentle leisure, then lean in to kiss me sweetly as his father chatted on about balance springs and wheel pinions.

Chaine and I met in secret every night, using our stairway behind Gitana's portrait as a portal to passionate interludes. When the weather would allow, we bundled up and had midnight picnics in the star tower, or waded through moonlit pools of hot springs in the forest. Already beyond companionship, we became confidantes and together learned the ways of love. Yet my betrothed refused to take my innocence until we shared the Thornton name.

With three months left in my mourning period for Mama, we opted to set the nuptials for March to meet society's rigid strictures. But Chaine and I were unable to wait, so we had a private Romani ceremony beneath the gazebo on a full-mooned January eve, with Aunt Bitti, Father Merril, Uncle, Enya, and Hawk's barren flower in attendance.

I wore a new riding habit Miss Hunny made of white cotton with lacy cuffs and collar. I left my hair down at Chaine's request and Enya tucked rosebuds throughout the strands.

Chaine decorated the gazebo with wildflowers, ribbons, feathers, and candlelight. But nothing compared to the vision of him waiting for me atop the misty platform, in a white wool frock coat hanging down to his ankles, a black vest, and fitted white trousers.

Even with his newly acquired color differentiation, he still had an affinity for clashing hues. I cherished this peculiarity as part of his heritage, part of the man I fell in love with. But on our wedding, he wore black and white only, in homage to who he had been before his brother's gift of color.

After our vows, so heartfelt and sincere our audience wept, Chaine and I rode into the forest on Draba to immerse ourselves in a hot spring and consummate our love beneath a star-filled sky.

For so long I had dreaded my first time with a man— concerned my deafness would impede our enjoyment, that I'd feel alone and awkward in the silence. Yet, I discovered when one has the right partner sensation becomes its own symphony, performed by two hearts. My husband played me like a beloved instrument, teaching me to play him, too. With each tender sweep of his knowing fingers as he bared my flesh to the night, part of my innocence fell away like broken notes. And I relished the raw harmony he exposed.

He led me to the water's edge, his eyes never leaving my body. There, I bared him of his clothes and couldn't resist learning every facet of his moonlit nakedness, each part of him lit-up in rhythmic flashes reflected off the water.

His sheer perfection beguiled me.

He lifted me to sit upon a smooth rock and stepped into the spring, his face level with my waist as he submerged up to his chest. He coaxed me to take a bow, my body arching like a harp, curled over him so he could strum my strings with kisses. My skin flashed from chill to flame upon the flavor and scent of him combined with the night air. His lips and tongue dragged lower and lower still, tasting every facet of my woman's body, even the hidden places no other man ... or ghost ... had ever laid claim to. He tortured, teased, and titillated, until I gasped with every touch.

When he brought me down into the water, the warm slickness of the spring offered a calming welcome—a contrast to his intensity. The song had reached its cadenza, and it was time for our duet to become a solo. Chaine's gentleness gave way to our fervent, fiery need to unite our souls. Until that moment, I never knew pain and pleasure could be as one. His mouth pressed unheard words of encouragement and love to my ear—his panting breath hot, his teeth nibbling. I didn't need to hear him, for his every touch sang to my flesh in a vernacular more potent than words or sounds.

At the peak of rapture, another song lit within me—the resurgence of Hawk's baritone—as powerful and enduring as when he shared my mind. It was the manifestation of his vow ... that I would never be without music again.

And beneath my husband's tears, for I could taste them on my face mingled with my own, I danced in the rain like I once did as a child. Only this time, I was powerful and uninhibited, dancing as a woman and a bride.

It was mid-July when Chaine, Father Merril, and I at last made a journey to Claringwell to attend Enya and Uncle's wedding. They planned to return to the Manor after a weeklong honeymoon. They enjoyed working in the boutique, and had come to love the estate with its vine-covered arbors, flowing streams, and grassy slopes, every bit as much as I.

By this time, Chaine and I had been married—publicly—for over four months. Although in truth it had been six.

After attending Uncle and Enya's nuptials, we visited with family and friends at the old house. My nightingale adored my husband like all animals did, and sang to him with fluffed feathers until he opened her cage and preened her with a fingertip. Uncle's spaniel followed Chaine from one room to the next as if his pockets were filled with mutton. And Enya's brothers and sisters idolized his gypsy heritage—the girls for his charming fairytales, and the boys for the card tricks he shared. I had never seen him so happy, to at last be surrounded and accepted by a loving family of his own.

In the late afternoon, Chaine and I slipped out to visit the cemetery wherein I had first seen him and contacted his brother's spirit ... the place where love had waited so patiently for me to find it.

We carried Hawk's flower stem in its terrarium. Ever since his departure, I had planned to one day plant it again where it belonged, in hopes it would bloom anew.

The sun cast a golden glow all around us and a warm breeze blew over the grasses. My husband and I walked hand in hand. He limped with grace, leaning on his cane as we wove through statues and headstones, the scent of honeysuckle and lilacs thick with the season. We paid tribute to Mama and Papa, leaving China roses upon the ground. Then, after Chaine took me in his arms and kissed my tears away, we passed the two angels that stood guard over the dead.

As we arrived at the enclosed grave, Chaine fished out the key his aunt had given him and opened the gate so we could enter together.

He wouldn't let me help dig the hole, for I carried his seed within my womb, a condition which brought about a most endearing protective streak in my Romani prince.

Lifting the flower from the terrarium and the pot, he settled it within its new home and raked soil around the roots. Once he'd patted the loose sod into place, he dusted off his gloves and studied the stem.

He looked up at me, curious. "There are buds forming."

I feigned surprise. In truth, I had seen them already— a month earlier. On the day I realized I was pregnant, two bumps appeared upon the barren stem, too tiny to be seen by anyone other than the plant's caregiver. It was a sign: God's way of righting a wrong brought about by the greed of arrogant, foolish men.

There was no question in my mind. I was carrying twins—Chaine's sons. Two brothers who would never be parted and would know more love, joy, and gentleness than any children who had ever walked the earth.

And they would be born with music in their hearts. For in them would live the songs of their uncle Nicolas, the brilliant architect who built a cathedral of melodies that now sprang eternal within the forgotten silences of my soul.

CPSIA information can be obtained at www.ICGtesting.com
Printed in the USA
LVOW08s2017260816

501474LV00001B/1/P